Confucius Jade

Published by Dudley Court Press, LLC
P.O. Box 102
Sonoita, Arizona 85637 USA
www.DudleyCourtPress.com

Also published by Dudley Court Press as an Ebook through www.Smashwords.com
Previously published in Singapore by Times Books International, 1993.

Paperback ISBN: 978-0-9819291-3-2
Ebook ISBN: 978-0-9819291-4-9
LCCN: 2009942709

Publisher's Cataloging-in-Publication Data:

Fisher, Frederick.
        Confucius jade / Frederick Fisher.
        p. cm.
        LCCN 2009942709
        ISBN-13: 978-0-9819291-3-2
        ISBN-10: 0-9819291-3-3
        ISBN-13: 978-0-9819291-4-9
        ISBN-10: 0-9819291-4-1

        1. Gemologists--Fiction. 2. Jade--China--Fiction.
        3. Confucianism--Fiction. 4. China--Fiction.
        I. Title.

        PS3606.I774C66 2010   813'.6   QBI09-600229

Cover design by Daniel Kiyoi
Interior design by Suzanne Hocking/Trellis Editorial

Frederick Fisher

CONFUCIUS JADE

Dudley Court Press
Sonoita, Arizona

For Jeffrey Carl Fisher

Prologue
GENESIS

MANGIN TAUNG, BURMA

Under gray skies, leaden with the September monsoon, the burros wound their way down the mountain, known as Mangin Taung in northern Burma. Twelve of the pack animals were tethered to each other. A drover led the train and another followed. An A-frame of rough hewn wood, strapped over hemp-pad blankets, burdened the sturdy animals. They bore fifty-kilo burlap sacks, containing jade boulders, lashed tightly to each side of the frame. Twelve hundred kilos of precious jade rough traveled on a route from the ancient mines at Hpakant in the Kachin Territory to Rangoon, far to the south.

A trio of guards followed them. They were of the Wa people of northeast Burma, fierce and wily. The cargo was valuable, subject to continual attacks from the bandits of the Golden Triangle, where the Burmese, Siamese and Laotian borders met. Raiders robbed the trains before they could reach the protected south. The loot went over the nearby borders to Chiang Mai in northern Siam, or Yunnan Province of China.

Caution of a quarter-century of near-death, clashes with bandits, and rain-weakened trails underfoot imbued the leading drover. His eyes scouted the trail ahead for trouble, seeking a cleft in the rocks to escape to in case of enemy rifles. He watched for signs of avalanches that could carry the caravan into the winding Mogaung River, far below. A tiny rivulet indenting the path ahead, he deemed inconsequential.

The large ears of the leading burro, more sensitive than the man's, flared up and pointed their sound tunnels ahead. Sharp eyes, alerted for self-preservation, saw danger more keenly than the human drover. The beast balked, digging in with trail-sharpened hooves. Eleven animals following stopped in unison. The drover, enraged at the balky animal, turned his back to the trail ahead. He wrapped the lead ropes tightly around one arm, and with a string of expletives that only a mountain burro could understand, beat the animal with his whip.

The drover stepped back to a forceful stance, his feet in the small stream coursing down the mountain. With a scream of mortal terror he felt the ground give way. Several meters of the trail dissolved. The burro dug in harder, instinctively, but the ground underneath disintegrated. The combined weight of the drover and the burro pulled them both down with the slide.

The rear drover and the guards watched helplessly. Lead ropes on the halters pulled each of the animals over the side of the narrow trail. Stunned, they watched, as the bodies, human and beasts, tumbled and turned, bounced from one ledge of rock to another to the bottom of the gorge. Heavy sacks spilled their contents as the A-frames broke away from the burros.

One of the boulders bounced high off an outcropping, with a crack echoing for miles. It came to rest in the middle of the stream far below, split in two, the halves not more than three meters apart at the river's edge. The waters of the Mogaung, coursing over the fresh split, made the translucent green center flash like molten emerald. A vulture circled high above, watching the drama below with his telescopic eyes. The predator began a slow circling descent, summoning his brethren to the carnage.

The vultures feasted on the carrion for many days. The bones bleached in the sun and the tale of the accident was soon forgotten, except by the widow and the family of the drover. The heavy halves of the boulder settled gradually into the silt of the river bottom.

A dozen decades flew by on the wings of time until the year of the great monsoon. Rains deluged the mountains for weeks on end. Avalanches formed deep trenches in the hillside. The waters overflowed the banks of the river. The Mogaung flooded, emptying downstream into the mighty Irrawaddy River. The deluge inundated small villages. Homes disappeared that had withstood a hundred years of storms. Silt boiled up from the bottom, joining encroaching jungle torn from the shore. Boats, parts of homes, and bloated dead animals washed downstream, taking the heavy boulders with them.

Storms abate. Rivers calm and return to their natural depth. Debris washes ashore, or settles into the river beds. Like twins that have preordained destiny, the two halves of the jade boulder settled near to each other, at a bend of the Irrawaddy River. They tipped against the soft bank, only a thin edge of green showing. The silt began building up again, secreting them for yet another generation.

Book One
THE FAMILY KONG

1

KUNMING, YUNNAN PROVINCE, CHINA

———— ∞∞∞ ————

KONG WAN YI

My name is Wan Yi of the family K'ung. Our famous ancestor is K'ung Fu-tze, scholar, historian, and advisor to governments of his day. The Jesuit priests anglicized his name to Confucius and our family was eventually known as Kong. Confucius lived twenty-five hundred years ago. He would have been proud of the University that bears his name at Qufu that recently celebrated its first commencement ceremony. My son Meng Li was in that graduating class. His ancestor, seventy-seven times removed, would have acclaimed the occasion as Meng Li's father and I did.

I am a jade carver, now living in the Eternal Spring City of Kunming, Yunnan Province of China, but born in 1936 in Burma. The University of Confucius asked me to record the story of its beginning, more than twenty-five hundred years after its namesake lived.

My celebrated ancestor's thoughts are like fine rare jade. Beauty emerges from the interior with understanding. When light shines through it, mystery, intrigue, and wonderment hypnotize the viewer.

Some events happened before I was born, told to me by other members of the Kong family. The tale revolves around a jade sculpture, myself, my immediate family, and those people whose lives it altered. The following background will help you understand the motives and the events that occurred, changing the lives of so many people.

China, my homeland, has a recorded history of more than five thousand years. The Great Sea in the east and the Himalayas, the grandest mountains on Earth, are China's borders. China survived the invasions by the Mongol hordes and, more recently, the Japanese.

European traders carried art treasures over the silk road to the east and ships plying the oceans to Europe and the Americas stuffed their hungry maws with China's valuables. Warlords fought with each other for supremacy and then combined to fight common enemies, twisting and turning the nation into a thousand shapes.

Our people managed to persist and breed themselves into millions. By the middle of the twentieth century, we were a thousand million or more. A billion people live in China now.

Survival is in the genes of the Chinese, as it is in the Jewish people. They migrated to nearby and faraway countries for the right to live.

The people of China endured pestilence, wars, and famines. They survived, but in much greater numbers than other races. Emperors ordered the construction of the Great Wall to deter the Mongol invaders. Its purpose failed but it became a wonder of the world.

Near the ancient capital of Xian, one Emperor had a massive army reproduced in clay and supplied it with replicas of horses, equipment, and arms. He buried the multitude, hidden until farmers discovered it centuries later. Millions of people would eventually visit his tomb, as well as others around the Sen Empire.

Each emperor tried to extend his lifeline into the future in one form or another. Described as SHOU (Longevity), many Chinese rulers commissioned art works in paintings, porcelains, stone carvings, metals, and woods.

Among these art forms, figures representing Happiness, Worldly Possessions, and Longevity emerged. Shou Xing Lao, the God of Longevity, is the one with the high bald head, long flowing white beard, happy face with bulging cheeks, and a twinkle in his eye. He carries a staff, accompanied sometimes by a red-headed crane and a spotted deer. A luscious peach in his hand symbolizes good health. At times he rides on the back of a turtle, denoting double longevity. Boy children often play at his feet.

Religions fostered and grew as each group tried to assimilate China into the rest of the world. The slavish idolatry of Buddhism, with its wishful thinking of peace, supported the vast army of monks. Taoism, the religion founded by Lao Tze, preached the pantheistic theory of communing with nature. The Shinto came from Japan, nature and ancestor worshipers. Islam shone the light of Allah for those that would believe in one God and allow themselves to be bound to the tightest of laws. Christianity prospered in China at one time with its proselytizers that drummed the stages for the glory of Jesus. The Hindus, who would not kill a fly or a cow, classed their adherents. They relegated themselves to that caste forever. A small number of Jews fleeing Russia's intolerance settled in Manchuria, establishing Judaism. Amongst these religious sects in China were the Confucians, followers of my ancestor's philosophy.

Born K'ung Fu-tze in 551 B.C. of a sixteen-year-old concubine, he lived to teach knowledge and reasoning. His words, both written and carved in stone, have survived to the present generation. The beliefs were pragmatic and he insisted on the issue of examinations to test the scholars, both to enter and to leave the premises of education.

My story begins in the early part of the twentieth century, when China endured hardships during the periods of devastations of war, pestilence, famine, and floods. The more barbaric of the people killed off or sold unwanted girl children to have less mouths to feed. Elders allowed themselves to die, rather than eat food necessary for the younger ones to exist. Indentured Chinese spewed out into the world like watermelon seeds. Their labor built the railroads of America, mined the goldfields of Australia, and served the ships at sea. They worked in the households and godowns of the British colonialists in Hong Kong and Singapore.

The more enlightened Confucians scholars mingled with these immigrants. Some went as far as San Francisco, the Golden Mountain. Others, when famine and floods hit their families, drifted to other parts of Asia, to survive. Thus it was for the two scholars, Kong Fan Shi and Kong Wen Xian, distant cousins, seventy-fifth generation descendants of Confucius. Wen Xian was my father. China suffered famine then, for three years. The Kuomintang under Chiang Kai-shek was fighting with the followers of Mao Zedong, devastating the countryside, tearing apart the communities they fought over.

For those three years, then, since 1932, there was no examinations, no way to further their studies. Fan Shi and my father, Wen Xian, lived here, in Kunming, capital of Yunnan Province in southwest China.

The land was bone-dry from the lack of rain. Even seed was eaten to survive. The scholars talked endlessly, trying to keep up each other's interest in life. Uncle Fan Shi and Aunt Chen Wu Xia had a son. My cousin Deng Huai was already two years old in 1935, when my story begins. I was still in the womb of my mother and was expected in the fall. Fan Shi, the elder of the cousins, was thirty-one years old. Mother and Aunt Chen, both born in 1915, were twenty, and my father was four years older than my mother.

According to Uncle Fan Shi, the two couples met with the family Kong in the winter of 1935 and told them of their joint decision to move west into Burma. Traders traveling through reported that the rains fell, the population was light, and there was much farmland for the taking.

British colonialism inspired education and in that very year, England's Parliament had passed The Government Of Burma Act, said to make a free and democratic country of the land. There should be much opportunity for scholars to teach and become important in the burgeoning country.

April was a good time to set off before the summer heat, they decided. The plan was to travel with one cart and donkey between them, carrying only meager belongings. They wore their most disreputable garments to discourage robbery by bandits said to roam the mountains.

Cooking utensils were necessary for they would eat by the roadside, scavenging food. Uncle Fan took important possessions, such as family scrolls, depicting the writings of Confucius in superb calligraphy and scenes of Yunnan. They needed to remember Green Mountain soaring high over Kunming, with its temple tacked to the side walls and the strange formations of the nearby stone forest.

They added books on Confucius, and the *Analects,* a record of the Master's sayings. Astrology, mathematics, and history would be with them, reminders of their home and their teachings. A roll of quilted padded coats and blankets would sustain them in the colder weather of the mountain ranges they had to cross.

Mother and Aunt Chen packed their wedding pillow boxes containing the treasures handed down from their mothers. There were exquisite eggshell-porcelain cups, painted on one side with the scenes of Kunming and on the other, the characters for Wedded Bliss and Double Happiness, wedding wishes for the brides.

Mother took her collection of jewelry, bracelets and necklaces of cloisonné and carved lacquer, silver and enamel brooches and hair ornaments decorated with the beautiful blue kingfisher feathers. She also had powders, rouges, tiny scissors and files for grooming.

Aunt Chen's treasures were more practical: herbs, medicines, ointments, photographs of her parents and her wedding. Her only jewelry was a phoenix bird carved in lavender jade, hanging from a thin pure gold chain.

Both had four pairs of chopsticks nestled in beautifully decorated wooden cases, which I still have. They are ivory, the square tops intricately carved, to properly serve guests.

The two scholars carried their most valuable possessions in cloth-lined wicker baskets. Pockets, stitched for each item, contained slate ink stones, slabs of ink decorated in gold, and small stone frogs that poured water for the ink onto the stones.

Each had a handful of brushes, with bristles of only the finest pig hairs, and antique soapstone-carved dishes for washing the brushes. A thick roll of rice paper wound around the scroll paintings to protect them and supply writing paper. Waxed paper covered the bundle, tied with silk ribbons, to protect the whole package from the elements. A false floor of the cart hid the valuables.

Deng Huai was to ride in a seat next to the driver. One person would drive and the other three walk, exchanging places each half day. Lack of food made the donkey, called Hsu Hsu, gaunt. They hoped he would last at least part of the way until they could cross the mountains, expecting to pull the cart themselves, resting the poor animal, if the going got too tough.

Aunt Chen remembered the beginning of the journey clearly. Starting an hour before daybreak, the family and neighbors came out to see them off as they passed by. They shouted words of safe journey, long life, good health, happiness and good fortune. The family's last view of Kunming was of Green Lake and the park around it.

Uncle Fan described the scene sadly. The lake was without water, the trees listless and silent of birds. Flowers that once decorated the paths were memories. The lotus leaves and blossoms, long gone, left pond beds of cracked dried mud. He hoped they or their sons might return to the city of Eternal Spring and see it once again in all of its glory.

The first few days of the journey were exhilarating. Hsu Hsu filled out with the lush grazing. Foraging in the jungle growth produced fruit and edible greens for a broth, augmented by an occasional wild bird or small animal. A farmer's wife, sons lost to the wars, offered them rice in exchange for help with the sowing of one rice paddy and the harvesting of another.

Feeling much more confident of their decision, the travelers took their time, often stopping in villages, sometimes for a few days. Food became plentiful as they neared the Burmese border; the war was remote. Higher in the mountains, water was available and the rice terraces produced healthy crops. The richest grains became seed for the next crop, improving the harvest. It was the custom to share food with strangers. The rural villagers craved news of the war and their conscripted men.

One of the villages invited the scholars to stay for a year to teach their children. Without teachers, there were no examinations to sit for, and no way to advance those with an aptitude to learn. The travelers agreed to stay for a while to rest, and build their bodies for the hardship of the remaining journey.

When it came time to move on, warnings were given them about dangers, crossing the border into Burma. Mountain trails slid into oblivion after the rains. Bandits, seeking jade caravans and the traders traveling the silk road into China, roamed at will. They would kill without mercy, steal anything, even a pair of leather boots. Individual travelers were non-existent, as all moved in groups with paid mercenaries to protect them. Aunt Chen told me the villagers begged them to wait for the next train to go through. My family decided to go anyway, concerned more about the August and September monsoons than the bandits.

The scholars were paid with necessities. "They appreciated the few weeks of teaching," Aunt Chen said. "The villagers gave us sacks of rice and wheat, delicate dried snake meat, dried fruits, and green tea from the hillside. The most precious gift was ten small sacks of seed grain, including rice, wheat, vegetables and flowers. I thanked them over and over. The grain would start my garden when we reached our destination.

"One family ceremoniously presented a Malay kris, left by some trader years before. It was of the sharpest steel we had ever seen and would come in handy for clearing jungle, if the trail became difficult. Your father welcomed it as a weapon to defend us. Another family offered an old pistol and six rounds of ammunition, as none in the village cared to use it. Neither your father or your uncle had ever fired a weapon, but they took it anyway as a show of bravado, in case of bandits. They were too young to be afraid. A student went with them to show a route across the border, bypassing the guards of China and Burma."

Uncle Fan admitted trepidation, when they moved over the mountain pass into Burma. They were in a foreign country for the first time in their lives, future unknown. The darkened afternoon skies warned of impending storms, furthering anxiety. He described the narrow trails twisting back and forth through the vast mountain passes. "We felt like tiny ants crawling through the world of giants."

The weather chilled, they said, requiring blankets and quilted jackets which added to our load. My mother, now in her seventh month, rode most of the time. They camped at night, managing a small fire and sheltering in a cave or behind a rock. After all, this was the very heart of bandit country and they did not want to draw too much attention on themselves.

One afternoon, a group of horsemen appeared several twists of the road below. Aunt Chen said, "Our bravado disappeared, we huddled back against the side of the cliff and turned off the road into a glen of dense trees. Uncle Fan went back up the trail, brushing it with tree branches to disguise our tracks. He predicted the men would arrive after dark and hoped they would pass us by. We welcomed the rain, as a shower began. It would help to obliterate the tracks farther down the trail.

"Your father climbed to a fork high in a tree to watch the progress of the men. The band of six approached at dusk. Dirty, unkempt, bearded, bandoleered with belts of ammunition, rifles in scabbards and across the pommel of the wooden saddles, they looked fierce. Each had at least two rifles; handguns and knives hung from belts and shoe tops.

"The bandits trailed three donkeys, loaded obviously with loot. The tough, small mules were overburdened, but trotted along at a pace that appeared could go on forever."

Aunt Chen would pause, re-living every detail of the moment. "Hidden in the tree, your father clung on like a tree frog fearing to even breathe. We prayed Hsu Hsu wouldn't bray in recognition of kindred souls around, or the baby let out a squeal. Loud voices of the brigands, evidently bragging and joking about their exploits, carried back to us. The rain lightened and the group stopped almost in front of the tree your father was hidden in. One of the men entered the small clearing directly under the tree your father was in. He checked the campsite and pointed to a circle of stones, used many times before as a fire pit. The group moved in and set up camp."

The near miss with tragedy became an oft-told story as I grew older. The bandits spent the night there, horses hobbled for graze nearby, a tarpaulin lean-to for a tent, heads resting on the saddles, a fire built, with a soup pot boiling, mutton turning on a spit over the fire. My father hung on for dear life, afraid he would doze and fall out of the tree. He imagined the bandits cutting him to pieces before he had a chance to run.

Mother, Uncle Fan, little Deng, and Aunt Chen had moved back in the glen one hundred meters, not daring to rustle around or make camp. The donkey was tied to a tree so tight, he couldn't crack a twig underfoot, his mouth bound with a cloth. Aunt Chen kept little Deng at her breast, suckling and sleeping, quieted by a few sips of wine from the leather container.

The danger passed with dawn. The brigands went on their way. My family survived their first life-threatening ordeal. Father was the only casualty, stiff and sore from the night in the tree. But mother took sick with fever from the wet and cold exposure of the traumatic night. Aunt Chen treated her from the small store of herbs. There was little improvement. They hurried on; rest was important, and better medical attention needed.

A day later, they were at the foot of the mountain, looking for the old trading route heading west and south to Rangoon. Later known as the Burma Road, it was a muddy trail winding through the jungle. Hundreds of caravans bore trade goods from China to Mandalay, Pagan, and the seaport at Rangoon.

They approached a small village and my father went ahead to find a doctor. He must have looked fierce with the Malay kris hanging from his side and the useless pistol across his hip, muddy and wet from the long trek in the mountains.

Uncle Fan related the incident to me at story-telling times. "The villagers closed their doors against him as he strode into the main street. It was here that the raiding party, who terrorized our family, had gotten their latest loot, we found out later. Your father was frantic with worry over your mother. He pounded on doors, shouting in the various tongues he knew. Suddenly there was a loud cry from one of the houses. He turned to face the sound, and a single shot from an old rifle rang out. Crying 'bu shi, bu shi' (no, no), he fell to the ground.

"An old woman came from another door nearby. She bent over him, seeing the gentle face, the high cheekbones, and the amulet around his neck carved with the character SHOU for the good luck of longevity.

"Eeeyah!" she shouted. 'This is no bandit. His face is unlike the murderous Mongols who plundered us.' Dropping to her knees, she cradled your father's head and whispered to him in the language of the Dai people of the Stone Forest. 'Who are you? What are you here for?'"

Every time Aunt Chen or Uncle Fan told the story, their eyes filled and throats choked with the memory. According to the sad tale, my poor father was in shock, worried about mother and unable to shout a warning. "We are but poor scholars looking for a new home," he whispered to the woman. "My wife is very ill and needs attention. Please go to them and help her. She carries my son."

I remember Uncle Fan always winking at me when he came to that part of the story. All Chinese families hoped for a male firstborn. Uncle would pat my shoulder and say, "We are fortunate, little Wan, that it was you instead of some miserable little boy that would never laugh and smile as you do."

I always thanked Uncle Fan with my smile and squeezed his hand as he continued the sad story of my father's death. "The old woman went with a small delegation to bring the rest of us into the village. They carried your mother into the hut and laid her next to your father."

Only an hour before they had exulted in arriving in civilized country once again. Now mother's world was falling apart. She was ill, distraught, barely able to whisper to him during his last moments. "I will bear your son, dear Wen Xian, and one day we will return your bones to Yunnan where you can join your ancestors."

Father answered, "Dear Yi Ku, my ancestors will meet me, wherever I am. You must live yourself and continue our journey to a new life for yourself and our child. Even if the baby is a girl, I will celebrate. Bury me here and remember always that I am with you wherever you are."

"We buried him in the village of Ho Pang, in the foreign soil of Burma," Uncle Fan related. "There was little ceremony, the shock over the sudden turn of events too extreme. The villagers were overwrought. They had, just three days before, buried six of their number, killed by the merciless bandits. Another innocent life was added to the toll. Had the bandits discovered us on the mountain, they would have killed for the sport, probably raping your mother and Chen."

Tears came to Uncle Fan from the pain of memory. He would pause, wipe his eyes and continue. "The old woman of the village stayed close by your mother, who tossed listlessly with grief and fever. None of the remedies would help. Aunt Chen urged her to live to save you. She forced nourishment of herb liquids and rich noodles in soup. Eventually, the patient became stronger, able to eat and drink.

"Your mother sat for hours by herself, ignoring us all in her sorrow. When she would talk, Yi Ku pleaded with us to go on without her. There were many days of uncertain travel ahead. We refused to leave without her, and said time and again that we are a family. We left China as a family and will remain together until the fates determine otherwise."

Aunt Chen sometimes took over the story at that point, always with tears streaming down her cheeks, her voice choked with emotion. "The labor pains came soon after. The village midwife moaned that it was too early, the baby should have another month in the womb. 'It's better this way,' said the old woman, disagreeing. If the baby stays much longer with the woman, it will never survive the birth. Yi Ku eats too little for both mother and child. The child is weakened by the grief of the mother.'

"Labor came that night and continued for three days. You were unwilling to leave the womb, traumatized by your mother's illness. You survived, but your poor mother died after giving birth. She held you for a short time, at first cried that you were a girl. Then she held you close, whispering that even though a girl, you had the genes of the family K'ung and would be very intelligent. I remember you held her finger tight with your tiny fist and smiled."

Emotion overcame dear Aunt Chen and I each time the story was related. It became almost a ritual. We dried our tears, hugged each other, and then smiled, knowing how close we were to mother at the time.

"A wet nurse in the village suckled you, tiny, physically weak, but very strong in spirit. We buried Yi Ku next to Wen Xian and ordered the inscription of the family K'ung on a stone. The villagers promised to tend the graves, as they would their ancestors.

"The few weeks in the village, while you were growing, allowed us to wait out the rains. Uncle Fan, with his wonderful ear for languages, quickly assimilated their tongue. It's similar to the Tibetan and Burmese, as the nearby lands were criss-crossed throughout history with the same peoples. He also taught some of the children basics in astronomy and mathematics. Fan is always the scholar, ever the teacher, no matter where he is.

"Life became tranquil for a time and little Deng was enamored of the new baby. You never cried, and overcame your premature birth quickly. We named you Wan Yi. Wan means gentle, graceful, gracious, beautiful, elegant, lovely and especially the word for smile. Yi means charming and gentle and is a definition for skill and art. These traits came to be, including your ability to carve gemstones."

2

LIFE IN BURMA

They followed the trade route south, as itinerant merchants had for centuries before them, crossing Burma from China into India. The springtime jungle was green and lush by the roadside. The kris sliced the tops off coconuts easily, providing the semi-sweet liquid, healthy to drink and cook with. Pieces of coconut meat carried in the pocket were pleasant to chew on while traveling. Papayas were hanging ripe, mangos plentiful in a dozen varieties. Clusters of rambutan hung like grapes from the trees, the peeled fruit looking and tasting like the Yunnan lychee they had known at home. Other travelers showed them how to eat the durian but the fetid odor from the opened fruit made them shy away from this local favorite.

My family dawdled, so they said, staying for days sometimes in a pleasant campsite near a stream and road. Villagers welcomed them, anxious to hear news from other parts of the world. Unlike Yunnan, the rice fields were rich with grain. They worked alongside the local people to earn rice and other food, increasing their supplies.

"In the evenings we gathered to talk about Burma and China. There were young men from the University of Rangoon, exposed to Marxism, carrying their ideals to the countryside. They called each other 'Thakin' like the Hindu 'Sahib', as a title of respect. Thakin Aung San and Thakin U Nu, student leaders, became well known in their fervor of defying the British system of government.

"Other Chinese asked your Uncle Fan to teach their children about Chinese history, astrology, and mathematics. There were small clusters of Chinese in each of these remote villages, and very little education. The British helped to establish some schooling in the larger cities of Mandalay, Pagan, Taunggyi and Rangoon, but they expended little effort in the rural areas. The peasants raised their children for labor. They grew food for the cities, picked tea for export, and supplied servants for the households and estates of foreign capitalists and wealthy Burmese."

Moving on to where the mighty Irrawaddy River convoluted with the smaller Mogaung, my adopted parents reached the village called Bhamo. It was here that awareness of life began for me. Bhamo was and is today a trading center, a staging point for caravans that gathered for the long treks north, east, and west. The people of Bhamo were familiar with travelers from China, India, Laos, Cambodia, Siam, and the Malay Sultanates. Strangers were welcome, especially one who had education, and could talk many languages.

The K'ung family, Aunt Chen and Uncle Fan, little Deng, and myself, the infant, were young and likeable. The scholar talked to the children as if they were equals, as a teacher, extolled the stars, proved mathematics, and recited history back to the days of his ancestor Confucius. Uncle Fan, my adopted father, is a consummate storyteller, repeating the tales of ancient China. He could retell the whole four volumes of the *Red Mansions* from memory. This epic of a high-living family in China, a century before, featured a jade amulet while other stories created morals to live by.

There were many Chinese families living in Bhamo, absorbed into the community with the Kachins, also called Jinghpaws, who wore black turbans. The Chinese were the Shan Tayok and the Kokang. We had a lot in common with the Shans. They were from Yunnan Province when the Shan principalities were under British Municipalities. The Shans told us that Rangoon had a large Chinese population as well, but they came by sea, became restaurant owners and merchants during the British colonial days. The Chinese prospered, sent their children to universities, and occupied a middle to high strata of society.

According to Uncle Fan, the Shans kept a low profile in the community of Bhamo, still considered aliens by many of the Tibeto-Burmese. The Chinese elders talked with us soon after we arrived there. The leader said, "It would be wise to stay with us in Bhamo. We yearn for a Chinese school. Our children have only the Burmese schools to attend. They know little of our Chinese history, and speak only the dialects we use at home."

"My son is learning accounts from you," said the rice merchant, addressing Uncle Fan. "He has made me much money already by checking the thieving traders who were cheating me. Stay and build a home. I'll rent you, for a low figure, some excellent farmland by the river, outside of town."

"The woman, Chen, has taught my daughter about medicines found in the jungle around us, and has already cured two of our neighbor's children of a racking cough," another said. "We will buy land for the school in town and build a school."

They reached an agreement. Uncle Fan leased the property, which became our home for the next two generations. The school provided income to pay the rent and eventually purchase the land. My adopted parents were comfortable by the river; it reminded them of Kunming. Fields, easily irrigated, allowed Aunt Chen to begin farming while Uncle Fan set up the school. Our newfound friends turned out *en masse* to help the scholar build his house. They constructed it on stilts high off the ground. The Irrawaddy flooded most years and the monsoons kept the ground soaked for weeks on end. Teak was plentiful in the neighboring jungle. Large logs, dragged in by the oxen, framed the corners and braced the roof.

Our living space was square, eight meters on a side. A sand pit in the center contained the cooking and warming fire. Shelves, shielded with bead curtains, lined one side to store our food and belongings. A covered porch extended on one side accommodated washing tubs. The toilet chute in the corner led down to a covered pit below ground. That pit in turn had an access trap so the excrement could be removed and used as fertilizer. Night soil was a necessary element for our farm.

A stairway ladder, pulled up at night, warded off any unseemly guests or animals. It came up through the living room floor. Aunt Chen told me many times, laughingly, "Deng was an aggressive youngster. I had to tie a rope on him so he wouldn't fall off the porch or down the ladder. You crawled very carefully around all obstacles and stayed clear of the ladder well. We knew we had a home when the scrolls from Kunming were unrolled, to hang on the walls."

Uncle Fan made a desk from left-over timber, set up his ink stone, watering frog, washer, and put the brushes in a bamboo cup. A friendly neighbor brought over short stools with bamboo legs and cane seats. Straw sleeping mats, rolled up during the day, provided clean beds for Deng and me. A niche secluded by a beaded curtain provided privacy for Aunt and Uncle.

Underneath the house, at the ground level, we tethered the goats and made pens to raise ducks. Our donkey, Hsu Hsu, grazed in the daytime, and spent the night in the small corral in the corner. Our family's dreams of a better life were now possible.

It had been a year since they had set out hungry, troubled by famine and the war surrounding them from Yunnan. Now they had this beautiful home, a chance to grow their own food and bring up the children in a clean and healthy environment. Aunt Chen often told me how they grieved for my parents. Deng and I never tired of hearing the sad story of my mother and father. Even at the age of five or six, I can remember talking about them as if they were still with me. Their treasure, as Aunt Chen used to call me. Wan Yi, the gentle one with the smile always on her face, tempered the tragedy of my lost parents.

Uncle Fan set up school in the store front, as promised, and duly registered with the village as 'The Chinese School of Bhamo'. In later years, it became a Chinese learning center for the whole province. The name stayed the same but the buildings eventually took up the whole block. Some of the more literate Burmese sent their children to the Chinese School instead of their own, for better university preparation. Uncle Fan, with a wry sense of humor, named the various buildings after famous cities in China. Kunming, of course, Beijing, Chongqing, Shanghai, Hangzhou, Suzhou, and Guilin. Each was decorated with scrolls depicting scenery from its namesake.

There were troubles and controversies. At first the monks from the local monastery objected to the school. The children, though Chinese, should learn more about Buddha, and less academia. Uncle Fan solved this problem by setting up a class in Buddhism, inviting the monks to come in and be guest lecturers to explain their beliefs. This grew into a whole school of comparative religions, where the students became familiar with every faith.

When the time came to admit the first class, there were no girls registered. Uncle Fan insisted that every Chinese child be given the chance. Many of the parents, who still thought in the manner of their past generations, objected. It was only necessary to teach girl children how to run a household, bear children, and help in the fields. Eventually, the first class had eight boys and four girls, ages from five to fifteen. They told me Aunt Chen went to visit each household, talking only to the women about equal rights for girl children in this modern world. She is a strong woman. Her name Wu Xia means 'without impurities', and this is evident in her beliefs. I can well imagine her working on these women, and they in turn on their husbands.

My adopted father, Fan Shi, began corresponding with Kunming. Direct mail service between the two countries was nonexistent in the early years. Traders took the letters, which were passed from group to group heading in the right direction. Waxed and sealed with the chop of the originator, it could take months to get a letter to its destination and sometimes a year to get a response. I can remember, even as a little girl, the joy and excitement in the house when a letter came from the family in China.

Life became complacent. Aunt Chen planted the precious seed grain in fields near the house. Our rice was the finest, the corn produced large luscious ears, long beans hung on the vines, cabbages sprouted. Uncle Fan toiled in the field after school, until we earned enough money to hire some neighbor boys to help. Deng, at the age of seven, was working as hard as any of them, and even I, only five years old, helped dry the grain and feed the growing livestock.

I remember my fifth year, 1941, the Year of the Snake. The rains came early in June. It poured steadily for forty days. Our road was so deep in mud that we had to walk and take the donkey cart high off the side of the road. The house, with its stilted construction, and set on a hill, was dry.

One morning, a tremendous roar woke me. The animals below us were rumbling. We now had two of the massive grey oxen, and Hsu Hsu had a companion. The goats multiplied to a half dozen and the ducks numbered twenty-five most of the time.

I remember Deng shouting from the porch, "The river, the river, it looks like it's coming right at us. There's a house floating down the middle, look at all the dead animals."

Uncle Fan hollered, "Come with me, Deng, we've got to move the oxen and donkeys to the high ground under the mango trees. Chen, try to save some of the ducks by putting them in the baskets up here. We'll let the goats loose and hope they will follow us up the hill."

The river banks had long ago disappeared; the water was now a foot deep in the pens below. Deng and Uncle Fan scrambled down the ladder in their bare feet, wearing only sleeping pants. They quickly untied the four animals and threw rope halters over their necks. Then they opened the small corral penning the goats. Deng and Uncle Fan jumped on the backs of the oxen. Each pulled a lead rope of a donkey, urging them out of the area toward the nearby hill. The animals were as frightened as we were, sensing the danger, and moved faster than I had ever seen them. The goats huddled together and scampered ahead of the train up the hill.

In the meantime, Aunt Chen was at the foot of the ladder, knee deep in mud, grabbing every duck she could lay her hands on. They were frantic and screaming, and milled about, trying to stay close to their flooded pen. She grabbed each one by the legs, looped a tie around them, wings whipping, their beaks trying to bite. As soon as they were tied, she climbed halfway up the ladder and handed the rope to me. Heavy as they were for my little five-year-old arms, I strained and lifted them into the big basket, slapping the cover down each time. We managed to save a dozen or so, before Aunt Chen gave up. "Maybe they will swim towards Fan and Deng. That way they may save themselves." It was not to be. We watched the silly fools swim right out and got caught up in the flood racing downstream.

Aunt Chen came back up, and we held each other as we went out on the porch to watch for our men. We could see them far up on the hill now, tethering the animals to the trees. They would be safe if the river didn't rise too much higher. "Stay there, stay there," Aunt Chen screamed at them, hoping they wouldn't try to get back to the house. The water below us was already waist high and the current running strong.

The weather raged on, the wind howling but fortunately, the rain was starting to abate.

We watched as Deng slipped, screaming as his head disappeared for a moment under the muddy water. Fan reached out for him and missed. He tried again and managed to grab his pants. They both got to their feet, holding on to each other. As they stood up, a pile of debris floated towards them. They jumped backwards to avoid it and started to climb back up the hill towards the animals. At that moment a bloated dead ox crashed into them. Swept off their feet, they grabbed for the animals' horns. The last glimpse we had was of the ballooned body washing downstream with Uncle Fan and Deng holding on to the horns for dear life.

I will never forget that terrible day and evening. The ducks complaining, were confined to the baskets. Aunt Chen, tears streaming down her face, strangely quiet, hugged me so tightly that I could scarcely breathe. We huddled together for hours, unable to sleep.

The light dawned on a grey, damp day. The rain had stopped but the water was still waist deep underneath our house. With credit to the builders, it stood firm and strong. We were afraid to think of Uncle Fan and Deng, hoping against hope that they had survived somehow. Aunt

Fan brewed a pot of tea and poured a cup for both of us. It was the first cup of tea I ever had, though half-filled with goat's milk. I became a grown-up person. We talked, Aunt Chen trying to reassure me.

"Oh, Aunt Chen, please tell me they'll be all right."

"Yes, Wan Yi, put that wonderful smile back on your face. They are all right, I can sense it. You know, when people live together like Uncle Fan and I, we feel each other's well-being. It's a communion of our minds. I know he was in danger, but I feel now that he is all right."

When the water subsided, we went back up the hill, and brought our stock back. Fortunately, some feed was stored high up on a shelf and they had something to eat. At the top of the hill we looked over the river, still raging. The brown water covered the land, the farm disappeared. Nothing showed above the surface of the water. There was no sign of a living soul as far as we could see.

As soon as we could get to the road, we hitched up a waterlogged cart to one of the donkeys and headed into town. Halfway there we saw, in the distance, a bedraggled pair trudging toward us. We took the stick to the poor donkey and trotted up to them, waving madly. Paying no attention to the mud, we jumped off the cart to run the last few feet toward Uncle Fan and Deng, crying out of happiness, and hugging each other in a tight cluster.

3

THE WAR YEARS

The crippled C-46 spun out of control, rudder smashed, engines trailing smoke. Deng and I watched it in the distance, twisting down behind the mountains. "There's a parachute, little sister. One of the airmen is escaping."

"Why is the airplane turning like that? What is a parachute?" We had watched the aircraft many times, high overhead, flying from our homeland of Yunnan to the country of Assam. Uncle Fan told us of airplanes taking supplies from India to the Chinese armies.

"Silly goose, the Japanese Zeros probably fired at it when it was crossing over. They wounded the airplane. It's out of control. A parachute is a big bag that pilots use to escape from broken airplanes. It has strings - look, you can see them - and the air fills the bag so they come down slowly."

My cousin Deng spent hours watching the skies, dreaming of being a pilot himself. This was the first time one had come so close to us. "Will he be safe, Deng?"

"It looks like he'll land way up the river. Look, there goes a Japanese patrol up the road to capture him. If he does land safely, they'll take him prisoner."

"Will they hurt him? What does being a prisoner mean?"

"Wan, don't ask so many questions. For a seven year old, you sure are a big bother. 'Prisoner' means they will keep him in a cage at the prison compound in Mandalay; he must stay there until the end of the war. They're not supposed to hurt him but we've heard all kids of stories about how little they give the prisoners to eat. Some of the Japanese officers are very mean, and sometimes torture them."

We saw the Japanese patrol truck come back down the road a couple of hours later and looked carefully to see if they had a prisoner. We saw the parachute piled in the back of the truck but no foreigner. Deng and I talked about it and figured the pilot must have died.

The Japanese landed in lower Burma in 1941 and easily established themselves in the major cities. We heard about the American, General Stillwell, escaping from Burma with some Chinese troops in February 1942, and laughed at his strange nickname, Vinegar Joe.

A platoon of Japanese soldiers were stationed in Bhamo. We knew all about them. They requisitioned a section of the school, forcing Uncle Fan to condense classes. Uncle Fan hated them. They forced him into service as an interpreter. Their commanding officer was young and very arrogant. He berated the Chinese as weak, and often said that the Imperial Japanese Forces would soon take over all of China in the name of Emperor Hirohito.

The war, following the year of the flood, made life difficult. The presence of the Japanese military was unsettling. Traders stopped traveling through. The Japanese confiscated our farm produce. News of the outer world and letters from Yunnan ceased.

It was all bad at first. The Japanese Occupation Army ravished the country after chasing the British and American-backed Chinese troops out of Burma. If anyone hid a soldier or gave food to the fleeing troops, Japanese soldiers retaliated by leveling a home and killing the occupants. Notices were posted at the school and in town warning against helping enemies of Japan. Punishment was instant death.

The morning after the plane crash, Aunt Chen was in town with Uncle Fan. I played by the river bank looking for mud crabs and pretty stones. A large, strange lump caught my eye, lying inert on the edge; it was a body. Frightened, I ran back to the house, shouting, "Deng, Deng, come quick." Deng was grooming the oxen, always a miserable job.

"What now, little sprig, are you filled with girl-questions again? Why must you always bother me? Ask Aunt Chen when she comes back."

"Deng, don't be mean," I said, after catching my breath. "You must come down by the river bank. There's a body there." Stuttering, I said, "And, and...I think it's dead, it's not moving."

We both ran fast as we could back to the river, Deng ahead of me as usual, with his long legs. He was kneeling beside the limp form when I caught up.

"It must be the American pilot. There's an American flag on his sleeve and he's still breathing. Pilot, pilot, can you hear me?" Deng tried to turn him over.

I squatted on the other side and saw his eyes flutter and focus on my face as Deng helped him turn over. "Deng, what should we do? I'm scared." I spoke Mandarin. We always used our mother tongue with each other. I heard a groan from the man.

"Ni hao, ni hao (are you all right)," I said.

"Silly, speak English, like father taught us. He's American and can't speak Chinese. Hello, hello, are you all right? Can you talk?"

"You speak English? Can you help me? Where am I? No, I don't feel very good, must have swallowed half of the damn river getting here."

"My father is a teacher. We speak a little English," Deng answered. "You are near Bhamo and there's a Japanese patrol looking for you. We saw them yesterday when they picked up your parachute."

"We must hide him, Deng. If they make him a prisoner, like you said, they'll hurt him."

"If we hide the pilot and they find out ...?" Standing up straight like a soldier himself, Deng thought. "You are right, little sister. First we'll help him hide. Then father can decide what to do."

The pilot watched us, warily. "For a young man, you think quickly. My name is Tony. What's yours and your sister's?"

"My name is Deng Huai, this is my cousin Wan Yi, of the family Kong. We are very happy to meet an American, the first we have ever seen."

"I am very glad to meet you, Deng Huai and Wan Yi. Now where can I hide until I get my stomach back? As soon as I can, I'll go away. I don't want to cause you trouble with the Japanese."

Puzzled, I said. "Where did you lose your stomach? We must look for it."

The pilot smiled. Deng chided me. "Silly goose. He means he's sick in the stomach. Let's take him up on the hill to the mango grove. The trees will hide him from the road and we can bring him food and dry clothes."

"You are very smart, Deng. You help him up the hill and I'll bring tea."

"Sweetie, if you could find me a piece of bread also, it might help me find my stomach. Ugh, I ache all over. Swimming down the river behind a log isn't the easiest way to travel. Give me a hand, young man. How far do we have to go?"

"It's just up the hill," Deng answered, giving the American a boost to stand up.

I watched them hobble up the hill and then ran to the house for something to eat and drink. There were mantou left from breakfast.

The steamed buns filled with minced pork would help. The water kettle was still on its hook over the fire. Aunt Chen always lifted the kettle, for fear I'd get hurt. Very carefully, with both hands, I lifted it off and poured some of the hot water into a bottle. I had seen Aunt Chen do it to pre-heat the container. Then I poured the water out on the sand pit. Next I pinched some fingers full of tea leaves from the can on the shelf, put that in the hot jar, and filled it up with the hot water. I wrapped the mantou in a banana leaf and put that into a basket, with the tea jar. "What else," I said to myself. "I'll take a couple of bananas and a bunch of lychee, Aunt Chen won't mind."

As I remember, it was the most exciting event in my seven years. I was grown-up and secretive, seeing and speaking to a real foreigner for the first time. Uncle Fan made us practice English all the time but we had never heard it spoken by a foreigner. Putting the basket over my arm, I slithered down the ladder, and gave a pat to Hsu Hsu, the donkey. His big ears raised like flags when I ran past him. "I'll be back, Hsu Hsu, don't worry."

Deng and the pilot were just where I thought they would be, deep inside the copse of trees. Deng and I played in a cave there many times, pretending to hide out from bandits. There weren't any bandits near Bhamo, but listening to my aunt and uncle's stories all those years, we always worried about fierce, bearded bandits getting us. The cave was tucked into the mango-covered hillside, hidden by clumps of banana trees. Their huge, floppy elephant-ear leaves could conceal anything.

"Tony, Mr. Pilot, said he has been in Kunming. That's where he flies from. Can you imagine, Wan? Uncle Fan will be happy to talk with him. Maybe he has even met some of our Kong family there."

Deng watched near the entrance, hardly containing his excitement. Our hero languished on a pile of rice straw we had brought in to make beds out of. I brought over the basket, and he looked up at me with the bluest eyes I had ever seen.

"Xie, xie (thanks), little one. The mantou look great." Ravenously, he ate them and reached for the tea bottle. The tea leaves had settled, the liquid a golden tan in color. He unscrewed the cover and took a long slow drink of the still hot liquid. "Wow, did I need that."

"Oh, you speak Chinese and know what mantou are," I squealed.

"Of course, sweetie, I can even use chopsticks. After eight months in China, I feel right at home."

"Tell us about Kunming. Is Green Mountain beautiful?" Deng

asked, anxious to practice his English and find out all he could about the land he had left at two years of age.

Relaxing, Tony leaned back. The food had temporarily relieved the stomach cramps and he sipped from the tea bottle. "Kunming is a beautiful city, called the Eternal Spring City, you know. Yes, Green Mountain is still there with the temple on the side of it. Every day, hundreds of people walk all the way up the winding road leading to it. I went myself, one time, with friends but I have to admit we took the jeep as far up as the road would take us and walked from there. The view of the whole city below is magnificent. We still haven't been to the famous stone forest but if I get back, I'll try to make it. Has your uncle told you about the stone peaks of the forest left over from some ancient ocean?"

We talked for a long time with the pilot until he fell asleep. While Deng sat outside the cave watching for any trouble, I went back to the house to wait for Uncle Fan and Aunt Chen. The clop, clop of the donkey pulling the cart sounded down the road. I hurried down the ladder to meet them as they pulled up under the house.

"What is it, little one, has anything happened to Deng?" My aunt always knew my moods and recognized my agitation.

"No, Aunt Chen... Deng is fine... but... we have a visitor. An American... We're worried... Deng is watching for the Japanese... Down by the river... He's up in the cave by the mangos... 1 gave him tea and mantou... He's blond." I stuttered everything until Uncle Fan stopped me.

"Wan, Wan, hold up, slow down and tell us exactly what happened. I've never seen you so wrought up. My quiet, peaceful little one is bubbling like a tea kettle."

We went up the ladder, and I very carefully told them the whole story. Uncle Fan went to get his flashlight and told Aunt Chen to stay in the house with me. He took off to see for himself exactly what the situation was. Aunt Chen, I remember, was very quiet, more concerned with calming me than thinking about the stranger.

The next few days were thrilling, with intrigue swirling around us. The American, well fed, soon recovered. Uncle Fan spent many hours, late at night, discussing the politics of America, China and Burma. They became fast friends.

The Japanese did not give up easily. They searched every home along the river, including ours. Aunt Chen just sat impassively, making me sit next to her, not saying a word. Uncle Fan was very polite, massaging the Japanese lieutenant's ego by telling him what a thorough job his men were doing. He diverted them by asking about the war events in Mandalay. How long, did he think, would it take them to conquer all of Asia? We were most afraid for Deng. He sat stiff during the questioning and started to say something about how they could never win the war. Uncle Fan stopped him with an order to muck out the corral.

One of the soldiers noticed the path going up the hill. He asked where that led to and Uncle Fan answered with a wink to the lieutenant, as if to say, 'another stupid one'. "To the mango trees, of course. There are some in the basket, take some for yourself and don't swallow the seed."

We all laughed at that, the Japanese officer especially. Everyone knows that only a elephant could swallow a mango seed. He lashed out at the soldier. "Take them, take them, you halfwitted cousin of a donkey. With intelligence like yours, we couldn't find a spy walking down the middle of the road."

After they left, Uncle Fan spoke more harshly than I had ever heard him. "Deng, stupid lout, you speak with stones for brains and your foot tangles your tongue. When you grow up, if you ever do, you will understand the way of the world."

"Did you notice the arrogant swine took the best mangos for himself?" Aunt Chen said. "They must be for his Burmese concubine."

"I don't want to talk in front of the children," Fan replied. "I've heard how he has the best rooms in the hotel, commandeered for his own use. There's a special hot water pool created in the courtyard, concealed with a high fence. Lin, the cook, hears screams of the woman when they go in the enclosure to bathe together. We know the Japanese love their hot water soaks, but this one is as mean as a snake. Prisoners are beaten often. They shot two of our citizens yesterday when they complained about the soldiers harassing their women. These are bad times. We must get the American out of here as soon as possible. Tonight I will talk to him. Deng, can you see where the patrol went to?"

"They have gone around the curve, father. I can see the trail of dust from their jeep far down the road. It's safe. I'm most humble at my arrogance when the soldiers were here. Please forgive me, father."

"You are forgiven, my son. The Master would probably say, *To escape the fangs of a snake, you must step around him.* I'll meet with our friend the American. Tonight, with the moon dark and an overcast sky, would be a good time to send him on his way. Get my oldest clothes, those that I work with in the field and don't wash often. The stench will not be pleasing, but they will be an excellent disguise."

I was with Uncle Fan as he discussed the plan with the pilot. It was my sad fate to give up something very dear to me to help him escape.

"Honored guest, I think it's an auspicious time for you to leave our nest. The moon is waning; there have been clouds for many days. You have the small compass from your survival kit and the map I drew for you. Deng is bringing up some old clothing. They will sorely aggrieve your nose but should have the effect of deterring strangers. The shoe polish in your hair has effectively turned it dark. I caution you to keep the peasant's pointed hat always on your head; rain would create havoc. The darkened skin from Chen's dye is good but be sure and keep your head down when you talk to anyone. Chinese do not have blue eyes. Now little Wan has something to say to you."

I stammered and blushed with embarrassment. "American friend. We wish ... for your safety. ... I ... want you to take Hsu Hsu ... my donkey ... to ride. He's ... much smarter than our other donkey. ... He ... came with us from Yunnan, before I was born ... and will remember the trails. ... It ... will be sad for me to lose ... my old friend ... but if it will save your life ..." I didn't finish the sentence, choking with tears.

"Little Wan Yi, I'll never forget your wonderful gift and the friendship of your family. Would you allow a barbarian such as me to put his arms around you as a token of love?"

Uncle Fan nodded agreement as I looked to him. I rushed into the arms of the big American as he hugged me tight, tears streaming down my face. My hand reached up to his cheek and felt his tears. These were moments of life never to be forgotten.

That night the American went on his way. Deng watched at the top of the hill, with a flashlight to signal if there was danger. Aunt Chen tied sacks of dried fruit and meat to the saddle, with two gourds of water. Uncle Fan explained over again how he was to keep traveling down the main Burma Road in full sight.

"Start at sunset and ride until dawn. Then rest under trees at the side of the road during the day, feigning or actually sleeping. Hsu Hsu will hobble easily and feed. Keep yourself hunched over, for the biggest problem you have is your height. Talk only to Chinese people - none are traitors, while some of the Burmese communists have toadied up to the Japanese. Deng will go with you to skirt the village and put you on the road beyond it. We wish you safety, American, and have great faith that your side will vanquish the Japanese. I'll remember with pleasure, the long hours of discussion. With good fortune our paths will cross again one day."

"Xie xie, my friends, thank you a thousand times. I owe my life to you and have the gift of your friendship. Especially Hsu Hsu, little Wan."

The tall American's legs hung down almost to the road. We stood there until the little donkey with his ungainly passenger disappeared. Deng moved down the hill and joined him as they went around the curve of the road. Just after dawn Deng returned and reported that everything went as planned.

The Japanese patrols searched many days for the missing airman.

Three months later, we heard a noise in the corral below, early in the morning. Fearing that something was attacking our meager livestock, Fan ran down the ladder, a club in his hand. Wan Yi, come to meet an old friend," he called up.

With shivers going up and down my body, I climbed down the ladder. A very gaunt donkey nuzzled me. A big ear turned to hear my whispering. Hsu Hsu was home.

4

POST-WAR BURMA SEETHES

The Master says, *When problems are ignored, they will
soon fall around you, as a blanket.*

"The war is over, the war is over. The Japanese have
surrendered." Deng ran down the road to our house,
hollering at the top of his voice.

August 28, 1945. The Japanese surrendered to the British in Rangoon.
The Bhamo patrol loaded weapons and personnel in their trucks, and
proceeded to Mandalay for the formal surrender. The final incident of
their occupation was when Uncle Fan found the Japanese lieutenant
down by the river bank, below the mango trees. Aunt Chen, Deng and
I stayed in the house. Uncle Fan told us later what happened.

"He was here and you helped him escape." It was a statement, so
Fan just nodded. "Was there a beacon used to bring him here?"

"There was no beacon, but my daughter Wan Yi has always believed
this part of our property is magical. I've found her many times just
sitting on the rock where you are, in a reverie. It was she who found the
American. We hid him in the cave up above until he could make his
way back to safety."

"I am Samurai, officer of the army that failed. Tradition demands
the ritual hara-kiri ceremony. I have embarrassed my ancestors. We
heard atomic bombs destroyed Japan. Millions of people are dead. The
cities, the buildings, the Empire of the Rising Sun obliterated."

From the porch we watched Uncle Fan and the young officer
talking. Their backs were to us, framed in the last rays of the setting sun,
transforming the muddy Irrawaddy into bright and shiny undulating
brown silk. There was enough breeze to stir the mango branches. The
buds of new fruit could be seen clumped high up in the branches.
Banana leaves waved from the hill. Fields green with new growth
promised a healthy crop.

Aunt Chen restrained Deng and I, surmising what might be
happening. Uncle Fan described the scene in detail. "The officer knelt
with the short sword in front of him, tunic open, baring the brown skin

of his body from groin to chest. A loyal aide stood by to complete the ceremony. He trembled, unsure of his mettle to chop the head from the body with the long sword. I feared there was little I could say or do to dissuade the suicide, but I tried.

"'Lieutenant, I'm a scholar and I know a little of your country's history of fierce warriors and conquering ways. The men you shot in the village were friends of mine; I can never forgive Japan for that. It was Japan and its nature that committed those crimes and eventually brought doom upon itself. The war has also devastated Burma, its destiny clouded. That cloud hangs over the future of my homeland, China. Seventy-five generations ago my ancestor Confucius lived. His sayings of twenty-five hundred years ago are valid today. It's proper to quote him, for he taught peace and pragmatic council amongst governments. The Master says. *How true is the saying that after a state has been ruled for a hundred years by good men, it is possible to get the better of cruelty and to do away with the killing.*

"'It's our fate to be here, knowing that within the next four generations, cruelty and killing could be stopped. There is something in the aura of this place that breeds Shou, longevity, to us. Go back into your world, lieutenant, forget the barbarism of your history that would split your belly. Let the hundred years begin. Hope for our future generations to enjoy a peace, instead of suffering war."

We watched Uncle Fan turn and walk away, his Burmese longyi skirt whipping in the wind. Hands clasped behind him, he looked exactly the part of the meditating scholar drawn on ancient scrolls. There are other moments and places to remember but this scene is indelible on my mind: the mighty river in the background, a lonely dejected soldier at its banks, the scholar walking up the path. Even then I knew that the world had reached a crossroads. History marked the date.

Burma became independent in January 1947. We watched history happen, as elections took place in April. Neighbors came to our porch to discuss the politics and happenings of the time. Sitting quietly in a corner, I caught snatches of the kaleidoscope of events through the words.

"Assassins killed Thakin Aung San. Good riddance, for he was a Marxist and collaborated with the Japanese."

"You're wrong, he was a good man, and saw the error of his ways. Assassination is seldom a weapon of democracy."

"And what of this Lt. General Ne Win, who has taken over the armies?"

"Thakin U Nu will be the first prime minister, if he can find an auspicious time to be inaugurated."

"Have you any word from Yunnan yet? The Japanese have left China, the warlord Chiang will try to oust the People's Army of Mao."

"I have heard that the Americans are supporting the Kuomintang. Mao will find it difficult."

Burma inaugurated Thakin U Nu at precisely 4:20 a.m. on the fourth of January 1948, an astrologically auspicious time. Burma became a Socialist Republic. In China, Mao Zedong warred with the Kuomintang led by the generalissimo Chiang Kai-shek.

Rural Bhamo insulated its citizens from the political turmoil of Rangoon, Mandalay, Pagan, and Taunggyi where the universities were. Uncle Fan's school enlarged as the Chinese population grew. Mao Zedong's People's Liberation Army routed the rest of the hated Kuomintang and chased them into exile in Taiwan. Landowners and former capitalists fled China by the thousands, fearing reprisals from the communists. Many came to Burma and some to Bhamo. They set up shops, restaurants, and roadside markets, and a few became farmers. Their children attended the Bhamo Chinese School, while the parents quietly integrated themselves into the community. They were good, hardworking citizens, avoiding the politics of the country. Other Chinese emigrated to the United States, Australia, Canada, and wherever they had relatives to take them in. They used up all the quotas available and then sneaked their way into Malaysia, Thailand, and Singapore. Hong Kong opened its borders to the millions that couldn't go elsewhere.

Traders returned to Bhamo, re-crossing the ancient trade routes, bringing letters from Kunming and some news of the lifestyle there under the communists. They told of communes formed for farming and factories. The Great Leap Forward plans for a common effort excited everyone for a while. Food became more plentiful, and clothing, though plain and uniform in style, was available. There were edicts from the government to restrict childbirth to one child a family so the motherland could survive. Petty and oppressive bureaucracy entrenched itself as members of the party flaunted their position and made cruel disposition of human rights. Uncle Fan received one of the little red books, *Sayings of Chairman Mao,* which he studied assiduously to understand the new emerging China. We read those letters and discussed them endlessly with others of the Chinese community, arguing the good and bad effects on the people. Everyone had relatives still living in China and many heard from them. As the world settled down into post-war peace, news came from Taiwan. The Americans helped Chiang Kai-shek set up his modern dictatorship.

Uncle Fan vowed to return to China one day and free the Chinese people, a paper dragon talking, as time proved. Once in a while news filtered in about America, the Golden Mountain. Everyone agreed that that was the place to go, if you could get in.

We of the Kong family lived a peaceful life as the years passed. Our farm prospered, and we helped Aunt Chen in the fields. There were rows of corn, tomatoes, long beans, cabbage, cauliflower, peppers, squash, and tiny hot chilies. Deng had ingeniously built dikes to ward off the common floods during the monsoon. We knew another major flood would wipe us out as before. Tethered underneath our house were two healthy oxen, and pens of chickens and ducks. The roosters woke us each morning. Four handsome ponies fed themselves in a nearby corral, and a riding cart stood next to the long farm wagon. Hsu Hsu became more cranky as the years passed. We seldom used him for heavy labor. He was a family pet and followed me without a halter around the farm, kicking at the ponies if they came near me.

Modernization set in. We had plastics to cover the seedlings so the birds wouldn't get in the field before the plants emerged. The hot-house effect accelerated the growth. Paved or hardened roads made transportation easier. We used bicycles on them more often than the ponies to go into town, unless there was a load of supplies to bring back or produce to deliver.

Uncle Fan, Aunt Chen and I sat comfortably on the porch one afternoon in the spring of my twenty-first year. We waited for Deng to come home for dinner together, each deep in our own thoughts.

"What is it, my husband? You are troubled." Aunty broke the silence. "Always before, you have told me when our lives met a mountain to climb."

"There is trouble, my wife." Fan turned from his gaze across the river and looked at Chen. I saw the pride in his eyes; she looked younger than her forty-two years. Uncle Fan looked older than his fifty-three, hair graying, a scraggly beard dripping untidily from his chin. "Yes, there's trouble. The school is to be taken away from us. New edicts from the Rangoon hierarchy have dictated the curriculum. Foreigners cannot teach any Burmese child. May the beard of my ancestor tell me what I am to do."

"There is another problem that we have to solve, my husband, wise one. The children are matured. There are few Chinese of their age to be with, and their blood must be rising. For some time I noticed they sit close to each other, and exchange secret glances."

"The change in the school and the children's future are troublesome. We must face the problems, dear husband. It's time for all four of us to plan the next phase of our lives."

"Trouble has always occurred in groups of three," Fan replied. "I wonder what will happen to complete the circle."

"Fan, your thoughts are drifting again, as the current in the Irrawaddy River. We must all talk and discuss our future. Maybe we should consider returning to China."

I listened to them talk. They appeared unaware that I was with them, so serious was the conversation. "Chen, I'm indeed fortunate to have a wife that can turn me around and point this senile mind in the right direction."

That day marked a crossroads in our lives, the right path chosen for our future. We three watched as Deng came up the road alone, waving to us on the porch. He scampered up the ladder, kicked off his shoes, stopped at the cold box to take the pitcher of cool coconut water and come out on the porch. Every night, we enjoyed the sunset together, before dinner.

Deng reached down to kiss his parents, an unusually affectionate habit for a Chinese. Our isolated lives, rather than tradition, dictated our emotions. Our love for these two old ones was greater than filial respect. Deng pulled off his shirt, turning the faucet and filling water into the large bowl on the stand. We had running water now, since the advent of electricity. The water tank was filled by a pump and light bulbs had replaced the old lanterns.

I realized we looked through three different sets of eyes at Deng's well muscled and tanned body, his shoulder muscles rippling as he scrubbed the day's sweat off. Like an actor, he smiled mischievously as he turned to face the audience, drying himself. Uncle Fan was proud of his strong son and happy that he had grown into a healthy young man. Aunty Chen's eyes took in the handsome face, still unbearded, with her husband's eyes that twinkled with inner self-confidence.

It was I who stared surreptitiously at the sensual mouth. Strong muscled arms protected me ever since I could remember. I imagined the hardness against me the last time we had embraced. My earliest memory is of Deng, who cared for me like a brother when my adopted parents were working. He defended me when dogs in the streets, or snakes from the jungle threatened. It was Deng who chased off the ill-mannered children when they teased us as ethnic misfits. We were Chinese and Confucians.

A spark was lit in us a year ago. On that stormy day, we huddled under a tree, waiting for the rains to soften, a loose poncho over both of our shoulders. The water ran off the outside of the plastic, steaming inside from humidity. Deng's arm was around me to protect me as always and I became aware that it was touching my breast, giving me a strange tingling feeling. I deliberately turned so that my breast curved into his palm.

Deng was afraid to move and I held his hand with mine, increasing the pressure in approval. He gazed into my face, our eyes boring deep into each other as we tried to understand what was happening. We kissed, faces wet with rain. I choked with emotion, trembling at feelings that were strange, wonderful, frightening, and demanding all at once. The rain, the humidity and the heat of our bodies under the poncho brought us together in an embrace as we explored each other.

Sexual coupling was part of farm life, ordinary occurrences among the animals. Aunt Chen had explained the wonders of the female body, at the onset of my menstruation. In the confines of our house, we easily identified Fan and Chen's actions in the late nights when they thought us asleep. We giggled knowingly when the sighs and soft words of love emanated from the bead-covered sleeping niche.

From that rainy meeting on, we dared only an occasional kiss, afraid to broach the subject to ourselves, let alone the old ones. Sleeping on our separate mats on either side of the living room tortured our young bodies. Dressing and undressing were suddenly embarrassing moments, after the many years of casual exposure to each other.

On the day so deeply imprinted in my memory, Deng and I sat cross-legged on mats in front of our elders. The two dearly loved people looked at each other. Uncle Fan gestured to Aunt Chen to begin, for obviously we had something very important to discuss. Aunt Chen lit up a new white cheroot and Uncle sipped from his bottle of local beer.

"Children," she said. "Forgive me, my children have grown. We must speak as adults and equals. Our problems are adult ones. We consider traditions and consult the sayings that we know the Master Confucius has left for guidance. Our lives have reached a plateau, a crossroads, and again we must seek an answer.

"Many years ago, when adversity descended on us, we came to Burma. Need, aided by Fan's courage and wisdom, saved the four of us. Now we have problems to solve and destiny to plan. The government requires the school closed, foreigners banned from teaching."

Deng spoke softly. "Yes, we have heard that news in the village. Everyone is against it. Burma is being run by the new leaders calling themselves socialists. None of the village leaders know the meaning of the term or what it may mean to them. All are afraid to oppose it.

"The wife of the wealthy shopkeeper at Maymyo was at the stand today and whispered that her husband was worried. She talked of leaving the country because the government would soon take over their trading business. Kyat, our money, would be worthless."

"Aha!" said Fan, his bushy eyebrows and wispy beard going in different directions that often made us laugh. "There had to be a third problem coming up. I knew it all along. What will we do with the hundreds of kyat we have?"

Deng, alert, spoke up again. "What is this 'three evils' that you talk of? We know only of the school and the government situation."

"It's you and I, dear Deng." I lifted my head slowly, eyes wet with tears, looking at the three people who meant the whole world to me. There was fear in my heart at what was happening, a terrible fear that somehow I had hurt the ones I loved the most. Looking at Chen with downcast eyes, I saw her nodding in assent. "We are adults, the childhood of brother and sister has ended."

Deng told me his thoughts later, in lover's detail. He looked at me, wanting so much to hold me at that moment, forcing himself to speak over natural shyness. "Tell me, father, what does the Master say about cousins marrying each other? We are miserable trying to hide our emotions from each other and you, our beloved parents."

In my memory, Confucius does not speak of inter-familial marriage, but there is appropriate advice he gives: "The Master says, *When problems are ignored, they will soon fall around you, as a blanket.*

"The medical texts are firm, however. They say that first and second cousins' merging of genes will magnify heredity defects and cause strange births. Our genealogy records Wan Yi's father as being from the Kong family, but a far removed branch from mine. Her mother, however, was my stepsister, born of my father's second wife. Therefore, in that relationship you are both first cousins, though a step removed, having the same grandfather.

"Neither Chen or Wan's father complicate the problem. To sum it up, a quarter of your genes are closely related. It is my inclination to favor the marriage. What is your opinion, my dear wife?"

"There is nothing I can say that would add any comfort. I must caution you both about bearing children, as much as I desire grandchildren. You are our only chance at Shou. You must rationalize in your minds exactly what might happen.

I hid my head and hugged my arms in embarrassment.

Deng continued. "We seek your approval and guidance but we have already decided. We like the life in Burma, especially as we hear more and more about the troubles in China. There are many stories you and the travelers have told us about the Golden Mountain called America. If trouble comes here, we would wish to go to America. In the meantime," he said, putting his arm around me, "we respectfully ask for permission to marry. We will vow to each other and have the local registrar prepare a certificate in proof that we have."

Aunt Chen and Uncle Fan simply nodded and reached for each other's hand. It was the longest speech any of us had ever heard Deng make.

The Immortals gave their blessing with a rosy sunset. That night, we feasted on crab. After we had stuffed ourselves and were ready to quit, we returned to the porch with freshly brewed green tea, to watch the full moon rise, unusually bright, a good omen for our future.

We sipped our tea silently, refilling the glasses from time to time from the thermos of boiled water. Breaking the reverie, Fan and Deng both spoke at once, laughing, then conceded to each other to start first. Deng finally began.

"Father, mother, lovely wife-to-be, I have a thought about our future. Father has worked many years, and deserves a partial retirement. Yes, I know he could never be idle. Mother has labored even harder than our oxen, from dawn to dusk for more years than should be necessary. It's my thought that we four should go into business together."

We all looked at this person, suddenly changed. Deng was a quiet child, a timid teenager, and now a serious adult with little social aggressiveness.

"There's a shop front in town, recently vacated by the grain merchant. It's available at a very cheap rental, needing considerable renovation. I propose we rent it and begin a restaurant and business like we have in the market. The itinerant merchants always ask for a place to eat where they can sit down for service. All they have now are hawker food stalls, which are often dirty, and make them sick. They have to stand up, squat, or sit on tiny stools on the sidewalk while they eat, and carry their own chopsticks. We could cook all our food from vegetables, chickens and ducks from our own farm and trade extra produce for meat from farmers we know and trust. Mother and father can journey to Rangoon on the train and purchase table porcelain, fixtures and equipment that we need. They deserve a vacation anyway. In the meantime Wan Yi and I will hire carpenters to help us remodel the building and erect a sign over the front." Deng stopped talking for a moment.

I became very excited, for I knew of Deng's dream. We had discussed it many times. "We could charge far more for our long beans, steamed and in bowls, than we are getting raw. They are the best in the village, few as large and tasty as ours. The seeds Mother Chen brought with her, many years ago, were more valuable than gold. In addition, we could sell carry-away and imported tinned goods. Deng and I will cook. Mother will serve the customers. Father will tend the counter, take the money and record our business dealings properly."

As the ideas were flowing, Mother Chen said, "I have an idea about the farm and who will tend the animals, plant the fields, and select the harvest. Our neighbors will be willing to share crops. We have to study the new government edicts to eliminate the possibility of being considered landlords."

Father Fan was strangely silent as we all talked excitedly about the new plans. It would be pleasant to sit at a counter and take in money, give his academic cronies a free cup of tea and provide game boards for them to play in a patio area during the hot hours of the day. After a while, he broke in. "And what about our wealth? The new government plans to change everything. Have you smart ones figured that out yet?"

Mother Chen answered, "As for the government decrees, our friend, the official registrar, will help us. I've heard that we can keep the land as long as it is a small portion and worked ourselves. We built our house long ago. Our personal belongings are modest. They will leave us alone, as we are the smallest peas in the pod.

"It's my suggestion," she continued, "that we quietly take our kyat and transform it into other forms as subtly as we can. The restaurant will need several hundred kyat. The fixtures and equipment we buy should be of the finest. Invest as little as you can into the floor, woodwork, and front. Good food is more important. We will convert some kyat into foreign money with the traders, bit by bit. If we offer more than the official exchange, they will jump at the chance. I have seen them carry India rupees, British pounds, Chinese renminbi, and even American dollars. I understand you can spend American dollars anywhere in the world.

"In addition, we can buy certain treasures from the traders and old families here. Fan, you can ask your friends at school if they have an exceptional piece of jade. Pretend it's a present for me, honoring our twenty-fifth anniversary. Wan Yi, solicit your merchant neighbor, the jewelry lady, and ask about fine rubies. Explain your interest in gems.

"She is familiar with your stone carving and might obtain hunks of rough jade material that can be carved later on. The criteria should be small and valuable. I've seen great pearls on the Maymyo shopkeeper's wife. Maybe they are worried too, and need money to bribe the officials with. If we all try, in a few years, we can convert most of our hoard into more marketable and portable value. We must be ready for whatever may happen in the future."

We all sat back in individual wonderment of what we had discussed. Far-reaching plans, promising to change our lives. The moon was descending, and Deng and I sat close to each other. We savored the approval of our elders. Our minds spun with ideas to add to the ones already proposed. Watching us were Fan and Chen, re-living their own decision to leave China and start a new life a generation before. They were about our ages then. They smiled at each other, holding hands, needing few words to augment their feelings.

5

THE WEDDING OF WAN YI AND DENG

The Master said, *To fail to speak to a man who is capable of benefiting, is to let a man go to waste. To speak to a man who is incapable of benefiting is to let one's words go to waste. A wise man lets neither man nor words go to waste.*

It's hard to believe that the girl walking down to the river is my thirteen-year-old daughter, Mei Hua. Her body is rounding with women's breasts and hips, most of the baby fat gone. The lovely long black hair, twisted into a single braid, hangs down her back to the waist. A bright colored longyi wraps around her stocky form, bare feet comfortable in the mud rows of the growing vegetables. Mei Hua, whose name means beautiful flower, was born in the Year of the Snake.

Mei Hua is intuitive. Her mind is that of a seven year old and will probably remain so. She has a phenomenal intuition and can tell what I am thinking or about to ask of her at the same moment I begin. Just now she was leaving to play by the river bank, and I was about to caution her. Before I could speak, she said, "Don't worry, mother, I won't go into the water. Crabbies are in mud. Mei Hua be careful."

She kissed me, picked up her yellow plastic bucket, skipped down the ladder and took off toward the river to hunt for mud crabs, one of her pleasures. From the height of the porch, I could see her setting the bucket down near the rocks. She hitched up her skirt between her legs and walked around the muddy edges of the river bed.

Our son Meng Li is nineteen, a duplicate of his father, Deng. Born in the Year of the Pig, he is very resourceful, as are all under that sign. He has unusual wisdom and talent. Taking over the chores of Father Fan in the restaurant, he also manages the whole grocery and packaged goods department by himself. Our restaurant, The House of Kong, is the finest in Bhamo, known far out into the surrounding province.

Deng, the ever famous chef, still does most of the cooking. Mother

Chen and I take care of the customers and supervise the half dozen young people we have serving them. I rush home to be with Mei Hua after lunch. She stays the mornings with our neighbor and waits for my bicycle coming up the road.

We are a close-knit family group and still gather most evenings on the joint porch of our homes. Father Fan remains the scholar and sage. Mother Chen, the keystone, wise and far-thinking, reminds us constantly of our heritage and China. Deng, my husband these many years, works very hard, saving every kyat that comes our way.

My afternoons, spent at my workbench, are my private pleasure. It is here that I work over interesting gemstones. I study the rough material for days or weeks to see what form a gem takes on the inside. A turtle, frog, or maybe a beautiful lady takes shape in my mind. Then comes the process of letting the image appear. I chip away at the outer matrix and detail the shape of the figure. Carving gemstones is another world for me to escape into. I keep the rarest sculptures that I love most on the shelf for our family and friends to enjoy. We sell the others in the shop, bringing amazing prices from the traveling traders.

The years have passed swiftly. I can remember every detail of our wedding. We festooned the hotel ballroom with red-tasseled lanterns. Undulating paper dragons decorated the walls to wish us good fortune. Paper fish hung from the ceiling to bless our marriage with children. We put aside the trepidations of inter-familial marriage.

Firecrackers were set off continually to let the Immortals know of our marriage. Almost every person in Bhamo was there to wish us well. Boxes of gifts, piled higher than we were, stood in one corner. Deng's pockets overflowed with envelopes of kyat good wishes.

I remember vividly that there was a strange guest at the wedding. The Karimganj family of Indian traders introduced him. These travelers from India became loyal friends over the years. They brought goods to sell from the world outside and often dined in our home.

The official government postal service was very inefficient. The Karimganj took letters for us into Yunnan and brought answers back on their return trip. It was our good fortune to have their presence at the wedding. Their friend was an Arab from a far-off Arabian Gulf country, the son of a famous sheikh. He wore his native garb for the wedding, a striking all-white flowing robe with a jeweled banded burnoose around his head. I knew enough about gems to recognize the precious emeralds, rubies, sapphires, and diamonds as real and very valuable.

Frederick Fisher

Tall and handsome, he looked every bit a prince. His Highness traveled with the traders seeking treasures for his father's empire. He knew of the world-famous Burma rubies and large pearls auctioned by the government each year. We all knew the finest gems never reached the government's tables. The borders were too vast and the clothing of travelers had many secret pockets for the small valuables.

Mother Chen told us about Prince Arum. For many days after the wedding, when Deng and I were on our honeymoon in Maymyo, the prince sat down by the river with Father Fan and debated world politics. The scholar was insatiable in his desire to learn of the world outside and the way governments operated. The two could be seen from the porch in silhouette, late in the day, their heads close in deep conversation.

That particular point of land where the river bent was meaningful for our family. It had a magical attraction for us, as well as foreigners. The American pilot had beached himself there. The Japanese lieutenant had intended his ritual suicide at that exact spot, when Father Fan stopped him. Mei Hua played at that point every day the weather permitted, collecting river stones and other river jetsam. We planned to erect a pavilion there one day to better enjoy the river view.

The prince was gallant and knowledgeable, so Mother Chen related, discussing the characteristics of fine gems with her when Fan napped: the peerless pigeon blood color of Burma's finest rubies, jade from the Kachin area, and pearls from Rangoon. Mother Chen trusted him and showed some of her collection. None but our immediate family had ever seen the valuables.

The collection impressed His Highness. He begged to buy two particularly rare gems. One was a large oval cabochon ruby, exceptionally flawless, without a whisper of a cloud inside, the curved striae through its grain proving it natural stone. The perfect pigeon blood red, when seen in the sun, transmitted a fiery beam that dazzled the Arabian wanderer. The other rare gem was a golden pearl, measuring twenty millimeters, its surface unflawed, without so much as a dimple. It rolled true as a crystal ball across the flat surface of the table, without deviating.

The pearl we acquired from the Maymyo merchant's wife, and the ruby from the fat jewelry lady in the marketplace. Both had needed money before the traders returned after the war. Mother Chen became an astute trader and offered more than the government company. She would only buy if the quality was superior, recognizing the value would increase over the years.

50

Arum, the prince, offered the enormous sum of 15,000 English pounds for the ruby, one thousand per carat. He added another five thousand for the pearl. It was more money than mother or father had ever seen before, irresistible. They added the twenty English thousand pound notes to the secret horde of other foreign currencies.

"May the Immortals bring you long life, honored sir," Father Fan said, as the sheikh's son left.

"May the same Gods bring you the freedom you wish and return to your homeland soon, honorable Kong Fan Shi. I will always remember the many hours we have spent in the company of your distinguished ancestor, Confucius."

Father replied with one of his favorite sayings of Confucius:

The Master said, *To fail to speak to a man who is capable of benefiting, is to let a man go to waste. To speak to a man who is incapable of benefiting is to let one's words go to waste. A wise man lets neither man nor words go to waste.*

"In this instance I must say that our association has been far from wasteful. With good fortune, we or our next generations will meet again." Fan bowed in respect, then extended his hand in the western manner to grip the Arab's.

They told us of the good fortune when we returned from our honeymoon. It might take many years, but when we leave Burma, we would go with treasure that could insure a peaceful old age for Fan and Chen. Also, the wealth would provide a fine education for our children and theirs for succeeding generations. We left the making of plans to conceal such treasure and transport ourselves back to China for another day.

Deng and I built a house for ourselves, but it had an adjoining porch with our parents' home. Our lives prospered as we finally dared to conceive Meng Li, a perfect boy child in all ways, allaying our fears of the family genes producing a defective baby. It encouraged us to try again and eight years after our marriage the immortals blessed us with Mei Hua. Like Meng Li, she was perfect physically. By the age of three, we admitted Mei Hua was slow. By that time, we were all so taken with the bright-eyed smiling child who seldom spoke that we considered her an exceptional gift from the Immortals.

At seven and eight she could compose simple phrases, though seldom a complete sentence. Intuition of what we wanted of her was almost magical and we knew we had a treasure. Father Fan and I became her teachers, the local school being unsuitable for such children. From the time Mei Hua was born, she never cried, even when she was hurting from falling down. When she desired attention, she needed merely to look up at any of us with that beatific smile.

Meng Li had the advantage of his grandfather's companionship. They would spend many hours of their lives at the river sanctuary, playing chess, fishing, or just talking. We built the small pavilion at the bend of the river with benches to sit on and the wide river to contemplate. The family history fascinated Meng Li. He absorbed all the information his grandfather could impart, then asked for more. He would study the *Analects* and come up with one of the Master's sayings that was particularly complex. For days after, the two would argue logic, sometimes heatedly over the words. What did the Master mean and how did it apply to today's world?

We celebrated our twentieth wedding anniversary. It was a tranquil world until one day I noticed Mei Hua coming up from the river. Her bucket overflowed with mud crabs crawling all over each other to get out. She washed the river mud off her legs. Blood oozed from the instep of her foot. "Hurt, mama. Mei Hua hurt foot. Mei Hua good girl, mama, come home when sun is straight up, like you said."

I instructed my daughter, if she was playing alone down by the river, to come home at noon. When the summer monsoons arrive, as they had for the past two weeks, the river swells and is dangerous. It changed the contour of the shore, often coming high up on the pavilion, then receding, leaving the trinkets Mei Hua loved so much. This time she had evidently cut herself on a half buried piece of glass or rock.

"Sit down, Little Flower, I'll clean and bandage it for you." I washed the wound thoroughly, dabbed it with alcohol, applied some tiger balm, and wrapped her foot in a banana leaf.

As always, there was never a whimper of pain or hurt, as if she were anesthetized. "Hurt gone, mama. Mei Hua bad girl?"

"Little Flower, you're a good girl for coming home. Look at all the mud crabs you have brought. The bucket is filled. How did you cut yourself?"

"Pretty rock, mama. Too heavy for Mei Hua. Mama come to see rock. Too heavy to carry. Mei Hua see rock in sitting place. You come now, mama, see pretty rock?"

"Later, Little Flower. Wait till your brother Meng gets home. He's strong and will bring the rock back for you to play with." Souvenirs found along the water's edge filled the shelf alongside Mei Hua's sleeping mat. She collected bits of driftwood, identified as a turtle, or rabbit, or egg in her mind. Endless river stones of all shapes, pieces of colored rope, and bottles thrown from boats plying the river were treasures.

"Here, go down the road and meet Meng, he'll be home soon. The lunch hour is over and he likes to study in the afternoon."

I could hear her talking to Meng as he wheeled up on his bicycle. "Meng, Meng, come get rock with me. Now, Meng. Mama said, you help carry rock. Rock too heavy Mei Hua. Meng, Meng."

"Quit bothering, you little pest. I'll go later. You are like a fly buzzing around my nose. Go away, fly." Meng adored his little sister and would sit for hours teaching her words or telling her stories of China. He knew she understood very little, but talked anyway. If her big brother Meng was talking, she would sit transfixed, nodding from time to time to make him think she comprehended. We know little about how much she does understand, and are constantly amazed at what she says.

"Mei Hua not fly, Mei Hua girl. Hurt foot bad on rock. Meng come quick to catch rock before bad water wash away. Please, Meng."

Watching from the top of the ladder, I could see Mei Hua tugging at her brother. "There's a rock she wants for her collection, apparently uncovered by the recent flood waters. Go help her dig it up, it was too heavy for her. Be careful, it's sharp. It cut her foot up somehow when she found it."

Letting her pull him by the hand, Meng laughed. "Okay, little fly, buzz, buzz, show me where your rock is. Your shelf is full, where'll you keep it if it's that big?"

Content that he was going with her, she gave him that ultimate reward we all coveted so much, the Guan Yin smile as we called it. Looking up at her brother, the whole face lit up with gratitude and happiness, irresistible. Limping on the injured foot, she pulled poor Meng down the worn path to the river. "Not fly, Meng. Mei Hua girl, not fly," I heard her say.

Meng returned a few minutes later, went over to the wash-stand to clean up, as he always did, and settled down on the porch. He loved to use Fan's chair in his favorite corner in the shade of the palm trees grown tall over the roof of the house. Fan would never disturb him, proud that he studied for hours in his place. This was his favorite time to drop deep into the reverie of ancient China, or the language of the Latins.

Before he settled down, I asked, "Did you get Mei Hua's stone for her?"

"Yes mother, there were two stones uncovered by the river. They must have been there for years, apparently one big rock that broke in half. I dug them up and put them in the pavilion so she could play with them. They're a green color inside, covered with years of mud and silt. Little Flower is washing them off and will play for hours. She just loves the river debris. May I have a cup of tea?"

It was a few nights later when Mother Chen called over from her side of the porch. "There will be a full moon tonight. Let's all go down to the pavilion and have our after-dinner tea there. The Irrawaddy is so beautiful when the moon is bright."

Mei Hua led as usual, skipping down the path ahead of us, always willing to go any place as long as her beloved family was there. Meng Li carried two hot water thermoses and I brought the basket with our cups and tin of tea leaves. Evening tea is ceremonial for us when we go to the pavilion. We use our finest porcelain teacups with the covers. They came all the way from Jingdezhen in Jiangxi China, hand-painted with famous scenic places. We played the games, climbed a steep hill, or sat in the pavilion and enjoyed the tranquility.

Mei Hua was playing with two halves of a boulder, apparently the rocks she had cut her foot on the other day. "Look, Mama, pretty rocks. Meng help Mei Hua get rocks." Turning to Mother Chen, "Look, Po Po, rock hurt Mei Hua foot."

We all watched her as she toyed with the heavy pieces, fitting them together like a puzzle then twisting them open again. Together they were the size of a soccer ball, apparently quite heavy from the way Mei Hua was struggling each time she moved them. We talked and laughed as we watched our Little Flower. Then, there was that moment that transfixed the scene, recorded forever in our minds.

The moon, reaching its full height, cast its ray upon the half-stone, as Mei Hua held it in a precise angle, by chance or direction. Moon rays lit the center of the half in her hands then reflected to the other half on the deck next to her, facing the five of us.

The phenomena affected each of us differently. For myself, I saw the center of the reflected half turning liquid, a green so vivid and intense that it burned into my memory. It appeared to boil, as if the lovely green syrup would spill from its bowl. Father and mother gasped, then reached for each other's hand. Deng and Meng Li abruptly stopped teasing Mei Hua about her pretty rock. I sensed immediately, as all gem lovers do, the aura of beauty far above anything I had ever experienced before. Shivers of excitement electrified my body. My heartbeat accelerated. Intuition stunned me into a comatose state.

Deng suddenly noticed my silence, reached for my hands, and said, "What is it, Wan Yi? Why are you trembling?" It broke the spell. I stuttered something unintelligible while walking over to my daughter, dropped to my knees alongside her and reached for the half of the boulder facing me.

"Is it really jade?" Father Fan asked. He and mother reacted as I had, having felt the impact of the phenomenon, the presence of something or someone taking hold of our lives. At that moment we sensed a change in our future. The Immortal controlling our destiny was in aura about us.

I found my voice in what seemed like an eon of time later. "Yes father, I believe it to be a boulder of jade, the finest I have ever seen. The wonder is that the other half of the rock is right alongside it. It could have been split in some far-off place a hundred or a thousand years before. To break such a rock required a tremendous blow. It would take many changes of the blade of the diamond saw to make a cut such as this. The molecules of jade hold to each other with the tenacity of a sister and brother in a great storm."

Mei Hua looked at each of us, perplexed by the sudden attention to her toys and the sudden quiet that had come over all of us. "Mama like Mei Hua's rock? Moon makes pretty. Look, Meng, pretty rock." Pushing it toward me, she said, "Present, mama. Mei Hua give present. Mama like rock?"

She was a giving child, always putting her treasures into our hands, sharing a stalk of sugar-cane, a pretty bottle. Anything she liked could be a gift for one she loved.

"Yes, Mei Hua, your rock is beautiful, I love your rock as I love you." Cupping her chin in my hand, smoothing her hair from her forehead, I bent and kissed her cheek. Only a storyteller could imagine how the jade came from the mountains of Kachin, split and lay these many years at this precise bend of the river, to be discovered by our Mei Hua. Only a storyteller could imagine what would emerge from the jade to affect the lives of so many.

6

THE KONG DESTINY

⎯⎯⎯⎯⎯

Wan Yi, you spend more time looking at the jade than you do your family. What do you see inside the rock?" Deng caught me in the late afternoon on the porch, the jade on a table angled to the setting sun.

"It's strange, dear husband. There's an aura about this jade that's different from any I have worked with before. A shape will usually disclose itself in a gem rock. Inclusions, oddity of the crystal formation, patterns of color reveal the object. This twin jade keeps staring back at me, daring me to penetrate its pattern. The color is thoroughly uniform, without a shade or a whisper of variation. The halves are as pure as mountain water. We must talk to mother and father about it. The jade is too valuable for my meager talents. If I were to make a mistake, it would be irreparable. We've talked about returning to Yunnan. This may be the sign we've been waiting for to make that decision."

That very night, in the autumn of the Year of the Horse, we gathered on the porch with our teacups. The moon was bright, almost full, stars sparkling in their vast array, each trying to help us. The golden Irrawaddy gleamed in the background. Mei Hua's jade was on a small table, its open halves facing us. We treated the split boulder as one of the Kongs, sometimes jokingly as the new twins coming to live with us.

Respectfully, we waited for Father Fan to speak. Since our marriage many years ago I called Fan and Chen father and mother. It pleased them and it was very natural for me.

"The moment has come, dear family. We have agreed to make the effort to return to China, each for our own reasons. Mother Chen and I because of the desire to join our ancestors when we die. We might even have the good fortune of a few years spent with the family in Kunming. Deng Huai and Wan Yi would live the dreams I have implanted in them, in the years of fanciful storytelling. Young Meng Li has the spirit of adventure that would probably take him in any direction if a good wind came up. We're blessed with our Little Flower, who desires only the security of the family blanket."

Mei Hua looked up at the mention of her name, noting the serious looks on her family. "Kong Kong, we go see Uncle Huo Huo?" The many stories her grandfather had told her about Yunnan always included the clown-like character of our Yunnan relative. Father remembered his younger cousin as always laughing, playing jokes, turning the somersaults of the acrobat. For our parents, he was symbolic of the joy awaiting our return to China. Father had spoken so often of him to little Mei Hua that to her, Uncle Huo Huo *Was* China.

"Yes, Little Flower, we'll surprise Uncle Huo Huo, but it must be a deep, deep secret. You must not tell any of your playmates even a whisper or it will spoil the surprise. Do you understand?"

We watched her get up, look all around, go to the edge of the porch and scan the area. Tiptoeing back, she held her finger up to her lips, whispering, "Secret, Kong Kong, no one knows secret. Mei Hua keep secret."

The humor of this marvelous seven-year-old mind, in an almost woman's body relaxed all of our tensions. We laughed so hard that tears came to our eyes, as she came to each one of us, pledging our secrecy.

Mother Chen, as always, brought us back to reality. "The Year of the Tiger should be favorable. It's a year for prowling and a time to be ferocious in our determination. Springtime would be auspicious for the long journey. In fact, it would be reasonable to tell our friends and neighbors that we are taking a vacation together for the first time in years. We have many months to sow the idea amongst them. There would be little gossip when we all disappear at once. Our treasures have accumulated. We have the English banknotes from the Arab traveler many years ago. Our hoard includes the American, Singapore, and Hong Kong dollars, exchanged on the black market with the tourists. There's some kyat in our bank account, which we'll have to leave there, to avoid suspicion. We will require some funds for traveling clothes and supplies. The balance will have the value of used newspaper."

Continuing, Mother Chen looked at me and the split boulder on the table. "Now, for the big problem; jade presents more difficulties than the valuables. Burma decrees jade and precious stones are the property of the government. If we're caught, severe reprisals would be our fate, as well as confiscation."

The jade swirled around my mind like a summer storm. "If I try to carve it, thus reducing the bulk, it would be a terrible mistake. First, no figure has presented itself to me, and second, my talents are limited. We must take it to Uncle Wang Shen, the jade carver in Yunnan you've told me so much about."

On the night of the full moon in the Chinese New Year, Mei Hua awoke crying. I thought it was the memory of the firecrackers and the undulating dragon celebrating in Bhamo two weeks earlier. "Hush, Little Flower, let's not wake the others. You never cry. What is it, my little one?"

"Mei Hua feel funny, mama. Something tell Mei Hua get up. Hold me mama."

"Everything is all right, Little Flower. Come, we'll go outside on the porch and watch the Immortal One in the moon." I took a blanket with us and we sat side by side on the bench outside. Our family spent the evenings talking late into the night and were all on edge because of the impending trip. Our nervousness had probably extended to the child. I knew she felt our trepidation.

It was the first full moon of the new year, described by the sages as having strange effects on the mind. It is especially on this night that realistic hallucinations occur, hard-to-explain visions of the future and the past.

My daughter and I snuggled under the blanket, warming each other. I loved the closeness of the child, as I had enjoyed the fulfillment of nursing her when an infant. She was gentle at the breast, eyes continually watching me while she fed, then holding tight with small fists as she slept. Her face looked up at me again, the oval eyes innocently beautiful in the moonlight. "Mei Hua's rock. Look mama, moon makes rock pretty."

The split jade was on a small table in front of us, left out from the evening's discussion. Its aura gave us direction and sense when we discussed our plans. One half had rolled, facing us on a slight angle toward the moon, the other, directly opposite, had tilted toward us. Our eyes were drawn to the lovely green gemstone. The rising moon lit the porch with floodlight intensity, brightening, changing the angle, focusing closer and closer to the exact center of the rock.

For a few moments, we were shocked. The moonbeam focused directly on the center. The jade appeared to melt, boil and come alive. A figure appeared within the stone, walking toward us. It was an old man with a high-peaked bald head, flowing beard and full robe whipping in an unseen wind. A staunch scepter with the head of a dragon was in his right hand. A fragile long-legged crane high-stepped alongside. To his left, a young spotted deer kept pace daintily, its eyes looking all around as if it was guarding its companion. The pretty pointed ears tuned into the wind to catch a sound of possible danger, the delicate nose twitching for a scent of trouble. The image of the Immortal smiled at us and proffered a luscious peach with his left hand. It was dripping with nectar.

Mei Hua recognized the figure. "Lao, mama, Shou Lao. Pretty Shou Lao."

It was Shou Xing Lao, the Immortal God of Longevity. Whether a dream, hallucination, or sheer imagination, at that moment it was real. The figure in motion so perfect in detail that the eyes moved from me to my daughter, delighted in her recognition. Shou Xing Lao raised the scepter in his right hand to wave at us. The peach dripped its nectar, so real we licked our lips in anticipation of the taste. The beam of light, diverted slightly, drew our attention to the other half of the rock. From it a mirror image of the longevity figure emerged, striding with opposite leg, the crane facing a crane, the deer's nose twitching at its own image. The figures moved simultaneously toward each other. I finally understood the meaning of the twin halves.

Art of our ancestors was often done in pairs. If one wished good fortune or happiness to someone, double gifts would signify double happiness, or double good fortune. The artist created two images, one mirrored the other as reflective twins. The degree of skill measured the exactness of the reflection.

The wonder of the Shou Xing Lao jade was that somehow the two halves of the split boulder had stayed together from its source. Centuries of river wear abraded the outside matrix of the jade. The inside was fresh, unaffected.

The story, often told by jade carvers, asserted that figures inside gemstones controlled their own destiny. They selected the sculptor to release them. In the mind of the carver, the figure develops, guided by a power within, recognized and acknowledged.

"Where Shou Lao, mama? Shou Lao gone."

The sharply focused moonbeam had moved on its way through the night's orbit. The images disappeared, leaving the emerald green sea of jade. Its velvety color glistened clear, depths devoid of the life we had seen moments before.

"Shou Xing Lao will come again one day, Little Flower. We are fortunate to have been here when he visited tonight. Did you see both of the gods with the spotted deer and the crane?"

"Yes mama, like seeing Mei Hua in water tank."

We had often watched our daughter leaning over the water tank to see her reflection. She would wave a hand, twirl her braid, turn the pretty face from side to side, and often talk to herself.

"We have another secret, Mei Hua, only you and I must know about Shou Xing Lao. Can you keep this secret too? Well, maybe we will tell the family. Can you remember to keep it secret?"

"Secret, mama, Mei Hua secret. I..." She struggled to make a full sentence as her brother had taught her, realizing the importance. I hugged her as her eyes began to close, tired from the experience, led her to her sleeping mat, and covered her with the blanket.

For a while I stayed in the company of the jade, trying to recreate the experience. Finally, I put the rocks together, tied them with twine, and stored them back in the room in the secret place under the fire box. Deng woke me in the morning, worried because I had overslept a full hour, well into daylight. It was the most pleasant rest I had had in weeks and I awoke refreshed, ready for the day, and our future. Mei Hua and I giggled all day long like schoolgirls, waiting to tell our family the secret that night.

It was six long years before we resolved our departure plans. Destiny guided us, though only I realized fully the identity of Destiny. My fears abated in the aura of my friends.

7

JOURNEY TO YUNNAN, SPRING 1986

The Master said, *If a man is correct in his own person then others will be obedient without orders being given, but if he is not correct in his own person, there will be no obedience, even though orders are given.*

Our departure from Bhamo that early April morning was festive, the sun bright with spring in the air. Almost the whole village came to see the Kong family off on our sabbatical; so we told our friends and neighbors. For the first time since the scholar Fan and practical Chen, with two small children, had arrived in Bhamo, our family was taking an extended holiday. We were a popular family, loved by everyone for our contribution to the community. Many remembered the education Scholar Fan Shi endowed them with before the government closed the school.

The House of Kong restaurant was a haven for good food and political discussions. The large round table in the back room constantly rotated argumentative scholars, pseudo-politicians, even monks and visiting lamas.

The announced destination was the village of Maymyo in the hill country. It was reputed to have small English-style hotels, a large botanical garden to walk in, and cool mountain air to escape the summer heat. Our friends assumed we would return in the fall. The capable staff cared for the restaurant and store. Neighbors gladly agreed to tend our livestock and farm the fields in our absence. The properties were sold years later but the Burmese government would not allow the export of the funds.

A mountain of luggage was piled on top of the garishly decorated Mercedes bus. We brought heavier coats and sleeping rolls for the expected cool nights in the hills. Underarm were baskets of food to last out the five-day journey. The 'farewell' crowd joked and teased us about becoming idle. Close Chinese friends wished us a special "Jai jian (goodbye)," sensing the deeper purpose of our travel.

The children carried backpacks, in the style of foreign teenagers they had admired traveling through Burma. Meng Li's haversack contained a soccer ball, much heavier than normal as the jade boulder was sewn inside. He stuffed sport shoes and playing clothes on top. Packets of dried raisins, cashews and coconut filled the side pockets. Meng Li's insatiable appetite required a considerable amount of constant fuel.

The morning we left, Mei Hua went to the grave of Hsu Hsu, at the foot of the hill near the bend of the river. It was a magical place for her. She talked to the stone replica over the grave often as if her friend was still alive. I saw her from a distance, arm around the statue, whispering in his ear. There were tears in her eyes when she returned to the house. "Mei Hua said goodbye to Hsu Hsu, mama."

It was difficult for all of us to leave our homes, fields, and the business for an unknown fate. A part of us stayed at the bend of the Irrawaddy, at the pavilion. I will always remember the jade figures appearing and walking out of the water into our lives.

According to plan, we left the bus at Kyaukme. We told the driver we would stay there for a few days. We were in no hurry to reach our supposed destination of Maymyo. Kyaukme is a pleasant town, famous for its spring festivities, called the Gokdekt Viaduct Shan Festival. The annual event, with its parades, dances, and open markets, was exciting. Road merchants came from far away to set up the brightly colored booths to sell food, clothing, medicine, toys, and the new plastic everythings.

Kyaukme occupied us for several days, then we boarded a train for an overnight trip to Lashio, also known for its scenic beauty. It was in the opposite direction of Maymyo, on the Burma Road. Mei Hua, excited by her first train ride, kept us up all night with constant chatter.

We rented a cottage on the edge of Lashio from a Chinese family. Like ourselves, they were restaurant operators in town. The camaraderie extended to comparing our businesses; Deng even went into their kitchen one day to show them some of his recipes. We dared not whisper a word of our intended journey, but I am sure they could feel our excitement.

Lashio days were pleasant for us, the effects on our family noticeable. Father Fan, now seventy years old, gained new vitality. His back straightened after a few days as he walked easily up the hills. Father entertained Meng Li for many hours with the tales of Confucius. I loved to sit near the two and listen to him talk about our ancestor.

"Shu Liang-ho was the father of Confucius, a large brute of a soldier, in the service of the Duke of Lu as a mercenary. He descended from the K'ungs of Sung, a neighboring dynasty. The K'ungs of Sung were famous: one a general, another founded a music school and library, a third a minister of the government. They say the minister's wife was a beautiful woman, and the wicked prince's designs upon her caused them to move to the State of Lu."

"Kong Kong, wife beautiful, like Mei Hua?" We hadn't even noticed our Little Flower quietly joining the group.

"Yes, Mei Hua, she was almost as beautiful as you. You're our little princess but listen carefully to the rest of the story. Shu Liang-ho was very unfortunate, according to the way of life in those days. He fathered nine girls and became impoverished with trying to provide dowries. It was tragic for there were no male heirs of the K'ung family, at least from his branch."

Mei Hua suddenly burst out in tears. "Mei Hua girl baby, no good. Meng Li boy baby, good. Mei Hua want to be boy baby."

Meng Li put his arms around his disconsolate sister. "Quiet, little one. Now, girl babies are more important than boy babies. What would we do without our beautiful girl Mei Hua? Here, have some of my raisins to make you feel better."

She pushed him away, knocking the raisins out of his hand. Glumly, she held her head in her hands, mumbling to herself, "Only girl baby, only girl baby, no good girl baby."

Father shook his head. Unable to do anything to calm her down, he kept on. "The old soldier, my age, took a sixteen-year-old concubine and from that union a son was born. She was promised a great reward if she could produce a boy child. In 551 B.C., our ancestor was born. At first he was called Chong Ni (Mud's Younger Brother), named thus because he was an ugly baby with a twisted nose and head all dented in. If you notice, my nose is twisted – and look at this dent in my head, like someone hit me with a stick."

Mei Hua, forgetting her dilemma, giggled at the name. She hugged her knees tighter, enraptured by the story. Father Fan leaned over, parting the hair on his head. He ran a finger through a small indentation in his scalp, then pulled at his nose to make it look more askew than it actually was. Mei Hua went over to father. Eyes sparkling with mischief, she bent his head down to feel the scalp. Putting both hands under his chin, she lifted his head and pulled at his nose.

Nodding her head in agreement, she giggled again. "Kong Kong, Confucius."

Father hugged her tightly, kissed the top of her head and continued the story. "Soon after the baby was born the father died and the young mother took her baby to Qufu, a town in Shandong Province. It's southeast of the capital, Beijing, near the town of Jinan. The halls of the K'ung mansion still exist today. People from all over the world interested in the life and sayings of Confucius visit there."

It was time for me to break up the storytelling. "Come now, all of you, let's walk into town and eat dinner at the restaurant for a change. It'll be sort of a party, and you'll have many hours to tell us more about Confucius, father. Come along, Mother Chen is waiting for us."

I remember being lavish with money, after hoarding all our lives. We indulged in a restaurant meal, splurging on the finest fruit, vegetables, and fresh meat was one of our frivolities.

The children and my husband retired early. Mother sat contentedly sipping tea. Father told me stories of the treasures created by Uncle Wang Shen, the jade carver. "Uncle Wang would be ninety-two now, ten years my senior, if he's still alive. There's a tale about the discovery of a jade stone so beautiful that a contest was held to see who could carve this treasure. The color was rare lavender, a soft bluish purple treasured by collectors around the world. Uncle Wang easily won the contest; there were none at the time with his vision or ability, yet he was only sixteen. A pair of matched lynxes, locked paw to paw, facing in opposite directions, leaped from the jade rock. He carved it so perfectly, their muscles appeared to ripple as the light passed through the translucent material."

"Do you know what happened to it, father? That must have been in the days when Qi Xi, the last Empress Dowager of the Manchus, still reigned."

"Yes, Wan Yi, the lavender jade lynxes were sent on to the Palace in Beijing. Huo Huo's father, the eldest member of the Kongs then, undertook the journey.

"It was sad. Though the jade was so rare and beautiful, the Empress Dowager rejected the color and gave the two pairs of lynxes to her protégé, Pu Yi. The young emperor-to-be adored the jade, and no one could take it from him. Traders told us that Pu Yi, when he became the puppet emperor in Manchuria, had to give the lavender jade lynxes to a Japanese general. It was necessary in those terrible days to curry favor to stay alive. Pu Yi, raised in wealth, could never understand privation.

"The Japanese general gave the precious carvings to General Chiang Kai-shek in exchange for his life, trying to escape just before the end of the war. He died anyway. The warlord Chiang had no respect for honor or human life. When the Nationalists escaped to Taiwan, the jade went with them in the possession of the one they call the Dragon Lady, Madam Chiang.

"According to the traders Karimganj, who are well acquainted with London collectors, the precious jade was sold by Madam Chiang for one million pounds to a private collector."

"History is sad, father," I said. "I hope the jade lynxes are in the hands of someone who appreciates their beauty."

Mother Chen, never the scholar but always the pragmatist, worked with Meng Li constantly, explaining the old system of examinations for students. There would be new systems to face. He would learn from the outer world. My son listened, drinking in all of the old woman's common sense. He knew of the modern inventions, of television and computers. He had seen the pictures of the Americans landing on the moon in the library. Meng Li hungered for knowledge that his grandfather and ancestors had. His genes had traveled through the labyrinth of generations from the venerable Confucius.

It was also Mother Chen who urged us on to complete our own plans. We bought two sturdy burros to carry our luggage, and a pony-drawn cart for mother and father to ride in. Three sturdy ponies completed the collection for Deng, Meng Li, and I to ride. Then we took to the task of repacking our possessions.

Meng Li, taking the jade as his personal commitment, concealed the boulders inside a brown earthenware jar of pickled vegetables. He wrapped it in raffia and tested the weight on the burros' load frames with other possessions. Similarly, we stored foods, pickled, dried, or wrapped in banana leaf, in the jars, ready for the long journey ahead.

Other earthenware jars contained the original ink stones, washers, brushes, my gemstone carvings, and family memorabilia. We sealed the family scrolls in waxed paper, as they were forty years before, to be concealed under the floor of the cart. Fan, yet the scholar, wrapped his precious horde of important books to hide them with the scrolls. Our coat hems and waistbands concealed the rare gems. Meng Li cleverly disguised the pearls inside plastic and wood beads, passed as cheap trade jewelry. Preparations were complete for the second part of our journey.

Two months had passed since we left Bhamo. We became anxious, the children irritable. The original joy of freedom began to wear thin. There were mountains to cross, the monsoon season would come soon and after that, winter.

"They're here," Meng shouted, bursting into the cottage one late afternoon. Impossible to hold down, Meng Li constantly roamed through the village, talking with the tradespeople, watching the trail for our friends. The pack train we awaited had finally arrived, crossing the breadth of Burma, from India.

"There are fifty burros, four families of herders to care for the animals and five members of the Karimganj family, our friends. I saw weapons concealed in the loads under the saddles, and three Gurkhas rode at the head, as guards. They're fierce-looking men with heavy black beards and carry big curved swords in belt scabbards."

Meng Li's excitement was infectious. Our friends were the traders we had known in Bhamo, bringing spices and rare foods for the restaurant. They have been to our home and drunk many a 'kam bei' with Chinese Mao Tai wine. Other townspeople respected the traders but never socialized with them, feeling superior to merchants of the trail. We, on the other hand, became very close, depending on their news of the world. Their connections spread internationally, from Bombay to London to New York to Hong Kong. They exchanged news from China with us and often carried letters to our family in Yunnan.

Meng Li raved on. "The eldest Karimganj recognized me and I told him where we were. He just nodded and went on. Do you suppose they know our plan?"

"Man, man (calm down), wild one." Mother Chen laughed at her grandson. He gasped out the words, breathless after the run from the village. "We are still in Burma and the traders are wise. The less said, the better. They'll appear soon enough. Let's make sure we have enough wine and food for them. Wan Yi and Deng," she said to us, "roast a couple of chickens with a lot of chili and red pepper. It won't be tandoori-style but you know how the Indian people love it. Have Mei Hua help make a stack of flat bread. Prepare large portions; it will be a long evening."

Later that night all five of the Karimganj were in the cottage, effusively greeting us. "You received our message?" Father Fan asked.

"Yes, the letter was waiting with my cousin in Imphal, as we passed through. We all agree with your decision to return to China. Burma will erupt in a few years, the blood of innocents will flow. The average Burmese is intelligent, and an independent people, contained under the ox yoke for too long. The students at the universities will lead them, as always. Education engenders democracy. What did your ancestor Confucius say about that, Fan Shi?"

"I believe you are referring to: *If a man is correct in his own person, then others will be obedient without orders being given, but if he is not correct in his own person, there will be no obedience, even though orders are given.*

"When students, in pursuit of knowledge, learn their leaders are deceiving them, it's only a matter of time until they seek freedom."

The eldest of the Karimganj added his thoughts. "On the other hand, China, under Deng Xiaoping, is loosening the yoke, seeing the need for democracy, even capitalism to a degree. By the next generation, it will again be respectable to think, educate your children, and open the gates to the rest of the world."

The Indians, with their own form of democracy, were straightforward and knowledgeable about the world. It was always mentally invigorating talking to them. Traders carried the threads of civilization. Governments tolerated them for commercial and often nefarious purposes.

Father Fan addressed the Karimganj. "How long will your caravan remain here, dear friends?"

"Seven days. Ten, if the villagers are loose with their money."

Deng explained what we had done so far, gathering transportation similar to theirs. He described the Indian-type saddles, pack frames and ponies for the journey. "We'd like to purchase passage with your caravan into Yunnan, as far as Simao or even into Kunming, if you intend to go that way."

The eldest of the Karimganj spoke, after a quick eye caucus of his family. "We would be proud to have you join us. You have paid us, these many years, with your friendship. However, there is great danger at the border. You must blacken your skins like ours and dress as we do."

The discussion continued until dawn, changing details, agreeing on a basic plan. We would leave Lashio quietly, early one morning and join the caravan in Hsenwi. I remember clearly the final words as the Indians took their leave. "There is no need for us to know what valuables you carry. It would be wise to disperse them amongst you in the event of fatal danger. The road you seek is full of unknowns. We fear the armed bandits more than weather and mountain traveling. The worst are the bureaucrats of officialdom, border guards."

We left before dawn a week later, to meet the Karimganj caravan in Hsenwi. Quietly, we merged our small group with theirs, and stained our faces and arms to match the darker skins of the Indians.

The older children and the adults were tense, sensing the possible dangers. I dressed as a man in the loose flowing clothes of the traders, wearing a burnoose head covering like Deng and Meng Li. We rode the ponies, helping to herd the burros and blend with the Indians. The caravan kept to the side trails off the road as much as possible because of the constant traffic of military vehicles. I remember the encampments at night, filled with pleasant food, music and the wonderful company of the traders. We felt free, like gypsies, without a care in the world.

The caravan stretched out for a kilometer, twisting around the winding mountain roads; overgrown jungle stifled the road bed. The afternoon heat lulled us half-asleep as we moved to the rhythm of the ponies. Deng and Meng Li were with me at the head of the caravan with the two elder Karimganj. The five of us were in the habit of leading the train. Far ahead, rode one of the Gurkha guards; the other two protected the rear.

Suddenly there were wild cries, gunshots, and the pounding of many hooves, alarming the whole train. We spun our ponies around and caught the fearsome sight of bandits coming down the trail behind the caravan. The rear Gurkha guards rendered their long rifles and prepared to defend the train.

"Bandits! Bandits!" shouted our Indian friends, quickly grasping the danger. "Hurry, get the train going on down the hill to the clearing below. Form a tight circle as we have planned." They rode back up the side of the caravan, shouting and whipping the animals into a frenzied run downhill. Guns suddenly appeared in their hands, concealed beneath their robes.

The sudden onslaught of danger stunned us. Our ponies began bolting downhill without our guidance. Meng Li shouted, "Chen, Fan, Mei Hua - they're in the rear of the train!" He fought his mount around and took off against the tumult of animals and people. Deng and I reined our ponies out of the stream and goaded them into following Meng Li. The Karimganj shouted at us to go the other way, but frightened for our family, we went on. The road wound uphill with its hairpin curves blinding us from what was happening at the rear of the train.

A crescendo of noise arose from the animals' pounding hooves; the bandits screamed battle cries to terrorize the victims. Rounding the last curve, we could see them, brandishing rifles and huge curved knives at their belts. Their plan of attack was to scare the people off the road into hiding while they herded the pack burros back to their lair.

Father and mother were just ahead of us up the trail. They had taken Mei Hua on the cart with them huddled next to Mother Chen for protection. The two burros, with our treasures, trailed behind, tied to the back of the cart. Father, whipping the pony, rounded the curve toward us. I was worried that they were all going over the side of the hill, as the cart careened on two wheels. Behind them, the two Gurkha guards stood fast on the trail, their rifles aimed at the descending horde. They held fire until the bandits were almost on them. The din was deafening. Dust rose in a cloud. Guns blasted streams of bullets. Screams of horses and men invaded the ear.

Deng and I wheeled our horses to take up position on either side of the family cart. The ponies needed no urging, the noise frightening them into frantic speed. Meng Li rode behind, brandishing a long whip he had been practicing with.

We heard more shots and pounding hooves behind as the Gurkhas caught up with us. One was bleeding badly. We could see his right arm hanging loose from a bloody shoulder. Riding his horse with his knees, his left hand brandished the terrorizing saber. Turning his horse, he waved to his companion to stay with us, and rode back into the oncoming swarm. The last we saw of him, he was standing firm at the curve of the trail where he could cut down the first to come around the corner. Not daring to look back, we heard fierce shouts, screams of pain, and finally gunshots, as the brave guard slowed them.

"Watch out!" the other guard called, and we heard pounding hooves once again behind us. Three of the bandits were still chasing us, having got around our defender. The other Gurkha wheeled his pony and swung the sword in a frenzied arc at the first attacker. The other two slipped by, trying to cut the lead ropes of our two burros. They came so close, I could smell the body odor of the men and the sweat of their ponies. For the next few moments, everything was a blur. I saw Meng

Li's whip cracking through the air as he defended us, heard the crashing of bodies as horses went down. There was no time to think. We just urged our animals faster and faster.

"Eeyah! Eeyah!" I could hear Meng Li's cry, as young warriors must have shouted in battle for many centuries. "Got them! Got them!"

He told us later, he aimed his whip at the leading bandit's pony, hitting right between the animal's eyes. Screaming in terror, it reared up, tossing its rider into the second bandit. The crash of animals and men hurled the mass off the side of the hill, tumbling one against the other to the road below.

Blood poured from Meng Li's hip, unnoticed until I pointed to it, terrified at the sight of the wound. We could do nothing for him in the rush to safety. Our badly frightened group finally arrived at the bottom of the hill to join the melee of the caravan. He slipped off his pony and collapsed on the ground before any of us could reach him. One of the Indian women rushed over to help, while we crowded around. She examined the wound and bound it up to stop the bleeding. "The bullet is still there," she said. "As soon as we make camp, we'll heat some water, remove the bullet and clean the wound. Your son is a strong man, he will be all right."

Mother and father were calming Mei Hua, whose only fear was seeing her beloved Meng Li wounded. The caravan had formed a circle, the armed men taking positions of defense. "They have lost too many men. We are probably safe now," the eldest Karimganj told us. "You have a very brave son to attack those savages with a whip. We saw the battle clearly."

The Gurkha guard went up to find his companions and led a sad cortege down the hill a half-hour later. He reported the two bandits Meng had battled, dead, with their horses, on the side of the mountain. A dozen other bodies, strewn along the trail, stripped of guns and swords, were abandoned by their companions. A pony carried the dead Gurkha's body. The other severely wounded one rode limp in the saddle, saved by his friend.

We made camp there to nurse our wounded and bury the dead Gurkha. The herders saw to their animals, unpacked the loads, checked for torn ligaments and damaged hooves. They fed and hobbled them in a nearby field to eat and calm themselves. The women bustled efficiently, setting up camp. They tended Meng Li and the wounded guard. I watched anxiously as the woman removed the bullet buried in the flesh; fortunately, it had missed the bone. Meng Li endured the pain stoically as they worked on him. I recall vividly the fierce grip as I held his hand. The woman that tended him had served as a nurse in the Indian Corps of the British Army, and was well trained in battle wounds. The nurse worked over the other guard for two hours, repairing severe sword wounds. There was little hope, she said, too much blood lost. The Gurkha died later that night, and was buried with his countryman the next day, high on a hill at the place of the battle. The whole entourage gathered around, the prayers mixed, of Hindu, and wishes to the Eight Immortals to protect their souls.

Our caravan camped for two days, where the Nanding He River widened and the people of Kunlong, across the river, came over in boats to trade for spices. The next afternoon, while Fan and Chen napped, Deng and I sat with Meng Li in the shade of the tent. We tried to look as inconspicuous as possible in camp. Mei Hua ran up like a frightened deer, screaming in terror. "Bad boys! Bad boys!"

The Gurkha guard told us what happened. Three young toughs from the village decided to tease the caravan's old women and children, camped near the river bed. The remaining Gurkha, now devoted to Meng Li, apologized for relaxing; he assumed there was little danger. Mei Hua apparently took their eye because she was more buxom than the slender Indian women. The young men pulled at her scarf and made lewd remarks, thinking she did not speak their language.

"Bad words. Bad boys. Mei Hua no like," Mei Hua interrupted.

The guard explained that the others gathered around to protect her. "I heard the frightened voices and ran over to chase the toughs, laughing and joking with each other. Unfortunately, one commented on the light skin of the girl's forehead where the scarf had been pulled off. He pointed out to the others that she wasn't like the other Indian women. I hope it won't cause trouble for your family."

We conferred with the Karimganj that night. "A friend in the village told us the young troublemaker reported to his father about the strange girl he had seen in the camp. He complained a group of soldiers with guns and swords chased them. The problem is that the father is the head of the Communist Party Cadre in Kunlong, the political chief in the area. We will have to be very careful if the border guards pay special attention to this caravan."

The Karimganj had warned us of the troublesome border guards.

The Burmese would confiscate our treasures, if discovered. They would treat us as criminals, and jail us as smugglers.

Deng, Meng Li and I went ahead to the next village, Ho Pang, a few kilometers from the border. We could see the mountains ahead of us. Deng said, "There is Yunnan, my son, China, which I have not seen since I was two years old. I must confess, there is nothing in my memory of passing through here but it does give me the feeling of heading home. This is the village that your grandfather and grandmother have told the story of. It is here that Wen Xian and Yi Ku lie, buried some forty years ago. I wonder if anyone remembers the incident."

The villagers of Ho Pang at first believed us to be part of the Indian trading party they had expected. Caravans often sent riders ahead to arrange a space to camp. The advance party excited the town by describing the goods to be offered. Invited into the cottage of the village elder, we asked if anyone remembered the two Chinese families that had stumbled into their village forty years ago. Others were called into the room where we had been sitting, having tea. They whispered amongst themselves, staring at us, the strange Chinese with the disguised black skin of the Indians.

"We remember your family very well. The story of their visit and the evil accident that took the life of the young scholar has been told as a parable to our children. A warning that to act in haste, even though frightened, can cause great harm. The young wife, who tragically gave up her life, has been wept over many times and thousands of leaves of gold applied to our Buddha on her behalf. Tell us, what of the child? A girl baby, if I remember. Did she survive?"

I shivered with excitement at the reception. "Yes, she survived. I'm the girl child, Wan Yi. Deng Huai, my husband, is the two-year-old boy child you took care of. Meng Li is our son, born and raised in Bhamo. We have darkened our skin to blend with the caravan and I dress as a man to be inconspicuous. We are with the caravan of the Karimganj, coming here in a few days. Fan Shi and Chen Wu Xia, the two survivors you met many years ago, are also with them and our daughter. It's our intention to return to China for the old ones to die peacefully in their homeland. Crossing the border is of great concern to us. We think the patrol know of our existence."

"Ayah," an elder exclaimed worriedly. "Just this morning we intercepted a friendly messenger taking a report to the border guards. Some people in the Indian caravan that were not from India. Being so close to China, we listen very carefully for border happenings, for our own safety. We are not in favor with the ruling party in Rangoon and we don't report everything we hear to the cadre chiefs. Our border families have been friends for hundreds of years, long before either the Rangoon or the Beijing communists thought of controlling us."

Shocked at the news of the potential danger, Deng said, "We must get back. It's our family they're talking about. We have to do something or they'll stop the whole caravan from traveling through, and may confiscate our belongings. We had intended to separate, the three of us to go over the mountain."

"Patience, my friend," the elder said. "Let me make a suggestion. We can atone somewhat for the terrible thing we did to your family many years ago. The old one you call Fan Shi returned good for evil, teaching our children while he was here. I was one of those children and to this day think of him every time I look at the stars at night.

"We know of a seldom used path over the border, impossible to guard properly. The trail is treacherous, winding upwards to more than twenty- seven hundred meters. From the valley beyond, however, you'll find your way into the village of our Chinese friends. They can show you where to meet up with the caravan on the other side.

"It is too difficult for the old ones, but you and the woman, Wan Yi, could make it across. Carry the possessions you cherish. The border guards will confiscate any valuables left with the caravan. Don't protest, we know what you probably carry. It is a pattern most Chinese follow when returning to their homeland.

"Your secret is safe with everyone in our village. The old ones and the young woman should cross with the caravan. The Burmese do not object to aliens, as they call you, leaving the country; the Chinese welcome re-patriots. Since Deng Xiaoping took over, there have been many changes in ideology, one of which is the return to tradition and respect for the elders."

We hurried back to our camp that very night and brought the others up to date with the happenings. The Karimganj agreed with the suggestion of the village elder. Deng at first refused to let me join him for the trek over the mountains. "The trip will be hazardous. You must travel with our parents."

Meng Li also agreed. "Mother, you stay with the caravan. I would be afraid for your life every minute of the way, the trails are narrow and dangerous. We will be many days on the backs of the ponies. If the

Burmese guards catch us, they would commit unspeakable atrocities with you, a woman."

"Enough of this silly conversation," I spoke up, in as firm a voice as I could muster. "I will go with you. Our possessions can thus be split up three ways, for easier carrying and safety. Enough talk, we have much to do this evening. Rearrange our packs and clothes, and select the proper animals to take with us."

Shaking their heads, they acquiesced to my wishes. The only problem was sending Mei Hua with father and mother. We had never been separated, even for a day, since she was born. She loved Mother Chen dearly, but it was to me she always turned. It would be difficult for me also, for I had decided to bring her into this world, responsible for her difficult life.

We packed the one burro and three ponies within the hour. Mother Chen removed the gemstones from the clothing that was to remain with them and added them to the waistbands of the three of us. The saddlebags of the ponies stored the books containing the paper money. A tarpaulin and sleeping rolls were lashed behind the saddles. Our burro's A-frame pack held the large pickle jars containing the jade boulder and my gemstone carvings. Our caravan friends loaded us with dried food, stuffed into the saddlebags.

One of the herders came over after we had packed the burro and asked if he could re-do the pack. Anxious as we were to get going, the elder Karimganj urged us to have patience. We watched as he made a special tie of the wooden A-shaped frame over the back of the animal. To the frame he added a second rope similar to the lead rope on the halter. He explained, "Keep this rope and the lead rope with you, as the burro follows you. If something happens to it on the trail, the load will release and hang from this rope. Thus, you have a good chance of recovering your valuables. May Vishnu guard you on your journey and bring you back to our caravan in safety."

There was little time for goodbyes. Mei Hua was crying with huge tears and deep sobs, not understanding the separation. Only the comfort of her grandmother could quiet her, for the two had become very close during the preceding days of dangers. We feared that, with her extrasensory perception, she sensed something would happen. We left in the dark of night.

8

OVER THE MOUNTAIN

꘎꘎꘎

The caravan arrived at Ho Pang two days later; Deng, Meng Li, and I were already on our way over the mountain. Meng Li was worrisome, still limping, favoring the wounded hip. He sat straight on the pony but I recognized his pain when he grimaced, mounting or dismounting. The surviving Gurkha presented the saber from his dead companion to him for his bravery. My son lashed the scabbard to the side of his saddle alongside the long whip, like badges of honor. Meng Li was no longer a boy.

The people of Ho Pang were delighted to see the Kongs again, recounting the story of forty years before. Mother Chen told me, months later, that the older people remembered them fondly, and asked about the seeds and seedlings they had given her. They spent many hours recalling the life of our family in Bhamo, and those of the villagers in this remote border community.

The elder reported that the three of us had stopped briefly, then proceeded quickly on through the village. His own grandson, Tiaung, had gone with us as a guide. It was a dangerous trail, difficult to follow from a map. He told them the plan was for us to take refuge the first dawn in a monastery on the mountain, where a friendly monk was in charge.

We arrived at the monastery early in the morning, weary from the past two days of tumult without sleep. The young novice, who answered Tiaung's pounding on the gate, recognized him through the small slide peephole. He unbolted and swung open the gate for us. "Wait here please while I attend his Eminence to advise him of your presence," he said.

He returned in a few minutes with another sleepy-eyed young man who took the lead ropes on our mounts and burro. The novice motioned us to follow him, through the compound, inner courtyard, around corners, and passageways, until we arrived at a large ornately carved wood double door. The young man rapped with the knocker and without waiting for an answer, swung one of the doors open. He entered first to announce us and prostrated himself on the floor, rapping his head three times before rising.

"The Venerable Aungsetkya Kyung, of the International Buddhist Missionary. Guests from Ho Pang, sir."

All my life I had seen and carved replicas of the figure we call Maitreya, Ho Ti. The Laughing Buddha traditionally sits with folded legs, bare feet facing forward, and wrinkled toes pointing out. A bald head and elongated ear lobes surround a face-wrinkling smile. The mountainous belly is bare, ready for rubbing each morning for good luck. Artists depict the hands in various prayer positions to bless the supplicant. Boy children quite often are playing around and on him, denoting happiness.

His Eminence, Aungsetkya Kyung, was the living image of Maitreya, even to the early morning dishevel of gaping robe, fat belly poking through. The happy face broke out into a welcoming smile. "Sit, sit, sit, friends, there will be tea shortly and maybe some dried fruit if this lazy novice of mine will take it upon himself to move." He commanded the young man, "Refill the thermos with fresh boiled water, and don't take all of the next ten minutes to do it."

We introduced ourselves and briefly told our story, leaving out mention of the valuables we were carrying. Tea, cakes and dried fruit appeared. The venerable one leaned back, rubbing his fat stomach and pulling at bare toes from time to time, while he listened as a confessor.

"You will rest in the sanctuary of our monastery. Your journey will be fraught with danger and stress. I am envious of the opportunity for a new life. It would take little encouragement for me to join your expedition."

After two full days resting in the delightful company of the Venerable Aungsetkya Kyung at the monastery, it was time to face the dangers of the mountain trail. "We'll spend the day in prayer for your safe journey," he said as we left.

The two-day rest healed Meng Li's wounds; he rode much easier in the saddle. The warrior was proud of his wound, though I shuddered every time I changed the dressing and looked at the ugly scar.

We talked constantly, while riding, of the problems we faced. The journey ahead and life in China thereafter were unknown challenges. Father Fan had dreamed of the time when the teachings of Confucius, the five 'constant virtues', would be the way of the world's leaders. I remembered vividly the figure of the jade Shou Xing Lao and his image, speaking to me one night in my dreams. He said, "I will help you, together we'll make the world see the real truth. Harmony of spirit will combine to win the greatest of wars, the fight for peace."

The elder's grandson, Tiaung, led the way up the switchback mountain trail, the pack burro on its tether behind him. Deng and I followed, with Meng Li in the rear, now assuming the role of guard. We had been going all night and daylight was breaking, the narrow trail becoming visible, less than a meter wide. The valley yawned far below, sending shivers down my back. It was better that we hadn't seen the trail, for a single misstep by our mounts would have meant instant death. Tiaung called a halt; we were to hide by day, out of sight of the border patrols. The growth around us changed, from bamboo, ferns, leafy plants, wild bananas, and coconut palms to the vegetation of a higher altitude, of firs, pines, and other evergreens.

We retreated into a glade off the trail, dismounted, and loosened the saddles of our ponies. Our hunger was sated, without a cooking fire, by dried meat, bananas, and a few clumps of lychee that Tiaung had spotted earlier. We went off into the bushes to relieve ourselves, returning with bundles of dead pine needles to make beds. Patches of snow were on the ground at this elevation; we needed insulation from the damp ground under our sleeping rolls.

While we wrapped ourselves in the bedrolls for a rest, Tiaung paced nervously, responsibility weighing heavy on his shoulders. Meng Li, with the confidence of youth and adventure, was sound asleep. My husband, worried for our safety, joined Tiaung.

"We are dependent on your judgment, young friend, what is your concern?"

"We've had early snow this year," Tiaung said. "The storm clouds worry me. It's possible heavy snow will catch us before reaching the peak, at least a day's journey at our present pace. If the weather comes in too heavy, we'll have to take refuge and wait it out. The advantage we have is, with the storm coming in, the guards can't see a hundred meters. We could cover considerable distance in the daylight."

"If you were alone, young friend, which would you choose?" Deng asked.

"You seldom speak, honored Kong, but wisely." Tiaung answered, a relieved smile on his face.

The decision made, we started up again, Tiaung estimating we were well past 2000 meters, with another 700 meters to go to get to the top of the first ridge. He pointed to the final divide and ridge beyond that. I shuddered at the awesome snow-covered spectacle, and retired my feelings into the comfort of a higher being controlling our destiny. Because of the impending storm, and the snow swirling around us now, our ponies and burro moved much slower. Tiaung and his mount, better acclimated to this altitude, moved ahead, often out of sight, and would wait for us to catch up at each bend of the trail.

By noon, we had reached the first ridge, and crossed over to the other side. There was little conversation; the altitude made us breathe much harder. Tiaung was waiting for us in a small clearing against an overhanging rock face, providing a partial cave underneath.

"We've done well, out of sight of the border guards now," Tiaung said. "We will stay here until the storm blows over. It's out of the wind and the snow won't drift over us. There's enough light to gather some additional firewood. The last traveler left enough dry wood to start the fire, as is the custom. The fire will dry out the new supply you'll bring in. The overhang will conceal the fire, so we can have tea and a hot dinner tonight. Meng Li, hobble the animals down the hill, in the glade to graze."

Tiaung and I unloaded our packs into the semi-cave. Deng and Meng Li went to gather firewood, while I piled the gear high in the corner, laid out the bed rolls, and started preparing food. Tiaung rigged a tarp over the front of the rest and lit a fire. We set a pot to boil with dried beef and pickled vegetables. I can't remember ever being as cold and wet in my entire life. Raised in the tropical deltas of the Irrawaddy, this altitude and weather bored right through me, in spite of the padded clothing. I stripped off my wet clothes and wrapped a bed-roll cover around me. Tiaung busied himself arranging the fire. We four would be cramped in the small area.

We stayed for three nights in that tiny partial cave. Fortunately, because of the snow, the temperature didn't drop too severely; the animals survived comfortably in the glen on twice daily grain allotments. On the fourth day, we decided to go, and take our chances of being seen against the new snow fall. We hoped the border guards would be too cold to watch the mountains very carefully. With luck, we would reach the last ridge by nightfall, the border into China. That alone was enough to urge us on.

We loaded up the pack animal again with our jars of valuables, stone carvings and the precious jade rock. Meng Li carefully attached the second rope exactly as the Indian herdsman had shown him. Tiaung watched him, pleased with the unique purpose. "That's an excellent idea. I've never seen it used before, but I appreciate the technique."

We moved slowly for hour after hour. The snow stopped. The altitude kept the air dry around us, but the wind-chill penetrated our clothing to the marrow of our bones. Tiaung led the way, walking his pony, testing the ground beneath the snow with a long pole before each step. We noted our tedious progress by looking back. Many times we dismounted to lead the animals over a small chasm discovered by Tiaung's careful probing. At 2500 meters, each step was painfully slow, my muscles ached and I felt my chest tighten with exertion.

Tiaung led. We were mounted again on our ponies. Endless curves dulled my senses, tightening their arcs as we came close to the top. Trees gave way to rocky tundra, exposing us even more to the wind. The cold bit deeper, snow swirling, the wind increasing. Meng Li was behind Tiaung, leading our burro. I followed next and Deng brought up the rear.

Our lethargy, brought on by the cold, difficult breathing and long trek, ended abruptly.

Tiaung's pony, evidently sensing danger around the next curve, suddenly reared up, screaming as animals do in fright. Tiaung tried to rein him down. The other animals jittered, nostrils flaring, ears flattened, their sense of danger alerted. With the sure knowledge of the mountain-man, Tiaung jumped off his pony at the moment a brown mountain of fur appeared around the corner. My heart pounded. I felt the sweat of fear oozing from my body, despite the cold.

Rearing up, the monster stood at twice the height of Tiaung facing him. A ferocious mouth opened with a frightening roar. The enormous head shook from side to side, giant arms waving, roaring again and again. Deng said later that I screamed again and again. I don't remember screaming, but the memory of that scene returns often in my dreams.

Deng and I were unable to think beyond controlling our own mounts, rearing and fighting the reins. The lead pony tried to turn and run. Tiaung, trying to escape the waving arms of the bear, desperately held onto the reins and reached for the halter. Meng Li's pony reared; the burro behind him tried to turn, all in the tight space of the narrow trail. The bear swung one of his sledgehammer paws, swiping Tiaung's pony across the head. The screaming animal tumbled off the narrow trail, over the side of the cliff, desperately trying to escape, hooves clawing at the crumbling edge. Tiaung crouched and let go of the reins. He grabbed the long ground-testing pole and thrust it at the angry and frightened animal, trying for its eyes. In the meantime, Meng Li threw the ropes of the burro to us. He hollered, "Tie the safety rope to your saddle."

The burro fought us, trying to back down the narrow trail. The threat of danger must have given me extra strength. I grabbed the safety rope and secured it around my saddle horn. Deng looped the halter rope around his arm, hoping to control the frightened animal. Our mounts bucked and reared leaving little room for the burro. The animal's hind feet slipped on the snow and loose ground of the cliff edge. Desperately it tried to recover its balance. Deng looped the halter rope around his saddle horn, hoping to stabilize the burro.

We saw the large ears bolt upright, the wild fear in its eyes as it slowly slipped away from us, disappearing over the edge. Deng's pony started to follow, until he let the halter rope feed out. There was a terrible jerk on my saddle, and for a moment my pony and I almost followed. Deng came alongside me to steady my pony. His right hand was bare, bleeding, the flesh torn. The glove ripped off during the melee, the halter ripping out of his hand, tearing the skin of his palms to shreds. In spite of the pain he must have felt, he grabbed the cargo line to ease the pressure on my mount. The knots had released. We could see the cargo frame suspended on the tether. The burro was out of sight, fallen to the rocks below.

Our ponies trembled in fear and exhaustion. Deng and I, paralyzed by the shock, were frozen by the scene less than three meters ahead of us. Tiaung and Meng Li fought for their lives against the monster. The roars of the bear horrified us. Meng Li had his sword out, kicking his pony to attack the bear. The animal wouldn't move, no matter how hard Meng Li dug his heels in. Shouting to Tiaung, he threw the sword to him. Meng then pulled up the whip that had been so lethal in the battle with the bandits before.

"Get down, Tiaung, down," he yelled as he whirled the whip in the air above him. Tiaung threw himself on the ground; the whip cracked on the nose of the bear. The monster reared up to its full height, towering over Meng, bellowing in pain and anger. The whip cracked again, this time hitting the bear right in the eye. Roaring ferociously, the bear shied back, trying to swat the stinging whip, now whistling a staccato of painful snaps at its head.

Tiaung crouched under the massive animal, grasping the saber in both hands. He levered the weapon by rising up and, mustering the extra strength of danger and survival, he forced the curved tapered blade upwards into the soft belly of the bear, and threw himself backward. The beast, in severe pain from the new attack, collapsed on top of the blade, forcing it further into its body. The gruesome mouth with bared teeth reached for the mortal enemy, blood running in a red river over the white snow.

"Tiaung, are you hurt?" Meng Li cried out at the still form lying centimeters in front of the bear. He didn't know whether the last swipe of the bear's paw had connected.

Tiaung slowly raised himself on one elbow, and looked at the pile of brown fur ahead of him. He turned around to see the worried look on Meng Li, still mounted. Deng and I were behind him, holding on with dear life to a rope hanging over the side of the cliff. He smiled, waved at us, and shouted, "We eat bear steak tonight. A gift of fresh bear paws will please grandfather."

We agreed Tiaung should take one of the two surviving animals, still trembling, bathed in sweat from the battle. We rigged the A-frame on our pony, with our precious cargo. Our bed rolls and other gear were bundled as backpacks for the three of us.

Tiaung looked at the mountain of fur and meat. "It will take me most of the day to butcher the beast and pack it down the mountain on a travois. Grandfather will treasure the paws, a special delicacy, you know, favored by the Manchus from Harbin in the north. Our family will prepare a feast with the bear meat, to celebrate your safe journey."

My last view of the battle scene was the mountain of brown fur, surrounded by bloodstained snow, the monstrous head as ferocious in death as it had been alive. We had to blindfold the pony to get it by the monster, led by both Meng Li and Deng.

We negotiated two more hairpin turns of the trail, on foot. The bitter cold, debilitating altitude, and heavy backpacks were neutralized by the energizing joy of being alive. We approached the top, the end of our journey in sight. Tiaung crested first and waited patiently until we caught up. He doffed his fur hat, bowed low to us and waved at the valley below. "Honored family of the Kong ... China. You are home."

Tiaung mounted his pony, bade us a safe journey and was about to leave when I pressed a small memento into his hand. "This is not for payment of your services, for we could never compensate you for our lives. It's a remembrance of friendship, Guan Yin, the Goddess of Mercy. May she watch over you and your family."

The Guan Yin, carved in ivory, palm-sized, was one of my finest creations. Her beatific smile was radiant; her delicate fingers offered gifts, the minute details from hair, dress to toes exquisite. The eyes of the goddess, set with tiny blue sapphires, sparkled with life. It was one of my early carvings. I had spent many months and much love on it. Mei Hua was my model.

Tiaung carefully wrapped the Guan Yin in a cloth and secreted it deep in a pocket. "We will remember your family always, and with good fortune, will meet again one day." Tiaung wheeled his pony, and without looking back, trotted down the mountain.

9

YUNNAN PROVINCE, CHINA

The Master said, *He who gives no thought to difficulties in the future is sure to be beset by worries at hand.*

Without talking, we proceeded down the trail, our pony following on a tether. Each of us was introspective of our own emotions. Meng Li, I suppose, felt the whole world opening to him below. Here was the land of opportunity, an inherited kinship with the past and hope for the future.

Whichever country the Chinese emigrated to over the centuries, they retained their heritage link with China, and their family's province. Often one, two, or three generations elapsed before one of the descendants returned to the motherland, be it the Guangdong Province for a returning Cantonese, or a Fujian whose ancestor had once sailed from Fuzhou or Xiamen, to look up any residual family still there. That spirit prevailed in all of us, but especially the younger ones. Meng Li had three-quarters of his life to live. Here was the province of Yunnan, origin of his grandfather.

For my husband Deng, always the pragmatist, I knew that survival was his weighty concern. The troubles of China were well known. Politics shifted in the wind. Mao Zedong and Zhou Enlai had struggled to fabricate the ideal society prescribed by Marx and Lenin. The new leader, Deng Xiaoping, supposedly was opening the windows and the doors to let in a fresh breeze. Deng questioned the process. What caused the revolution of the Red Guards? Why would young men and women abuse verbally and physically their elders? The Chinese had always venerated their parents and teachers. What hidden evil had erupted? Would Meng Li, if he had been there at the time, have criticized his grandfather? His grandfather the scholar, who believed and preached the sayings of Confucius? Fear spread over the China we could see far below, and a shiver went down my spine for him.

For myself, Wan Yi, the orphan, I cried for the mother and father I had never known. My thoughts were of family. The night at the village of Ho Pang, I knelt by their graves, lighting a paper effigy of a winged dragon, carrying a man and woman on its back. I wished them the power to fly with us, back to China and join their souls with our ancestors'. A mere daughter, I had the responsibility to carry their spirit and genes into the future. Little Flower, Mei Hua, my daughter, would never bear children. Her brother Meng Li, had the responsibility to continue our branch of the family Kong.

The miraculous jade Shou Xing Lao was constantly on my mind. I thought of how the sculpturing might be done. My humble talents were insufficient to begin such a serious task. Reconciled to this, I would allow only the most expert to touch the friend who had evidently adopted our family. What if the figure in the stone was my illusion, unseen by others? Another carver might see an elephant, a family of lions, or traditional figures of classic beauties. The image was too strong. The Shou Xing Lao and his mirror image would determine their own fate.

That night we walked down the mountain without a word between us, each deep in thought. Daylight found us on the outskirts of the settlement, near the home of a friendly farmer. The whole family came out to welcome three very tired travelers. They cared for us, as if we were long lost cousins. We delivered a note from Ho Pang, sending greetings and introductions.

Meng Li met Li Wan, a young man of his age, and gave him a private letter entrusted by Tiaung. We appreciated the warmth of the farmhouse and the pans of hot water to wash off the grime.

"We're speaking Chinese," I said, suddenly aware of the transition from Burma to China. The family crowded around, each of us talking to a different person. The family elder absorbed Deng with the problems we might face in Yunnan.

Meng Li told the story of the great brown bear to Li Wan, the size of the monster growing by many kilos in the telling. The two women, mother and daughter, discovering I was female, chattered until my ears dulled.

We slept the whole day and that night, waking up to the sounds of the farm the next day. The roosters crowed; the cottage stirred with the morning chores. We were in a familiar atmosphere, our clothes freshly washed, folded next to us. Stretching with the lassitude of a long sleep, I pulled my coat on, and, shivering, went outside to the toilet building. The temperature was freezing in the early morning. The squat toilets were neatly kept, with buckets of water nearby for flushing. It was hard to get used to the fetid smell, a small inconvenience to pay for the wonderful welcome we had received. Our more modern facilities in Burma had little odor because of the distance from the collection pits.

The large porridge pot overflowed with rice congee containing bits of vegetables and pork. Boiled fresh eggs, twisted fried bread, a basket of mantou, and the steamed rolls filled with bean paste or pork conveyed tantalizing odors. Holding blue china bowls, chopsticks clicking, the strangers and the family of seven joined in the bedlam of the beginning day. To us it sounded like music to be back in a family environment again. We only wished that father, mother and Mei Hua were with us.

The women chattered, the men silent except for the click of chopsticks against the edge of their bowls. They would stop for a moment to spear a mantou or fried bread, and then continue. Delicious Yunnan green tea filled our glasses, replenished from a large metal pot on the cooking fire. It had a delightful smoky flavor, and was grown on this very mountain, they said.

The meal was over. Courtesy demanded that serious conversation wait until we finished. We apprised the family of our intention to meet the caravan on the Simao-Kunming highway. We thought to travel as unobtrusively as possible and rejoin the caravan, as if we had crossed the border together. Bandits were rare, but there was still the problem of confiscation of our valuables by the government if they discovered our treasures.

"You will still have to conceal whatever valuables you brought out of Burma. We can have renminbi in any reasonable quantities, but the official trading groups like the China National Arts and Crafts Import and Export Corporation supposedly market all artifacts, gems and jewelry. If you claim old family possession, they will purchase it from you, but at a ridiculously small percentage of its real value.

"We suggest you trade your clothes for our old farmer pants, Sun Yat-sen jackets, and loose blouses. It's cold enough to keep your padded coats. You'll take your pony and one of our rice carts, as if you were a farm family going to market."

We talked for a long time, reviewing the happenings in Burma and China for the past forty years. Education was still the dream of all Chinese for their sons and daughters. This farmer was very proud of his grandson, Li Wan, with a mind quicker than a cat's. "He should become a scholar," he said, "though only fifteen years old, the local education of visiting teachers has only taken him through a minimum of knowledge."

We offered payment for the services the farmers supplied us. They dismissed it out of hand as unnecessary.

"Why doesn't Li Wan come with us?" Meng Li suggested. "We plan to go to Kunming, and there should find advanced schools. We have family to help when we arrive, and you can send money for his books and upkeep." The boys were ecstatic; they had become instant friends. Li Wan's parents, shocked by the aggressive plan, agreed only to think about it.

We stayed another day to rest up, and, late in the afternoon, left for the final leg of our journey. July, the monsoon season, makes it difficult to travel, though it was a danger much less threatening than anything we had gone through before. We hitched our pony to a cart about three meters long, enough to carry the rice sacks two deep and five abreast. We loaded twenty of the sacks, leaving room for the rest of our belongings. They were reduced to the bed rolls, extra coats, the books and scrolls, a tent tarpaulin, cooking utensils, a sack of cooking spices and oils, and water bags hung over the sides. One rice bag at the bottom rear had a thin green thread woven through the sacking, so fine that only a very close look could identify it.

The long chamois tubes, into which the gemstones had been sewn and then inserted into the hems of our coats, were now sewn into the belt lines of our baggy pants. My collection of carvings in their leather pouches were in the rice bag with the jade rock. We intended to pass through the towns and villages, and sell the rice when we reached Simao.

The departure, like many we had experienced over the past years, was tearful; Li Wan, the favored offspring, was going with us. The whole family, in from the fields, came to say goodbye, handing him mementos to remember them by. Two young ladies from the neighboring village, who had been vying for his attention, openly cried heavy goose tears, as we call them. They reminded us of a goose skittering through water, kicking up a wake behind itself.

I left one of my favorite gemstone carvings with the family, as a gift for their kindness. A pair of Qilin, the strange animal with the horn of the unicorn, wings of the eagle, head and body scales of the dragon, and feet of the deer. The strange combination of gemstone material called rhodochrosite was an exquisite pink and grey blended color.

"May the Qilin guard your home from all evil," I wished them with the presentation.

Li Wan took it upon himself to be the guide. In two days we descended the mountain, avoided a village, and crossed the stream we had seen from the other side of the valley. We camped during the day in a jungle-like glen of the valley floor, and that night took the trail up the mountain on the other side. Easier to negotiate, this route took us only two days up the near side, and another down the far side.

The chance of encountering border guards was slight. An occasional mountain family tending their terraces of rice or vegetables waved at us. A common rice cart drew little attention.

We crested the mountain, panting and heaving from pushing the cart to help the pony up the last steep curve of the road. Li Wan pointed down to the valley. "There is the north-south highway, and if you look far up the road you can see a dust cloud. If my reckoning is right, that should be your caravan."

Meng, my very curious son, asked, "How can you tell from this distance?"

"Most travelers on this road are single carts or small groups of people. The only long caravans are the military, and a rare group of the famous Indian traders. That dust cloud is moving far too slowly for military trucks, so I assume it's your friends. They are probably watching this very mountain pass to see if we're coming over."

Too excited to rest, we hurried down the mountain. With luck, and the pace of downhill walking, we would have a good chance of joining them by nightfall.

And so it happened. Li Wan, the smart one, was right. We began waving and shouting to each other for a kilometer before we converged. I recognized Mei Hua running down the road ahead of the caravan, as we did, leaving Li Wan to bring up the cart. Breathless, tears streaming down all of our faces, we could do little but mumble names and take turns embracing. Our Little Flower, with the false coloring removed from her face, showed the golden skin and facial beauty we knew so well, happiness lighting it up in an ethereal aura. Her voice bubbled: "Mama, papa, Meng Li. Mama, papa, Meng Li, Mei Hua happy, Mei Hua happy." Finally she calmed down and walked arm in arm with us to meet Mother Chen and Father Fan, striding boldly toward us. Their pace was as strong as ours. Father walked as straight as he had twenty years before.

The half-month we were parted was an eternity of worry, our reunion, a pleasure of life beginning anew.

We introduced Li Wan, who was immediately accepted into the family as another cousin. Mei Hua, with an arm through each, now had two loving protectors.

The Karimganj rode up on their ponies, dismounted and greeted us warmly, delighted to see we were safe and sound. It was time to make camp, and at the next clearing the whole entourage pulled off the road to set up for the night. We exchanged tales of the past days, taking turns talking around the campfire. The eldest Karimganj acted as a referee, laughingly pointing out the next one's turn to tell part of their adventure.

Burmese customs and border patrol, alerted by the rumor of possible smuggling, had given poor Mother and Fan a thorough inspection. They refused to believe that they were indeed Chinese re-patriots, and tore apart their cart and luggage, even making them remove the clothes they were wearing for examination. The officials terrified Mei Hua. Mother Chen said it was her backpack that finally caused the customs officials to give up. Thinking that the older people would hide their real valuables in the girl's belongings, they had made Mei Hua empty her treasures on a table. Mother Chen explained to her that it was a game. They wanted to see her collection.

Little Flower, with more perception than we gave her credit for, took out each little stone, unwrapped it carefully, explained just how she had found it, and what the shape meant. One of the guards became impatient and started to turn the bag upside down to dump out everything. "Don't break. Mei Hua's treasure. Don't break." When the tears started to well up in the angelic face, the chief of the border guards stepped in and called a halt. Patting her on the head, he took a small piece of jade from his pocket and handed it to her.

"Here, little one, add this to your collection. I have carried it for years just waiting for a goddess to give it to." Brusquely, he ordered the guards to let them re-pack and go on their way.

"The last we heard," Mother Chen said, "as we left, was the chiefs loud, angry voice screaming at someone over the telephone. It was something about being stupid as a donkey, and Rangoon would hear about his incompetence.

"China's guards were just the opposite," mother continued. "They took a kindly interest in father, the returning scholar of the famous house of Kong. Mei Hua has a faculty of encouraging interest, because of her extraordinarily beautiful face."

"Did they ask you to declare anything or inquire about the rest of the family?"

"Yes, they asked us to declare what valuables and technical equipment we might have, laughing and pointing to Mei Hua. They had heard about the incident with the Burmese guards looking so foolishly at the little one's valued collection.

"Welcome home, old ones," the Chinese border chief said. They accepted the customary cigarette and liquor gifts from the Indian traders, and sent them on their way."

We decided to separate from the Karimganj and proceed to Simao. The caravan reversed and proceeded north to Kunming, and later Chengdu, both large cities, good for business. Simao was where we had last heard of Uncle Wang Chen. He was our priority.

Again, it was time to take leave of old friends. I had saved one special soapstone carving from my collection, just for this occasion. It was a beautiful rendition of the Hindu god Ganesh. I knew the sitting figure of the half-man, half-elephant was a favorite of theirs, the Karimganj thanked us profusely for our rare gift. They prized it, especially because their friend Wan Yi had carved it.

Our journey with their help created a closer friendship than before. Danger shared is a warm embrace. We promised to visit them one day in Kashmir. We knew of their headquarters in Srinegar, where they return at the end of a journey.

We parted and they agreed to carry a letter for us to Kunming. Our family would learn of our safe arrival in Yunnan. The morning rain hinted at the monsoons coming. The gloomy day put a pall on our parting, which changed quickly to joy as the sun broke through by noon.

Three days later, we entered the village of Simao. The villagers saw a common sight: a pony cart loaded with rice, two oldsters astride ponies, two middle-aged people in pointed farmer's hats, and three youths walking ahead, eager to find out what went on in a Chinese city. The first leg of our long journey was over. A feeling of peace and accomplishment came over me, as we entered Simao. It reminded me of a hug and a pat on my head from Mother Chen when I was a child and did something exceptional.

Each of us was immersed in our own thoughts of what the future might bring. Father Fan, the Confucian scholar, managed to bring it all in focus with a quote from the *Analects*. As we stopped at the edge of town, almost hesitating to cross the line into our future, he quoted our ancestor:

The Master said; *He who gives no thought to difficulties in the future is sure to be beset by worries at hand.*

Confucius, the scholar of seventy-five generations ago, has brought us into full focus on this day. We must think of the future, otherwise small unimportant problems would cloud our minds.

10

SIMAO

O ur entry into Simao was unsettling, with the proliferation of soldiers and military vehicles on the road. An entire People's Liberation Army encamped, protecting the Laotian border.

Jeeps, military trucks, bicycles and an occasional Shanghai Special crowded the center of town. We all stared at the four-door sedan, a novelty to our rural life. Shanghai produced thousands of this vehicle, painted grey or black. Military or political officials used the black ones; the grey ones were for the tourists that somehow found their way this far south.

We decided to fulfill our first mission, and asked the way to the nearest grain warehouse where farmers sold their crops. A passerby pointed down the road. "The military buys everything around here, including rice. Their trade office is down the street, where you see the Red Flag of China."

We joined a line of carts bringing rice, wheat and other produce to the warehouse. They bought our rice with no questions asked about the source, except the one sack with the green thread. We told them it was for a gift to local relatives. Expecting money, we asked the farmer behind us why they were giving pieces of paper to the people.

Suspiciously he looked at us and said, "You must be strangers. The military pays with chits, and you take them to the Bank of China office over there to get your money. Is this the first time you've been here?"

Smart Li Wan quickly sized up the situation and spoke up in the local accent. "My cousins here are from way up north and my parents had me bring them here. They are really dolts and don't know the system."

The man turned away, satisfied we were country bumpkins. Li Wan took the chit into the bank, and brought out a stack of ten yuan notes. We saved the funds for Li Wan's education, as promised. In the meantime Meng Li struck up a conversation with a young bicyclist. He told us where Kong Wang Shen lived.

"Everyone in town knows Uncle Wang. He carves chops for us, and tells us stories of Confucius. Please let me lead you there. It would be an honor for me."

Quickly picking up an entourage after leaving the main street, the boy kept calling loudly, "Famous Kong family, famous Kong family, coming to visit Uncle Wang Shen. Old relatives returning." All the neighbors came out of their houses to see what was going on and followed us down the street. It was a spectacular parade. The boy on the bicycle led like a drum major. Li Wan and Meng Li followed with the almost empty pony cart. Father Fan and Mother Chen walked behind them, the excitement making them swagger proudly. Mei Hua was between Deng and I, with a hand in each of ours, skipping and dancing. The people following us talked amongst themselves, trying to guess where we had come from. They enjoyed the diversion of a group of strangers visiting their neighborhood.

The parade was a hundred-strong and the noise growing as we reached the end of the street. The boy leading us leaped off his bicycle and hollered for Uncle Wang. We crowded into the house of our Great Uncle.

Uncle Wang told me later, it was like a mirage materializing - something that happened to him often when he was contemplating a gemstone crystal, trying to fathom its depths. His first thought was that his brother, long since gone to his ancestors, had returned. The brother, too, had Confucius' features resembling Father Fan's. At his age, he often day-napped, dreaming, so that when we arrived, he heard the voices through his subconscious, and awoke to find the dream was real.

Kong Wang Shen in his youth stood more than two meters tall, with a massive frame carrying over two hundred pounds. The craggy head appeared dented, with a long nose askew. Ninety-two years of age, eighty-two of them working at the carver's bench, had bent his back. A wispy white beard hung from his near-emaciated face, and his once full body was honed thin by years of near starvation and hardship. He was the image of his ancient ancestor Confucius, and bore an uncanny resemblance to Father Fan.

The old one limped as he crossed the room to greet his nephew, Fan Shi, eyes shining bright with tears of joy. Great Uncle Wang, the famous jade carver, alive and well, threw long arms around Father Fan. Tears rolled down their cheeks and ours, as we watched them.

We crowded into the small room amid the bedlam of greetings and introductions, everyone laughing and crying. Neighbors and friends surrounded the house, unable to enter because of the crowd inside. They pointed and gawked at the strange sight of seven lost relatives suddenly appearing, covered with the dust of travel.

Uncle Wang Shen was well known in Simao as the venerable descendant of Confucius and a noted carver of gemstones. Our good fortune continued. He had survived China's traumas of the past two generations.

There would be time later to talk of the hardships, who was still alive in the family, and who had been born since our family departed. A neighbor told us later, the riots of the Cultural Revolution caught him in a fight to retain his possessions.

The art works and books were saved, but at the cost of his beloved wife. He broke his hip when he fell under the onslaught of the crazed students of the Red Guard. She held them off his crippled body with a kitchen knife, screaming epithets to scare them. They shoved her against the wall so hard, she fell on the knife, blood spurting all over them. Shocked at the sight of her blood, they retreated, recalling some of the respect they had once felt for their teacher. The neighbors found them, Uncle Wang with his back propped against a wall, holding his wife; she died in his arms that very night.

This and other tales would occupy our family reunion for many days to come, but in the meantime the room was full of joy and happiness. Father Fan and Mother Chen brought me into the tight circle around Uncle Wang. "This one, Wan Yi, has inherited your talents, uncle. Without teaching, she has created beautiful stone, wood, and ivory sculpture work, much of which paid our way here from Burma. We call Wan Yi 'Double Happiness' - an adopted daughter, daughter-in-law, wife of our son, and mother of our grandchildren. She brings us double happiness in each of her roles."

"You are indeed fortunate to have two daughters in one person. We lost our three children many years ago during the flood and famine years. Wan Yi, you must have a protector, leaving China in your mother's womb, and returning as a grown woman with two wonderful children. You're a charmed person. We must spend much time together, second niece. When the greetings subside, show me the work you have done, and tell me the materials you have used. Have you worked the famous Burmese green jade? What tools have you?"

Great Uncle Wang's tone gave me the immense pleasure of equal treatment, as a peer of this legendary patriarch. I replied, "I worked for my pleasure. I dreamt, often, of returning here to work under your teaching. When just a child, I carved with a knife in wood and bone material, then began working with the multi-color soapstone.

"Father Fan encouraged me with tales of your accomplishments. Eventually, I secured carving tools, polishing equipment. The Karimganj, our trader friends, brought me an electric drill and a stone polisher from India, when Bhamo had electricity."

"When the excitement dies down, Wan Yi, we will show each other our accomplishments and discuss what further education you might need. The feeling of stone in your hands is a special talent, and we can only teach the mechanics of the trade; artistry comes from within."

I nodded agreement, happy to be there in the same room with him. We had decided to conceal our jade until there was some privacy, especially from the inquisitive neighbors.

The picture of Great Uncle Wang and Father Fan sitting on the porch the next morning will always be with me. Tiny stools lost to sight beneath them, the curved backs of both bearded men leaned against the wall. Both were smoking the farmers' long pipes with the tiny L-shaped bowls, a leaf of tobacco rolled and inserted vertically. Mother Chen was on the steps, her back to a roof pillar, listening to the two catch up on the family happenings. The boys had earlier gone with Mei Hua into the marketplace and were exchanging views near the porch. I joined the three elders on the porch, sitting on the step opposite Mother Chen.

Uncle Wang told us the Yunnan branch of the family was smaller now, only three left of Fan's generation. The younger couples were of Deng's and my generation, each with one child, under the government's edicts of birth control. Uncle Wang lived alone in Simao, preferring to live out his life in the more remote city. It was quiet, he said, before the military took over and crowded the town's facilities and streets.

The Kunming branch of the family, cousin Huo Huo the leader now, had contact with members of the Kong family in Hong Kong and overseas. Sometimes he heard from other parts of China - Guangzhou, Fuzhou, Harbin, Shanghai, and Beijing - where there were still Kongs. At the Kong Mansions in Qufu, one woman and her daughter resided, the last of the direct descendants living at K'ung Fu-tze's birthplace.

"I retired many years ago from the jade carving factory in Kunming.

Most of my generation had to retire at 55 (60 now) to leave room for the younger workers. Unfortunately, the Cultural Revolution caught up with us, and I lost my dear wife."

Tears came to his eyes as he choked out the last sentence. After sipping at his tea to recover, he continued. "I carve chops for the local people, and act as a scribe to write and send letters for them to relatives. The government pays a small pension.

"For carving, there is some soapstone from the local mountain, but no important material. It's suitable for my own pleasure and to keep my fingers from getting stiff. Rice and vegetables are cheap, and once a month a neighbor brings a small piece of pork for soup, bartering a favor I have done."

Father Fan related the story of the original trip to Burma, the loss of Wen Xian and Yi Ku, and the good fortune in saving me. I remarked that I was now older than they had been at the time of the journey.

"Our Burmese kyat is worthless here, but we've managed to conceal a few small treasures. Will there be a place to change them for renminbi, dear Uncle?"

"Yes, but it's difficult. The government took all valuable possessions at first, under the socialist ideology that the government owns everything. Then there were periods of relaxation, followed by stern times. The Red Guard, during the Cultural Revolution, destroyed antiques and seized valuables as bourgeois, against the teachings of Mao."

Uncle Wang spoke softly, stopping often to wipe a memory tear for the losses and terror suffered. "Fortunately the wiser heads of Zhou Enlai and Deng Xiaoping took over. Now there is a period of modernization, and people can earn money with their own talents and effort. The government instructs the People's Liberation Army to make friends with the local populace, and often help them in the harvest. They aid as well during nature's travesties of flood, fire, storm, and other national disasters."

Uncle Wang looked around the street. The neighbors, for the first time since our arrival, had returned to their daily routine. Even then, I remember, he whispered. The fear of the past years was ingrained in his actions. "Don't breathe a word of your articles. Act as if you are very poor and will depend on me to care for you. The Party line taught the people to inform on any deviation. When you get to Kunming, Huo Huo will advise you. We have family connections in Hong Kong and San Francisco that are free.

"First you must register with the local authorities. Tell them of your re-immigration from Burma, because of all the political turmoil. That is acceptable. Many of our people returned home due to the modernization of Deng Xiaoping's edicts. The local authorities will be very happy you are going on to Kunming. That relieves them of the responsibility of finding jobs for the younger ones. Fan and Chen are too old to work, of course."

Mother Chen started to bristle at the words. Great Uncle Wang's eyes wrinkled with a smile. She laughed at her own reaction and listened carefully to the old one's advice. "Tell us, uncle, who are we to fear? Certainly neighbor wouldn't steal from neighbor. We desire, as you do, to spend the rest of our life in peace, in as much comfort as we can. We hope our children will have control over their lives, educate their children, and have the happiness of grandchildren."

"Confucius, our revered ancestor, spent his life wandering from one state to another, seeking to convince the leaders that all sane people desired the roads of peace," Uncle Wang answered. He paused for reflection, refilled his pipe with a fresh twist of tobacco, and blew a cloud of smoke in a halo.

"Today's world has crooked roads. The countries on all sides of us have continuing wars. You've heard, more than I, of the terrible massacres in Cambodia. The frightful loss of life in Vietnam has made the people the losers of the war amongst themselves. Our leaders tell us the whole border with Russia must be guarded continually.

"On the local Simao level, petty officials are jealous of the new wealth of the farmers. They spend their days securing their own positions, pushing their children to attend universities, disregarding talent. They stuff themselves with extravagant food at banquets, when higher officials or foreign visitors come to visit. The ones we fear the most are an occasional mean neighbor who will reveal our secrets or make up stories to tell the officials. They do this to get favors for themselves."

Mother Chen went in to fetch the tea basket, using the cloud tea brought down from the mountain. Great Uncle Wang delighted in the change from his inferior fourth grade oolong tea from the local market.

Deng joined us, with the three children. Quickly, I brought them up to date with Great Uncle Wang's advice and warnings.

Settling down with a fresh cup of tea, and invigorated at having the whole family around him, Uncle Wang continued with his cautions.

"In addition to the petty officials, there are evil ones in Kunming and more in Hong Kong that would steal and murder. I have heard that the old Tewu Secret Service from Shanghai still exists, fostered in secret by the government. They have no regard for life, only the directions from their leaders. You must talk in confidence, and only to a direct member of the Kong family."

"Uncle Wang," I said. "Venerable great uncle, we have something even more important to ask your help with. The Gods have seen fit to transfer into our hands a treasure. I am younger than you, with little experience in the handling of fine gems. I believe it to be rare and very valuable. We've risked our lives, as we've told you, to bring it out of Burma, especially for your eyes. The Immortal that governs our fates has seen fit to extend your life and safeguard ours. Will you help us?"

"Child," for he thought of me as his own daughter, "you tease an old man. Who could resist the challenge of such a plea? The lure of a rare treasure is in the genes handed down to me from grandfathers as far back as the recorded history of our family. There has always been a jade carver, in every generation appearing from one or the other branches, often from father to child. I am fortunate to be the carver of my generation, and you give me reason to believe you are the carver of your generation.

"Tell me first how you came into possession of whatever it is you wish to show me."

"Let us wander separately into the house," I said. "It should appear as if we were preparing to have lunch together. Your wonderful neighbors are so very curious about us, and even now, they watch from their porches and windows. We must be careful."

The others all played the game. Even Mei Hua, bless her heart, played around with the boys for a few minutes and then came into the house. As briefly as I could, I told the story of Mei Hua finding the rock by the river. I left out the strange incidents that had happened to us since the discovery. There would be time for those later.

Uncle Wang was patient, sitting back in his favorite chair, still smoking and drinking his tea. "And where is the treasure, dear Wan Yi?" he said, finally unable to contain himself.

"The rice sack dumped in your kitchen room, dear uncle, is its temporary hiding place, with my own carvings. Meng Li, please bring it out. Li Wan, sit by the door and watch for any strangers that might be heading towards the house."

Meng Li brought out the jade rock and shook the rice off. Ceremoniously, he removed the twine holding the halves together, and set it down in front of Uncle Wang.

Kong Wang Shen, the descendant of the Kong family jade carvers since the fifth century before Christ, caressed the outer rough surface. Seventy-three generations had gone before him. There were other gemstone carving families, of course, servicing the various warlords and dynasties. None had the combined veneration of the teachings of Confucius and the talent of envisioning the secrets inside the stones, as did the Kong carvers.

The room was soundless; all eyes focused on the familiar rock. The two halves fell apart in Uncle Wang's hands, as if waiting for the moment he touched them. Even in the poor light, he could see the intensity of the color, mesmerizing, creating an aura in the small room, permeating the minds of the people watching it.

Uncle Wang stood up, carried the jade to the window on the north side of the house, overlooking his workbench. He turned the halves to catch the light at different angles, then carefully matched the halves again, covering the precious material.

As if a pressure gauge suddenly gave way, we all breathed out, then looked to the venerable carver as he set the jade rock back on the small table.

Uncle Wang Shen's bent back straightened visibly, bringing his body almost up to the height it had once been. He didn't speak, and wandered over to the doorway to gaze down the street. Then he walked over to Mei Hua, cupping her chin and rubbing her shoulders. Pacing, he walked over to the south window with the high ledge and watched the clouds playing in the sky. Father Fan gestured to us all to keep silent with a ringer to his lips. The family fidgeted, sitting around on the mats and stools in the room.

Mother Chen went into the kitchen to light a fire under the soup pot, and add water to the kettle for tea. His pacing became more uniform, hands clasped behind his back, pulling his shoulders as if he could completely unbend his curved spine with sheer strength. He was oblivious to the rest of us in the room. I imagined his mind reviewing everything that a lifetime of his craft had taught.

He told me later. The images in his memory recalled every piece of green jade he had ever carved or seen. Some were famous sculptures in museums toured in the days when the government allowed limited travel. From the camaraderie of jade carvers and friends, he knew all the principal art carvings that had once been in the Forbidden City. The National Museum in Taipei held many of those treasures, looted by the Kuomintang. Gossip attributed the sale of many of the treasures to Madam Chiang Kai-shek to enhance her personal fortune.

Our attention was riveted on Kong Wang Shen. His eyes re-focused on me, mind returning to the present, aware again of the family's presence. I thought the scene had gone on for hours, but in reality only a few minutes had elapsed. Mother Chen poured fresh tea as he sat down again in his chair, staring at the jade rock.

Finally Uncle Wang spoke. "There is much to study of the jade and what may be inside. Even in this miserable light, its superb beauty is obvious. There is nothing I have ever seen, had in my hands, or even heard tell of, to compare with it."

We all started to talk at once, but Great Uncle Wang held up his hand and continued. "There must be mystery to the separation. A split of this nature is unique in my experience. The molecules of jade are so tenacious, a solid piece never cleaves in half. We saw it with the dust of diamond on the wheel.

"It will take time to unveil the secret inside, and determine the reason for being in two parts. You told me the story of Mei Hua finding it down by the bend of the river. The pieces must have traveled together for a long distance, as if they had a common soul and body."

"I have experienced the aura you speak of, great uncle. I will stay with you to help unravel the mystery. My poor hands could never accomplish what you have, but I want, very much, to watch you work."

Uncle Wang broke the solemnity with an eye-wrinkling wink and a smile. "Wan Yi, I suspect that you may know more about this precious treasure than you are telling me. I'll be patient and listen when you feel it is time to reveal the secrets you suspect or know. You are welcome to my humble house. A higher authority has chosen us for a task that occurs but once in our lifetime. The Immortals will guide our hands to birth a monumental treasure."

11

THE JADE OF CONFUCIUS

Mother Chen and I exchanged monthly letters. Fortunately, we saved them, and they are now a part of the University memorabilia. We missed each other. The close existence of life in Burma entwined our lives more than ordinary filial love. We are, even to this day, as identical twin sisters. Our minds exchanged thoughts without words uttered. Mei Hua was more than a common bond; we lived in her world, as she did in ours. Our men, Father Fan the scholar, Deng Huai the ever-dependable rock, and Meng Li the future, gave us peace and security. The letters tell their own story.

Dearest Wan Yi,

We wished you were with us when we neared Kunming. Father Fan and I remembered every moment of our departure more than fifty years ago.

The bus rounded Green Mountain, winding its way down the hill. The whole of the city appeared below us. We cheered, infecting the rest of the people crowded into the bus. Meng Li and Li Wan kept pointing out the city scenery to Mei Hua, until she was bobbing up and down in her seat like a bouncing ball. Your Father and I were body-sore and weary from three days on the bus. We could only wash our face and hands at the stops during the journey.

The feeling was eerie. We were back in Kunming, the Eternal Spring City. You should have seen Mei Hua when she finally met Uncle Huo Huo. Her eyes lit up, as if she was meeting one of the Immortals in person.

"Uncle Huo Huo! Mei Hua waiting many moons to see Uncle Huo Huo." It was one of her longer sentences.

I stood in the middle of the noisy crowd, trying to talk with Huo over the bedlam. "Huo, you were but a child when I saw you last. I'm Chen Wu Xia, wife of Fan Shi, your cousin. This is Mei Hua, our Little Flower, daughter of our son Deng Huai and Wan Yi. Wan Yi is the daughter of Wen Xian and Yi Ku, the cousins who traveled with us to Burma."

Uncle Huo is a short man, completely opposite from your father and Wang Shen, always bubbling over with enthusiasm. He actually talks with a laugh. The words pour out so fast, you have trouble sorting out what he is saying. His arms went around Mei Hua, with an immediate attraction, as water flows into the dry stream bed.

Now Fan goes to the park every morning to play chess with rediscovered old friends. Deng is a chef in the Green Lake Hotel. They were delighted to get his services. He has made an application to the authorities to open his restaurant on the street at the back of the hotel where it winds down into the heart of the city. It will take many months but with the new liberation policy of the government, it is possible. Meng Li and Li Wan are enrolled at the University. You would be proud of Meng as they asked him to become an associate teacher because of his knowledge of languages. They have a class there to teach guides for the Luxingshe. His experience in Bhamo, familiarity with the English, Indians and other travelers who came through Burma is invaluable to them. Mei Hua takes care of the apartment for Huo. You know what a neat housekeeper she is. The apartment really was a mess, for Huo never married and when his parents died, he did little housework. Your daughter cleaned those four rooms so thoroughly Huo thought he was in the wrong place when he returned from work that night.

We stayed with Huo until he arranged housing for us. Our apartment is one of the few bordering Green Lake, built before the war. Fortunately Father Fan, the scholar, impressed the official. Huo also impressed him with cartons of American cigarettes and two liters of English gin. Huo explained the system of getting favors from the bureaucracy. Because he worked with foreign tourists, exchange currency was available to get the imported black-market goods. With these items he could trade for favors.

We stayed with Huo for weeks, until the apartment became available for us. This will be your home as well as ours when you come to Kunming. There's a bedroom for you and Deng, another for Fan and I. The main room, opening on to a porch overlooking the lake, is a delight. It reminds us of Bhamo. Unfortunately, we are on the third floor, a little difficult to climb. But then, the exercise is good for your father and me.

We all miss our dear Wan Yi very much. With good fortune I will visit you before the rains begin. Please tell Wang Shen we wish him good health and happiness.

Mother Chen

Dear Mother Chen and Family,

It was very lonely for me when you left. I became depressed for days on end, worried that I had made the wrong decision. For the first time in my life, Deng and I live separate lives. The bed is cold without his presence. Mei Hua's absence is an emptiness, hard to bear. Knowing you are there with her is my only comfort.

Mother Chen, I miss you especially, though we have lived in separate houses these many years. I long for the family dinners, the many hours of talking with each other, even the worries and trauma we experienced together. I fall asleep each night thinking of the time we will be together again.

Uncle Wang Shen is wonderful, and giving him my company is rewarding. We spend many hours discussing gemstones, the art of carving, and the traditions of our craft. There's so much I don't know. Their structure, and how best relating to the cleaving, polishing, and carving absorbs me completely.

We work every day and spend the evenings contemplating the jade boulder. I miss you very much, mother dear. I am anxiously waiting for you to visit us.

All my love to Mei Hua, Deng and our family.

Wan Yi

Uncle Wang and I took the Kong jade in the evening and sat, like devotees of Buddha, in the presence of it. We knew that somehow, sometime, the soul would manifest itself. I knew, from past experience, it was a stone of the moonlight. During the day's light the jade was very pretty, the color brilliant and interesting. However, it was the moonlight, when it was bright enough, that brought life to the stone.

My loneliness abated; I became absorbed in my work, and obsessed with the jade. I didn't tell Uncle Wang what I had seen the year before in Bhamo, though he suspected there was something I withheld from him. For one so inexperienced as I, it would have been presumptuous to suggest to the artist, Wang Shen, what was inside such a stone.

The Year of the Rabbit ebbed; the Year of the Dragon arrived. Each night we enjoyed the same routine. We relaxed in our chairs with the last cup of tea of the day in the main room of the house. Sitting outside with the jade exposed might induce unwanted curiosity from the neighbors. The windows were open to let in the cool tropical night air and the moonlight unhampered. We lit jasmine or pine incense and Uncle Wang puffed on his pipe. The jade halves were open, and set on the small table in front of us. We basked in its presence. The new year's first moon neared, enlarged, and grew brighter each night. Uncle Wang and I sat dozing one evening, unsure when it would occur. As usual, we arranged the jade boulder halves on the table in front of us. We angled one to catch the beam coming through the window, the other mirrored toward us.

Suddenly we both sat up, startled, as if a bell had rung to shake us awake. The moonbeam had struck the dead center of the jade, revealing the life inside, as it had before. The green depths swirled and became liquid in appearance. In the aura, the Shou Xing Lao slowly materialized, the crane and deer at his side. He looked directly at Uncle Wang, waving the staff with the dragon head carved on it, a peach dripping with nectar in the other hand. He appeared to stride right out of the green sea, smiling and waving.

As the light grew brighter, the beam reflected to the other half of the rock. The mirror image of Shou Xing Lao appeared distinct, as before. Uncle Wang was transfixed. He sat bolt upright in his chair, straining to rise, as if to go meet the Immortal One. Details that I hadn't seen before sank into my mind. The cloaks had a pattern to them, of woven brocade. There were slippers on the old ones' feet that turned up at the toe. A small netsuke hung from each pouch at their belts, carved in a replica of themselves. The split-toed hooves of the deer were bold and sharp. The two cranes' lower wing feathers showed, a shade darker than the rest. The two figures walked toward us in tandem, reflecting each other's image. Dragon-headed crooks waved at us from opposite sides.

Moments later the concentrated light beam passed over the jade. The figures melted back into the emerald green sea. Uncle Wang turned his head to me; I nodded 'yes', before he asked the question. "This is the same figure I saw years ago at the first full moon of the New Year. Shou Xing Lao, and a mirror image emerging from the twin half of the rock."

He sat back, folding his hands over his stomach, and stared again at the jade. "Shou Xing Lao, the God of Longevity. Of course, what else would suit the perfectly split jade. Somehow he has managed to keep himself and his image together. Jade, which is virtually indestructible, the eternal stone, fashioned into the Immortal, God of Longevity.

"It's as if I live only to release this one from his shell. The Immortals honor us, my niece. In delivering you, Wan Yi, the inherited talent of the Kong family carvers, to Simao, they prove their existence. Shou Xing Lao may be one soul with an image, or two immortals joined by the likeness. Whichever, they have arranged for release.

"For perfection, we must carve them identically and at the same moment. We will duplicate each stroke of the chisel against the stone. That's why my aged body survived my wife and children. They directed Mei Hua to the boulder. You journeyed over the mountains to join me here. Together we will give birth to the Immortal and his image."

"Honored uncle, am I qualified for such an important task? You said this was the finest jade in all the world, and I have done only minor work, little of it in the fine Burma jade."

Uncle Wang smiled at me, took both my hands in his and said, "Wan Yi, the powers that live in the jade have honored us. These four hands will remove the material bonds that conceal the figures. What their purpose is afterward will materialize, as their images appeared. Yes, you have the talent, and my hands have resisted the trembling with age, as they should be now at this time of my life.

"There's much work to be done. When the sun rises tomorrow, we will gather the tools needed, build another workbench like mine and begin the most important work of our lives. The hardest part will be to keep our labors a secret. The importance of this jade could tempt evils beyond our conception."

The very next morning, we engaged a local woodworker to make another bench for me. We went into town to purchase the necessary tools. We ordered a new grinding and polishing machine from Kunming. The carpenter placed mirrors overhead and behind the benches, angled down. We could thus watch each other and stroke in unison.

For the first few months, the work went slowly. It was necessary to remove the outer shell of the rock before blocking the figures. Then the real task began. My memory recalls it more as a dream sequence than as an actual happening.

To maintain the secrecy, we pretended to be working on other carvings when the neighbors came over. The jade pieces dropped into trapdoors fashioned by Wang in the top of the benches. When the moon was bright enough, we continued the work at night. However, most of the sculpting was done in the early morning when the north light gave us the ultimate in visual clarity.

In the afternoon we did the local trade work for the neighbors and store customers. We kept this up, reluctantly, to allay any suspicions on the part of the local authorities or neighbors. Anyone newly arrived in Simao was suspect because of the local military base. Soon, everyone accepted my presence and I melted into the community.

When Mother Chen visited us, I asked about other details. "What about your hoard of gems, Mother Chen? Do Uncle Huo and the other members of the family know about them?"

"We revealed them only to Uncle Huo; there's a very clever mind inside his clown exterior. When we spoke of our collection and showed him a few rubies and pearls, he wanted to know if they were real, jokingly. Then he went to his cabinet, took out a jeweler's eye loupe and examined them more carefully. 'Just as I suspected, we have a problem,' he winked at me. 'They are definitely real. We'll have to get them out of China somehow.' Huo arranged to send a small packet each time a reliable visitor left for Hong Kong or the United States. Many overseas relatives visit Yunnan regularly.

"It's amazing how many relatives our Kong family have. One of them, fortunately, is an officer in the Hong Kong and Shanghai Bank. He has taken it upon himself to store them in a safe deposit box in our name. Passing them off as estate gems from some deceased bank customer, they're sold slowly, one at a time. The money accumulates in an account for us. And we have a cousin in San Francisco who is a gemologist. Your Uncle Kong Sham Choy is marketing some of the gems. Another Kong relative, called an investment something or other is safeguarding those proceeds. According to Huo, we are very rich in Hong Kong and San Francisco."

Mother Chen became nervous when she talked about the money. She always whispered. "There's enough money to take care of our family for the rest of our lives, if we are careful."

Uncle Wang and I devoted as much time as possible to our task. We plotted each stroke of the chisel. It often took hours to discuss one motion. We removed the skin, the outer matrix of the rock, and blocked the figures. This consisted of outlining the proposed figures, then carefully removing the extraneous bulk material. We sat facing each other, our benches back to back, day after day, mirrors focused on the work.

Uncle Wang would hold his figure, which I could see easily in the mirror above, the next blow already calculated. I then held mine in the exact same position. He saw and made sure each move he made, I duplicated in reverse simultaneously.

As the Year of the Dragon came to a close, our work appeared to go faster. We tediously fringed the beards, and shaped the smiling mouths, exposing precise rows of teeth. We etched the robes in a brocade pattern, the folds appearing to wave in a wind.

"Wan Yi, do you feel as if the details are happening without our initiative?"

Nodding, I answered, "Yes, honored uncle, when I make a stroke or etch a line, my hands move by themselves. Have you ever experienced this phenomenon before?"

"It is strange, dear niece. I must credit it to weariness and experience. Like riding my bike from the city home, I often can't remember passing certain landmarks, though I must have. You are an accomplished carver and probably experiencing the same reactions."

Pulling his long nose, and exaggerating a wink, he said, "If I'm correct, the honorable Shou Xing Lao is finishing up the job himself through our hands. I would have to believe it, because the New Year approaches, and he is planning to appear again."

It was, as Uncle Wang predicted on that night of the full moon of the Year of the Snake, especially auspicious. In Chinese lore the Dragon is associated with the Snake, making those years the most powerful of the twelve-year cycle.

Our last stroke finished the tiny eye of the deer. I will never forget the small friendly face, looking up at me as I fashioned the pupil of its eye. The delicate eyelid closed and opened in a wink Uncle Wang looked at me, and I at him. He nodded, the wrinkles of his eyes webbed in a smile. The resulting wink was in slow motion, as if time now beat a slower cadence.

The figures took up positions on the table in front of the window as the moon brightened the room. Our eyes soon adjusted to the glow. We settled back in our chairs, weary from the strain of the past months. The urgency of the last few days and hours centered on this evening. We looked at each other with satisfaction. We expected the transference to reality, the third emergence for me and the second for Uncle Wang.

Our work bred intimacy on the figures. A wisp of beard, a tiny fingernail, the curl of a lip made them personal and real. They were far more than friends. Like children, the Immortals were part of us.

Shou Xing Lao and his mirror image appeared that night. The light rose in the room. The direct beam of the full moon crept over the sill of the window, hit the table and then focused directly on the pair of figures. They faced each other, one angling slightly to the window, the other toward us. The beam of light reflected from one to the other. You may believe it was hallucination, or a simple fantasy of our minds. But Uncle Wang and I saw the figures move in unison, one creating an exact reflection of the other. The Shou Xing Laos strode on turned-up toed slippers, and waved their dragon head staffs in greeting. Beards moved in the assumed wind, mouths voiced silent words. We saw a tongue that we had no recollection of carving. Tall cranes walked delicately by their sides, lifting their slender legs high in the air. Spotted deer bounded on the opposite sides, their heads bobbing. The peaches dripped with health-giving juices, so real we licked our lips and salivated.

Uncle Wang and I sat, numb, staring, mentally communicating with our creation. Maybe it was their creation, I thought. Confucianism teaches reality. I wondered at the mysticism and pleasure confusing the reality.

The concentrated moonbeam passed. The jade figures were passive, positioned exactly as we had placed them. The green jade, appearing liquid a moment ago, now was translucent ice. Uncle Wang and I exhaled at the same moment and sat there until all light faded, the figures a shadow. We had finished the creation and now the Kong family would decide their future.

In the morning, we planned that Uncle Wang would return with me to Kunming. He appeared wan and drained, as if the tremendous effort had sapped his strength. It was obvious he wanted to see the family again, as he felt his life fading.

We swathed the delicate parts of the carvings with cotton, then settled them in leather pouches. The pouches, surrounded with clothing, were in a string sack of red, white and blue synthetic material. Tough, the bags were now used universally in China by travelers.

We were a common sight, the middle-aged woman taking her ancient relative on a trip to visit their family. It was easy to secure permission to make the trip, and buy tickets on the bus. The driver wanted us to put our bags up on the roof of the vehicle, but we fussed and kept them inside under our feet the whole trip.

Entering Kunming, reunion with my loved ones remains a joyous and vague memory. Huo Huo's magnificent efforts to arrange a journey for Mother, Father, and myself are as fuzzy as our first airplane adventure. Hong Kong and then overseas to the Golden Mountain appear more dream than reality as if stepping through a moon gate into another world. San Francisco is another world.

12

SAN FRANCISCO

⸻⸺⸻

Tsu-Kung, addressing Confucius, said, *If you had a piece of beautiful jade here, would you put it away safely in a box or would you try to sell it for a good price?*

The Master said, *Of course I would sell it. All I am waiting for is the right offer.*

Tzu Lu, an adherent, was asked by the Master, *What is it you have your heart set on?*

His answer was, *I should like to share my carriage and horses, clothes and furs with my friends, and to have no regrets even when -   they become worn.*

It was a normal answer but then Tzu Lu turned the tables and said to K'ung Fu-tze, *I should like to hear what you have set your heart on.*

The Master said, *To bring peace to the old, to have trust in my friends, and to cherish the young.*

We were tired, awed, and very ill at ease in our exit from the long ramp to the customs area at San Francisco International Airport. Only those who have entered a strange country for the first time know the feeling of trepidation. Excitement, a warm feeling of comfort breaking out into smiles replaced the fears. A hand-held sign read WELCOME KONG FAMILY in Mandarin and English. Next to the three people holding that sign was a larger delegation holding another sign. It read WELCOME KUNMING SISTER CITY COMMITTEE. In the commotion, no one noticed Fan, Chen, and myself slipping away from the larger group.

Recognizing us at once, Uncle Kong Sham Choy embraced his cousin Kong Fan Shi, and actually kissed Mother Chen and me. "My wife, Ai Lin, and my miserable grandson, Jie Lie. We brought him to make sure we old people found and brought you home."

The woman bowed slightly to my father. "We are honored to meet the famous Confucian scholar, Kong Fan Shi, and his family. Please excuse the American manners of my husband who has forgotten how to welcome distinguished visitors properly. You are Chen Wu Xia, and your daughter Wan Yi? It's our honor and pleasure for you to stay in our home. We look forward to showing you our fair city."

"My wife the diplomat. Must you do anything with the delegation you are arriving with?" Uncle Choy said.

I answered, "The arrangements are to leave us out of the formalities, and join them again on their return to China ten days from now. Our cousin Huo managed to include us in this sister city delegation from Kunming to San Francisco. He is remarkable at organizing devious plots."

My tongue was garbling the words. "Please excuse our lack of animation, honored uncle. Our first ride in an airplane, worrying about the trip, and finally arriving at our destination have combined to numb us."

Father and mother bowed shyly to Aunt Ai Lin and thanked her for the hospitality. I turned to the young man introduced as Jie Lie. He wore blue jeans with a tee-shirt, emblazoned SAUSALITO. "What does Sausalito mean?"

"Wan Yi, I guess you are an aunt, or a cousin sort of. Your visit has excited the whole Kong family. Gramps hasn't slept for the past week, making plans. Grandma Ai Lin has been getting the apartment ready, laying in enough food to feed an army. Oh yes, Sausalito, it's a small town over the big bridge, loaded with street shops, artists, rock music, and all kinds of good stuff. We'll take you there for the day if you like."

Tired as I was, I had to laugh at the exuberance of this young man. Meng Li would have to meet him some day; they were kindred souls, waiting to conquer the world. He took over the cart with our luggage. Mother Chen and I kept the two red, white, and blue striped plastic stringbags, our carry-on bags. "Wait here, everyone, I'll get the limo and return for you." "Limo?" Mother Chen said. "What's that?" Aunt Lin replied. "Unfortunately part of the slang our young people speak now. A limo or limousine is a larger car, usually used for chauffeur-driven guests. Our car is not really a limousine, but our grandson jokes that it is. Jie Lie is an undergraduate of Stanford University, but sometimes talks like one of the street people we call hippies."

By the time we reached their apartment, our minds and bodies could take little more excitement. San Francisco at night was a fascinating kaleidoscope of lights, freeways, and more automobiles than we could have imagined in all the world. Sitting in the soft leather seats of the luxurious car was an adventure. Mother and father were in back with Uncle Choy. Jie Lie drove with Aunt Ai Lin and me in the front, explaining some of the sights.

We arrived through the Grant Street arch, into the warrens of streets they called Chinatown. It reminded me of Kunming with the Chinese signs, small crowded shops, and people on the street, even at this late hour. Young Choy turned the car up a side street and parked in front of a narrow shop. The sign read, SAM CHOY, JEWELRY AND ANTIQUITIES. We entered a door next to the store entrance and climbed stairs leading up to the second floor. The flat above extended over the whole building and was like entering a palace, compared to our Kunming home.

"Welcome to our home. Please consider it yours while you are here," Aunt Ai Lin said. "Come, I'll show you your rooms. Wash up a bit, then come in the living room and we will have a cup of tea before you go to sleep. You all look very weary and need some rest."

I giggled like a schoolgirl when I came out of the bedroom. "You know, Aunt Ai Lin, when I turned the faucet and saw hot water gushing out, I really thought I had broken something. That's why I called out to you. Other than public baths, we still boil water for our washing. I've heard some of the new apartments have both hot and cold running water, and a privileged few have air-conditioning."

Mother added. "The room you've given us is wonderful. Having a private bathroom is a luxury I never thought we would have."

The neat white enameled machines in the kitchen amazed me when I went into the kitchen to help Aunt Ai Lin with the tea. "Maybe tomorrow, you'll show me what these machines are for. The kitchen is larger than our whole apartment in Yunnan, shared by two families."

Aunt Ai Lin laughed, hugged me, and explained. "Too often, we take for granted the lifestyle we have. This extra faucet on the sink has very hot water, hot enough for tea. Be careful not to burn yourself." She opened overhead cupboard doors, revealing packed shelves of fascinating food containers. "The tea is in here, help yourself."

I couldn't resist opening both of the refrigerator's double doors. The shelves were loaded with food, one side frozen packages, the other vegetables, fruit, bottles, jars, more than in our market in Kunming. Aunty squeezed my arm gently, obviously enjoying my reaction.

"There's fruit, salad, cold meats and cheese. I know you don't enjoy milk products at home but you might like to taste it while you are here. You may wake up very hungry in the night, so just make yourself at home."

I was quiet for a moment. Taking her hands in mine, "You knew my mother, Yi Ku, when you were both children in Yunnan, didn't you, Aunt Ai Lin? Do you remember what she was like?"

"Yes, dear Wan Yi, we knew little of troubles in those days because we were so young. It was our parents who took the brunt of the problems. To us it was an adventure to leave Kunming for a new life. Your mother and father went to Burma. Sham and I were fortunate enough to come here to the Golden Mountain a couple of years later. I do remember your mother. Yi Ku was a happy young woman, never worried too much, always laughing and teasing your father. She was a beautiful person. It was sad to hear, years later, that they both died during the trip."

It wasn't a dream. Daylight and street noises were coming through the open window. We were really there. I could hear mother and father in their room, murmuring quietly. Cooking odors perfumed the apartment, making me very aware of being hungry. I stretched luxuriously under the fine cotton sheets and comforter, wishing only that Deng could be with me. My thoughts then were focused on the hope we could return together one day. I would have so much fun showing Deng the wonderful way of living in America.

Aunt Ai Lin explained. "Uncle Choy is in the shop with an important wholesale customer from Arizona. I've prepared breakfast, some boiled eggs, sliced pork cutlet, pickled vegetables, and hot cream of wheat cereal. It's something like congee. There's a bowl of fresh fruit, and doughnuts. Jie Li insisted that you have some American junk food, as we call it, while you are here."

Mother Chen answered for the three of us. "You are too kind, dear cousin, our poor stomachs will be bulging with all this food. I must tell Jie Lie that we have junk food too, except our doughnuts are long and twisted. We call them fried bread."

Father Fan looked twenty years younger that morning. He was always invigorated by a new adventure. A good night's sleep and the prospective wonders of the new world was better than a whole ginseng root. "It's actually a Golden Mountain, this San Francisco. We are fortunate to have rich cousins such as you. Your success must have been the result of many years of hard work."

"Yes, honored Fan," Ai Lin answered. "There have been countless hours of tending shop, negotiating with sellers and buyers, saving *each nickel,* as they say here in the United States. My clever husband bought this building some years ago, just after the War, and rents out the other stores you see downstairs. His other properties are the treasures he has in the shop, purchased from Chinese friends and customers all over the world. Sam's reputation as a gemologist and honest friend has brought him many valuables on trust, such as your collection.

"His reputation also brought him credibility with collectors and dealers; They take his word on the validity of an antique or the value of a rare gem. Sham is an expert on jade, often paid by the auction houses and museums to verify and appraise items for them."

"Why do you call uncle Sham sometimes and then Sam? What does he prefer we use?"

"His Chinese name is Sham. The English word means fake, if they don't pronounce the long *a*. His customers made a lot of jokes about it. Other than formal introductions, we call him Sam, like the Americans use Uncle Sam. Now let's have some breakfast before it gets cold."

"What about Jie Li, is he in school now?"

"Jie Lie is on vacation, spring break, from Stanford University, not too far from here. He'll be your tour guide while you are here. He planned to take you across the Golden Gate Bridge to Sausalito. You'll enjoy the Embarcadero and the ferry tour around the harbor. One day he wants to show off his Stanford Campus at Palo Alto and maybe take you to a baseball game. All the cousins, in-laws, aunts and uncles are coming to a family dinner at a local restaurant called 'The Spring Garden' to meet the Kongs. They are clamoring to have you as guests for dinner or a day."

"It's too much," Mother Chen said. "You must explain who each of our relatives are before we meet them. Are they all Kongs?"

"Yes and no, dear Chen. There are a few direct descendants and a great many in-laws with their families. We use the custom of family names over here, which makes it very confusing. Sam keeps a detailed family tree, showing both names to make it easier. Cousin Huo keeps him up to date with the China and Hong Kong branches. Together they maintain the family archives. Jie Lie created a program on our computer that shows as much as we know about the whole Confucius clan, as far back as recorded history. There's a niece you will meet at the family dinner, a professor at Stanford, also deeply interested in our family history. She has created a course at the university in Confucianism. It's very popular with the Caucasians as well as the Chinese students."

We sat in the comfortable main room and talked the whole morning. Mother Chen recalled our mission. "We are filled with happiness, Ai Lin, but have a small problem. There is a precious article in our luggage. Can we put it in some safe place until we get a chance to show it to you and Sham?"

"Of course Chen. Sam has a safe in his laboratory next to the kitchen, where we can leave it for the day, and tonight you can show it to us."

Bringing them out of our room, I showed her two carved wooden figures of Shou Xing Lao, nestling in their brocade fitted boxes. "They are a small token of our respect, but they do have a secret within them. We have heard so much of crime in the United States. Will they be safe here, while we are touring around?"

"Perfectly safe," Ai Lin said.

I saw her smiling to herself at the modest wooden carvings, amidst the wonderful collection of antiques in their room. "We have an alarm system everywhere in the building that rings directly in the police station not more than a block from here. Those little discs you see on the ceiling are smoke alarms. They alert us to fire and trip the police alarm. We will lock your beautiful gift in the lab room, however, so you won't worry."

Beads of perspiration appeared on Uncle Sham Choy's brow, as he stared at the Jade figures on his laboratory bench, late that night.

We had spent the day touring San Francisco, thrilled at the Embarcadero, the waterfront, the carnival atmosphere, family crowds, browsing through the shops, the wax museum, and eating crab with our fingers out of the little plastic bowls. By early afternoon, we returned to the apartment for a nap. The long journey the day before and the day's adventure wore us out. After dinner, we coaxed Uncle Choy, Jie Lie and Aunt Ai Lin into the lab room to get a reaction to our treasure.

The array of equipment in the laboratory impressed us. Jie Lie explained the function of the binocular microscope, polariscope, refractometer, spectroscope, specific gravity liquids, electronic scale, ultrasonic cleaner, and all the other gemological paraphernalia. "With these, and a little deduction, we can identify any gems tone that comes our way," Jie Lie said. "As far as determining value, that depends on a knowledge of the world market and a specific grading system. I keep a record on my computer of current sales we are aware of. Lists from other sources are added to the data. We can determine a value by comparison with known sales of such items."

Certificates on the wall accredited both Sham Choy Kong and Jie Lie Kong with the various courses taught by the Gemological Institute of America, and coveted membership in the American Gem Society. We quickly got in the habit of using the Americanized Sam, and the family name last, as everyone did here.

"I don't believe what I'm seeing," Uncle Sam said.

Jie Lie, for the first time since we had met him, was quiet. He hadn't said one word after examining the figures.

"The perfection is absolute, not so much as a grain of pepper. The carving, the mirror image preciseness, is exquisite. The size and weight of the two figures is larger than anything recorded of this color and clarity. They weigh within a gram of each other. Without running any of these tests, I would declare them authentic jadeite jade. Speak up, Jie Lie, you're the one that has studied the description of the articles in the National Museum at Taipei, and the jewelry collection in the Forbidden City of Beijing. Have you seen any recorded like these?"

Father Fan and Mother Chen sat quietly on stools in a corner of the laboratory, holding hands, looking in awe as the professional gemologists went about their business. I was busy focusing on one of our rubies in the diamondscope. Jie Lie had explained the fingerprint, included so dramatically in the center of the ruby. I likened it to approval of the Immortal, adding his chop mark to seal the authenticity.

"Grandfather, my youth and inexperience bow to your forty years of dealing with treasures of this magnitude. Frankly, it's beyond my comprehension. Technically they are jadeite jade, of a color and quality far superior to any I have ever seen, except in a small gemstone. If you are asking me what they are worth, we had better spend a lot of time searching the results of auctions. Christie's and Sotheby's have held notorious sales in Hong Kong. I have some of the results in the computer, but we need more.

"We know that the Chinese and Japanese collectors paid high prices over there. There was one sale recorded last week, of an extremely fine piece of jade carved in the shape of a pepper, with an insignificant diamond filigree cap. The hammer price was eight hundred seventy-five thousand U.S. dollars plus the 10% Christie's buyer's commission. Therefore, these two Jade pieces, weighing more than a hundred times the pepper, could be worth a billion dollars."

Uncle Sam was quiet for a while, turning the figures around and around in front of the special back and under-lit panels of the examining stage. He took repeated photographs from every angle with the appraisal camera aimed at the small platform. Finally, he spun around on his stool, his back to the figures, wiping the perspiration from his forehead.

"Your method of carrying them was ingenious, probably better than any fancy locked box. When Ai Lin told me about the wood figures you worried about, neither of us had any idea what you were carrying. The Shou Xing Laos in wood were well done, but of no great value.

"I noticed the weight when I first picked them up, but attributed that to exceptionally heavy ironwood or teak. Wan Yi, when you removed the bottom panels, exposing the real treasure, my heart began to pound. I almost put a nitro-glycerine tablet under my tongue, for fear my heart would stop.

"You must have suspected, they are of inestimable value. The story you tell of the phenomena is believable to me. There are skeptics, but in my years of experience, I too have felt strange auras, and inexplicable happenings connected with gem-stones. Bad luck and good luck have been associated with rare gems since recorded history."

He chided Jie Lie with a loving hand on the shoulder. "You are a skeptic, but you'll become a believer as you mature."

Uncle Choy turned back to the figures, studying them again. I assumed he was still trying to convince himself of his own expertise. "We must have more security than we have here, however. My safe will be okay for tonight, but tomorrow we get them into the bank. A museum would have electronic safeguards, and armed security for a treasure like this.

"By the way, we must talk about your investments. From previous sales, your account already is into six figures. You'll have to tell us what you would like done with the proceeds. I have opened a trust account for your family, invested in money market funds, for the time being."

Mother Chen, always the practical one, asked, "Please tell me what you mean by six figures, money markets, and trust accounts. My poor command of English does not comprehend those terms."

Uncle Sam spent the next half hour explaining high finance in America. We were groggy by the time he finished. "We'll arrange a more detailed explanation when you meet Kong Ren Quan, one of your cousins, who happens to be an investment banker. He is a partner in Rothschild, Oppenheimer, Cookson, & Kong, known internationally."

I could tell this technical conversation was well over father's head, mother tried hard to concentrate, and I barely understood the general concept. The large amounts of money Uncle was talking about, converted into renminbi, were astronomical. I giggled, slightly hysterical, when I thought how much top grade tea it would buy for Uncle Wang Shen.

Uncle Sam was still talking. "... this magnificent treasure of jade you have brought. We are now thinking about millions of dollars. Jie Lie and I will have to spend many hours discussing the potential market. For you, the inevitable problem is what to do with wealth. As citizens of China, there might be serious repercussions and demands by your government. If we negotiate a sale in the U.S. through your trust, taxes could be enormous. Money begets problems in our world today.

"Let's put these elegant friends of yours in the safe, and relax in the living room. Maybe we can figure out a plan."

We settled ourselves in the living room, the inevitable teacups warming our hands, mentally exhausted. Uncle Sam Choy took up the conversation once more.

"I suggest we consult with certain members of the family when we gather for the reunion tomorrow night at the Spring Garden Restaurant. In particular, Kong Ren Quan, who is already privy to your wealth and working on your behalf. Then there is Kong Jian Yi, at 35 a full professor at Stanford, a solid academic. Jian Yi teaches Genealogy and Confucianism.

"The third person I recommend is Kong Wei Tang. Cousin Wei Tang is a retired Lieutenant-General in the United States Army. Now he operates the Kong Safety Net Company, specializing in protection against kidnapping, hijacks, and technology thefts."

Father Fan had been extremely quiet during the past hour, listening carefully as always, absorbing the conversation, trying to understand, and extend the eventualities that might occur. "Cousin Choy," he said, "the Shou Xing Laos are leading us into a labyrinth of probabilities and possibilities. They would confound even our venerable ancestor K'ung Fu-tze." Father often reverted to Confucius' real name when reference becomes serious.

"In my estimation there are two points of great significance, involving our future and the Kong family. One is the future home of these rare and magnificent creations.

"No matter how they came into our possession, whether through celestial destiny or accident of nature, we are responsible. I choose to believe that destiny has played the larger part, thus there is a grander purpose in their arrival. We must find out that purpose and do whatever possible to achieve it for them.

"Now on the other hand, the unimaginable sums of money you speak of, frightens me. Money, even in the days of Confucius, was an evil as much as a benefit. Good has always fought with greed, inherent in most men. I remember what Tzu Lu, an adherent, was asked by the Master: *What is it you have your heart set on?*

"His answer was, *I should like to share my carriage and horses, clothes and furs with my friends, and to have no regrets even when they become worn.*

"It was a normal answer but then Tzu Lu turned the tables and said to K'ung Fu-tze, *I should like to hear what you have set your heart on.* The Master said, *To bring peace to the old, to have trust in my friends and to cherish the young.*

"I interpret those words to have important meaning in our world today. This passage, as recorded in the *Analects,* is the answer to our legacy. With my beloved Chen Wu Xia and Wan Yi we'll try to answer your question of what to do with the money. We must direct it away from the greed of men to fulfill the good intentions of the Shou Xing Lao destiny."

Father arose, and straightened to the fullest height allowed by his curved back. The large frame, indented head, rather askew large nose, which some might even call ugly, was a duplicate of how his ancestor Confucius was described. His hands, clasped behind his back, sought to pull his shoulders erect. He paced back and forth across the room in the manner of ancient philosophers.

I imagined our ancestor twenty-five hundred years before, attired in long robes, sandals on his feet, beard twisted, contemplating a similar problem. Mother Chen, myself, Uncle Sam and Aunt Ai Lin sat back and watched, an audience to a rare happening of world importance.

"*To bring peace to the old,* K'ung Fu-tze said. I interpret that for our situation, as not just old people like ourselves, but the world, tired and old, weary of wars and strife, badgered by conflict of races and ideologies, torn by the thought of possible destruction. It's my opinion that he would have peace for the world."

Kong Fan Shi, the scholar, continued with his interpretation of the Master's words. "Trust in my friends. It's my belief that the Shou Xing Lao and his image are saying to us, *Trust in me, the Immortal of Longevity. I and my reflection are your destiny. We will direct you to the proper use of our incarnation. We have brought you here, far from the edge of the Irrawaddy, through Burma and China. Trust in me, and the destiny.*

"The last part, *Cherish the children.* The meaning is more than our love of Meng Li and our Little Flower, Mei Hua. It's obvious, the meaning is to cherish the children of the world in order for them to fulfill their purpose in life. Give birth to them through love, raise them to adulthood with care and attention. Then give them of your knowledge and way of belief, so they may spread that gospel out into the world."

Father Fan Shi paused, pulled at his beard, stood before us as if a reincarnation of Confucius. We were mesmerized. "Let us create a special place for people to acquire that knowledge and spew it out in such a manner as to infect the world with virtue, decency, and morality. I believe the Shou Xing Laos came to us, the Confucius clan, to create a mighty university in the image of what K'ung Fu-tze preached. That school should be at Qufu, his birthplace. It's our mission to fulfill it. The means are this enormous amount of money you envision."

The Jade Shou Xing Laos, even from their concealment in the lab safe, had spoken.

13

THE KONG PLAN

In ethics, Confucianism upholds the five 'constant virtues' of Ren (human heartedness); Yi (righteousness); Li (propriety); Zhi (wisdom); and Xin (sincerity or good faith); in politics, Yin stresses the moral importance of human relationships. In its last analysis, virtue alone constitutes the ultimate goal of man. Knowledge creates intelligence, and intelligence can solve the most complex problems.

It was a memorable evening. The crowd was raucous, wanting to know everything about us. Most of the younger generations had never been to China. Their interest was avid. They promised to visit the homeland as soon as they could. It was the first time we three had been together with affluent and modern Chinese, our own family of Kong. During the dinner, we went from table to table, trying to place each in the family relationship. 'Kam bei!' echoed throughout the room, like an order from a military commander, making everyone stand up to hear one good wish after another.

The restaurant outdid itself, bringing course after course, stuffing us to the brim. The family quieted down, subdued by the food and drink. As is the custom of Chinese banquets, the final soup course signified the end of the meal. The last 'kam bei' by Father Fan ended the affair with a quotation from Confucius. It was one I didn't remember. I suspected the toasts had caught up to my dear Father. Partly supported by Mother Chen, he spoke in a rather wobbly voice. "Friends, family Kong, descendants of the Master, I make a final toast: "The Master said, *Joy is to be found in the warm comfort of the family nest.*

"You have brought us the joy of our famous ancestor and we thank you and the God of our destiny who has brought us here tonight. May you all benefit from that destiny. Kam bei!"

We bundled Father into the car; he was asleep the moment the door closed. Mother Chen and I managed to get him into bed. I remember how shocked I was by his lean, bony, aged body.

Aunt Ai Lin prepared strong coffee for the few members of the party that returned with us. Uncle Sam invited Wei Tang, the burly general, Jian Yi, the petite professor, and Ren Quan, a small, immaculately dressed man with grey hair and gold-rimmed glasses.

Jian Yi and the wives of the other two men were in the kitchen, chatting with Aunt Ai Lin and helping with the coffee. Uncle Sam summoned everybody into the lab.

"Before you all get comfortable, bring your coffee. I have something to show you."

Jie Lie and I stayed in the living room to give the others more room in the laboratory. A very sober group of relatives rejoined us afterward in the living room. Mother Chen came in from the bedroom and announced that father was sound asleep, snoring so loudly she might have to sleep with me.

Aunt Ai Lin refilled the coffee cups, and sat down without saying a word. Uncle Sam looked at each of the sobered relatives, then spoke. "Well, members of the Kong family, what are your thoughts?"

Wei Tang spoke first in his deep, resonant voice. "I don't know what the intentions are for this treasure, but I do know we have a security problem when word gets out that such a valuable treasure is in existence. Have you estimated the possible worth yet, Cousin Choy?"

"It's impossible to estimate, other than in the millions of course. The intentions of Fan Shi and his immediate family are to sell the figures. Strangely, Confucius himself had something to say on owning such a jade treasure. Yes, we have a problem, in fact two problems. One is to find a buyer; second, we must invest the funds wisely for Cousin Fan and his family. Fan Shi suggests the stupendous idea of creating a University of Confucius, assuming the yield is enough. In addition, according to Fan, the only suitable location is Qufu, Shandong Province, Confucius's birthplace."

"The formation of an international university? In the middle of China? What a fascinating idea. Does the government of China know anything about this?" Jian Yi said, shaking her head in disbelief.

Uncle Sam answered her. "Dear Jian Yi, esteemed niece, Fan Shi must tell you of his dreams, or rather the dreams of Confucius. I am in awe of the idea. I am in awe of this rare treasure. Since meeting the Jade Shou Xing Laos, I've talked to them in my dreams. They came to me with encouragement and tell me it can be done. When I wake up, it's all crazy.

"What of the funds, Cousin Ren Quan?" Uncle Sam asked. "Up to this time we have been talking of a few hundred thousand dollars. The yield from Chen's collection of gems is to be put in a trust for their family's future. Now we are talking in multi-millions and then the income from such a fund. It's beyond my comprehension."

Ren Quan always spoke slowly, quietly, and only after much cogitation. The room quieted. We all looked at him, and waited many minutes for an answer. "Choy, I'm known as a conservative investment banker, and have handled enormous funds around the world. My firm has dealt with kings, governments and individuals for fifty years. Our Rothschild partner is a descendant of a famous family like ours. The Oppenheimers made their fortune in diamonds, and the little known Cookson is a director on more private family trust funds than you can conceive or even know of.

"They know me as the Hong Kong connection, advising our Asian clients. Collectively, we are known as the ROCK, an acronym for Rothschild, Oppenheimer, Cookson and Kong. This will be a monumental challenge for our firm. Assuming we must meet again, I ask permission to consult my partners. The investment of the money is a solvable problem. Tax ramifications and the possible greedy fingers of various governments are easy to avoid. Build a University of Confucius in China? I don't know. Physically it is no problem ... but I refuse to think of the enormity of operating such an institution. Fan is a dreamer. Confucius was a dreamer in his age. Maybe, just maybe, the dream could become a reality."

Uncle Sam wound up the conversation. "It's late. I'm sure we will get little sleep tonight. Fan Shi, Chen Wu Xia and Wan Yi must leave with their delegation from Kunming in five more days. Would it be asking too much for us to have another meeting before they leave?"

For busy people, it was difficult to arrange a date. They finally agreed to come on Sunday, the day before we were to leave. We would meet at noon, here at the apartment.

The next five days sped by in a whirlwind of invitations to relatives' homes and side trips to see the countryside. I remember Sunday, the day before we left. Mother Chen and Aunt Ai Lin packed our bags early. I made contact with the Kunming group to rejoin them at the airport early the next morning. The immediate Kong Tong, as Jie Lie laughingly called it, assembled. Aunt Ai Lin prepared an American Sunday brunch, set up on a buffet table, and everyone helped themselves to the array of food. Finishing, we sat around the living room, nibbling on sweets, almost everyone drinking coffee, including me. Until I came to the United States, I never used the highly caffeinated liquid. Now, I drank coffee for breakfast every morning and saved my tea for afternoons and evenings.

Uncle Sam Choy, the self-appointed leader, began. "Thank you all for coming, we are anxious to hear what exceptional wisdom will come forth from this elite group."

Father sat on the sofa with Mother Chen on one side and Aunt Ai Lin on the other. I'd taken a large, comfortable chair in a corner with a pad and pencil to take some notes on what might happen. The others were scattered around the room in other chairs and at the antique games table in the corner. Jie Lie paced, looking very nervous, with a notebook in his hand, reading it every few minutes, as if rehearsing a speech.

"Jian Yi, please start us off with the dream. You've spent many hours with Fan Shi to understand his thoughts, derived from our ancestor. Tell us, is there a chance to accomplish the dream?"

"Honorable Fan Shi, and our family. When you first spoke of this, I admit to being very skeptical and incredulous at such an idea. Like our esteemed elder Fan Shi, I too have studied the *Analects,* and the history of Confucianism. The University of Confucius is a dream, but it's possible, given the funds to start. I'm fortunate to be a member of a group called the Mensa Society, named for Mencius, our ancestor's famous disciple.

"Each year, when we meet, a designated member proposes a topic for discussion, to challenge the brilliant minds. I've talked to our program director about a subject entitled: A World Class University; based on the five virtues expounded by Confucius.

"The idea is so exciting to them that they immediately agreed to use it for the program during our next Mensa conclave. We'll have the best minds of the world helping us. I'm sure that if our plan succeeds they will be most anxious to participate. At this early point it's impossible to do any financial or operating proposals. It will cost vast sums of money. The financial support must be entirely free of any government, especially the host country.

"My initial thoughts are: Tuition must be voluntary. Admission standards unique. Freedom of mind and curriculum undisputed. It's possible we can set up a tithing system, such as the Mormon Church uses, for all graduates. A voluntary contribution of one percent, for instance, of income after graduation would guarantee a continual flow of funds far into the future. If we have but five thousand students each year from around the world, that number would multiply to one hundred thousand in twenty years.

"These are but seeds of thought, naive, preliminary, but the possibilities are mesmerizing."

"Ren Quan," Uncle Choy said, addressing the mild-looking banker. 'Money Uncle' sat quietly in a corner, trying to be as invisible as the famous gnomes of Switzerland. "Does the financial wizard of the Kong Tong have any thoughts on our plan so far?"

"It's a strange challenge for my associates. 'How to invest an unknown amount, for a blind trust, that crosses international currency lines, for the probable use in a foreign country that has little or no reciprocal agreements with our country."

"They were inclined to think it was a teaser question to test their mental acuity. However, I assured them it was a real probability. To get them to accept the reality of the situation, I revealed that the funds would be the yield of a hitherto unknown gem sculpture, unique in the world.

"My partner Oppenheimer took up on that. It was his family's company, the De Beers, who marketed the six hundred and thirty carat Cullinan Diamond, the largest ever discovered.

"Rothschild, whose family criss-crossed the European continent centuries ago with financial dealings that saved governments, is well aware of international and governmental dealings.

"The other partner, Alexander Cookson, was a famous astronaut. Few people know that he was a vital planner of the space program during the Kennedy days. We need his ethereal vision for uncharted waters. With this man's brain, everything is possible, it only needs development to make it work.

"There is little that we can do, until you give us more data, but rest assured the ROCK Group is thinking, and very much intrigued."

"I suppose it's my turn next," Uncle Wei Tang said. Our principle of operation in the Kong Safety Net Company is to keep an event from happening. If we can prevent the occurrence of a kidnapping or theft, it eliminates the need for an expensive and quite often life-saving operation.

"The second principle of security importance is to realize that there is no such thing as a secret, as long as two persons are aware of a fact. We always assume that greed, deviousness, the need for power, can and will infiltrate the best-kept plans.

"For instance, Sam and Jie Lie, with my knowledge, thought it necessary to get an outside, unbiased authority to verify the treasure. They also thought it expedient to prepare a taped film of the Jade to eliminate most of the exposure that might be required in selling it.

"For the outside authority, Choy has called on an old friend, the retired director of the Gemological Institute of America. This esteemed person is known worldwide, has written many books on gems, and ran the Institute for more years than Jie Lie is old. As a favor, for he was always reluctant to appraise anything outside of the laboratory, he did come here and spend three hours with Sam and Jie Lie. Together they prepared a certificate of verification of the size, weight, color, and identification of the Jade, as well as the instrumentation used to make the appraisal."

Uncle Wei Tang took his commanding 250-pound bulk back to his chair. "That's all I have for now, folks. The Confucius Jade is now safely stored, waiting for its coming-out party."

"That leaves us with my part," Uncle Sam Choy said. "You have all surpassed our fondest dreams. I see cousin Fan's eyes shining as bright as the Shou Xing Lao.

"The major problem is whom do we sell it to, and how do we go about such a sale? I've negotiated the sale of millions of dollars of rare antiques in my career. I have top-drawer access to the major auction houses. In my own computer file I have three thousand names of worldwide collectors who might be approached privately. None of these systems is adequate for the scope of what we have to offer.

"Along with the General we deemed it necessary to keep the secret amongst ourselves. Jie Lie and I have talked endlessly the past few days. In spite of the few number of years he has lived, I value his advice as a peer. Please listen to what he has come up with, and then give us your best advice. Unless we are able, as Confucius says, *to negotiate the correct price* our dreams will be out the window."

Jie Lie was small for his generation, skin light honey colored, smooth and taut as a woman's. He had high cheek bones, owlish eyes, covered with large tortoiseshell-framed glasses. The glasses really distorted his face, belying the intelligence I had come to realize. He stood, nervously opening and closing a notebook, and spoke.

"Honored elders, my meager talents and humble abilities are at your service. My respected grandfather has asked for an opinion from my generation." Uncle Sam gave him a broad wink, and indicated his approval to continue.

"Auctions bring much public attention. Famous paintings like the Van Gogh sold recently for forty million dollars, bought by a Japanese company for prestige. There were many persons and museums bidding against them. Sotheby's invited the most potential buyers. It's called 'marketing' in our school.

"The Confucius Jade is also a question of marketing, even though it has a personality of its own.

"Question: what will it bring? Answer: it will bring whatever the buyer will pay for it."

The young man paused, now obviously so intent that he had lost his nervousness. "We have a product of unique use to a very small market. The Confucius Jade has the rarity of an art treasure, with a legend and phenomena. It is of the most value to a collector who desires those attributes.

"The buyer, in addition to the usual requirements of having money, must believe in the Shou Xing Lao philosophy of long life. He, or she, must desire long life more than anything in the world, including money. If we present our treasure to the commercial world of the auctioneers, key buyers will shy off. Advertising and media will hype the publicity. Despite agent purchase, the trade knows the score. Security is involved, taxes are involved. China or Burma may claim ownership. The net result is possible trouble and little, if any, monetary result."

Jie Lie smiled. His face expressed the pride of solving an earth-shaking problem. "The answer of whom to approach was simpler than we thought, as is usually the case in good marketing. This very week three national publications reported in detail on the leading billionaires in the world. They have done our research for us, differing somewhat in their approach and classification. The articles reveal three persons who have no similarity at all in character, but have aims in life that are identical.

"The short bios - excuse me, biographies - augmented by a little research of my own, expose almost everything we need to know. The interesting part is, they are the only ones to fit the pattern. Grandfather calls it destiny. I, the skeptic, refer to the coincidence of the Jade's arrival, the magazine articles, and the path opening in front of us."

The phenomenon was apparent to me. I agreed with Uncle Sam. Jie Lie continued. The audience, including me, were sitting on the edge of their chairs. He paused, looked around, smiled, removed his glasses. The names he revealed then would stay with us for the rest of our lives.

"One of the candidates is known as Arum ibn Mohammed al Par ad, Ruler of the Emirate of Par ad. He holds the key to the OPEC oil sales, since the Saudis have been having so much financial trouble. The Paradi have the capability to turn on or off five million barrels of oil production a day." Jie Lie smiled again.

"The Sheikh has sixty-two wives, according to the Forbes article, and lives only to take more brides. His father, Mohammed ibn Abdullah al Parad, left him a jewelry collection, estimated in the billions of dollars. Forbes calculated the financial assets of the Emirate at one hundred billion dollars. A rare treasure and the chance of extending his life and harem will attract this man. The article quoted an unidentified source. 'His Highness has a goal of one hundred wives.'"

Jie Lie's impish grin was contagious. A rumble of giggles went through the audience.

He continued. "Then there's Anthony Gossett of New York, a newspaper baron, president of Gossett Media Incorporated. By takeovers, and other financial strategies, he has accumulated ownership of hundreds of small newspapers and supposedly insignificant magazines.

"The article about him in *Fortune, supported by Newsweek's* information, says that Gossett's accumulation of readership is greater than the American, Rupert Murdoch, and Great Britain's Manchester, combined. He collects small town weeklies and dailies, publications in the suburbs of the big cities, sport, hobby, and trade magazines. Apparently Mr. Gossett savors the challenge, as his business plan is to own the world of minor publishing.

"Gossett shuns the beautiful people, crowds, and publicity. He prefers to travel in his own private yacht, moored at Australia's Gold Coast, and owns a Boeing 737. He does collect items of rarity and large value, but only to beat a competitor. According to the article, Gossett considers items of less than a million dollars unworthy of his attention. The collection is for his own enjoyment, scattered amongst his various residences in New York, England, Australia, and Sonoita, Arizona.

"One of his hobbies is to play cowboy, and he often talks with a pseudo-western affectation. The key line in the articles is a quote from

Gossett: 'This old Cayuse has got a lot of range to cover and enough hay in the bank to do it, before I become a sky rider.'"

Jie Lie paused again, to see if he was boring the audience yet. The people he talked about overwhelmed me. The worlds they lived in were beyond my perception.

"There is one more person mentioned, who we think is a possibility. Unlike the others, details are few about his life. This person takes a delight in hiding his personal life and assets from the world. All three magazines report his name, but with qualifications. They estimate his wealth to be on a par with the other two. Thanks to the diligence of the magazine reporters, who do take a delight in ferreting out details about people.

"They call him Emperor of the Pearls, whose base of operations is Kobe, Japan. The name is Ru Kokomoto, the largest distributor of cultured and freshwater pearls in the world. Individually owned, the company, Empire of the Golden Pearls, is run autonomously by Ru Kokomoto. He displays evidences of wealth far in excess of his reported income.

"There is a rare picture of the man in color in one of the magazines. He is shown entering his new twenty-five story office building in Kobe. The tower has a dome, consisting of a replica of a golden pearl, measuring fifty meters, over one hundred and fifty feet in diameter. The dome is Ru Kokomoto's personal office and sophisticated communications center.

"Ru Koko has a collection of jade, reported to be finer and more valuable than any in the world. When asked why he favored it so, he replied; 'Jade symbolizes strong character and longevity, for it is the toughest of gemstones, and gains patina with age, like I do. I would like to live forever, as does jade.'"

Turning to Uncle Choy with a look on his face of utter contentment, as if he had just swum across San Francisco Bay, Jie Lie wound up his long speech. "We believe, honored elders, that each of these three persons could easily expend as much as one billion dollars, that is one thousand million, for our rare treasure.

"It behooves us to create a plan where the three compete for the Confucius Jade. If Great Uncle Fan will allow me to quote our ancestor Confucius, he said, as reported in the *Analects. Knowledge creates intelligence, and intelligence can solve the most complex problems.*"

The young man bowed, thanked us for listening, and put his notebook into the back pocket of his blue jeans.

Uncle Sam spoke first. "And a child shall lead us."

The hour of speeches made us all hungry again. We spent the next hour re-attacking Aunt Ai Lin's buffet, talking amongst ourselves, trying to absorb all we had heard. Father Fan appeared tired, in a reverie, sitting in a corner of the sofa alone. I walked over, sat down and picked up his hand in mine. The skin was smooth, thin as parchment stretched over the bones.

He tightened his grip on my hand, turned his eyes to me and said, "Wan Yi, I have been listening to this exciting talk. It is gratifying to know my dream is possible. Something is bothering me, though. I feel deep inside that I missed some information that should have coordinated with my memory. Perhaps it is the Shou Xing Lao trying to communicate with me. I fear my age is dulling my memory. I am fortunate matters are in more agile and competent hands. It's possible that K'ung Fu-tze's dream will come true, though it's doubtful I will live to see it."

I remembered the emaciated form that Mother Chen and I had put to bed a few nights ago.

Book Two
THE EMPIRES

1

KOBE, JAPAN

KONG AI MEI

The Master said, *Is it really possible to work side by side with a mean fellow in the service of a lord? Before he gets what he wants, he worries lest he should not get it. After he has got it, he worries lest he should lose it, and when that happens he will not stop at anything.*

The flight from Los Angeles to Osaka is a dreary eleven hours, softened by the wonderful attention of the Japan Airlines flight crew. Bloomies popped for business class, giving us a little more seat-squirming room, free drinks, a toilet kit, and more personal service from the attendants. Ruthie Stein and I requested Japanese-style food trays. We ate every grain of rice and every bite of the sushi, sashimi, tempura, pretty vegetables, flaky seaweed, and other delectables I didn't recognize in the compartmented trays. We ordered hot sake first; it goes down leaving a pleasant warm glow. Delicately flavored green tea after dinner helped to put us both to sleep.

John Hemply, our team leader, and Marianne Pless, the snob from Fifth Avenue, sat across from us, gorging themselves on calories and cholesterol, and guzzling free drinks. They had several scotches before dinner, refilled glasses of wine during, and soaked up the port after dinner. Soused at 35,000 feet, the two would have monumental hangovers and jet lag tomorrow.

My name is Kong Ai Mei, rhymes with I May. Close friends and people who can't pronounce the Chinese version call me Amy Kong. When they're in a teasing mood, they call me Daughter of Kong, especially when I come on too strong or authoritative on the job. Hemply, Marianne, Ruthie and I are a buying delegation from Bloomingdales department store in New York. Hemply is the head buyer for the jewelry and cosmetics department, trying desperately to finish his twenty-five-year stint with the company without making a serious mistake and endangering his pension. Ruthie Stein, Brooklynite, is a buyer for the costume and bead goods, while Marianne handles the fine gold and designer division. I'm the kid of the group, only twenty-five years old, and in charge of pearls.

Our mission was to firm up a contract and advertising plan I started with the Empire of the Golden Pearl Company in Kobe, Japan for Bloomies. The idea had mushroomed into 'The Year of the Pearl' promotion for next year, and the hierarchy didn't trust their junior buyer. My project might involve hundreds of thousands of dollars of inventory purchases and a few million dollars in potential retail sales. Like all department store administrative groups, we have our internal jealousies and territorial complications. Hemply is over the hill and drunk most of the time. He holds on to his staff by delegating the open-to-buy privileges to those who support him. Section heads need inventory to do a good job and get recognized.

Marianne, our Fifth Avenue snob, came from the once rich Pless family, and keeps her position because old friends of the family still patronize her department. She has no use at all for me, an ethnic Chinese smart-arse with a degree from Radcliffe in Art and Asian Languages, plus a Masters in Business Administration from Columbia.

Actually, they hired me because I had taken a course one summer, on a whim, at the Gemological Institute's New York Branch on Pearl Identification and grading. This, with my MBA knowledge of Japanese and Chinese economics and language, impressed Personnel. They were really looking for Japanese-speaking staff, for the Tokyo tourist invasions hitting the store.

"Please put trays up, set your seats in an upright position, make sure your seat belts are fastened and put out all cigarettes. We will land at Osaka Airport in eight minutes. Local time is 6:10 p.m., the weather is rainy, temperature 68 degrees Fahrenheit, 20 degrees Centigrade." I winked at Ruthie and squeezed her arm.

The landing was smooth. The excitement flush of being in a foreign country was on everybody's faces. The multiple immigration stations stamped our visas in minutes. By the time we got to the baggage carousels, our luggage was already spinning around. Customs was an easy formality, waved through with oral declarations. Within a half hour we were in the public area.

A uniformed chauffeur held up a signboard with a row of lighted gold light bulbs around it, looking like pearls. 'Welcome Bloomingdales' identified our greeters and moments later we were at the curb. The uniform held the doors open for us, while another stowed our luggage in the mammoth trunk of the longest limousine I'd ever ridden in.

Hemply and the snob took the back seat, relegating Ruthie and I to the jump seats. Fortunately, we faced forward so we didn't have to watch the souse-birds.

"You'll find hot towels in the compartments on the elbow rests. The bar is in the table between you, and in the back of the front seat there's a small microwave oven with yakatori ready for re-warming, if you're hungry. Our trip to Kobe will take about one hour, and reservations are waiting for you at the Portopia Hotel. I suggest you dine in the hotel and rest this evening to recover from the jet lag. This limousine will pick you up at nine o'clock tomorrow morning and take you directly to company headquarters. If you need assistance during the trip, please use the telephone in the console. Konbanwa, good evening, and welcome to Japan."

I leaned over and slid open the window to thank the speaker. The driver ejected a tape with the pre-programmed reception from the dash and inserted another that produced the familiar songs and voice of balladeer Linda Ronstadt.

"Wow, this is class," Ruthie said. "I could learn to like this service. Do you suppose, boss, you could have a limo pick me up in Flatbush every morning and bring me to work?"

Hemply had already put ice in two glasses for himself and Marianne and was reaching for the Haig & Haig pinch bottle. I wondered if they were even going to bother getting separate rooms while they were here. "No way, Ruthie, not a shance for a limo for you," he slurred. "If any one gesh one, it'll be me first. Wanna drink, girlsh?"

We both shook our heads, more interested in watching the lights of the city go by, as we drove through Osaka, out on the freeway to Kobe, our destination. Hemply was awash from the sleepless hours and liquor and Marianne looked comatose. I giggled in Ruthie's ear. "Wait'll you see her tail dragging tomorrow morning."

Ruthie and I watched the lights of continuous urbanization from Osaka to Kobe, surprisingly similar to our big cities. Only the signs in Japanese were different.

The hotel was new and modern, equal to any of the Hyatt or Hilton class, with a towering lobby. Reception clerks efficiently found our reservations on the computer. Minutes later we luxuriated in rooms high up on the twentieth floor. Hemply changed the rooms for himself and the snob to a suite with adjoining bedrooms. Ruthie and I shared a twin-bed room across the hall.

Fraternization is frowned on by Bloomingdale's management. However, some buyers play any game they can take advantage of the largess of suppliers and the willingness of subordinates. In the rag business, the vendors used to pimp male buyers with models from the company. With women's lib and more female buyers, they now opt for dinner, and then try to come on to us if they can get away with it.

The turned-down beds invited two very weary travelers. Starched blue and white kimono lay on each, and a pair of leather slippers on a small foot towel alongside. We took turns for a long soak in the deep tub, put on the kimono, and relaxed on the beds, tossing local tourist brochures back and forth to each other. Kobe promised a fascinating week.

I called Hemply's room to see if they were ready for breakfast. "We'll meet you in front of the hotel at nine. Ruthie and I are going upstairs to the buffet breakfast on the top floor instead of the coffee shop. See you, boss." His grunt for an answer sounded like he was suffering.

The view from the dining room was superb. The hotel was actually on a peninsula of reclaimed land, according to the information booklet. Toward the sea was an enormous dock decorated with container ships. The boxes were stacked like parts of a Lego set, cranes moving them on and off truck trailers and the ships' decks. Around the perimeter of the peninsula was an elevated track. From our view, the trains looked toy-like, starting and stopping at the depots. They moved around the island, over a red bridge, and into town on the other side. The maitre d' explained. "They operate automatically. Drop a hundred yen coin in the gate slot, board the train like you would an elevator, and get off wherever you like."

Hemply and Marianne appeared in the lobby on time, avoiding us and breakfast. Bleary-eyed, and complaining about jet lag, they said they had had coffee and openers in the room.

If Bloomingdales has to depend on the likes of them to negotiate a contract for hundreds of thousands of dollars, I feel sorry for the company. I whispered to Ruthie, "If these two screw up the contract, I'll probably get the blame. Try to keep them busy today so I can work out the program."

"You're a hundred percent right, kiddo. They aren't worth a dried herring. I'll do my best to play nursemaid while you do the work. Go get 'em."

The limousine waiting outside drove over the bridge, giving us a panoramic view of Kobe, the port city, packed into the waterfront and up the hill rising in back, San Francisco style. Far ahead of us, as we turned into the main boulevard, was a high cone-shaped building, with a golden sphere appearing to float on the pointed top. We had seen pictures of it in a magazine article, but the actual sight was dazzling in the morning sunlight. The pearl-like globe shimmered and appeared to revolve slowly. The whole building rose like a futuristic temple, a form of glistening gold, drawing gasps from all of us.

The moment it came into view a tape recording, with the same melodious voice we'd heard the night before, rendered a tour guide's description of what we were seeing. "You are in Kobe, the city of pearls, looking at The Golden Pearl Tower. The unique tapered cone shape is twenty-five stories crowned by the golden globe. This landmark can be seen for miles out to sea, used as a landfall by mariners traveling the Inland Sea.

"The sphere makes one revolution each ten minutes on its base, the twenty-fifth floor of the building. It's the nerve center of the Empire of the Golden Pearl Company. Windows girdle the diameter, gold-tinted to blend with the outer shell. Monks from Burma were engaged to cover the surface of the pearl with twenty-four karat gold leaves, in the manner of the Shwedagon Pagoda in Rangoon. They used one hundred thousand ounces of pure gold, worth about fifty million U.S. dollars.

"The four outside elevators in the shape of scarab beetles are gold-tinted glass. Tourists are taken on these elevators to the combined twenty-second and twenty-third floors, our retail gallery. A glass tank simulates an underwater environment, similar to that of our oyster beds in the sea. Customers pay a fee and a diver swims to the bottom, selects an oyster to bring to the surface. If desired, our jewelers drill and mount the pearl for a pendant or a ring, while they wait. A spiral escalator moves completely around the gallery taking the visitors by our cases of pearls and pearl jewelry. They step off the moving ramp when they want to look at something, and make their selection. Prices range from twenty-five dollars to one million U.S. dollars.

"The twenty-fourth floor is the wholesale business area for customers like yourselves. The twenty-fifth floor is for dining, social affairs. The sphere above contains the business offices. In the door pocket you will find coded identification badges for you. Every entrance and private area electronically reviews your classification."

Precisely at the moment we reached the building, the voice finished with "Domo arigato, thank you very much, may you have a pleasant and productive visit to the Empire of the Golden Pearl. The doorman will escort you to your elevator."

"Ohio gozaimus, honored visitors from Bloomingdales."

Hemply, getting his act together a little bit, coughed and answered. "Thank you. My name is John Hemply, this is Marianne Pless, Ruth Stein, and Ai Mei Kong of our staff. Thank you for the arrival courtesies."

Our two greeters straightened up from their bowing and introduced themselves as the sales representatives in charge of our promotion. Dressed identically in tailored black silk suits with white shirts and gold ties, the young woman's and the young man's dress differed only by his trousers and her skirt.

Ignoring his assistant, the man motioned us to a lounge area on the south side of the building.

"Please come over and sit here. We will acquaint ourselves with each other and discuss your program. My name is Nu Kokomoto, second son of my esteemed father, Ru Kokomoto. Because of the magnitude of your program, I will oversee it myself. Yoko Kashimoto will assist on the project," finally acknowledging the young woman at his side. Ms. Kashimoto bowed to us again, her face registering not an iota of emotion.

Ruthie whispered to me, as we followed the others over to the lounge area, "Boy, these guys sure treat their women rough, don't they?"

I nodded, agreeing, distracted by the view twenty-five floors below. The city teemed with people and cars, like an ant colony. Low hills framed the background. The elevated trains moved in slow motion over the streets across the red painted bridge to the peninsula and back to the city.

Yoko spoke excellent English, obviously much more practiced than her senior, with the indomitable r's causing a slight accent. "Please sit down. May I have coffee or tea brought in?" Hemply and Marianne ordered coffee; Ruthie and I elected tea. Two kimono-clad hostesses arrived moments later with exquisitely appointed china, large cups for the uncouth Americans' coffee, and paper-thin, delicately decorated cups for our tea. Tiny silver chopsticks accompanied miniature doughnuts, an apparent whimsical touch for the American clients.

The next order of protocol was the exchanging of business cards, like a farcical comedy.

Eventually, we began to discuss our project. The big shots finally let me do my job and explain what we wanted to do. "Our promotion is, The Year of the Pearl, to begin next spring before the Easter and Mother's Day selling periods. We'll devote five thousand square feet of space to it. An idea occurred to me as we were driving in. The tape-recorded guide said something about the retail store below us with a re-created undersea environment. It sounds like something we should duplicate as a background for the promotion. We would like assistance in the ambience, such as screens, art works, tea ceremonies. Could you arrange for cultural entertainment groups to perform? We can get a lot of free TV exposure with them. If you have it, we would like some video backup to show the history and mechanics of pearl growing and harvesting."

I paused to sip my tea, checking my audience reaction. Hemply had never bothered to look at my plans in detail; his mouth hung open in amazement. Marianne had a disgusted look on her face, realizing I had one-upped her and she had better do something about it, before the big brass in the ivory tower got wind of it. I'd have to watch my rear end carefully. This bimbo might knife the project completely, or worse yet, try to take credit for it. Nu, the second son, was another story. I really couldn't figure him out until I realized he focused on my anatomy showing through the glass-top table. In my excitement, my split tight skirt had worked up, magnetizing the guy with a lot of exposed leg. This could mean trouble.

"Now about the inventory," I continued. "From what your New York sales office advises me, and our projected sales figures, the opening order should be around five hundred thousand dollars broken down according to the analysis already worked out. Here's a spreadsheet on the goods. Cultured pearls, freshwater pearls, and Marianne's department of gold and pearl jewelry." I thought I'd better throw a bone to the snob before she fermented and boiled over. "Ms. Stein will coordinate the less expensive goods and silver-decorated gift items through her costume jewelry department. Ruthie has plans for coordinating the cheaper pearls with gemstone beads, such as coral, turquoise, amethyst and lapis."

Ruthie kicked me under the table; I hadn't even told her what I had in mind for her. She picked up on it real quickly, however, and was busily writing figures on her work-pad.

Trying not to be obvious, I straightened my skirt and continued. "I suggest that you designate members of your firm to work with each of us separately while we are here. It's also very important that you supply certain expensive show pieces on a memorandum or consignment basis. We don't want to invest our money in slow-moving inventory, but will be able to create a sale or two in the fifty thousand and up category, if we have it on hand. In addition, we will require assurance of a re-order supply. I understand there are considerable ecological problems with your freshwater pearl farms. We know that Japan is purchasing a lot of their goods from China at the Guangzhou Pearl and Jewelry Mini-fairs. We have attended the auction and put in our own tender offers for certain types of their freshwater pearls. We want it understood there will be no effort on your part to block either our entry into the fair, or unfair competing on goods we want to buy. There will be enough business on your part with Bloomingdales. If we want to play around in the open market ourselves, frankly we don't want any sour grapes on your part. That's why I am putting it on the table now, up front, so you won't think we are sneaking behind your back to supplement your goods."

Niban, which means 'second son' in Japanese, lost his composure, stopped eyeing my legs and stared. Hemply was trying to send me signals to slow down. This wasn't his way of operating. He was obviously worried that I would blow the whole deal.

If I followed his system, he would simply allot the amount of dollars to the supplier and have them put on the whole show. That wouldn't be to the best advantage of Bloomingdales' profit side. We could make more by feeding in some choice lots at a better mark-up and soup-up our average margin. Also, I wasn't about to be stuck with high-priced goods that would tie up my open-to-buy figures. They could give us the big stuff on memo.

The men, Hemply and Nu, looked at each other and decided to call an intermission until they could swallow all I had thrown at them. "Please may we adjourn for a short tour and lunch. It's a little early, but I do want to introduce you to my father. He takes pride in his bubble above us, and will want to show you all of his electronics." Nu lisped this out, stood up and nodded to Yoko to do something quickly.

"Before we go upstairs to the social and dining floor, may I take time to show you the sales offices on the north side." Yoko took over, and led us to the other side of the building, facing the Inland Sea. In the far distance we could see the outline of Shikoku, the large island forming the major part of the body of water. "There are plans to build a bridge from Kobe to Shikoku," Yoko explained, in describing the picturesque panorama before us.

The sales area consisted of several partitioned areas containing conference tables with white formica tops, special lamps, a scale, millimeter measuring devices, and jeweler's trays. Each area faced the north-lit windows. "This is where we actually show the merchandise to potential buyers. The inventory is brought up by the runners, you see, from vaults below, according to whatever the customer is interested in. Each buying area has a computer communicator with the stock rooms, and a complete file of the inventory available, by size, grade, style, and quantity."

A spiral escalator took us up to the next floor, Yoko and I following the others. Ruthie, bless her heart, was sticking to Hemply and Marianne, who were still nuzzling up to Nu Kokomoto. Smaller in size than the floor below, because of the cone shape of the building, the twenty-fifth or social floor was superbly simple. It rotated slowly, the base for the globe suspended above us. Floor-to-ceiling windows, the motion contrasted with the city below, gave me a lightheaded feeling. Low lacquered tables were set around the outer edge, seat backs placed on the floor for western visitors having trouble sitting cross-legged.

On the next tier up, western-style tables were set, with padded chairs. The third tier had lounge furniture and small cocktail tables for greeting and drinking. The central core, Yoko told me, concealed interior elevators. The pantries for serving were behind decorated eight-panel screens. Tables appointed with rare porcelains and cloisonné accented the elegance.

Yoko winked at me as we stared at the moving panorama of Kobe. "If 'the Emperor' takes a liking to you, he might show you around the office in the bubble. It's an electronic wonder; he likes his toys to play with, including young ladies like you, so be careful of any special invitations."

We watched the small groups of buyers and their sales hosts arriving for lunch. Graceful young women in kimono passed cups of sake, glasses of wine and champagne, and trays of hot hors d'oeuvres.

Nudging me, Yoko turned her head toward the inside. "Watch the show, the Emperor is about to join us. Notice the flashing gold bulb above that panel. It's his personal elevator." A door slid open soundlessly, revealing a cocoon-like chair, not unlike a throne, if you associated it with the occupant. "The elevator takes him from the ground floor to the bubble. He is actually sitting in his desk chair, which goes right through the top of the elevator cab to the office above."

A small man rose from the chair, and with a military-like stride entered the room. Hair of silvery grey, impeccably trimmed, topped an impassive face. He wore a gold silk suit and a cream-colored shirt, opened at the collar with a pure white foulard as a background for a golden pearl the size of a quail's egg. Pausing for just a moment, as all eyes focused on him, he bowed slightly. Ru Kokomoto was at the top of the ladder, and others must bow more deeply to him, as did all the staff members in the room. It was interesting to see the people bend down almost to the floor, while his son Nu bent only a quarter turn.

"We are honored," Yoko said. "He will join us at the luncheon table, though I warn you, he may elect to sit only with Mr. Hemply and his son, leaving the women at another table."

An aide escorted him around the room, where he greeted each of the clients warmly. Yoko and I moved over to join the others, as Ru Koko approached. The son started to introduce us, waved off imperially by his father. Ru Koko greeted Hemply by name and acknowledged Marianne and Ruthie with a slight bow to each. He turned to me, speaking Japanese, "May I assume you are Kong Ai Mei, who I've been told, originated the Year of the Pearl plan?"

I felt like curtsying, but instead bowed to waist level and held the position for a few seconds in respect. "Hai! Honored sir, I'm pleased my plans have attracted your attention. Domo arigato gozaimaste."

His eyes bored into mine, and although they did not move downward, I felt naked under his gaze. My nipples hardened, poking embarrassingly against my silk shirt; I was sorry I hadn't worn a brassiere. This was a man who recognized the body response of a woman, no matter what the words. He existed for conquest. Yoko was correct, I would have to use everything in my command to hold off the Emperor of the Pearl.

2
CONTACT

A business lunch in Japan is a formal affair. At the lower level carpeted with tatami mats, we removed our shoes before walking down the few steps. Hemply was visibly uncomfortable at his own ineptness in settling down with crossed legs, stretching them under the table. He leaned heavily against the back rest and looked longingly at the chairs and tables on the tier above us.

Ru Koko motioned me to his left. "Please join me, Miss Kong. I would like more details of program." He spoke in the stilted English of the self-taught Japanese student.

My plain blue linen skirt was form-fitting and tight around my derriere, with a split up each side for walking comfort. The one drawback was that there was no way I could prevent showing my legs halfway up my thighs when sitting down. My legs folded gracefully as 'amah' taught me. Rising to the occasion, my skirt automatically shifted into high, giving my voyeuristic host a good show. There was no applause, but everyone at the table was watching me, with different reactions. Ruthie and Yoko presumably admired my aplomb and nodded with approval. Hemply licked his lips. I'm sure if his snobbish friend wasn't along, I would have faced a come-on that night. Niban rubbed his palms, never taking an eye off me, while his father simply took everything in and nodded, as if to say, "Well done."

Marianne gave me a look that would, if she had the power, have consumed me in flames on the spot.

The luncheon was delightful. Graceful hostesses brought dozens of tiny serving dishes, filled with sauces and condiments, colorful pickled vegetables and tasty treats. The centerpiece was a model boat filled with an assortment of raw fish. The tuna was pink and inviting, the squid so pure a white it looked artificial, and bite-sized filets of fish, each a shade different in color and texture. There were shrimp lightly cooked to a pastel pink, stripped to their tails. My host, ignoring the other guests at the table, concentrated on explaining to me each of the delicacies from the sea. He insisted that I sample them, spearing morsels with his own chopsticks to put on my plate, suggesting particular sauces from the dozen tiny dishes in front of me, and watching for my taste reactions.

Following Ru Koko's lead, I ignored the rest of the company and paid full attention to His Highness, the lord and master, Emperor of the Pearl.

I explained the program in detail, which he absorbed and commented on, with professional marketing perception. He suggested a few additions to the show, and special consignment pieces, promising to arrange it personally. Ru Koko ate delicately, emptied each cup of sake, constantly refilled, trying to get me to do the same. I fudged, sipped sparingly, and focused on de-sensualizing the relationship. I had the feeling I was sitting there without a stitch on, while he feasted on me as well as the food on the table.

After lunch, my attentive host took my arm and led me over to the window, pointing out various ships in the harbor. "There at pier, Golden Pearl yacht. Look like naval destroyer. We use for pleasure and shipments from Nippon ports to Kobe vaults. Security better than commercial shipping."

Ru Koko was about my height. His hand firmly clutched my upper arm to keep me close. For a moment the others were far enough away. I spoke quietly in Japanese, just a few inches from his ear. "Mr. Kokomoto, you may have recognized my family name, Kong. I have a personal and confidential message for you from the family. A superb jade treasure has recently surfaced. We plan a private sale because of financial complications. We are aware you are a collector with interest in rare jade. I can provide further details. I'll get on the elevated train leaving from my hotel this evening at 7:30, and ride it around the circuit and back to the hotel."

Ru Koko's eyes narrowed to a fine slit, and his hand tightened on my arm, brushing against my breast, the message evidently received.

The Emperor of the Pearl abruptly dropped my arm, turned to face the other guests and thanked them for coming. "Domo arigato, Golden Pearl very pleased with Bloomingdale. Golden Pearl wish successful and profitable promotion."

Hemply answered for us. "The President of Bloomingdales has asked me to extend a personal invitation for you to be his guest in New York, at some time during the promotion. We will arrange our end whenever you find it convenient."

"Domo arigato, Mr. Hemply. Accept president's offer. Niban make arrangements. Compliment very good plans. Miss Kong Ai Mei interesting person, very knowledgeable about pearls. Please appoint Miss Kong special person with Golden Pearl. Many visits to Kobe necessary for promotion."

"In all fairness, it's been Amy's plan from the start, Mr. Kokomoto. The rest of us are here to support the other details. She has our permission to return as necessary."

Listening to these two talk about me really scared me enough to wet my panties. It looked like they were going to carve me up, put the pieces on the dinner table and attack me with giant chopsticks. At least Hemply had given me credit. Ru Koko might think we cooked up the promotion to cover the greater plan. Actually, I worked on the Tear of the Pearl' before Aunt Jian Yi called me and said the family needed my help.

During the research into the three clients for the Confucius Jade, my name turned up as a possible contact to Kokomoto. The strange part is, the Bloomingdale promotion plans were already bubbling in the pot. The family grilled and then coached me like a CIA plot in a spy thriller.

The story of the jade and my far-off relatives was history in the making. The danger, the challenge, the thrill of being a part of the Confucius Jade plan was irresistible. They had every detail on Kokomoto's private life, family and rumored sexual habits, classed as mean and nasty. Research was thorough and extensive on all three of the billionaires. The whole scenario reminds me of a Ludlum spy novel, except it's real. I'm here, and have made the initial contact.

I boarded the elevated cab from the hotel side station at 7:30. Blue jeans and a sweatshirt, with a bright red bandanna around my neck, I hoped made me a normal tourist. The mall below was visible, the fair still going on. Farther away, at the pier, lights revealed the loading of ships with containers. There were only a half dozen other people on the car that I was in. I took a seat in the rear and played tourist with my camera hanging around my neck and tiny binoculars to enjoy the distant scenery. The train traveled over the bridge and into town. I started to get nervous. The plan wasn't working. No one even tried to sit next to me. Stopping at the various stations, the train circled back over the bridge to the peninsula.

Great stuff, Amy. The last of the Mata Haris. You think that palooka even heard what you said about the jade? For hours you studied the reports on Koko and he hasn't done anything except look at your legs. Maybe he's hard of hearing and didn't even know what you said. Now what are you going to do?

Talking to myself is a bad habit, but then I'm a total team of one person, so who else? A young man got on at the first station next to the bridge, looked around, and came over to sit next to me, deliberately close. It's difficult to estimate the age of any of us orientals, but he appeared about thirty, dressed in expensive sport clothes. I recognized the class act; he crossed his legs and dangled one alligator Bally slipper in front of me. If I hadn't known who he was, I would have been up and out of that seat, hollering as loud as I could. This was a typical New York subway come-on.

"Konbanwa, Miss Kong, I am here to receive the message you said you had for my father."

The voice was condescending, designed to put me, the Chinese female, in my place. His look, deliberately focused on the tight crotch of my pants, calculated an approach. I know the type; I've seen and heard it all.

Number one son didn't waste any time. His hand went right to my knee. I jumped up, faced him, eyes flashing, and in a whispered tone, my lips barely moving, gave an Oscar performance.

"Look, buster, I know who you are and what you are. You got thrown out of school at the University of California, Santa Cruz, for a scene no one wants to talk about. If you hadn't been the number one son of your esteemed father, you probably would have gone to jail. Your reputation as a spoiled playboy who romps everywhere except at home is well known. Keep your hands to yourself, quit the drooling and get back to papasan. My message is for him alone. Tell Mr. Kokomoto I'm not a salesperson, I'm a courier. Take it or leave it. You have until this car stops at the hotel in about five minutes to arrange a meeting."

Iu Kokomoto, Ichiban, the number one son of Ru Kokomoto, gave me a look spewing hate and venom. I may have made a mistake in antagonizing this one. It wasn't very smart of me, but I couldn't control myself. He was typical of the chauvinistic oriental male. They consider women something to satisfy their sexual needs, collecting enough bodies to take care of their house, home, office, bath, and food.

Ichiban got up, turned without a word, took off at the next stop, and was waiting for me when I arrived at the hotel stop five minutes later.

"Okay, smart-ass, follow me. Against my advice papasan has agreed to see you." He walked fast, almost running down the steps to the street. When he looked back to see me leisurely following, he stopped and waited. I laughed to myself, knowing what he was thinking: *This was going to be some tough babe to get into, but when I do, she'll be sorry.*

A black Nissan President limo waited outside the train station steps. A uniformed chauffeur held the door open for me; Ru Koko waited in the back seat. When number one son tried to follow me into the car, papasan spoke a couple of words too fast for me to catch. Ichiban slammed the door behind me and climbed into the front seat next to the driver. Ru Koko pushed a button, raising a window and a curtain between the front seat and us, and spoke briefly into a telephone, as the car started up.

Impassive face, in halting English, Ru Koko spoke. "You have meeting, Miss Kong, we talk while drive? Very private, no one hear. Ten minutes, because your name Kong."

He turned to me, put his hand inside my upper thigh without any preamble, squeezing it with an iron grip, and said, "Begin, please."

Grabbing his forefinger in a classic defense movement, I quickly bent it up with such force he cried out as his hand came free of my leg. Anger at the Kokomoto's standard hands-on approach, I spewed out in Japanese. "I'm a courier, as I told your son, not here to provide an evening's entertainment for you or him. You should know that my education includes a complete defense and offense system taught by my brother. He received his education at the Shaolin Temple in China. Need I say more?"

The eyes closed to mere slits and he clamped his teeth to keep from letting me, this she-tiger, know the pain in his finger. I knew enough about oriental chauvinism to realize the damage to his pride. This kind of a tyrant would boil inside, having underestimated an adversary. Retaliation would be uppermost in his mind.

Ru Koko nodded for me to continue.

I explained the background of the treasure, the discovery of the jade rocks, evolution of the Immortal Shou Xing Lao, and his reflected image. Ru Koko's eyes never left mine. I detailed the sculpting done by our family in China and described Wan Yi's unique experience on the night of the first full moon of the Years of the Goat and Dragon.

"It's our family's opinion that the Shou Xing Laos Jade will bring a peaceful and protected existence to the owner, and longevity for his family line as far into the future as time will record. There are no markings or inclusions, every centimeter is clear as liquid emerald to its very depths. We have certificates of authentication by the retired director of the Gemological Institute, whom you may know. It's our intention to offer it for sale and erect a university to honor our ancestor Confucius. We wish to bring his philosophies of the five virtues into the troubled world we live in today. Mr. Kokomoto, you are one of three persons in the world to be offered the treasure."

He listened without interruption, nursing his finger. I stopped short of dislocating the knuckle, but I knew it hurt, and that he would be reluctant to show pain. Strangely, as I reported back to our family, he asked only one question, this time speaking Japanese. "Do you know where the great uncle you speak of lived at the time of the jade rock discovery?"

"Yes, Great Uncle Kong Fan Shi and his family lived in the small town of Bhamo in Burma. Their home, according to the story I heard, was at a bend of the Irrawaddy River, just outside the town."

Ru Koko, obviously mesmerized by the story, said nothing, staring ahead in a trance. We drove through the hills above the city, the road curving in S's to the top. The driver pulled into a viewpoint looking over the whole area, and parked.

Ru Koko started from his reverie, and turned to me, actually shifting his body away from mine to allay any fears that there would be more advances. "Thank you for the message, Miss Kong. The story of the jade treasure is interesting. I am not sure whether it is fate or the intelligence of the Kong family that found me. Please excuse the touching. Our Japanese way is different than your country's. I need proof of the treasure before making an offer. Please tell the Kong elders, there is no reason to tell the other two persons."

Careful not to offend, I answered. "Honored sir, they say there is no negotiation. The price is one billion U.S. dollars. My family has faith the Shou Xing Laos will determine their own destiny. There has been enough phenomena in their finding and creation to convince us that they are directing their own future. I have in my possession all the proof you will need to confirm the existence and value of the Confucius Jade. If you can arrange a suitable place to view a video tape, I can assure you of the reality."

"Miss Kong, honor me. Dine with my family this evening. Your celebrated ancestor, Confucius, would have said, *It is proper to enjoy an important moment with free mind and full stomach.* My sons will join us to learn from you."

The man actually winked at me, slight traces of a smile at the corners of his mouth. I thought for a moment, and then decided, why not? Trying to calm my excitement at getting this far, I answered with as little emotion as I could. "It would be a rare pleasure to dine with your distinguished family. Please excuse my casual dress."

"Wives will find you a comfortable kimono."

The offer was interesting; the tone of autocratic chauvinism was disturbing.

Picking up the phone at his elbow, he spoke a few words, too low to hear. The limousine headed downhill. We stopped about halfway down, entering a short wooded driveway. Two massive wooden doors opened automatically. The car proceeded down a narrow tree-lined lane, and circled to a low structure half hidden in the trees.

Iu opened the car door and handed me out in a gentlemanly manner. Another pair of heavy wooden doors, carved with dragons, opened to reveal an exquisite garden. River stones paved the grounds, and a graceful bridge with carved strange figures on the rails arched over the small stream. The dim light of the lanterns showed dwarfed branches of bonsai trees. A miniature mountain rose dimly in one corner of the yard; water gurgled in a tiny waterfall within it. A pair of carved stone dragons arched and faced each other at the house entrance. Shoji screen panels slid open. Two women appeared with Nu, the second son and a younger man, apparently the third son, whom I had yet to meet.

I admired their poise. They bowed low, murmuring greetings to the lord and master, with not a show of surprise at the strange guest. Ru Koko introduced me, switching to English for my benefit, I suppose. "Miss Kong, you know Nu, second son; please meet third son, Sanban. First wife, Midori, second wife, Saki, welcome guest our home."

I caught most of what he said to his family in Japanese. "I have brought an important guest to honor our home. Kong woman is descendant of ancient one of China, Confucius. See that she change clothes Japanese-style. Ichiban, Niban, Sanban, you will dine with our guest and remain after. Miss Kong has an interesting video tape to show us."

Again turning to me, "Family eat then enjoy bath together before sleep. Miss Kong welcome to stay for evening."

The boys' heads came up in unison like martinets, and the women giggled at the possible fun of teaching this one the bathing rituals. I had to laugh at how quickly they accepted me into the intimate family circle.

I answered. "That might be pleasant, honored sir, but first let's enjoy the early evening. We will need time to view the tape and discuss the reaction you and your family might have."

Before I could bend down to kick off my shoes, Saki, the younger woman, dropped to her knees and undid the laces, helping me to slip out of them. Midori left to prepare for the extra guest at the table, and sent young Saki with me to find a suitable costume for the dinner. This promised to be a very unusual evening.

Saki, about my age, acted more like a sister than a wife in the family. "How do you handle a husband who has another wife living with you, and is old enough to be your father?"

"Oh, demands Nippon way. Midori help when master call me to futon," she said, thinking I was asking about her sexual relations. I guess that was all she was in the family for.

"Wife number one knows desires. Help arrange positions for bamboo rod and jade gate comfort. Saki make life easier for Midori. Midori not called to futon often now to service master. Midori teach me to start screaming early, when he presses too hard or pinches my tender places. Be careful not to encourage the sons; a strange jade gate is tempting."

I stripped off my sweatshirt, and rolled down the jeans, leaving me in socks and the tiny lace briefs I liked to wear. Saki looked curiously at my nakedness, and shyly cupped my breasts.

"They are so firm and large compared to my flat ones, and mamasan's droop like empty plums. Take care if you join us in the bath tonight. One look at you and all the men will have swollen bamboo rods between their legs. It will take most of the night for mamasan and me to drain their shoots after you leave.

"You mean you and their mother have to have sex with the sons too? I don't think I'd like that, even if I were a second wife."

Saki giggled again at my naiveness of Japanese family life. "Oh, they do not enter me, my jade gate for master only. If they call at night with big sword, I massage them until they spurt. They often try to play with me, but I only allow them to look and not touch. The maids can spread their legs, as long as mamasan doesn't catch them. Papasan, the master, prefers they use special ryokan and pay for service. Unwanted children are a problem."

Saki spoke halting English and I helped out when she needed a word. Both of us giggled like schoolgirls as I tried on one kimono after another from Saki's ample wardrobe. Rather than the formal costumes and dress of the Kokomoto women, I opted for a simple bright kimono with a red obi.

Tying the obi around me and standing back to see the effect, Saki continued with more family gossip. "Ichiban's wife in seclusion, she pregnant and sore because he hurt her."

The Kong family data voyeurs will have a ball when I report all this, I thought. Saki led me down a passageway, slid open a pair of translucent doors, and stood aside for me to enter.

A long, low, black lacquer table inlaid with a mother of pearl seascape dominated the room. Its beauty made me gasp. The fish appeared to move, guided by mermaids floating through clouds of waves. Ru Koko and the three sons were seated, leaving a place for me next to the lord and master. The men, drinking hot sake, took in my entrance like a first night at the opera. I acted the diva and bowed to the audience.

Ru Koko motioned me to sit at the place next to him, oriental courtesy bending enough to have me at their table, but not quite to the point where they got up at my arrival. Midori smiled approvingly. Evidently the women would not join us at the table, but would serve. Papasan led the applause. "The proper dress complements your beauty, Miss Kong. Welcome to our table."

The warm sake loosened inhibitions. Conversation flowed with the array of dishes arriving as constant as the waves on the seashore. Midori and Saki alternated in bringing the stacked containers, bowed, sank to their knees, uncovered the delicacies, removed the empty bowls, and drifted out noiselessly.

The sons, especially the youngest one, after he lost his shyness, bombarded me with questions about life in the United States. Ru Koko sat back, seldom injecting a word, preferring to enjoy the entertainment of my earthy responses. Expecting questions about our program or marketing, Sanban surprised me with his interest in current rock groups, Madonna, and the popular black singer that wore white gloves and sparkling suits, and danced backwards when he sang.

Ru Koko unfolded himself gracefully from the sitting position we had been in for the past three hours. "Enough talk. Time for show tape. Sanban, please arrange with Miss Kong."

We moved into a small sitting room with low upholstered chairs, and a wall of equipment. It contained every conceivable style of electronic entertainment equipment the Japanese had ever manufactured. Settling down in a chair, I took hot tea; Ru Koko and his sons took coffee with Suntory whisky. Sanban bowed and took the proffered tape from my hand, looked at the label with the dragon and phoenix on it, went over to one of the VCR's, set it up, and handed a remote control unit to his father.

The image of far-off mountains appeared, the faint sound of Ravel's *Bolero* beginning in the background. The camera approached the mountains as if flying, gradually focusing on a ribbon-like waterfall. The crescendo of the *Bolero* paced as the lens eye approached the mountains, spewing out their excess water, increasing in volume and tumultuousness, coursing downward. The white water grew fierce, through the camera's eye, and eventually calmed as the music softened, flowing into the wide river. Superimposed on the scene, two women in traditional Chinese dress appeared on either side of a temple-gong, taller than they were. I recognized them as my cousin Sha Li and Rui Xia, Jie Lie's girlfriend. In unison, they struck the gong three times, the sound reverberating into this room and around the walls. Across the screen a title appeared: 'The Jade of Confucius'.

I hadn't seen the complete tape, but I know my cousins had used stock film from the U.S.C. film library for the background. It was spectacular, realistic sound filling the room, so perfect that the roar of the rushing waters made you shrink back. The temple gongs rang, echoing in stereo around the room.

The waters of the muddy river appeared to recede and a figure of shimmering green emerged from the mist. The illusion of animation and actual form created the image of a person striding towards the screen, getting larger and larger. The moon came up overhead, causing a reflection on the water, piercing the inside of the jade figure. That reflection then took form, and rose up alongside the original figure, joining it for the walk towards us. A delicate, long-limbed crane walked on the outer side of each figure, spotted deer beside each on the inside, duplicating each nuance of movement. For a moment, the Jade Immortals, moonlit, translucent, filled the screen, their eminence dramatic and vibrant. The bald old men with long beards offered peaches with one hand, juices dripping from them, and each carved dragon-headed scepter raised to symbolize his power in the other. A clear, vibrant mature voice spoke softly.

"It would be wise to remove malice and greed from the heart. No one who would think evil may have my friendship, nor the power of my dragon's scepter. My companion, the crane, brings wisdom to those that she approves of, while the spotted deer by my side bears peace and goodwill to those he favors. A bite of this peach will bring good health, but if one is not righteous, it will turn sour in the mouth. Take care. Amongst those you trust, are the ones who seek power for themselves."

Light swirled in the interior of the figures, the green jade alive with reflections, the detail of the faces so perfect, the eyes blinked, the lips moved, the beards waved in the breeze. The figures turned around slowly, exposing every minute surface and interior in close-up views. A woman's hand appeared to stroke the bald heads and cup around the base to show the size. Shou Xing Lao and his mirror image receded into the Irrawaddy River background; they disappeared in the swirling mist.

A scholarly face appeared. "I am Dr. Richard Liddecoat, retired director of the Gemological Institute of America. I have examined the figures you have seen, using spectrography, magnification, and spot identification for refractive index. My conclusion is, the material is jadeite jade, of a natural green color, flawless under ten power magnification, probable origin: the Kachin Mountains of Burma.

Dr. Liddecoat faded from the screen and the scene of the jade figures again came into view, repeating their performance, filling the screen. A pair of carved doors slowly closed, the Immortals receding into the waters beyond. The two women stood ready with wooden mallets, moving in slow motion to strike the gongs three times in unison. The last frame repeated the tide, 'The Jade of Confucius', signed in the lower corner, 'Presented by the family of K'ung Fu-tze, Confucius, who lived more than seventy-five generations ago.'

There was silence in the room. The lights turned up. I looked around. Iu stood in the rear of the room, scowling as usual. Midori and Saki were kneeling on the floor on one side of the room, holding each other's hand, bowing heads as if in prayer. Nu, the second son, and his younger brother sitting lotus-style next to their father, looked at each other then at Ru Koko, not daring to make a sound that would break the spell.

Ru Kokomoto was in a trance, his heavy breathing the only evidence of reaction. He got up slowly, went to the VCR, removed the tape, slipped it into the long sleeve of his robe, and then walked out of the room into the garden, not looking at anyone nor saying a word. We all watched as he knelt in front of the miniature mountain and waterfall, kowtowed three times, forehead hitting the ground audibly, then sat back on his haunches and stared into the falling water.

Ichiban whispered in a corner with his brothers, so low I couldn't hear them. One voice was contemptuous, the other two trying to placate it. Midori went to prepare coffee and whisky for the master. Saki came and sat on the floor next to me, holding my hand, not saying a word. The Confucius Jade absorbed the House of Kokomoto.

A few minutes later, Ru Koko stirred himself and motioned me to come sit beside him. "Miss Kong, what else can you tell me of the jade?"

"We believe it has visionary power. Everyone who has been in the actual presence of the jade figures has experienced a dream, or a hallucination, call it what you like, of visitation and conversation with the Immortals. We hope you will see them at some time in the future."

"Possible, Miss Kong. They meet me in waterfall. No dream. Real. Laos repeat five virtues of famous Kong ancestor. Fate says jade is mine. Please, what next in Kong plan?"

"Honorable Ru Kokomoto, my family informs you there are two other persons interested in the jade. They suggest you prepare the necessary funds for electronic transfer. The final determination will be at an appointed place in the Fiji Islands on the date of the first full moon of the Year of the Dragon. The Kongs suggest you travel there with your ship, the *Golden Pearl*. Notify me of your departure date, I will arrange to sail with you or meet you en route."

"Will three parties bid for possession?"

"We know only that the Shou Xing Laos themselves will designate their future home."

A half-hour later, I got out of the chauffeur-driven car in my kimono, in front of the hotel, feeling like a courtesan of the night. Ruthie saw the strange sight come in, and had to look twice to recognize me. "Come along, my little friend, I can see you have a lot to tell me."

Marianne and Hemply were going into their room as we arrived at the door. They were drunk as usual and looked at me like I was an apparition. Without a word of explanation, we waved goodnight and went into our room.

3

THE EMPIRE OF THE GOLDEN PEARL

———⟨∞⟩———

The long black limousine arrived at precisely eight a.m. Portopia Hotel's formally dressed doorman held the door open for me, and saluted the man inside, obviously impressed. "Ohio gozaimus, Mr. Kokomoto," I said, as I took the far corner opposite my host. My co-workers were ushered into a following limousine, shocked speechless.

After responding to my 'good morning', he was quiet for a few minutes. Piercing eyes and a low imperious voice in English forced my attention. "You cause mixed feelings, Miss Kong. I angry you use door of business. Yet, Shou Xing Lao jade interesting."

"I assure you, honored sir, the business affair is no facade. The plans began long before I learned of the Jade treasure." I tried to break the deadly seriousness of the moment with a smile. "Unless the gods have created the stage before we humans entered."

It worked. He broke the stare for a moment. I continued. "My family is considering the details now. I advised them of your interest."

"One billion dollars? You test me. Famous art works, rare diamonds bring big price from Japanese companies. Millions, not billion."

He pumped me, as we had expected. "Mr. Kokomoto, as I mentioned before, I'm a mere messenger for our family. Its worth is a price you or another buyer would be willing to pay. Confucius himself mentions the possibility of selling a jade treasure only if a price is determined. On the other hand, there are few men in the world who would consider paying a billion dollars for a rare treasure. It's a compliment to you. How would your children react to your spending so much of their inheritance on a whim?"

He laughed. "Iu already suggest stealing. Nu thinks father very foolish. Intrigue, beauty, phenomena, fascinate Sanban. Sanban not money-conscious. My ancestors, like yours, famous many generations. Kokomotos always samurai, soldiers of Emperor. My generation fight with finance and power, not sword. Today, my empire more value than Nippon Emperor. My life more interesting."

"Please tell me how you gained your wealth."

"You are person with intelligence and beauty. Your family choose courier wisely. I try to get information. Instead I speak of matters I never tell strangers. Kokomoto raised in wealthy family. I only male survivor of Kokomotos from the war, a defeated military officer. Samurai warrior supposed to hara-kiri. Strange happening. I did not. Return instead to rebuild family fortune.

"I know American occupiers, only money in Nippon. I collect pearls from every source, resell to soldiers, later to tourists." A slight smile escaped as Ru Koko continued.

"Maybe steal some, sometimes buy pearls at first. My family need food. My business need inventory. Now, I control thousand times more treasure than fools at Mikimoto. Golden Pearl sell all over world. Golden Pearl own hundreds pearl farms. Golden Pearl buy harvest in China, Indonesia and Australia. I copy system of De Beers. De Beers control diamonds. Golden Pearl control pearls. Their secret, control marketing, good years, bad years. Empire of Golden Pearl control more than fifty percent of world market."

The limousine drove up to the other side of the building from which we had entered yesterday. A concealed gate rolled up, the dark interior swallowed us. Inside was much more than a garage. We circled up a ramp to the central core. Guards lent a quasi-military ambience. Concealed panels that opened and closed like the Starship Enterprise honeycombed the bustling interior. A guard opened the door, saluted Ru Koko, and escorted us across a golden carpet to the gleaming cylinder I had caught a glimpse of yesterday.

Wordlessly, I followed Ru Koko, who took his seat in the cocoon-like chair, beckoning for me to stand alongside it. The door slid shut. I felt the cab rising, the lack of sound numbing the senses. Ru Koko noticed my curious expression and this time laughed outright.

"Compressed air source of power, like bullet in gun. Look up, see entrance like in camera lens."

I saw flat black discs recessing to reveal an opening the size of the cab. The floor platform rose through that opening into the golden bubble, and clicked into position, the discs below us closing to make a solid base. It was eerie, a feeling that was probably shared by astronauts catapulting into space.

The electronic throne was dead center on the axis of the globe. The staff, on three tiers below, stood up from their desks, as if on cue, as the mighty one appeared. "Ohio gozaimus!" resounded. They all bowed in unison. A returned bow and a wave of his hand returned them to their activities.

Impressing me further, Ru Koko pressed a button on the arm-rest console, rotating our whole platform, or throne as I thought of it, forty-five degrees. He pointed to a desk on the tier below. "That man vice president in charge of inventory. Please watch, we have morning review." Another button on the console controlled a twelve-inch monitor screen that suddenly appeared like a Porsche headlight from the flat desk. A keyboard ejected at its base. The menu flashing up on the screen listed twenty-five major departments in alphabetical order. Accounting, Inventory, Sales, Security, etc. He moved the cursor to Inventory, and pressed the 'enter' key. The screen immediately responded: INVENTORY – V.P. SASHI LOCATION – CORE.

"Core here. Program tracks person and department. Have complete worldwide information in moment."

For the next half hour he continued to show off the organization, and then a signal appeared on the screen: URGENT HONG KONG URGENT. Ru Koko abruptly dismissed me with a wave of his hand.

"Domo arigato, Mr. Kokomoto, your personal attention is appreciated. With good fortune, we will meet again before I return to the United States."

Yoko met me on the tier below, bowed and said, "Ni hao ma?" then straightened up and extended her hand for a western greeting.

"Hao, qing, ohio gozaimus Miss Kashimoto. It's good to see you again," I said. She had a firm handshake. I felt a warm camaraderie with her, as a sister.

We walked slowly down the steps, watching the various executives, aides, assistants, each working his or her video monitors. The concealed printers spewed sheets of paper through slots on the desk surface. On the lower tier, we walked the whole perimeter of the globe, watching both the people at work and the superb outdoor views. As the globe turned with barely perceptible motion, the scene changed around us as in a panoramic exhibition.

Yoko interrupted my reverie. "Come, enough sightseeing, we'll have a cup of tea in the dining room below. I want you to meet a good friend of mine."

Going through a passageway underneath the tiers, we came to a circular escalator spiraling around the central core. A pretty young woman, dressed like Yoko, met us at the foot of the escalator. "Miss Amy Kong, please meet Nikko Okusu, the assistant director of security."

Slipping off our shoes, we went to the lower level, and dropped to our knees at one of the delightful lacquered tables. A hostess brought and served tea in the traditional ceremonial manner while we explored each other conversationally. Nikko spoke American idiomatic English. "You went to college in the States?" I asked.

"M.I.T. all the way, after I finished university in Japan. Like Yoko, I am one of the few lucky women who are allowed by their families to have a career."

Yoko spoke up. "Here we are, three smart, educated women with important careers that we're proud of, but at least you, Ai Mei, can have a husband, family and still have your profession. Nikko and I, if we want to get married, must resign and go back to being a housewife. I am in love with Niban; we have talked of getting married. If I do, all the years of education, the struggle to achieve an important position in the company go down the drain. I will have to resign, go to live in the Kokomoto household, have babies, and cook dinner for my husband. He, on the other hand, will seldom come home for dinner, go to bars and geishas after work, and once in a while show up to have some fun with me and make a baby. The system is changing in Japan, but it will take another generation or more to release us."

I thought a few moments and answered, "What would worry me, if I was in your shoes, is what will happen when the lord and master passes on. Ichiban becomes the head honcho. He is one tough macho samurai, from what I have seen. Yoko becomes a subjugated wife of the second brother, and lives under the knuckles of his nibs."

Yoko looked at Nikko and received an affirmative nod in return. "We have plans. Maybe we can run the company some day. For now, we collect information to know what's going on. The brothers are very secretive about certain phases of the business that are not public. Nikko will show you her offices and a peek into our network. Maybe you will help us?"

The security office, on the second floor, had a battery of monitors. Nikko explained, "They cover all departments, including the vaults downstairs." Using a hand-print identifier, Nikko opened the door to her inner office, and gestured us in. She used another hand-print ident, with her left hand. A console came up on her desk, ejecting a keyboard, the same as I had seen on Ru Koko's desk. Nikko explained. "Ru Koko's hand-print ident secures his private communications. It doesn't take much hacking on my part to gain access when I want to. Here's what happened after you left his desk this morning."

A face appeared on the screen, with the override, HONG KONG, TOJO STATION CHIEF. They exchanged the customary greetings. Tojo reported. "Freshwater pearls are hot with the tourists visiting Hong Kong now. I've found out the boat people are smuggling some heavy goods in through Fujian and Guangdong Province. The high speed hovercraft they tried to use are too visible, so they are going back to the fishing junks and bringing the goods in through Aberdeen. The problem is, they won't sell to us, preferring to sell to the wholesalers and retailers directly. They're getting double from the wholesalers, and three times from the retailers, than what we offer them."

Ru Koko's voice came in, hard and cold, using the few terse words he communicated with. "First send out a warning that we will not accept the current condition. Second, get the exact sea routing they use and approximate times of sailing. I will activate our group of two-man armed submarines, and the mother ship. A little piracy will correct the situation."

I gasped. Armed submarines, mother ship! I wondered what else he used his navy for.

Hong Kong disconnected. A heavy-set Semitic woman appeared next on the screen with the locale reading TEL AVIV, ISRAEL, SELMA COHEN STATION CHIEF. "Morning, boss man, what's cookin'?"

Apparently Ru Koko endured this effrontery. Yoko explained. "Israel is not friendly with Japan. It is difficult to get loyal contacts. Selma Cohen is resident agent for the company in the Middle East, therefore Golden Pearl's listening post in the Arab world. The seed pearls of the Iranian Gulf are an important commodity for us. The Iranians want to trade for sophisticated armament, which the Chief refuses to deal in. It's Selma's job to get the pearls another way, by trading for diamonds. It's a complicated process. Israelis trade through the French connections. Listen."

Ru Koko was speaking in his stilted English. "Selma, we need one thousand carats full-cut melee for workshop and special promotion for American customer. Calibrated three, five and ten pointers, clean white. Can use three hundred carats four grainers. No heavy girdles. Good make, eye clean. Ichiban meet ten days."

"No problem, boss man, but you'll have to come up with U.S. dollars in currency. They love those packages of one hundred dollar bills. I'll meet Ichiban at Shangri-La, Hong Kong myself. The last time I sent my daughter, your kinky son tried to make time with her. No invoices, no paperwork."

The military voice responding, clipped the words, irritated. "No need remind me of senseless Israel currency and trading laws. Your government learn some day, advantage of free trade."

"Yeh, boss man, I know all about Japan's system of free and easy trade, going out that is, not coming in."

Ru Koko cut his connection, but apparently Selma Cohen had not shut off her video phone transmitter and Nikko's tap kept the line open. We heard: "That's one tough bastard. Some day I am going to hear about someone shooting the yellow globe off the top of his building with him in it. Gertie, get Hyman on the phone and tell him to come over to dinner tonight with a couple of his friends."

The line went dead.

"You two really have something going here. What happens if Ru Koko ever finds out?"

"We're very careful, and so far have little use for the information we have accumulated." Nikko spoke in a quiet, tight-lipped voice. "If he ever does try to retaliate, we have some films of his other activities that he would not care to have revealed. The major newspapers in Japan and United States will get them automatically, if anything should happen to either one of us."

"What other activities?"

Yoko answered for both of them. "Not right now, Miss Kong. We like you but haven't known you long enough. See if you can extend your stay, until we can check you out."

Yoko's voice changed, the friendly tone dropped. I was afraid I had spoiled the relationship. "Please forgive me if I have angered you. I'll talk to Hemply and get a couple more days to solidify the orders. In the meantime, if you have a contact in Hong Kong, I can give you a number there to verify my credentials."

4

KOKOMOTO, KOBE

The weak-chinned face on the screen was thin and angular, topped with stringy brown hair, eyes dressed in academic half-glasses. HOUSINGLY, LONDON read the location strip at the bottom. We heard Ru Koko's abridged English spitting out commands, Housingly nodding from time to time to show attentiveness.

"Watch for unusual jade sculpture come on market. National Museum, Taipei might unload treasure for cash. Chiang's son always need money. Possible Madam Chiang has valuable items in closet. Old Nationalists worried about Mainland merger not too far off. Sailors say, rats leaving the ship. Maybe need liquidate secret treasures. Asian Wall Street Journal reports cosmetic company purchase Gumps in San Francisco, maybe liquidate Jade Room collection.

Neville Housingly's British accent responded with a thoughtful, delayed tone. "I'll have our company's agents scout around in the hope that we'll be the auction agent. Nothing has come into my office for appraisal in the past month except boring junk, not worth the effort for us to put up for bid. Did you receive the information I sent you about the large jade auction in October in Hong Kong at the Mandarin? I understand Sothebys limited the invitations to one hundred buyers."

"Yes, have catalogue, and invitation. Nothing interests me. Will send Niban for show. Report personally with information. Private, my ears only."

Nikko, Yoko and I gathered around the television in my hotel room. They brought a VCR unit and edited tapes of the day's conversations of Ru Koko's video phone system. A lacquer-tiered wedding basket contained a stack of food trays. Yoko began, between popping the goodies into her mouth with chopsticks, "we made the phone call to Hong Kong, as you suggested, and our friends there know of your family Kong. They said Kong Ai Mei can be trusted, as the thoughts of Confucius are trusted for twenty-five hundred years. The Treasure your family proposes to sell will cause an earthquake in the Kokomoto Empire."

We listened to the Britisher first. Nikko explained. "Housingly is an appraiser with Panderly Auction House. The Chief has a special line to him. Because of Housingly's position, he looks at many articles before the firm officially accepts them. The rat sometimes diverts an item to Ru Koko. It's simple enough for the seller to withdraw an item if he gets a cash offer, and doesn't have to pay a commission to the house. The company loses the commission but the contact, Housingly, suddenly finds shares of stock in his portfolio on the London Stock Exchange. His broker is the same one our firm uses in its transactions with London by a strange coincidence."

Yoko stopped to sip her tea and savor a sweet. "Now this next one is a real tender slice of raw tuna. The Chief just got him. The name is Rick Davis, and he did a research interview for one of the U.S. business magazine's annual economic edition. You may have seen it, about the world's richest men. Listen to how Ru Koko sucks him into the net. We have people all over the world, indebted to the Chief personally and kept on with strings of cash, as your Chinese Immortals used to say. We've read about military and technical spies in the United States giving away the nation's secrets. Well, the lord and master is on the receiving end of info, for the strings of cash."

"The rest is voice transmission only. Ru Koko contacts many of his agents in their home, or at secured locations." Nikko explained while she set up a tape cassette. We sat back, sipped our tea, and listened to gossip like back fence amahs.

"Richard Davis, here."

"Mr. Davis, I am Kokomoto, the pearl baron you write article about." Ru Koko had switched masks for this person. His voice was conversational, with none of the abruptness he used with the others. "Domo arigato for modest view of Golden Pearl. Your overview and little detail appreciated."

"My boss did call me down on your portion. He complained it was too weak and not enough actual figures on operation, that should be available. They accepted it anyway, and there is no reason for the whole world to know about some of your other affairs. I destroyed all my notes by the way, except those that were on the material actually reported."

"Again, thank you. I hope the new Haslebad camera equipment arrived in good order."

"Excellent, I'm forever indebted. Especially since it was gift wrapped and on the seat of the new Accura Legend that I found in my driveway last month with a title in my name. You asked me not to contact you. Your gifts are very kind. Domo arigato.

Ru Koko answered. "You honor me. Coin needs two sides to be valuable. I ask favor please. Research files. Tell me which multi-millionaires your magazine wrote about, also would be interested in valuable jade. Auctions soon, I hear serious competition amongst them."

"I'll contact my office tonight; the information you want should be on file there. Where would you like the details sent?"

"Fax Tokyo office, disguising the information as follow-up interview questions to me. The header should read "FOR EYES OF RK ONLY." They will send by special courier to me. Sayonara, Mr. Davis."

Nikko interrupted, "We only have another hour or so until your friend shows up. Let me run through the rest of these for you. Most of it is just business, but it will give you a key to the kind of an organization the Emperor runs."

The traffic was international. Each was a replay of force, giving no quarter to the competition, considered the enemy by Ru Koko. There were far-reaching plans proposed for absorbing all the pearl farms in China through joint ventures, Indonesia by acquisition, Australia by financial pressure. The web of Ru Kokomoto, the Empire of the Golden Pearl, was global in scope.

"You mentioned the company has other trade interests. Would you care to let me in on that also?"

"They include the oldest son, Iu," Yoko said. "Niban and I are very close. It's difficult for me to reveal secrets of the family that I am aware of to him. He is an honest person, doing a fine job for the company. His father thinks little of him because his plans are of efficiency, the growth of a finer product, a better life for the workers in the field, while his older brother mixes with the drug lords of the Golden Triangle. He would like to reintroduce opium to the Chinese and exploit them as the British did in the last century."

Nikko sat forward on the edge of her chair. "I don't know everything. I'm going to tell you what I've seen and heard. While setting up security lines in the vault rooms below, I overheard conversations by Iu with the ship. They bring cocaine in with the pearl divers. The *Golden Pearl* acting as the mother ship, takes small two-man submarines out into international waters, contacting coastal freighters from Southeast Asia. They pick up waterproof containers suspended from buoys dropped overboard by the contacts, and drag them underwater back to the oyster beds. Special divers load them into pearl baskets. From there they go right into the vaults with the pearl harvest, diverted into a special area.

"The whole operation is run by Ichiban, I assume with the knowledge of his father."

"Would you like one more glimpse into the Emperor's life?" Yoko said.

"With an opening like that, how could I resist? What else could be in the great one's style of living, other than the yacht and private airplane he uses?"

"We caught a phone call to the Ryokan Edo. Ru Koko has reserved the whole Ryokan for tomorrow evening, for himself. Mamasan, who runs it, is an old friend of ours, once a famous Geisha. If you're game for some sorority capers, she's offered to let us in the voyeurs' viewing room. The Emperor is known to get a little rough. We want you to know exactly what kind of a man you are dealing with." Nikko looked me straight in the eye, looking for the slightest hesitation on my part.

"Okay, this is probably the one and only time I will ever see the inside of a geisha house. I'm game. When do we meet?"

"I can't go with you," Nikko said. "Yoko will take you and see that you get safely back to the hotel. I'm sure you'll learn a lot about Ru Kokomoto." The last sentence concluded with a wink and a rare smile.

The phone rang. Nikko picked up the receiver before I could reach it, listened a moment, then hung up. "Your friend Ruthie is on her way up, we'll have to split, as you say." In a matter of seconds, they grabbed the basket, VCR tapes, even the empty glasses we had been using, and were out the door, heading toward the stairway. I quickly checked around for other traces of our party, turned the television on, and plopped down on the sofa, pretending to be asleep. A key turned in the door and Ruthie entered.

Ruthie, Hemply and Marianne left for the States in the morning, and I went to the Golden Pearl Building to work out some more details with Yoko on our promotion. Ichiban came up to the lunch table, bowed, and turned on the charm.

"Your visit is ending, I understand. It would give me great pleasure to entertain you for the evening tonight. It's only a short journey to

Osaka, where I know of a famous restaurant and night club. The food is memorable, serving only the finest Kobe beef, and the entertainment stimulating."

"My regrets Iu, it's impossible for me to go out tonight, there is a lot of paperwork that I must finish. Aside from that, my honored parents have instructed me never to accompany a married man."

In a low voice, exploding each word as if shot at me with a gun, Iu said, "You'll regret your indifference to the Crown Prince of the Golden Empire." He rose, turned his back, and hurried out.

"The Crown Prince will no longer be your friend," Yoko said, overhearing part of the conversation. "If you are to continue the association with the family, however, watch out for this black snake, he reeks of venom."

For the night's adventure, Yoko advised blue jeans and dark clothes, to look as unobtrusive and neutral as possible. When I went downstairs to meet her, there were two motorcycles waiting for us. She asked, "Have you handled one of these before?"

"I popped my first wet T-shirt on my brother's Harley, riding through San Francisco's North Shore area. The dunes and the mountain trails were our favorite Sunday jaunts." I winked and gave her a thumb up. "Yes, I think I can handle this toy." I tucked my hair under the helmet, buttoned up my denim jacket. We gunned the throttles and spun out, looking like a * couple of bikers on the prowl. We couldn't talk much on the way, except to give directions at the occasional stop for a red light. Avoiding the main road up the mountain, Yoko led me up a narrow deserted dirt track, a little scary on the turns, almost to the top. We turned into a hidden path to face a wood gate, shrouded in pine trees.

Yoko spoke softly into a speaker box by the side of the gate. "Two shadows in the night."

There was an audible click and the gate swung open. Inside we stored the bikes in a small shed. We walked up a narrow path revealed only by the tiny flashlight in Yoko's hand.

5

RYOKAN EDO

⸎

The Ryokan Edo bustled like a miniature inaugural ball. Mamasan was a dear. Considered a madam in our part of the world, she ran a legitimate, up-market and respected business in Japan. The sign at the gate said CLOSED FOR PRIVATE PARTY. She explained; the Pearl Emperor would pay triple their normal income for the evening. The whole staff attended him in one way or another. It would be a long night.

We heard a car drive up in front, and Mamasan excused herself, directing one of the women to take us upstairs. Nuki, the geisha, rushed by in ceremonial robes, face painted white as a blanc d'chine sculpture. The carmine lips and dark eye paint created a theatrical effect. Yoko explained, "Mamasan, Nuki, and student geisha Pai Shan will greet the Emperor. We must disappear."

We left our shoes in the passageway and entered a sitting room, furnished with lounge chairs, tea tables and a group of four television screens inset into one wall. A bar was at one end, and a bathroom peeked out from a partially opened door at the other. The young woman escorting us said, "I am only a lowly second year novice, not needed at the affairs tonight. It is my good fortune to be with you, Miss Kashimoto. Will you require a selection of tapes, or is it your pleasure to enjoy the monitors?"

"The monitors will be enough, little one. Please bring us tea and some cakes."

My adrenalin began revving up with trepidations similar to entering an adult movie theater for the first time. I wondered how my relatives would view this research project. Uppermost in my mind was the effect it might have on the Jade and the business relationships.

Yoko must have sensed my palpitations of conscience. "You are worrying about the propriety, aren't you Ai Mei? Please trust me. Nikko and I want you to know the part of Japanese life style that is seldom seen by foreigners, in fact deliberately hidden from them. If you are going

167

to do business with our world, we feel you should have full knowledge of the personality cults our men create around themselves. Strangely, most of the wealthy clients are aware of this room, often using it for their own pleasure. Mamasan does not allow any photographs to be taken, and uses it herself to supervise the activities.

"Nikko's first job before she went to work with Golden Pearl was to install cameras and monitors in the Ryokan Edo."

Temporarily mollified, I sat down and watched the scene at the front entrance. The three women greeted Ru Koko with a low uniform bow. The picture was perfect, the voices clear when Yoko activated the remote control. We could sit back and use any of the screens, reporting from thirty-two stations, she explained. A chorus of "Konbanwa Honored Guest!" echoed from the three greeters. "Welcome to our house of relaxation and pleasure!"

Returning the bow, Ru Koko beamed. "Congratulations, mamasan. The stress of my business affairs has faded since the car began to ascend the hill to your Ryokan. These are difficult times. I need to relax, as well as meditate on a particular problem." Turning to his chauffeur, he said, "you may return for me at eight tomorrow morning."

Once in the dressing room. Mamasan supervised the removing of Ru Koko's business suit, shirt, tie and underclothing. Handing it all to one of the attendants standing by, she said, "Wash clean and press everything." While talking, she held a kimono for Ru Koko, standing with his back to the camera. We saw the pale olive hairless skin, firm legs and buttocks.

"You are strong master," mamasan said, as she faced him closing the robe and tying the obi around his middle. "Your bamboo rod is heavy with juices. Rarely have I seen a man in such splendid physical shape. You have the organs of a man half your age. I wish you many happenings tonight, and will instruct my staff to exert every effort to please you."

I cringed back in the chair. Ru Koko strutted like a peacock, gloating in the compliments. "Maybe you should taste and feel the pearl of pearls yourself, Madame," he said, reaching to fondle a breast. "You are young enough to scream with pleasure. I have rarely seen you smile or express any emotion."

"You honor this ancient bag of suet, Lord of the Pearl, but you jest. The tight tunnels of the younger ones will give more pleasure. Pai Shan is waiting for you in the bath. Please be kind to her. She remembers your terrible strength from the last visit. It was many days before the bruises healed."

"She is warning him," Yoko said, switching to the gymnasium garden. "Mamasan knows her client well. Take it easy and don't bruise the women. Even with his clout, he knows she can and would refuse service if he became too abusive."

Yoko rotated the camera to show me the whole room, created with rocks and tropical greenery, replicating a jungle forest. The pool itself was large and freeform, meandering around the rock formations. Four smaller pools surrounded it, each with a small sign indicating the exact mineral content. Two steamed, the others were flat, looking ice cold. Focusing back with the wide angle, we saw the paraphernalia of a typical Japanese bath: small stools, wooden buckets, bars of soap, and plastic bottles of shampoo. Against the wall were a series of mirrors, and shelves with shaving gear, brushes and combs.

Yoko explained, "In busy times there could be more than thirty men here at a time. The attendants keep busy with their chores, thoroughly soaping, scrubbing, and rinsing their clients. They concentrate on the heads and genital areas, for not a speck of dirt or loose hair is to enter the main pool. It's social. They negotiate business deals, talk, soak and wait their turn for massages and other services."

A matched pair of doll-like attendants waited at the entrance, wearing thin white towels, rolled into a scarf tied around the waist, the ends dropping in front. They looked like miniature sumo-wrestlers girding for battle, bowing almost to the floor as Ru Koko entered. Their bodies glistened with sweat; Yoko said that they would have exercised with each other to loosen up hands, elbows, knees, and feet, all used energetically during massages.

My friendly tour guide gave me a running commentary on the scene. "The masseuses are twin sisters, finest in the Ryokan. They perform the massages, but Pai Shan will help with the washing and then enter the pool giving him attention while he soaks."

Pai Shan entered the room from off stage, attired identically to the masseuses. She bowed low before him. Her tiny breasts, perfectly formed, fell forward like ripe mandarin oranges ready to fall from the tree. She raised up and smiled at Ru Koko, now sitting on a stool before her. Almond eyes, black silk hair, flat abdomen, protruding buttocks, almost twenty years of age, a talented actress, Yoko told me. "She can portray herself in any role a client requests. Pai Shan is an assistant to the geisha Nuki. One day if she studies and trains enough, she will become a full geisha in her own right."

The twins came up with buckets of water from the pool, and unceremoniously dunked the human object in front of them. Pai Shan soaped the small wash towel, and began scrubbing Ru Koko's back and shoulders, underarm, and chest, repeating the action time and again, while the masseuses continued to bring buckets of water. The twins took turns shampooing his head, raising a foam and knuckling him as hard as they could.

Pai Shan acted the attentive handmaiden, kneeling, washing between his legs, and giggling as she lifted his penis. "It looks like a sea cucumber, dark and limp." Apparently all the activity had softened the member. She talked constantly to Ru Koko, though we could hear little of the mumbled sing-song voice. He responded by playfully grabbing at whatever part of the women he could reach, not being able to hold on because of the wet soapy bodies.

My mental state was a confused mess. I spoke to Yoko, who was complacently sipping tea, and watching my reactions. "I am a voyeur, with mixed emotions of sexual stimulation and guilt at the fear of being caught."

"The rough part comes next. Pai Shan will give him a shave and then join him in the bath to let him get his fun in. Ru Koko has some grotesque habits of twisting, pressuring, pinching, and other routines you may not want to see. He enjoys inflicting pain. Pai Shan will put on a good show, trying to evade his little tricks and screaming as loud and realistically as possible. The twins will watch and take over when Pai Shan gives them the signal to pull her out, then work him over pretty good on the massage table. They manage a lot of elbow and knuckle rubbing with some arm and leg twisting of their own. This will take the steam out of him for a while and give Nuki a chance to gradually bring him around again. Let's turn it off for a while, have something to eat and talk."

I nodded agreement, still trying to self-justify my presence. Mamasan joined us; the young novice served dinner and we spent a pleasant hour talking about everything except the scene I had watched. Mamasan explained. "The pleasures of the flesh reaffirm the confidence of the man in his male prowess and strength. He has a natural fear of growing old and impotent. Ru Kokomoto, for instance, desires to re-live the fantasy of his ancestors, the ancient samurai who commanded their lands and households as an emperor, so we cater to those whims. Tonight Nuki, his favorite geisha, will entertain him in the manner of ancient Edo.

"I must leave. The green light on set number two means that Nuki is about to take over for the evening. This will be an experience for you, Ai Mei, that foreigners seldom see."

Yoko punched the remote control for the set and then a combination of numbers to get the room. "This is Nuki's work room." She whispered as if they could hear us. Ru Kokomoto was stretched out across a double futon sound asleep.

Nuki entered the room silently, fully dressed in the multi-layered kimono outfit she had been wearing before. Other women brought a lacquer table, a kettle of steaming water, tea service, and a container of green tea leaves.

Yoko said, "Watch now. Nuki will awaken him soon. I know what she is thinking. He's samurai, bold, demanding, forceful, and cruel, and could be as mean as a nest of hornets if antagonized. We know he thinks women are objects to be owned and played with, services bought like any commodity. Wealth and power control his mind. Maybe he will send her a necklace of fine pearls that other geisha do not have. She's probably thinking about what she could do to amuse him the most, to tease him into granting a special compensation. Should she play the bee and attack him, or the butterfly and let him chase her around?"

The man stirred, awakened, looked around, not remembering for a moment where he was. "I'm brewing tea for you, Master," Nuki said. "You are in the time of your ancestors, a samurai, in the Realm of Edo, to enjoy the pleasures of the evening. I am Nuki, the most beautiful geisha in Nippon, to attend you." He sat up looking at the familiar painted face, the kneeling figure dressed in layers of magnificent silk, woven with pure gold. The formal robe fanned around her, as a queen might look on a throne. A single pearl, which Yoko said he had given her last time, gleamed atop her hair braided into a coil on top of her head. She rose with the grace of a leaf in the wind, and brought the small lacquer table to his side. Her long tapering fingers arranged the tea ceremony: heating the cup, emptying the water into the waste bowl, a tiny pinch of leaves for the bottom, and then the boiling water, raising a delicate aroma. The rites were a poetry recital; the soft voice made the scene so realistic, I imagined the perfumed aroma of the tea.

Yoko gave me a running commentary, whispering as if we were in the room with them. "The tea must be slightly acrid, as the flavor of the first cup should be. The liquid hot, just below the tongue-burning point, for too hot and you cannot taste the tea, too cool and the flavor ebbs. Her hands are cool in his, as he covers them bringing the cup to his lips. These hands will bring such delight, with their feather touch, exploring his body, like a Guan Yin with a hundred hands all at one time."

We watched as Nuki put the cup down, opened his robe to see if the bamboo rod needed immediate attention, or could wait until after dinner. "Lie back, great samurai, your sword needs sharpening." Nuki tapped on the floor twice with her knuckles and two attendants slid the doors open so quietly that Ru Koko didn't even look up. They went to her and unlayered her formal regalia, a ceremony in itself. Ru Koko watched intently. It was done quickly, Nuki never losing eye contact with her guest. She settled down beside him, humming a soft melody, as she bent to open his kimono fully. Tonguing each nipple with a feather touch, while running the long tapering fingers inside his thighs, up and back of his aroused body. He moaned, reaching for her breasts, larger than Pai Shan's. Yoko had told me she had a quarter ancestry of Portuguese sailor.

My guide stopped talking for a moment. We had both become silent voyeurs, watching the artistic manipulations of the geisha.

Now I was succumbing to arousal myself, and stared at the light brown nipples upturned to the top of the mounds, as perfect as an artist could carve out of ivory. The teasing went on for better than half an hour, giving credit to her trade, and finally when she decided he was ready, she assumed the mounted position, and, squeezing and manipulating with her jade gate, produced the wind and the rains. She caressed his forehead, massaging the temples, as he pumped and then subsided.

Another couple of taps on the floor and the attendants quickly appeared with warm water and cloths to bathe both of them. They brought fresh simple kimonos and quickly folded the futons into the wall closet. A table replaced them. Ru Koko arose, and went into the corner to relieve himself in the night soil container, not paying any attention to the maids fluttering in and out setting up dinner. It took only moments to turn the sleeping chamber into a dining room, a cushioned back rest placed for the samurai's comfort. Screen doors slid back to reveal a secluded part of the garden, lit by the moon. Yoko panned the camera to see water cascading over rocks, and a miniature bridge. Golden fish surfaced in a swarm when the doors opened, expecting someone to feed them.

A delicate, narrow-necked porcelain bottle supplied warm sake. The tiny cup was filled, quickly emptied, refilled again, until the bottle was emptied. Another bottle waited on the tray.

The attendants began to bring in the dinner trays in their carrying stacks, until the table overflowed with delicacies, each in a separate bowl or dish. Nuki speared the morsels with ivory chopsticks, and fed the hungry guest. Ru Koko drank countless cups of sake while Saki fed him every mouthful of food. He finally leaned back, propped up his hands, and belched three times. "Enough, enough, leave me alone; I must meditate. After that I will attend the evening's entertainment."

Nuki quickly had the table cleared and removed, as Ru Koko got up, walked in the garden, hunkered on the miniature bridge, and stared into the waterfall. I imagined his thoughts. "Who are my competitors? Which minions can be trusted to act for me? They're talking a billion dollars, which is foolish, but is it? If the Jade is as fine as they say, there is nothing like it in the world. Money is unimportant... Will Shou Xing Lao guarantee me many more years of pleasure like tonight?"

I could well imagine those thoughts and many more. His nature was cruel and possessive. He might try to take the Jade through ruse or force. He would have no compunction about eliminating others that might get in his way. It was also apparent that he had the money available, for the drug trade must provide deep pockets of unspendable money. I would have to report back to the elders with an analysis of the man's nature, and predictions as to what he might do.

"I've seen enough, my friend. Is it all right if we go back to the hotel now?"

"Okay with me, Ai Mei. The rest will be mere emptying of the rod, and a long sleep for the guest. Now you know what kind of a life this man leads. Anything Ru Koko can do to extend his life is very precious."

Forty-eight hours later, losing one day from the calendar, I arrived back in San Francisco, and called Uncle Sam Choy.

6

LONDON, ENGLAND

KONG FENG WA

The Master said, *If in word you are conscientious and trustworthy and in deed single-minded and reverent, then even in the lands of the barbarians you will go forward without obstruction.*

My official business card bears the crest of the United States of America, and identifies David Kong, staff of the United States Ambassador to the United Nations. I am a natural born citizen of the United States. Had I been born in China, the name would read Kong Feng Wa, and I doubt if I would be on a diplomatic staff of the People's Republic of China.

It's my good fortune to have been born into the family of Confucius, with whom I have much in common. My ancestor of seventy-seven generations ago, also served governments, not too successfully as the history records. His philosophy of peaceful negotiations and freedom of thought live today, however.

Some day, we hope, the followers of Confucianism will convince governments that wars do not solve problems. Conflicts merely create new problems and breed new dictators in another place.

Kong Sham Choy, Uncle Sam to the family, asked me to contact a certain Sheikh because of my international credentials. His name is Arum ibn Mohammed al Parad, Emir of the Emirate of Parad. It didn't appear to have any conflict of interest with my position in the U.S. Diplomatic Service. I admit, I did not tell the Ambassador what I was going to do. Ancestral obligations would have to mollify my conscience in this instance.

By a convenient coincidence, the Ambassador delegated me to attend a meeting in London, called by the Ethiopian Relief Committee of the World Bank. You may have seen the article in this morning's London Times:

Addis Ababa... fighting between the government and rebel forces in the regions of Tigray and Eritrea continues, exacerbating the famine problems of 1984 and 1985. The relief effort has brought world attention. An estimated seven million Ethiopians require basic food. The United Nations Food and Agriculture Organization has delivered one million tons of supplies since 1984. They estimate another 1.3 million tons are urgently needed. Tigray is an inaccessible area. In April of this year, only 300,000 people received minimum aid. Over one million need immediate relief.

The Ambassador coached me to work on the delegate from Parad. The oil-rich Sheikhdom had given only token amounts. My assignment was to persuade them to give considerably more.

At this morning's meeting, speakers prattled on with statistical warnings, about how the first world nations were responsible for the less provident. The delegates were blasé, knowing that only part of the relief supplies actually get through to the people. The Ethiopian government officials divert a good portion to their own benefit and sell the goods to other countries.

The delegates were here to discuss a world problem. What I actually heard around me was gossip about the gambling clubs in London, and what to do about Muammar Qaddafi, the wild one from Libya.

The meeting re-convened that afternoon. The crowd thinned out, with some of the delegates pursuing other interests. I picked up my identification plaque and moved over to an empty place next to the Paradi delegate. Ahmed ibn Arum, oldest son of the Sheikh's first wife, was dozing, from the previous night's excesses I guessed. He roused himself as I sat down, greeting me with a "Hi, David."

Arum was in the graduating class at Harvard the year before me. We had done some boozing together in my wilder days, before I got married and settled down. We shook hands and listened to the dull drone of the speaker for awhile.

"Ahmed, are you still trying to outdo your father in his efforts to increase the harem of Parad?"

"Not me, and especially not in this part of the world. All I want is a one-night stand, and to be sure not to sire any children." He smiled at his humor. "There is enough siring done in the kingdom. The ones I like to meet should have experience and maybe an odd talent." He looked at me, with a wink and a concealed finger motion under the sleeve of his robe.

"Have dinner with me this evening." I changed my tone to diplomatic formal. "I have a message for the ears of your respected father that will be of extreme interest to him." The low hum of conversation around us covered up the diversion from the meeting's purpose.

Ahmed's ears perked up at the unusual insert of conversation. I knew the Arab psyche; they love intrigue. He said, "It's difficult, even for me, to get the attention of my revered parent. If the message is of sufficient importance, I'll listen. You may join us for this evening's entertainment or have tea after the meeting."

"High tea in the Dorchester's lounge would be most acceptable, Your Highness. Thank you for the invitation to join your group this evening, but it's impossible. I'm booked on this evening's flight from Heathrow to San Francisco." I had had one experience with the outrageous sex partying with the groupies that Ahmed attracted. It wasn't my idea of entertainment.

The soft leather chairs in the Dorchester lounge embraced us. The formally dressed waiter wheeled up the tea cart. Ceremoniously, arrogantly, he set service on the table in front of us, rinsed the silver pot with hot water, and poured the residue into the waste bowl. He placed three teaspoons of Earl Grey in the pot and added the steaming water. Another waiter placed Staffordshire cups and saucers with a silver strainer on the table. A heavy silver demitasse spoon, drip container for the strainer, starched white linen napkins, small butter plates, and matching butter knives were added. Crumpets and jam and butter pots were added until we both fidgeted with the lengthy service. Finally, "Will there be anything else, gentlemen?" The waiter bent stiffly.

It was too much to resist for me. "That will be all, my good man, please enter the bill on my ledger," I said with a wink at Ahmed.

"Thank you Mr. Kong," bowing again, "Your Highness." Bowing to Ahmed, the waiter marched off.

"During the war, there would have been time to plant a bug, and give the MI5's a chance to pick up our secrets," I said, while pouring tea.

"We could have eaten a danish, swallowed two cups of coffee, and finished our conversation in the same time, at the UN cafe," Ahmed said, trying to be the urbane American.

An Arabian Prince in traditional white flowing robe and head covering, and the courtier, an impeccably dressed Chinese, in a shantung silk tailored suit, light gray shirt and a striped maroon silk tie, drew little attention in the sophisticated ambience.

176

Ahmed's dark skin, pencil-thin mustache, and tightly trimmed goatee was as perfect a villain casting as Hollywood could dream up. Not a word was spoken until I had eaten half of the crumpet, and settled back, cup in hand. "I need the energy after all of that blurb this afternoon. Tell me, Your Highness, will the Sheikh of Parad donate to the relief fund?"

"His Highness has authorized ten million dollars. I will pledge only two million. When the committee assures that the money will go directly to the people, I will authorize the balance. There's too much graft in Ethiopia. We are tired of lining the pockets of the leaders. The Ethiopian leaders are thieves, concerned more with their lifestyle than with the deaths of thousands of their own people."

"We understand your concern. I will advise the Ambassador of the reserve. He is working on a method of getting the relief directly to the people, as we have the same problem you have. Our honorable Congress is continually criticizing us for waste in our support of the third world."

Without losing the same cadence of voice, in case someone was listening, I continued. "My family has a jade treasure of rare qualities and exceptional value. Please inform your honored father that I wish to visit him and relate the story of its origin."

The Prince didn't like that at all. He scowled, sipped his cup of tea, broke off and ate a piece of crumpet, taking elaborate time to spread the butter and jam on it. "Is that the message? Just tell me the story and I will see that it gets to the proper ears. Tales of rare treasures often come our way, and seldom are they as represented. The people of the auction galleries consistently tease us with such reports. Our family has professional buyers, They only take it to His Royal Highness after the purchase is complete.

"Father concentrates personally on brides for the harem. My uncles, brother princes and I take care of the oil business and investments. If that's all you have to say, I'll take my leave. The club has promised unusual entertainment tonight. I must go to my room to rest up for the evening."

Returning his arrogance, with my own attention to the tea serving, I refilled my cup and took a long draught. I pursed my lips, lowered my voice to a stage whisper, and shot the words right into his face. "You know of the family Kong, descendants of Confucius. We do not play with words or people, nor do we choose to do business with the commercial houses of auction. We will present our treasure to only three persons in the entire world, each carefully selected for his taste and ability to acquire it. My message is for the ears of the Sheikh himself. I can tell you that it will prolong his life."

I paused to let the first shot sink in. "We are aware of his ambition to have a harem of one hundred wives, and sire twice that many offspring. We know the current count is only sixty-two flowers opened to this time. He will have to live many more years to make the goal. If you have not the stature to provide me with entree, there are others."

The Prince's anger leaked out of his trembling chin, shifting eyes and pursed lips. He probably recognized my ploy of attacking his position in the family. He spat out the words, "I will telex your message, but I can't guarantee any results."

Reverting to my diplomatic cloak, I softened. "I respectfully suggest that one as wise as yourself would see the need of taking the message to your father personally. Others who see a written communication might try to intercede and rob you of due credit. I personally selected Your Highness as the most intelligent of your family for the contact. You know I'm intimately familiar with your diplomatic corps."

"Very well." He calmed down, realizing I was right. "I'll bring the message, but tell me again, specifically what I am to relate?"

The hook was set. The Prince was leaving in two days for the Kingdom. "Please tell His Royal Highness that the family of Kong has the rarest jade treasure in all the history of the world. It carries an attribute to aid longevity. Long life. I suggest your pledge to the Relief Fund accompany a request to the US Ambassador to the United Nations to assign me to assist.

"Invite me to your country to complete the arrangements. There'll be ample time for me to spin my tale while there. I understand your uncle Abdullah, the Minister of Finance, is concerned over the Emirate's money tied up in property. It's possible that I can devise a method for your kingdom to recover from the terrible market crash of 1987. It would not be wise for the Sheikh to know the true state of the Emirate's investment portfolio."

Arabs are as inscrutable as the Chinese, but this time I detected a definite intake of breath and tightening of the eyes. He was about to question me then shook his head, conceding defeat. His lips formed a tight ghost of a smile and said, "Before I left the Kingdom for school, my honored father gave me this advice: 'In battle, if you are out-gunned, always give ground to live another day, my son. Your grandfather lived for ninety-three years. I intend to acquire more than one hundred markings of my birthday. Look at Allah's fools in Iraq, Iran, Libya and Lebanon, who beat each other into genocide, while we and our neighbors, the Saudis, live in peace and luxury. The world comes to our doorstep for our underground gold, presenting us with wealth far beyond our dreams. Live to enjoy it, my son.'"

It wasn't hard for me to follow the workings of Ahmed's mind. He would tell his father that he was following his advice, and if the treasure was real, his prestige in the Palace would be immense. If not, he could only be accused of trying to help the old fool live long enough.

My first task was finished. The bait dangled, I caught the plane for San Francisco and the Prince went on to his nightly revelries.

Within twenty-four hours after the Prince arrived home, a flowery invitation was hand-delivered to the United States Attaché in Parad. The Sheikhdom was considering the UN committee's request for ten million dollars to the relief fund. It would be of great benefit if the United States could provide the services of their delegate David Kong.

I noted the change from the two million to the ten million that the Sheikh had apparently authorized in the first place.

My boss, the Ambassador to the United Nations, called me into his office and showed me the relayed message as soon as I arrived in New York. "I don't know how you got by the guards of the Paradi Purse, but it looks like your meeting in London was a success. Pack a bag, and don't hurry back. Helen should have your ticket by now, and some petty cash. Congratulations, David. This project will look impressive on your record.

"The Secretary of State has heard about you and asked for a transfer to his personal organization. I'll hold him off until the next administration gets in. It's not practical for you to move over there and then have to move out a year later with a new group taking over. You are destined to become a valued career diplomat, and I want to keep you insulated from politics as much as possible."

He put a fatherly hand on my shoulder and shook hands to wish me well. The Ambassador's son had been my roommate at school. The many hours I had spent tutoring Hal to get him through was well worth the appreciation shown by his family.

7

THE EMIRATE OF PARAD

The Royal Paradi Airlines Boeing 747 flew directly from New York to Eden, the capital city. Pressure in my eardrums signaled the plane's descent. Below were the shoreline and the Straits of Hormuz. I turned the television screen to the on-board camera and caught the pilot's view, ahead of the plane. From time to time they switched to telephoto lens, enlarging the detail. The Bay of Eden came into view, the city nestled along the shore, white against the beige sand of the desert surrounding it. Palm trees and greenery surrounded the buildings. The palace sat up on a hill behind the city, in a lush green setting surrounded by an undulating wall. Terraced cubes and oblong blocks stacked inside the compound formed the building, decorated with azure blue swimming pools and colorful awnings.

When the camera switched to telephoto, tiny figures became real people, tending the vegetation, strolling on the porches, someone lapping one of the pools. Moving dots on top of the wall became white caftan-garbed guards with weapons on their shoulders.

Oil derricks filled the bay. Arms pumped elliptically like puppets dancing in the water. A massive tanker flying the Rising Sun flag of Japan stood offshore at a pump station, the pipes leading into the large storage tanks at the corner of the Bay.

I reviewed my notes on the Kingdom. Eden was the only large city in the country. Foreigners increase the one hundred thousand population by fifty percent. They work the oil fields and supply other services for the Emirate. Half of the Paradi live in and around Eden; the rest are nomads of the desert.

An estimated ten percent of the nomads are members of Sheikh Arum ibn Mohammed's tribe. The other Bedouin tribes live in small villages or tent communities in the desert, pursuing the life of their ancestors. The leaders gather once a year to council the ruling family, voicing their support or opposition.

Parad is an enlightened country, compared to some of their fanatically religious neighbors. The country prays to Allah at dawn, midday, mid-afternoon, sunset, and nightfall. Their women are secluded and veiled when they go out on the street, but can choose husbands through elaborate, discreet introductions. Female and male students, abroad for education and travel, are not required to observe religious and dress codes out of the country.

The plane touched down with smooth precision; Prince Ahmed met me at the arrival gate. I had my briefcase and garment bag over my shoulder. We simply walked through the customs and immigration area, the officers saluting as we passed.

"No more luggage, David?" Ahmed laughed. "I forgot, you travel light. I travel with eight or ten suitcases, empty of course on the way out. Forbidden fruits fill them on the return. Welcome to the Garden of Eden."

A white stretch-limousine waited outside. One front fender displayed the Royal Flag of Parad, the other the United States Colors. Four attendants held the doors open to usher us inside. One became the driver, encased in his own section. The seat next to the driver swiveled around facing the rear. The occupant was to serve us en route to the Palace. The other two guards mounted small running boards on either side of the car, grasping railings, riding shotgun.

"Surely, you don't need security here in your own city," I asked, "the enlightened and peaceful Parad?"

"No, not security, the footmen will clear away any crowds that appear as the Royal Limousine travels through the city."

The attendant in the car poured chilled Perrier water and presented a plate with fresh dates, figs and small almond cakes. Ahmed said, "I have succeeded in intriguing father with your story. He will meet with you in private in the late afternoon. His Highness requests you dine and share the entertainment with the Royal family this evening."

Ahmed's ingratiating way of presenting the Royal permission was a facade. The reply to the Ambassador came too quickly from the Emir. Only that august person would make such a quick decision.

Ahmed continued to patronize me. "Two attendants will serve your quarters, provide you with a suitable wardrobe, and help you with the bath and dressing. There is a private pool outside your room, if you care to take a swim this afternoon."

"Please explain the Palace courtesies; my visit is more than a diplomatic mission. There may be some manners not covered by the Royal Etiquette course at school. I'm aware of the eating with right hand. Will my clothes be appropriate for the dinner? Am I allowed to leave a small gift or money for my servants?"

"The Filipino maids will be far more interested in your leaving a sample of your semen inside them than money, I am sure. They lead a rather dull life. Paradi do not associate with them. You will wear soft slippers inside the Palace, left at the doors of the prayer, audience, and eating rooms. The women will provide proper attire. I will aid you in any other courtesies necessary."

It was my turn to laugh. "I'm one of those husbands strangely monogamous and faithful to my wife, so please advise the maids. I wouldn't like to offend any of the Palace faithful."

Driving through the narrow streets of the city, the attendants shouted for people to clear the way. I was impressed. It was unusually clean for an old city of this size. Gutters were swept, buildings newly painted, urchins neatly clothed and, apparently, well-fed. The women, though covered, stopped and stared through their abbayas as we went past them.

Ahmed watched my tourist stares, and commented. "Don't look so surprised. We have sewers and waste disposal. Every home has electricity and indoor plumbing. The markets are full with our own agriculture and air freight brings in everything else we need each day. The Bedouins who still prefer tents and the desert can choose to live there, and many do, in the ancient manner. Silk and brocade line their tents, the floors covered by the finest Persian carpets. We have a modern hospital in the middle of town. Our doctors graduate from your American schools and hospitals.

"Every citizen gets a monthly allowance from our oil revenues and pursues his own activities. Schools provide a desert education to all the children, according to the Koran. The privileged ones of the Royal Family have permission to go abroad. We do have special intelligence examinations for the average citizen, and only those with IQs over one twenty-five apply for extended education.

"We expect the oil to expire in the next generation. We are busy making plans to turn our country into a hot house. We have a hydroponic agricultural society, furnishing the whole peninsula with fruits and vegetables.

"You see, my friend, we are modern, and using our money well. There are some within the Kingdom that do not agree with the welfare type of society that the Emir dictates. They see no reason for throwing money at the rabble, and would prefer to keep it for themselves. I hope your project does not intend to deprive Parad of any substantial assets."

It was a tease question. I knew he would stew and brood until he heard the story and knew what I was up to. The only problem, in a society like this, would be the difficulty in separating the ones loyal to the Sheikh from those that continually sought to replace him with their own coterie.

"Which side of the fence does your princely rump sit on, Ahmed ibn Arum? There must be a cabal within the Palace that would desire to take over?"

Ahmed looked at me, bit his lip, and started to say something, but the limousine was turning into the Palace gates. He explained there was electronic surveillance of the perimeter and only two gates. One, the front gates we entered, was used by the Royal Family and guests, the other by the town's tradesmen delivering supplies or seeking audience with the government.

"You look at me quizzically, as if to say, who are our enemies? Dictators like Qadaffi and Saddam Hussein are greedy, ready to pounce on a weaker neighbor. There is immense wealth in our Kingdom, and our families are precious. With turmoil in the world, one day, we will be subject to invasion, or trouble. Our small army is terrorist-trained, better than your army retaliation groups. Our Navy consists of three ships, one destroyer class and two patrol boats. The latest model of the French Exocet Missiles arm them. We have six of your F-16 fighters, concealed at the airport, and a girdle of SAM sites entrenched around the city.

"Our forces are small, but could inflict terrible damage to any country or group that would choose to annoy us. We share military technology with the Saudis and have a mutual agreement to protect each other."

Pure white marble facades decorated the palace interior. Paving and walkways of porous sandstone absorbed the heat. Walls rose in a series of blocks and cubes. Like icing on a cake, filigree-decorated galleries and minarets laced the edges. The grounds were lush with date palms and fig and olive trees. Fountains gurgled and colorful awnings shaded the doors and windows.

Ahmed, my Royal tour guide, commented. "The Palace has one hundred and fifty rooms plus the royal quarters, and five swimming pools. The kitchen and serving facilities are in the center core and special hallways take the servants out to the private rooms of the Royal Family. There are five tiers in all, the Sheikh's at the top, rooms of the harem below. Guest wings are on the third level. The family and courtiers that live in the palace occupy the second floor. The ground floor is strictly for entertainment, with gardens to walk in and a grand banquet room, which you will see tonight."

"Out of curiosity, do all the wives and children live on the one floor?"

"There are rarely more than ten wives actually living in the Palace at one time. Most of the flowers, the new brides, remain for the first years. If they have borne two or more children, they may choose to live outside the palace and even take another husband. The Royal offspring remain in the palace, reared as princes and princesses until they reach sixteen. It's a rare honor for a man to gain a wife who has borne children for the Sheikh. The favored wives and their offspring live in the Palace.

"My father has many brothers, also Princes of the Royal Blood, sons of my revered grandfather. Their families have their own courts in the other parts of the Emirate, or in the hills around us."

Inside the palace, hallways spun off from the entry hall. Ahmed said that the large area became a throne room, where the Sheikh gave audiences or judged crimes on specific days of the month.

It was midday. There was little activity, the air hot and breathlessly still. Attendants appeared, and Ahmed directed one to take me to my quarters. "Get some rest, David, I'll come or send for you as soon as His Highness is ready to give you an audience. Please relax, but don't go wandering around the Palace by yourself. There are forbidden areas, and you could easily get lost." He winked. "We once had a guest who disappeared for three days."

Diplomatic training served me well, for I heard and understood the subliminal instructions as well as the real ones. Ahmed was actually going to be friendly, judging from the conversations so far. The treasure intrigued the Sheikh. Ahmed, the messenger, stood to gain by the association.

My guide led me up two tiers and then to the right, down a passageway, through several of the cubic sections, climbing short flights of stairs and descending others. We came to a galleried arch. Strings of beads covered the entrance. "I will wait for you here, honored guest, please have the maids summon me if you need anything." He settled cross-legged on a mat outside the entrance, and immediately closed his eyes. Siesta time.

Brushing aside the beads, I entered the foyer, fantasizing myself as a modern day Humphrey Bogart. Mysterious, what is beyond the veil of beads?

Two women, instantly aware of my arrival, rushed to the doorway and bowed low. It was a large room, maybe 30 feet across to another arch that opened on a terrace. I caught a glimpse of the ocean beyond and the blue water of a swimming pool on the deck. The women stood aside to let me in, bowing slightly with prayer hands. They were modestly dressed in pantaloons and blouses, and bare footed. Pretty Hispanic faces raised to look at me, and smiled.

"Buenos tardes, señor. Bienvenidos de Los Eden."

One of the women noticed my surprised look and smiled again broadly. "We are Filipinas, senor, hired to work in the palace. Paradi women do not attend to foreigners."

I smiled in return, relaxing from the tension of arrival and dueling with Ahmed. "Buenos tardes, senoritas." They took my val-pack and briefcase, leading me in; I could see a sideboard laden with fruits, cheeses, breads, and gourd-shaped bottles. One side was apparently a bath and dressing room, the bathroom concealed by bead-string curtains. On the other side was a mound of pillows, a sleeping pad, and a low table. My luggage disappeared into the dressing room. I looked around, and went out on the balcony to see the pool. It was sparkling and inviting, and I had been sweating in a white linen suit, in and out of air conditioning, on the long walk through the palace. I could feel the heat of noonday Parad, in all its intensity.

I pointed to the pool and made swimming motions with my arms. "Es possible, señoritas?" I asked, in my best Spanish. I knew some but my specialty is in Arabic and Hebrew languages. "Have you swim trunks? I neglected to bring any." In the bright light of the outside, I could see that both women were olive complexioned, had dark hair with a tinge of red, and had perfect features; they looked to be in their late twenties. Their teeth gleamed snow white as they giggled at me.

"Si, es possible senor, there is no need of wearing trunks. No one is here to embarrass you."

"I am pleased that you speak my language, ladies, but it's not the custom in my country to bathe in the nude with women present."

"We are but maid servants, not ladies, senor. It's our duty to dress and bathe you without embarrassment to you or ourselves. We could not be here if we were children of Islam."

Oh well, I decided, I'm in the Garden of Eden, fig leaf or not. I stripped down, with the kind and giggling help of my female valets, and jumped in the pool. It was delightful, and fifty laps later, I emerged. The señoritas were standing by with towels and a richly woven cotton robe. A table was set out on the balcony with tea, dried meats, and bowls of luscious-looking figs and dates. It was a new experience for me to be waited on, literally hand and foot. There were no sensual overtures, though the smothered giggles when drying me off were evidently pointed at my modest genital equipment. There were some asides between them in their own Spanish, but spoken too rapidly for me to decipher them.

As I relaxed on the pillows, they brought plates of delicacies. I ate the grapes with my own fingers. "Please to rest now, young master, for the evening may indeed be long." The pile of pillows and the low bed beckoned. It was only moments before I drifted off, reeking with guilt, of dreams, of how the maids were going to wake me up.

My wife would have to understand, there were certain customs observed, courtesies endured, if I was going to spend my career life in foreign countries.

The prayer call at dusk woke me. The ladies sat quietly nearby, staring at my disarrayed robe, probably discussing my attributes again. They brought a basin with warm water, bathed me, combed my hair, dressed me in a fresh white robe, and put soft leather sandals on my feet. This kind of life I could get used to. I wondered again if and how I was going to describe all this to my naive bride.

There was a swish of the beads at the door, and my guide or guard, whatever, entered. Emir of Parad, Arum ibn Mohammed, requests your presence, honored sir."

8

ARUM IBN MOHAMMED

Through the maze of passages, up and down levels and mid-levels I followed the hurried steps of my guide, trying to keep my sense of direction. We reached the top tier, Sheikh country. A pair of stolid armed warriors guarded massive carved doors. Gold-leafed swords surrounding the Royal Crest emblazoned the surface. Without a word, the guards opened the doors and stood at attention. My guide stood aside and beckoned me in, pointing at my feet to remind me to remove the slippers. The light was dim, the carpet liquid-soft underfoot. My eyes gradually focused to the light, revealing tapestries on the walls, like a Bedouin's tent. Louvered sliding doors, slightly open, hinted of the sunset on the opposite side. A massive, tall figure rose spectrally out of a pile of cushions in the dimness.

Bowing slightly, I said, "I am Kong Feng Wa, Your Highness, honored to have this audience with you. It's a privilege to meet the ruler of Parad, Sheikh of the Realm, Protector of the Golden Sword. My Ambassador and my family send their respects. It's said that you are a man of peace and education, just as my famous ancestor."

"Welcome to Eden, young Kong. I have studied the sayings of Confucius, and traveled the lands of the Far East in my youth. It has been my good fortune to learn much from his wisdom. Come, sit beside me and tell me of the secret that has brought you to my kingdom."

With a wave of his hand, a shadowy form rose from the pillows, pulling a black filmy material over its head and around a feminine form. The wraith-like shape disappeared behind a bead curtain, the tinkle of tiny bells and aroma of delicate perfume following it. A pervading scent hung in the air, and flowed from the cushions as the Sheikh led me out to the porch. We settled in deep-cushioned chairs. Pitchers of cold milk and water sat in buckets of ice on the small table between us. I looked up to see a black, shiny, impassive face, bald and beardless and attached to a heavy, obese body, standing over us.

We both indicated the milk, and he poured it into tall glasses. The body disappeared with the same cat-like silence it had emerged with.

"Mustafi, an old retainer from my father's day, yes a eunuch." The Sheikh responded to the questioning look in my eyes. "The other shadow you saw leaving my pillows is Silk, my newest wife. You enter this inner sanctum because it is the safest place in the palace from gossip and intrigue. It's enough that Ahmed knows about our meeting. The young woman will hold her tongue for awhile, until the other members of the harem wean her away from my side. Drink, young Kong, and weave me a story of jade and treasure."

"My congratulations on your recent bride, Your Highness, number sixty-three is it?"

His laugh was deep, and the strong Semitic face broke out into waves of wrinkles. "You have done your homework well, young man, your Ambassador should be proud of his well-trained diplomat. Yes, last month I took another wife. Silk is the sixty-third, according to Erik, the keeper of the records of the harem. Begin, it will be dark soon. There are plans for the evening's entertainment that I hope will please you."

The scene for relating my story was perfect, as I told my family later. We were on a marble-floored terrace, silk carpets underfoot, with pillowed cane chairs to sit back in, and sipping cold goat's milk. The setting sun painted its red glow over the vast bay of water in front of us. High up on the hill, from the uppermost tier of the white Palace, the desert's edge on either side of the blue horseshoe lake was an unforgettable panorama. Lilting music, as the poets say, from the harem on the floor below us wafted upwards, completing the ambience. The ears of a royal personage were waiting for my speech, and I, for the moment, was suspended in time.

"You are different from my sons, young Kong. Your eyes have the depth of your ancestors, and reflect the wisdom of your genes. My sons acquire fast cars, learn from the finest universities, and spend their seeds on many strange houris, but have much to learn of the maturity that shows in your person." The voice was soft and emotional, belying the fierce visage and massive frame, evident underneath the loose flowing robes.

I wove the magical tale of the Confucius Jade. Out of breath, I stopped for a moment. I watched my host, whose eyes stared as if hypnotized. After a few moments, realizing I had stopped talking, he blinked, re-focusing, as if coming out of a trance, and stared at me and smiled. Meditating for a time, with hands palmed, he then asked, "Why would your family want to dispose of such a treasure? Money is of little consequence to them, so I've heard. The descendants of Confucius are more conscious of life and line of life than any of us. If we believe the will of the Immortals, the possessor of such a treasure would live more than a lifetime, and his descendants after him."

"You are correct, Your Highness. The family of Confucius has a recorded history of seventy-seven generations already, since K'ung Fu-tze's birth in Qufu, five hundred years before Christ. The elders of the family have decided there is a greater purpose in the emergence of the Shou Xing Laos. They desire to initiate and dedicate a university to further the teachings of Confucius. There are serious plans for the promulgation of world peace. The sale of this Jade makes all this possible."

"Yes, I can understand the thinking of your family. The House of Parad has collected rare jewels and treasures for the royal vaults. The last diamond my agents acquired cost an un-Allah like price." He turned the ring on his finger to the setting sun, reflecting the blood red of a large cabochon ruby, as if asking it a question.

"If your story is true, and you can offer proof, am I privileged to be the only person to present an offer? What princely sum is asked for such a treasure?"

"There are two others my family selected as worthy to own such a treasure. The price has been set at one billion U.S. dollars. If all three persons choose to contend, then we will arrange a meeting place. We believe that in some way the Shou Xing Laos will decide their own future. The God of Longevity is a symbol of peace, therefore we caution no forceful measures. We think they have a power of their own."

Arum sat back again, whistled, drummed his fingers on the chair arm and laughed. "Beautiful," he said after calming the laughter. "Your family is the world's shrewdest business negotiator. It will be a three-way chess game. We must try to outwit each other, and then, of course, outwit you. That challenge alone should make it worthwhile. I assume you have heard of my inclinations as to long life. You suspect there is another more secret motive for my wishing to outlive my sons' generations."

It was my turn to smile. "The Kong elders advised me to be awake when I talk with you. Yes, honored sir, they know of your harem and the family that intrigues around you. We wonder at the facade of your taking so many women. Our wish is to see you fulfill your desires. We believe the Confucius Jade will bring health, happiness, worldly goods, and long life. It will be a prize for you and your succeeding generations, far exceeding the treasures now in the Sheikhdom's vaults. To change the subject, would Your Highness grant me the privilege of visiting the famous Paradi Gallery of Treasures?"

"Ahmed will be so instructed. I have become bored with the acquisitions, except rare ones, like this ruby." He offered his hand, the ruby bent toward the last ray of the sun, the blood red gem absorbing, then reflecting, the rays of light through its depth.

"The Keeper of the Royal Treasures advises me that our collection of artworks, rare gems, rare coins, and antiques will one day be far more valuable than the portfolio of equities and bonds that is under the administration of my brother, the Finance Minister. I find it amusing to keep them in competition with each other. As an aside, I instructed the Finance Minister to meet with you. Please help him to make some sense out of the complicated morass he now has our capital in. I have also instructed him to grant the funds for the Ethiopian Relief. You know of my reluctance for such gifts, often a waste. Deep pockets skim these funds before the poor devils that need the goods get anything. There is little sympathy in my heart for those evil ones that call themselves leaders of their countries."

"Parad is a model for the world. It's well known that all Paradi share the wealth of the Emirate, and rumored that most of your brothers and sons are honest." I winked.

"Yes, I try to keep them honest with certain pressures, but they wait for my passing, and vie incessantly for territory at the court. My sons need maturing. Some of my daughters are smarter than the sons and are now seeking to assert themselves in the palace business. It would be a most interesting turn of fate if some of them attended your University of Confucius one day. They might learn and then put into effect peace amongst the Paradi's neighboring states."

"The honor would be ours, Your Highness. I'll be happy to forward the request to my elders. May I assume by the tenor of the conversation that I can relate a positive response to the Confucius Jade Shou Xing Lao chess game, as you put it?"

"A thousand yeses, young Kong. You have proof of the existence of this rare treasure? Allah himself could not keep me from the challenge of my life."

His imperious tone commanded. "You will attend the banquet

tonight. If I seem distracted, you alone will know where my mind is. Go now, Mustafi will escort you back to your quarters. Ahmed advises me that you reject the services of a sleeping companion. I understand, but hope that your lifestyle is open enough to enjoy the entertainment of my dancer, Shalimar, and her retinue." He winked.

"I accept, Your Highness. A wise diplomat must conform to the lifestyle of his host country. My instructions include one more detail. I have in my possession a video tape provided by the family that will prove, as you questioned, the existence and beauty of the Jade. If you can arrange a viewing time, I would be most happy to present it."

The Sheikh looked at me strangely, then nodded. "I will arrange it." Mustafi appeared by some set of ESP signals, beckoned me through the doors of the terrace, and out of the Sheikh's quarters. I saw a woman enter as I left. She nodded to me, her face veiled. The eyes were those of an older woman, and I supposed that this was the favored first wife, Ahmed's mother, the love marriage wife. She carried a tray on which was a pot of coffee, strong enough to waft its aroma across the room to me.

As I left, I caught the strong vibrant voice addressing the woman. "You're as old and wobbly as the camel's humps, woman, but serviceable and a comfort to me. Your son has done me an impressive favor in bringing the young Chinese delegate to me. Tell me the gossip of the hallways."

9

SHALIMAR

⊸⊱⊰⊷

hmed came to escort me personally to the dinner and festivities of the evening, in my honor. "You have a very interesting court, Prince Ahmed. Tell me about Shalimar, who my attendants described as the Red Witch of the Palace." We were hurrying down a narrow passageway to the main ballroom for the impending dinner.

"It's a long story, but I will shorten it as much as I can. Shalimar came into the palace ten years ago, about the time I was leaving to attend Harvard. My uncle, Assiz ibn Mohammed, Minister of Security and State, discovered her singing in a gambling club in Estoril, Portugal. Using his usual nefarious methods, he promised her an entertainment contract of twenty-five hundred U.S. dollars a week in Parad. She demanded a written contract. Instead, he drugged and kidnapped her that night and brought her here. Assiz's wife, who is very jealous, helped her escape one night and luckily she ran into my father in this same passageway. His brother's action shocked him. To make amends, he set her up as a director of entertainment for the palace, at the same salary Assiz had promised her."

"She must be very rich and independent now," I interrupted, rapidly computing the totals of ten years times $2500 a week, re-invested and compounded.

"Shalimar is very wise, and has her accounts in Switzerland earning for the day when she may have to leave. Whenever the Emir travels without his family entourage, Shalimar accompanies him. Gossip of the harem says that she has never entered the pillows of my father, instead providing only the entertainment he requests. Because she is no threat to the wives, she survives the harem politics, but Assiz has never forgiven her. He smolders with hate and waits for the day he can avenge his pride."

Ahmed told me that his mother had seen me leave the Sheikh's quarters. After she had served him and left, the Red Witch had come in. "According to mother, Shalimar sweet-talked my father. 'I have arranged a very genteel evening, a little ballet and a silver flute ensemble of chamber music. There will be nothing to offend the senses of the American envoy. I doubt the innocence he pretends. The Chinese were as adept in the enjoyment of sexual pleasures, centuries ago, as any in the world.'

"Our Master answered the arrogant hellcat. 'It would not please me to have the young man take word back to his people that I am living in a flesh pot. The chamber music you mention is a strange term, as the only chambers your women know is their own tunnels. You chide me, woman. Give him flesh to look at, but keep it clean. Send a woman to his room only if he asks. I don't want a United Nations delegate to accuse Parad of bribery.'

"Mother told me that a strange event then happened. 'Your father looked around the room to see if anyone was listening. He may have known I was nearby. Arum beckoned Shalimar out on the terrace. I could only get snatches of the conversation. *There is a favor...Family of Kong... Hong Kong friend? Jade...* That was all I could hear.'"

We approached the banquet room. Ahmed whispered a last word to me. "We have much to talk about, David. You haven't told me about the Jade Treasure."

The Royal Family was in full attendance. The Sheikh and his four brothers were there. Several of the wives were secluded behind gauze curtains off to one side. The first tier was for the Sheikh, with his brothers on either side. Below them were the sons, the oldest in the center, the younger ones strung out on either side of the horseshoe-shaped table. They had reserved a place for me alongside the Emir. I requested instead to sit with Ahmed on the second tier; no use offending the Princes.

Ahmed told me how Arum, his father, took over the kingdom when his grandfather died many years ago. There were seven brothers originally, each dreaming of how he could become the Emir of Parad. Arum was the second son, and his father's favorite, openly groomed to take over. Mustafi and Erik discovered a plot. Arum's older brother, the first son, was a weak, malleable person.

The third brother contrived the plot to kill all five of the others, to put the first son on the throne. Thus, he would run the kingdom through the weak brother.

The brothers gathered one night, in this very room, to dine and discuss their new roles, after the death of their father. The two plotters sat together, waiting for a signal. Armed mercenaries were to come ashore that night, and raid the banquet room, killing all the males, except those wearing red headbands on their gutras.

Instead, Mustafi gave a signal to Arum. Loyal soldiers intercepted and killed the mercenaries. Arum stood up behind his brothers and pulled off the red-banded gutras of the two plotters. He grabbed the two heads of hair in one of his enormous hands and drew the Golden Sword with the other. One mighty swing decapitated the plotters. Blood spurted over everyone within ten feet of the bodies.

Ahmed said his father made a very short speech. "Thus, the Golden Sword has spoken against all conspirators. Allah, by my hand, will spare the sons and wives of these two. The families and their descendants are banished from the Palace and Eden. They must live as their forbears in the tents of the desert. If so much as a toe is set within the limits of Eden, it will be severed."

Arum drew himself to foil height, and brandished the Golden Sword. "I declare myself Emir, leader of the Sheikhs of Parad, protected by this blade, the Golden Sword. Let there be peace and prosperity during my reign. May my sons follow the path of Allah."

"There have been plots since then," Ahmed said, "but only for money or position within the administration, or women of the harem."

This conversation went on during the meal, while servants scurried back and forth, attending the guests. Court jesters and clowns performed during the dinner. Acrobats came out to toss each other into the air, pyramiding bodies, then jumping over our heads.

The Sheikh leaned back against his pillows, belching loudly enough for all of us to hear, immediately followed by a chorus of belches from those wanting to compliment the chef. He raised his hands, clapped once, then folded them across his stomach.

The lights went out completely. Only the flickering candles decorating the tables lit the room. A single spotlight hit the center of the stage. A single flute began a plaintive wail. A single drum echoed, hard fingertips on its surface. There was a pyramid of red silk in the center of the light, clinched with a ruby-set ring. The ruby began to rotate, shooting red rays around the room. The red silk rose in the air, as if a specter created by a magician. A white form emerged as the whole pyramid grew taller, twisting around, uncoiling like a spring. Two arms of white flesh undulated, fluorescent red fingertips flashing. The red silk with the ruby on top shook back like the mane of a horse flying in the wind. The now exposed face revealed high, prominent cheekbones, a full, bold nose, and eyebrows matching the red silk hair. The lips were full and sensuous, painted with an exact shade of color to the fiery hair.

The body became more exposed as the arms spread, uncoiling in slow turns. It could have been a life-sized doll spiked to a musical turntable. She was nude, except for a tiny G-string pear-shaped patch of gold held by a slender rope of woven gold chain. The glittery adornment was paved with brilliant diamonds. Shalimar's breasts were firm and full, carried without the semblance of a sag. Large Slavic nipples and aureoles inherited from her Russian mother swung a single gold chain attached by a tiny gold ring around the tips. A diamond swung at the end of the chain, sparkling in the tight beam of light. The breasts swayed, the slightly rounded stomach began to rotate and tiny tassels of gold chain, flecked with diamonds inserted in the navel, shone like fireflies. As she rotated, the twin globes of her buttocks moved up and down, pumped by heel and toe movement. Muscled thighs and dancer's calves shaped long legs hinting at acrobatic powers.

Arum sighed audibly and a low murmur of similar intakes of breath waved over the room. I was spellbound, and couldn't take my eyes off the performer.

The sound of other instruments joined the single flute, lute, and drum. The raucous rattle of tambourines and bells joined in, building to a crescendo as Shalimar moved around the small circle of light. Belly rotated. Hips followed and humped back and forth to the beat of the drum. At one moment, the music stopped, she stood straight, hands on her hips, legs spread wide. First one breast rotated, the tiny tassel sparkling, then the other in the other direction. Only the drum beat to the rhythm of the rotating globes. The tassels then moved with her hips in a belly dancer's fashion. Arum began to clap his hands to the beat, and others took up the cadence, until we were all clapping in tune to the dance of Shalimar.

The performance fascinated, captivated, and titillated every one. I could feel an erection straining at my robe. Nude dancing was not novel to me. During my tenure in Hong Kong, I saw many of the fleshy bars in Tsim Sha Tsui. One meeting in Bangkok had ended at a particular nightclub where the show was gross and obscene. It disgusted me, and I walked out.

This was an artistic performance by a beautiful woman, a rare treasure. The Sheikh appreciated fine art performances. Yes, he was a good choice to participate in the affair of the Jade of Confucius. I would inform my family.

Colored spotlights appeared one by one on the stage around Shalimar as she stood still as a mime, not moving a tassel or muscle. The lights moved to each of the twelve women. They joined Shalimar in the center of the stage, costumed as she was. Each wore a G-string and a full gauzy veil hinting at exquisite faces underneath. As they appeared, breast tassels showed, individually decorated with different gem stones; ruby, emerald, sapphire, blue zircon, amethyst, carnelian, garnet, peridot, aquamarine, opal, topaz, and pearl, the twelve birthstones.

They became a kaleidoscope of color and olive-colored flesh as they wove themselves around the queen. Circles formed, facing outward, bodies bent back to touch the floor with their hands, and then in rotation stood on their hands, legs straight up in the air, turning slowly. The stage suddenly erupted in a kaleidoscope of acrobatics, the performers doing somersaults, cartwheels, and air-borne leaps, ending in leg splits. The audience called out cheers to their favorites, identifying them by their jewels.

Shalimar stood statuesque on a small rotating platform in the middle of the mayhem. Still, and as white as an alabaster Grecian Goddess, she surveyed her group. They now began to circle her, at center stage. The lights gradually snuffed out, one by one. The dancers faded into the darkness. Shalimar remained on the platform, folding herself down, until only the red silk of her hair fastened with the magnificent ruby remained. The spotlight grew smaller and smaller until only the ruby could be seen, and then winked out.

Arum arose from his pillow and clapped his giant hands like cymbals. Everyone in the room followed his lead. Lights relit the center and the troop came to stagefront, each covered by a silk cloth, matching her jewels. Shalimar was the last to take her bows, in a gauze-thin red cape that accented the pure white skin showing underneath.

The Sheikh nodded to me and said "Good night, young one, sleep well, and give good advice to my finance minister tomorrow. I cautioned him to listen well to your advice."

The evening over, Ahmed escorted me back to my room. The maids waited with a cool sponge bath and a light cotton sleeping robe. My mind was a blur of dancing women, twirling breasts, and in the background, shadowy figures of green jade looking over me. Tomorrow would bring wonders of another nature, with a visit to the gallery and an insight into the financial treasure of Eden.

A delicate hand on my shoulder awakened me, as Shalimar was finishing her dance in my dreams. Her graceful body was stark naked, twirling like a top in front of me, finally disappearing in a cloud of genie-like smoke.

"It's time, Master Kong. The Emir summons."

Suddenly awake, my eyes tried to focus on the dim form next to my bed. A subtle aroma of perfume pervaded the room.

I arose, checked my briefcase, and sighed with relief when I found the tape intact. A special combination secured the diplomatic case. A secret compartment concealed the tape, but I had been lucky. If Ahmed had suspected, he would have taken the whole briefcase without qualms.

It was dark in the passageways, unlit by the moon outside. My guide held me close, with her arm through mine. We bumped around every corner, the soft warm lightly clad body nudging me in the right direction. The palace exuded sensuality, making it difficult to keep my mind on business.

"I can return to your quarters tonight young master, if you desire me," the young woman whispered, sensing my libidinal confusion.

Shalimar's women, Filipinas, were tuned to the male from an early age. "Thank you for your offer, kind lady, but I am loyal to my wife and cannot consider lying with another woman."

She giggled at the uncommon answer. "As you wish, young master. I am also schooled in the art of massage, and can relieve you that way if it will not be too much of a burden on your conscience."

We arrived at our destination without meeting one person in the corridors. A door opened and my escort disappeared with a squeeze of my hand and a whispered name. "Enid."

Shalimar and Arum were waiting for me, talking quietly in the dim light of the room. I saw the outline of a stage-sized round bed in one corner, fluffed with pillows. A bead curtain with a soft light behind it showed the bath and toilet room. Sliding doors along one wall were barely visible under the curtains drawn over them. That would be the balcony. The center of the room was a round pit, pillow-lined for lounging.

Shalimar whispered to three shadows that I hadn't noticed before. "Cover the balcony, hallway and secret passageways until you hear a signal from me. If anyone at all approaches, use your karate chop to take them down and lock them in the next room. We will deal with them after we're through." The three shadows disappeared, while I found the VCR and set the tape cartridge in the slot. Shalimar lowered a viewing screen on a platform from the ceiling to eye level.

"You have the remote control next to you, Your Highness." The screen lit up with the mountain scene, the rushing torrents, then the tranquil wide Irrawaddy River. THE JADE OF CONFUCIUS title spread across the screen, and the same story followed that only two other people in the world would see. We watched in complete silence; it was the first time I had seen the completed tape. Shalimar gasped when the jade figures first appeared. I heard the Sheikh suck in his breath. When the tape finished, Arum started it over. Three times during the display, he stopped the tape when the Shou Xing Laos were in full screen and turning. Finally, he turned the machine off. I removed the tape and handed it to him.

"There are only three men, including yourself, outside the Kong family that have seen or will see this tape. They may have confidants like Shalimar that are privileged to view it also. Are there any questions about the authenticity?"

"I believe what I saw, if that is your question, young Kong. I felt the aura of the Immortals as I was viewing them. If the feeling was this strong in just a video tape, I can well imagine what one would experience in their presence. Have you seen them yourself?"

"Yes, Your Highness, I was fortunate enough to be in the laboratory once when they were preparing this video document. My reaction was like yours, exaggerated ten times over. They appear alive, vibrant, the color an intense liquid green. Aunt Wan Yi told me of the three times she has seen the figures in the first full moon of a new year. The aura is so strong that one feels in a trance."

Shalimar was still in a trance, with her eyes closed. Without asking I knew she was communicating with the Immortals. She opened her eyes and looked up at us as if she had no previous knowledge we had been with her. "They've warned me of danger to you, Your Highness, and have asked me to watch over you. There has never been an experience in my life like this."

"What is the rest of the message, young Kong? I must confess that

I too felt a kinship, as if I had been in their presence before. If I have had such a strong reaction, why is it necessary to bring in the other two men? Money? No it can't be that, for greed is not the nature of the Kongs. There must be more to the plan than money."

"Your Highness, Sheikh of the Kingdom of Arum, the scheme is to invite you all to a remote place in the world. You will be in the presence of the Jade, away from any possible interference. There we're confident the Shou Xing Laos will select their own future home in some unpredictable manner.

"I am to remind you of the five virtues of our ancestor, Confucius. We request that you have ready a minimum of one billion dollars ready for transfer electronically, should you be the one selected."

Shalimar whistled, while Arum stared at me without an expression on his face. I continued. "The meeting will take place in the Fiji Islands at the first full moon of the Year of the Dragon. Assuming you are participating, please advise me of your sailing date and route to be taken. With your permission, I will join your ship either here or at some convenient point along the way."

"Your family has thought out an interesting plan." Arum finally said after a long, interminable silence. "Thank you, young Kong, I would hear more of the plans before you leave Parad. Your secret is sealed on our lips. I'll give you an answer by nightfall tomorrow. Shalimar's maid will see you back to your room, safely I hope."

"Goodnight, Your Highness, and goodnight to you, Shalimar, I thank you for allowing me into your private world." As I stepped out of the room into the dark hallway, I could see nothing. A soft arm linked mine, again keeping herself tantaliz-ingly close. Body heat and feminine curves continually brushed against me in the narrow confines of the dark passageway.

When we reached my room, she spoke for the first time. "Your women will have retired. I will come in and prepare the bed for you."

Too tired to protest, I can remember vaguely slipping out of my robe. A warm cloth washed my face and wiped my body before I fell asleep. On waking in the morning, I could not separate dreams from reality. The fact was that I awoke from a deep and satisfying sleep, hungry and ready to face the day, whatever it would bring.

The early morning was cool before the heat rose from the desert. Ignoring my former embarrassment in front of the Filipina valets, I jumped in the pool sans trunks. Shalimar was waiting when I finished my fifty laps, and held up a terrycloth robe for me, with not so much as a leer or an ogle. It is an adage: *When in Eden, dress as Adam and Eve might have.*

"Good morning, Shalimar. Will you join me for breakfast?"

"It was my intention to invade your privacy, Mr. Kong."

"My wife and close friends call me David, a translation for Feng Wa. As long as you come in peace, bearing gossip of the palace, it would please me if you used it instead of Mr. Kong."

"So be it. I come in peace but there are a few tales to relate this early in the morning. The future is more interesting to discuss than the past anyway. For me this is the best time of the day, the air still fresh, before the sun attacks me."

"You are a beautiful woman. Your enemy, the sun, glorifies that red hair. A story teller might say, *fire of the sun inflamed the smoldering tresses.* Your daytime dress is modest."

"White-skinned redheads have a big problem with the sun, and I'm no exception. If you notice, I'm taking the shadiest spot under your table umbrella, and wearing this sun hat. The slightest exposure turns me a bright pink." She laughed at my raised eyebrow and then added, "I'm an actress, employed here as a performer, and part of my characterization of Shalimar of Eden is physical appearance."

"I've never known an actress, Shalimar. We in the diplomatic service are on a different stage. Your past must be fascinating compared to my dull history."

Shalimar smiled and winked. "Dear David, the real story would bore you, but if you promise to spend an afternoon with me, I'll concoct a fancy tale that you can tell to your family. The fantasies of my life often merge with the reality until even I can't separate them."

"If His Highness chooses to meet us in Fiji, will you sail with us, Shalimar?"

"Probably. I maintain the entertainment, and act as a buffer between him and the palace entourage. I'm also his token Westerner, and Arum loves to show me off."

"Would you hazard a guess about the Sheikh's attitude toward the competition for the Jade?"

Shalimar thought for a moment, and removed her hat, letting the red mane flame in the reflection of the sun. "The money means nothing to him. Acquiring the rare treasure is the key. Arum's father and grandfather were avid jewel collectors. The Palace vault has a vast collection of jewels. Arum allows me to borrow pieces, as you saw in last night's show.

"Then there is the challenge of competing against other bidders. He'll find out who they are and make every attempt to discredit them or undercut them. This is not your biggest problem, however, and that is why I am infringing on your breakfast privacy."

"Tell me, oh beautiful fountain of wisdom, what is my horoscope reading for this glorious August day?"

Turning a glass goblet upside down, Shalimar waved her hands over it like a fortune teller uses a glass ball. "The sun is shining in the Garden of Eden, oh curious one. I see a cloud on the horizon that is moving slowly over the palace. The ship at anchor in the harbor is rolling, as the sea roughens under the cloud. There are forces of evil in the palace that would thwart your project for their own personal aims and ambitions. Thus, I see dangers that can rock the boat. I warn you. The sea will be rough and the evil forces on the inside will cause even greater turmoil."

"You make a good Red-Headed Witch of the East, Shalimar. I appreciate your warnings and will watch my tail feathers closely. Tell me why you are taking this trouble to tell me?"

"The answer to that is simpler than you think, descendant of Confucius. When in the Palace of Eden, one has to side with either the good guys or the bad guys. The only problem is identifying one from the other. My protector Arum is the only good guy I trust. I've decided that you are also a good guy. That makes three of us, and I hope, enough to even out against the bad ones."

"Thank you, Shalimar. The combined power of the Golden Sword, a red-headed witch, and a humble Chinese servant should be an unbeatable team. Please don't take offense at the term 'witch' for they properly described are fearless women of power, some good, some bad."

Laughing out loud, Shalimar shook her red mane and said, "I respect the term witch. It's when some call me a bitch that I take offense. No David, you don't offend me. I disagree with the 'humble Chinese servant' bit. You and your family probably have as much power in their combined intelligence as any kingdom on earth. If the family of Kong ever started teaching the world how to get along, it would be a different place to live in." It was difficult not to say something to this woman with a brain. I decided that when the University of Confucius gets started I would recommend her for the faculty. Shalimar's mind could run level or ahead of any diplomat I had ever run into.

Two days later I arrived back in Washington with three items on my agenda. There was a report due the Ambassador on the events in Parad, regarding the Ethiopian Relief Fund. Then, the usual debriefing by the State Department.

And there was my young wife to greet, and to tell about the fantasy world I had just come from. As it actually happened, I related the whole story except for the confidential government stuff. She just laughed and said I had a wonderful imagination and was just trying to make her jealous.

Two days later I flew to San Francisco to meet with Uncle Sam Choy and Jie Lie. There would be much planning necessary when all the reports were in.

10

NEW YORK CITY

KONG KAI TAI

The Master said, *When you meet someone better than yourself, turn your thoughts to becoming his equal. When you meet someone not as good as you are, look within and examine your own self.*

ANTHONY BLAINE GOSSETT, my laptop computer read. Born 13 March 1923, New York City. Father, Theodore Roosevelt Gossett. Mother, Georgina Louella Blaine. Exeter Preppie University of Arizona, Freshman and sophomore years, majoring in Journalism. Enlisted United States Air Force 1942. Discharged honorably 1946 with rank of Major, U.S. Air Force Reserve... Returned to Arizona for junior and senior years, graduating 1949 with B.S. in Journalism. Quarterback on the Wildcats Football team. Harvard School of Business 1950-1951.

PERSONAL SUBJECTIVE ANALYSIS OF OFF-RECORD INFORMATION FROM FELLOW STUDENTS, BUSINESS ACQUAINTANCES AND LOCALS IN ARIZONA.

Tony Gossett born of southern belle mother, old money, the Blaines of Georgia. Father, T.R. Gossett, wealthy Yankee, publisher of the New York Post...

Tony spent boyhood summers on the ranches of Northern Arizona with the Flake Family of Snowflake, Arizona. They taught him how to ride, work the cattle round-ups with the cowboys, and participate in the annual Tucson Rodeo. Gossett survived a three-day summer storm one year, lost on the Mogillon Rim. The storm finally abated. He rode out safely without help and met the search parties sent out to look for him. According to one of the Flakes in the search party, the only request he had, on meeting up, was for a farrier to replace two shoes on his horse, thrown during the storm. Tony did not continue the rodeo games after breaking a leg in his first year of entry. Mother and Father Gossett laid down the law. Football was bad enough, but no more rodeo.

The Mexican Women of Canal Street in Nogales taught him and most of the other members of the football team the raw side of sex. Arizona co-eds took turns trying to catch him before the eastern society dames targeted the ideal bachelor, and lost. On completing MBA degree at Harvard, it took Gossett two weeks to find and marry Lauranne Peterson, an art student from Santa Fe, New Mexico. The family bought Tony the Tucson Daily Citizen and threw in a radio station, KCEE, as an extra.

Tucson society welcomed them, as it did the young Pulitzers, publishers of the competing Arizona Star. An old, rambling home in the exclusive Tucson Country Club Estates was a good place to raise the two children that followed. They built a second home in the ranchland of Sonoita, south of Tucson, horse country. The 5,000-foot altitude provided welcome relief from the desert heat of the summers. They named the ranch property "Casa Amor, de Los Arroyo." The early years of marriage were pleasant. Gossett was outgoing, a leading citizen of Tucson, active in backroom politics of the community and state. Lauranne was reluctant to join the social world, preferring to paint.

EMPIRE BUILDING... THE GOSSETT DOCTRINE... El Paso, Texas, Wickenburg, Arizona, Bakersfield, California, and the tiny Brewery Gulch Gazette in the old mining town of Bisbee, Arizona. The Brewery Gulch Gazette became an outlet for satire and political opinion; the others formed a western base of operations. Circulations of the acquisitions ranged from 5,000 to 100,000.

Quietly Gossett bought up small and medium sized city newspapers in Arizona, Nevada, California, Texas and New Mexico. He allowed their existing editorial staffs to operate as they had in the past. He took over the business management.

Advertising revenue was the game he played. Gossett sales staff solicited national advertisers. Enticing bulk rates placed the client in all of the small urban communities of the Southwest. Sales return per dollar advertising costs were three times the national average.

Like Walton, of Walmart Department Store fame, Gossett discovered that middle America was where the action is. Stock market convolutions, foreign competition, big factory closings and textile woes had little effect on the small communities of the Gossett conglomerate. He seeped throughout the United States, as the years went by, and then invaded Canada.

Mexico was next; that was a disaster. He was about to close a group of deals purchasing papers in Nogales, Sonora, Hermisillo, and Guaymas when the local politicians brought up the subject of 'mordito', the Mexican system of payoff. The law required fifty-one percent of ownership by a Mexican citizen. Bundles of U.S. $100 bills had to change hands to get legal approval. Gossett, disgusted, backed off. He settled for the Nogales Herald and the three border radio stations.

Gossett then created a division of slick magazines, again avoiding the large ones. He acquired monthly hobby, sport, and trade journals with their subscription lists and rack sales.

In the 70s he began to travel abroad to see what the foreign market might bring. England, France, Italy, Australia and New Zealand were next on his hit list.

PERSONAL LIFE CHANGES... Gossett's lifestyle spread from coast to coast. Lauranne blew the whistle on their marriage when he began to go international. Tony's business life was amongst women who fleshed out the advertising industry. Denied presidencies and C.E.O. positions in the big companies, the more talented and aggressive women found their niche on agency staffs and in Tony's bed. It was into these vulnerables that he inserted his business charm and rumored sexual prowess. Lauranne had enough of filial time share.

Melinda, their daughter, born in 1949, was 21 when they broke up; Anthony Jr., two years younger. Linny worked with her father, groomed from her high school years to become Tony's heir apparent in the company. Young Tony, artistic like his mother, refused to go to Arizona's universities. He moved to Santa Fe, New Mexico to pursue his fondness for sculpture and bronze-casting. His world is the artists' colony; Grandma Peterson lived there to feed him, if he got hungry.

The divorce was amicable, Lauranne taking only their Sonoita home, what she desired of their possessions, and an investment annuity created for her and the children. It was more than ample to cover her simple needs. She had become a noted Western artist, painting the Arizona sunsets, the occasional cowboy, a ghost town, and the extraordinary cactus flowers of the desert when they were in bloom.

MELINDA "LINNY" GOSSETT...

I turned off the screen, as the stewardess said, "Miss Kong, would you like a glass of wine before lunch?"

"Chardonnay will be fine. What time do we arrive?"

"4:52, New York time. Don't forget to change your watch. There's a three hour time difference between San Francisco and New York."

My young cousin Jie Lie had supplied the disc I worked on inflight, with the Gossett data. Newspaper and magazine morgues revealed most of the information, kept as background for articles. In addition, I had another disc from my own office in Hong Kong, with all of the statistical details of the Gossett empire. The flight from Hong Kong to San Francisco gave me ample time to review that information, with some dozing in between.

Anthony Gossett was often described as the Baron of the publishing world. The conglomeration was known to own 5236 small and medium town newspapers outright. There were 1724 monthly and quarterly magazines, ranging from "Health and Nature," a nudist magazine published in England, to "Black Leather," for the bikers, in his media empire.

Five percent were in the United Kingdom, another seven percent in Europe. Australia accounted for seven percent, Canada for five percent, and the rest throughout the United States. The numbers changed daily. Gossett moved around the world, making personal approaches to local owners of publications. Legal teams then flew in to close the deal and fund the money.

The numbers experts arrived next to analyze and detail the circulation, classify the market, and estimate the future potential. An advertiser seeking worldwide distribution could buy, from one source, a demographically identified market in any one or all the areas covered.

I was to present a plan to include Asia. Phoenix Advertising had studied the mighty media giant for a year. There is a large untapped reader market of millions in the developed and emerging countries of Asia, plus the billion in China. There are thousands of vendors that desire to sell their products to the rest of the world. Ours was a brilliant plan, concocted by the Phoenix Birds, as they call us, an organization of all women, with the second highest billings in Hong Kong.

Uncle Sam Choy asked me to visit him in San Francisco on my way over. I had no idea of what my favorite uncle wanted. The blockbuster he unloaded really blew my mind. Uncle Sam, Jie Lie, and I talked all night, with Aunty Ai Lin keeping us awake with tea and food. The magnitude of what they were planning made my business project look puny. Sleep was impossible after the session. My mind kept jumping from one to the other, dominated by the vision of the Jade trying to talk to me. When I actually saw the Jade of Shou Xing Lao, it was love at first sight.

I folded the laptop Compaq LTE, stored it in my briefcase, and leaned back in the seat, sipping the wine. I didn't often drink while flying, but it tasted good and the long journey from Hong Kong was about over. I admit to prejudging this arrogant publisher with a reputation as a womanizer. What little publicity seeped out always showed Gossett at some beautiful people party with a sexy young woman hanging on to his arm for dear life. How would he handle a little Chinese woman, almost forty years old, a business executive, interested in advertising contracts and not his bed?

I said to myself: Well, Kaytee, you've handled the likes of him many times before, without using the jade gate technique. You've fought your way up through the male chauvinism of Hong Kong to own the second largest advertising firm in Asia. The dragon Gossett can also be slain, heeled even.

The Gossett Empire was big. Their contracts with my clients would put me far ahead of the competition, Abercromie, Bartholomew, and Creighton. If they hadn't refused me a partnership ten years ago, I wouldn't be in business for myself today. Phoenix Advertising would never have started. Yes, for an innocent-looking, middle-aged Chinese matron named Kai Tai Kong, you haven't done too bad. Maybe some of the genes of my ancestor of seventy-odd generations ago have seeped into a mere woman.

An hour later, I folded up, tightened the seat belt, and prepared for my white-knuckle landing at La Guardia. I've never gotten over a fear of landing in the blunderbuss modern aircraft. Taking off and cruising don't bother me, but every time the pilot comes on the air to announce the landing, I prepare mentally for a crash.

Leather purse and briefcase in one hand, pulling a luggage cart behind me with the other, I joined the crowd rushing from the plane. My cousin found me before I saw him. He radiated sophistication, dressed in a light grey silk suit, white shirt with a maroon striped tie.

He also radiated a pleasant aroma of Tiger Talk cologne. "Kai Tai?"

I smiled, glad to see a friendly look.

He broke out in a grin. "I'm Kong Xi Ku, please call me Scot. Welcome to New York City. I've re-confirmed your reservation at the Waldorf."

"Thanks for meeting me, Scot. I'm ready for the Big Apple. I understand you are a busy young attorney."

"Good fortune has been with me, especially tonight. It's a rare privilege to meet the famous and beautiful Kong Kai Tai. My family has described your business talents, but they didn't tell me you have the beauty of women portrayed in the art of our ancestors."

"Come now, Scot, you are very kind, but if you keep staring at me, we'll never get to the hotel." He blushed and quickly grabbed my luggage cart, heading toward the doors and parking garage.

"Your traffic is worse than Hong Kong's, if that's possible," I said as Scot wove his little Porsche through the rush hour traffic. "Do all young smart lawyers in New York drive bright red Porsches? If I had this one in Hong Kong, I'd be the envy of the office. Tell me about your career. What type of law do you specialize in?"

Laughing, he stole a quick glance at me. "The Porsche is a graduation gift from my family. They're proud of my Summa Cum Laude diploma, and honored me with this hot rod. I work for a large legal firm, in their business merger division. Our mutual cousin David, in Washington, is trying to get me into the Diplomatic Corps. Another government organization is working on me too. I think it's the CIA. Frankly, I don't know which way to go. The law firm could be big money but becoming a partner may take twenty years."

We talked about the family as the traffic and lights became a blur, the skyline a magnified Hong Kong. This was not my first visit to New York, but the immensity of it still thrilled me. The young man next to me, fifteen years my junior, was just starting, and in a way I envied him. He was born in the United States, with opportunity for education and career available. I was born in Shanghai, my parents escaping to Hong Kong when I was five. They continually bragged to their friends that I, a woman, am a big shot in business. I wondered where I would be if I had been born in New York.

My escort broke in. "You are quiet, cousin, caught up in the raptures of New York's lights? Can you tell me what you'll be doing while you're here? Will you have time to meet my family? Jie Lie told me when he called that you are single. How about fixing you up with a date? There are a couple of guys in my office that would love to know a beautiful woman like you."

"Slow down, Cousin Kong. Let's start by you calling me Kaytee, so I won't feel like the older generation. I'm here on business and won't have much time to play around. I'd like to visit your parents. Give me a couple of days to settle down and I'll call you as soon as I know what time I have. Tonight I'm going to have dinner in my room and hit the pillows. This client Gossett I have to see tomorrow is sharp, and I have some jet lag to get over."

Scot whistled, "You mean *the* Anthony Gossett, the media guy? That's big stuff. We take care of some of his contracts in our firm, and he's big league. May I ask what you are working on with him, or is it a secret?"

"Not a big secret. Phoenix Advertising, my company, is proposing a contract with Gossett Media. If it works you can spread the word around how good we are. If he turns us down, don't even whisper it in your sleep. Getting an appointment with him took some real doing. If it hadn't been for one of my clients who happens to know him personally, I probably wouldn't have gotten past the daughter. I understand that she is a real tough cookie. Have you met the mighty Melinda Gossett yet?"

"I haven't met her, but I play squash with a lawyer with the Department of Justice. Eddy is Melinda Gossett's official escort and occasional roommate. He says the lady is brilliant, educated, well-heeled and very moody."

My ears perked up. Lucky coincidences were useful, I discovered years ago. "Scot, if you can find out anything more about the Gossett family for me, I would appreciate it. I'm not asking you to spy or reveal professional information. It's personality traits and how they live that will really help me. Essentially, I am just a lady with big ideas about advertising. If I can convince them, it will result in a big plus for me and my company."

"You got it, cousin, anything I can do to help. Maybe you will need a hot shot lawyer for your New York affairs. I'm good on contracts and mergers. Here we are, the famous Waldorf-Astoria, a good address to have in New York. They'll take care of you, I'm sure. In the meantime here's my card. I wrote my home address and phone number on the back. It's a real pleasure to meet you. Please, please give me a call when you have time."

Soaking in a bubbly hot tub, I recapped the past three days. Events that began then would probably affect the rest of my life, one of the many crossroads I had come to. Tomorrow morning was the appointment with Gossett and his daughter. They were, according to my information, powerful people, making quick decisions. My approach would be straightforward, no subtlety, pure data. The Phoenix staff did a good job, I thought, on the demographics, facts, and potentials.

We, at Phoenix Advertising, are known as the Dirty Dozen, the Phoenix Birds, or the Zodiacs, in various publicity articles written about us. Twelve women, each with a different talent, hardworking and successful as a team. As coincidence would have it, each of us was born under a different sign, and we gave ourselves nicknames based on our signs. I was born in the Year of the Rat. We are bold and daring, optimistic, well-liked and successful. They call me "Mousey" in the office, and caution people to watch out for my sharp teeth.

Self-reflecting, I mentally gathered my assets, preparing myself for the big sales pitch. Every time I approach a new client, I've learned to step back and check myself out first. Studying my ancestor Confucius has taught me the art of self-examination. Selling is using your talents, professional and personal. Appearance is the first impression. What should I wear? Almost forty, I avoid thinking about my age. I noted that the body is still in good shape. No wrinkles around the eyes, skin tight around the cheeks of my face, and my derriere. Breasts a little larger than most Asian women's, and still pointing the way. Flat tummy, fat never a problem. Long legs, in proportion to my height, looked great peeking out from the side of a cheongsam split skirt. Sex? Sure, at the right time and place. Yes, I would get their attention, and then my brain takes over to prove we could do what we said. My big chance.

Go to it, Kai Tai, K.T., Kaytee, Mousey, whatever they want to call you, go get 'em, K'ung Fu-tze is watching over you, Confucius and Kaytee are synonymous, I told myself, as I fell sound asleep.

11

THE GOSSET EMPIRE

"**M**r. Gossett, you already know from Linny that Phoenix of Hong Kong is an important advertising agency. Our executives are all women, not predatory, but the finest advertising team in Asia. Our billings were 500 million U.S. dollars last year, and growing, because we do a good job for our clients. Frankly, we don't know what our limitations will be with a Hong Kong headquarters, when Mother China takes us over in 1997. Our firm, however, will be world-wide within the next five years. Taking a card from your deck, we intend, with mergers and acquisitions, to broaden our horizons. We might even find some men acceptable to our organization."

This got a chuckle from my audience and gave me a little breather. My first shot at Gossett was cool and efficient. Inside I concentrated on repressing the butterflies fluttering through my blood vessels, stirring up a lot of heat and stress.

Melinda Gossett came out to greet me at the reception area in the very impressive offices of G.M.I. – Gossett Media Incorporated. High ceilings and massive windows looking out over the city from the top floor of Gossett towers makes the visitor feel a little subdued and insignificant. Melinda dispelled that feeling somewhat with a very cordial handshake. "Welcome to Gossettland, Miss Kong. You come from a part of the world I am not familiar with but would like to visit some day."

Linny gave me a professional once-over. I'm glad I decided to dress conservatively in a pale lavender knee-length snug skirt, side-slit for easier movement. A white silk shirt, open at the throat, and a suit jacket to match the skirt to give me a businesslike look. I wore several rope-length strands of multi-color rice-shaped fresh water pearls twisted into a choker. An attractive lavender jade twister clasp held them together at the throat. My black hair fell straight, framing my face, emphasized by my favorite light lavender lipstick and eye shadow. A lavender jade ring rimmed with diamonds and an antique gold bangle bracelet completed my jewelry accessories.

Linny escorted me into a programming room, outfitted with blackboard, movie screen, and some television monitors. I carried only the LTE, Little Tig Er, I called it, and cables to plug into the bigger screens. The man walked in through a side door while I worked on setting up the computer.

He had some papers in his hand, hardly looked at me, took a chair and said, "Tony Gossett, Miss Kong, welcome to New York. I hope fifteen minutes is enough time for your presentation; I have an urgent appointment."

That did it, I started to burn. "Mr. Gossett, our company has been working for a year on this proposal. I have personally come halfway around the world to pitch it. If you're not interested in listening to a plan that will add a half-billion dollars of advertising revenue to Gossett Media, I'll be happy to close my case and take it to Rupert Murdoch," I ejected the diskette from the computer and started to close it up.

Up to this moment, Gossett hardly had given me a glance, having come in as I was bent over the computer, greeted me without looking, and taken a seat at the table. After the explosion, he looked up and stared at the spectacle of a flaring fire coming out of my nose, breast heaving, eyes flashing. He looked stunned.

Anthony Gossett stood up slowly, holding up his hands. Towering a full foot over me, I had to look up to see where the top was. "Now whoa there little filly, settle down. Linny knows I don't like to sit through long boring presentations. I figured you were just going to give me another pitch for some deal my staff could look at. Sorry if I put a burr under your saddle. Go ahead, let's see what you have."

Whatever happened to change his mind, I could only suspect. Linny gave me the high sign, and when I began with the half-billion pitch, he straightened up the tall lanky frame and paid attention. I continued the program, the screen keeping up with my patter as I punched keys.

"We select our target for their ability and personnel, not their clients. Those will come to us automatically, as the industry notices our scorecard. You can see by this list that we intend to service only the foremost companies in Asia, selling the finest products that have world-wide potential. This information you have on file already. I assume Linny has done her usual efficient investigation of our company. I wouldn't be here now if she hadn't approved."

I booted up my first blockbuster. "This map shows the Gossett Empire. The filled circles are your current holdings, the open circles, those you are working on, and the triangles, possibilities that are up for discussion at the moment."

Breaking, I walked away from the screen with as much of a feline grace as the tight skirt would allow me. I watched them as Linny stared at the screen and Gossett followed every move I made. It should shake them up. Much of the information we had was confidential. Gossett Media was essentially a holding company, controlling a mass of corporations and sub-entities. The new possibilities would be the biggest surprise; they were unknown to all of the acquisition teams. Each group worked independently. From what I had found out about Anthony Gossett, even his own daughter didn't know which backyard he was in at any given moment.

Walking back to the table, I could feel the laser beam eyes of the cowboy piercing my back, or was it my backside. "The second part of my program, Ms. Gossett, Mr. Gossett."

He held up his hand again, addressing Linny. "Cancel the rest of my morning appointments, and make a reservation for two at Donnie Trump's place down the street. This little lady and I are going to have a long talk over lunch. Now keep on pitching, bright eyes, you have my attention. By the way, what do they call you besides Miss Kong?"

"Kai Tai is the rest of my name, Kaytee for short," I answered, giving him the biggest grin my tiny mouth allows.

Melinda's smile changed to a frown. Big Daddy's imperious commands apparently irritated her. I imagine that being excluded from the lunch also miffed her. She left for a few minutes to take care of the details.

Office politics. I decided to stay out of it. Obviously, I had the Dragon's attention, and possibly a little panting as well. Business is business. I would handle the other part if I had to. There was a lot of experience under my garter belt for diplomatic brush-offs.

Continuing, I punched up another map. "This is the Phoenix Empire made up of clients in Japan, Korea, Taiwan, Hong Kong, India, Singapore, Malaysia, Thailand, Indonesia, and the Philippines. Our expansion plans include further density in these countries, and then going into the South Pacific Basin. Some clients in Australia, New Zealand, and other island countries have already solicited our services. A few are manufacturers. Others, like Fiji, want to sell their copra and cane sugar products. All the national clients have a major interest in tourism, their cash cow. Your media has the best access to travelers.

"Let me roll a few advertisers for you; some might be familiar. Corporations show their country of origin, headquarters, capital, annual volume, profits, and advertising budgets."

I tapped the cursor quickly until a big one popped up, held it, and then continued. My immediate audience drummed his fingers on the table, eyes going from the screen to me as if he were watching a tennis match. Linny was in the back of the room, making notes on a clipboard. Cutting off, I punched up the next program.

"Now, this is some advance work we have done for you." Japan appeared on the screen, with twenty-four small triangles overlaid on it. The potential sources ran from Hokkaido in the North, Honshu in the middle, Shikkoku Island in the Inland Sea, and Kyushu, the lower island. The southernmost was a tiny triangle on Okinawa. "These are small towns and cities that have daily newspapers, with substantial readership. We have a personal contact with the owners that are willing to sell. They will trade for property in the United States. They want mostly small hotels or resorts. Japan's income tax is as much a problem for them as it is for you in the United States." Quickly, I unrolled maps of the other countries, each showing locations we had researched. "We have the details on every triangle. Amongst our group of executives, we speak the language of each of these countries. We know the best way to complete a deal, given the intricacies of its government, and methods of doing business. We have tax-beneficial plans for acquiring every paper."

Gossett listened carefully. I imagined his mental computers whirring, evaluating the information. With a boyish grin, like plucking a cherry out of a cocktail, he spoke.

"You left out something, little lady, how about those billion people in China's mainland. I don't see it on any of your charts." He drawled the words, half teasing.

"I thought you would never ask, Mr. Gossett. By the way, if you don't mind please call me Kaytee. Filly and little lady both sound like you are addressing your favorite stable mare." I pressed the return key, and the sub-list file returned to the screen, identifying all the countries he had just seen. The last item on the menu was titled 'Zhongguo'. "This program will take 30 minutes to run, and it promises you a new medium for the Gossett Empire, billboards."

"You're pulling my leg little... excuse me, Kaytee. What on earth would I be doing with billboards?"

It was time for me to toss out a little charm. I cat-walked over to his end of the table, perched a cheek on the edge, my skirt hiking up a few inches, swung a leg under his nose, and leaned forward enough for him to catch a sniff of my scent. "That, mighty mogul of the media, is precisely why you need us. No one buys newspaper advertising in China. There are few papers and practically no distribution. We're working on a joint-venture arrangement for thousands of billboards. The electronic companies and watch companies can't wait to buy as much space as you can provide. The Chinese people will buy anything we can get through their customs to sell, and the list is getting bigger every day. Our demographics of Chinese buyers reveal a different story than your reports."

"Whoa there... excuse me, wait a minute, Miss Kaytee. Our research teams reported that there is no use working on China, because they only make the equivalent of $65 to $100 a month."

I laughed, hiked up my skirt another inch to make sure he was listening. "That's what I mean Mr. Gossett. Your researchers never left New York to get their figures. I'll bet their data is from the U.S. Chamber of Commerce, or misinformation from the Chinese Consulate. Whoever sold you that report ripped you off. I saw a copy and it isn't worth the cost of the print-out.

"What they didn't find out is the important data. The Chinese earn modest income, compared to the Western world, but they save. There is little to spend their renminbi on. Housing costs them two or three dollars a month, food is cheap and price-controlled by the government. If you drop alcoholics from their budget, everyone has money to spend. Apartment dwellers pool their funds to buy a Japanese television for three times what they cost you and I. High-priced, tiny washing machines and refrigerators sell out the day they arrive on the floor. Can you imagine what would happen if a big G.E. or Whirlpool hit the coast over there? Farmers have so much extra spending money, they carry it around in satchels. Times have changed. The government encourages spending to circulate that cash. People can now buy imported goods in the Friendship stores, previously reserved for foreigners.

"Look at what the cigarette companies are doing with their joint ventures in the mainland. So far the Chinese consume more cigarettes than the rest of the world put together. That's a guess by the way, not a verified fact. Yes, Mr. Gossett, China is the big number. All it needs is a little joint venture between thee and me, and then with us and them."

I stopped the leg show, slid off the table, walked over to the computer, pressed the F7 to exit, and then turned off the power when it finished saving. "Is that lunch invitation still open?"

"My pleasure, Miss Kai Tai Kong," he said, extending his bent elbow for my grasp. "Do you trust your programs staying here until we return?"

"Unless you get me drunk, and I divulge the access code, they are perfectly safe, Mr. Gossett."

Linny looked up and said, "Coming back this afternoon, you two?"

"Mebbe' yes, mebbe' no, take care of the gear in the conference room, just in case we don't." Gossett responded.

We were a strange couple walking out of the conference room, through the office, and the reception room. My five-foot-three, a petite oriental, walking next to the lanky, six-foot plus cowboy in alligator boots, his Stetson adding another ten inches. The incongruity drew gasps and giggles from the staff.

The doorman looked up in alarm. The office usually notified him when the Chief was leaving and would need his car or a limo.

"Don't bother, Ben, we're walking." Off we went, show-stopping even the blasé New Yorkers. "Do you always get this much attention, Mr. Gossett?" I said to the head far above me.

"Pahdnah, let's have a truce, you call me Tony, and I'll enter you in the race as Kaytee out of Kong. City folks aren't gawking at me, they jus' ain't seen nothin' as purty as you. Now me, for instance, ah'm having trouble keeping my mind on the horse race and not the horse."

"Okay Tony, tell me, do you use that cowboy lingo to impress the ladies? I detect a Harvard override in there from time to time. Must you keep comparing me to some horse you have in your stable? It really is very irritating."

"Smart one, ain'cha Kaytee, you've found me out. I like to twiddle folks with my best horse manure. My apologies again about classifying you. Horses are beautiful to me. I have a bad habit of using their terminology in everything I admire. As far as the natural voice, I admit to learning the finest Bawston-ese at Hahvad. I also confess to speaking a passable French, and being able to fake an Australian twang that makes some people think I am actually Dundee.

216

"Hope you like tacos and enchiladas, señorita," he said, sweeping off his hat, as we entered the restaurant.

"Buenos tardes, señor Gossett," the maitre d'hotel greeted us. "Como esta amigo, que se llama las muy bella señorita?"

"Esta bien, Manuelo, muchas gracias. Se llama señorita es Kaytee Kong, from Hong Kong."

"Bienvenidos, señorita Kong, mi casa es su casa. You are a very beautiful woman. What are you doing with this bandito? He is a very dangerous caballero."

Quipping back, I winked and said, "I lost a hand at show-down poker, tough luck."

Winking, he picked up two menus and beckoned us off to a secluded booth in a corner.

"Margaritas, senor Gossett? And may I arrange the luncheon?"

"My pleasure, mi amigo, remember señorita Kong is a visitor."

The margaritas arrived. Sitting down, I could look into Tony's eyes without straining my neck. I sipped the green foamy liquid, enjoying the bite of salt on the rim of the glass, letting the tequila base seep into my inhibitions. I couldn't help wondering what kind of a lover he would make.

I refused another margarita. Lunch began with two-bite tacos, tostados, enchiladas, chorizos, chimichangas, and a half dozen others that I lost the names of in the haze of the margarita.

"Tell me, oh great caballero of the West, how am I supposed to go back to your office and finish my sales pitch?"

Slipping back into his cowboy boots, verbally, Tony tossed his lariat, hoping to rope in the mare. "Tell you what, little filly... whoops, Kaytee, consider the rest of the afternoon lost, and let me take you out on the range of the big city. We can hitch up a couple of mounts in Central Park, or take the ferry around Manhattan Island. My casa is about thirty floors above here, and we could wind up there for a private dinner overlooking the city. Teracita, Manuelo's little sister, is my cook and bottle-washer. She can whip up French, Chinese or Italian on a moment's notice."

Removing my hand from his, I pulled my legs up under my chair. The other pair of very long legs were cozying up to effect a subtle massage. I threw off the inebriated act. "Mr. Anthony Gossett, if you have finished your lunch, and are through playing kneesy with me, we can return to your office. As long as your schedule is free enough to take a tourist around town, I suggest we return to the office and work over our program.

"I want to present the money side of my proposal. In addition to the customary fifteen percent, we want block contracts on position, and specific demographically identified market share."

I learned that when Tony Gossett really wanted to laugh, the whole room could hear him. He bellowed so hard, tears flowed from his eyes, and even Manuelo came over to see if he was all right. "Wai, I never seen a mare toss a rider quicker than that. Here I am sneaking up gentle like with my rope, figerin' this one's going to be easy, and got thrown before I touched the horn. Kaytee, remind me to give you the tequila straight, from now on. Never mind that green goo to hide it."

"Tony, honestly, we aren't going to have a lasting business relationship if you are going to try to come on to me. You're an intriguing man, but give me a little of the space that you talk so much about. Without all of the fol-de-rol, what do you actually think about the program we are presenting?"

"If I told you I was already hooked on your half-billion dollar proposal, you wouldn't believe me anyway. I'll play the hand straight. You're a very intriguing woman. You probably know from my bio, I love women, especially exotic, sensual and beautiful women. When I see one like you, plus all that business sense and brains, I admit to making a grab at your skirt. It was a serious mistake. I realize that now. Can we be friends, and maybe get to know each other? Who knows what may come out of it?"

Tony pushed his chair back, sat up straight, folded his arms on his chest, and focused his eyes right on mine. "Regarding your well-planned business proposal; I'm a quick decision maker. It's good, has the potential in the area I am interested in. You've done your research and both Linny and I are impressed.

"My suggestion is, assign a small team from your office to work with some people from ours, and set up a flow chart of implementation. You're familiar with the theory of test-marketing. As for dollars, income, who's going to make what, I have a further suggestion. If it's a go, after a market test, we set up a new company on an equal basis as a joint venture."

We walked back to the office. I hadn't said a word since his long speech. The data bank on Gossett showed an enterprising, forceful personality. Yet, he surprised me. In a sparse outline meeting, he absorbed the complete idea of our plan, decided it was viable, and then came up with a way to get it started without overpowering our organization or his.

It was time to change the subject. The business plan accepted, there was no further selling needed.

"Tony," I looked up, and he leaned over to hear my half-whispered voice. "Have you ever heard of my family, the Kongs, descendants of Confucius?"

"Yes I have, Kaytee. During the war I spent two years flying the hump, and spent many of my free days in Kunming in Yunnan Province. There were scholars there that spoke fine English. I talked with them for hours about your ancestor, K'ung Fu-tze."

"That's right, K'ung Fu-tze, Confucius, lived seventy-five generations ago. His philosophies and thoughts are viable today. There's a story I must tell you about my family and a discovery they have made of an extremely rare jade sculpture. It has meaning far beyond its artistic value. It'll take some time however, and we must have a detached-from-business atmosphere."

"Mystery and intrigue, along with a newfound friend, how could I possibly resist? Tell me, Kaytee, would you trust me enough to come to my apartment for dinner tonight? I promise to give you all the time you need to tell me the strange story, and won't mention the advertising business. There will be no advances made, but you'll have to forgive me if I happen to drool from time to time."

The twinkle in his eyes, smile on the lips, and the squeeze he gave my hand was irresistible. I returned the twinkle and smile. "What time would be convenient? May I request a curfew of midnight just in case I should be the one to lose control?"

"The stagecoach will pick you up at sunset, ma'am. You can recognize it by the twelve horses hitched up under the hood and the 'A' leanin' on the lazy 'G' branded on the withers. You won't need your chaps or spurs. Duds are informal."

The rest of the afternoon sped by. Linny was angry at something or someone, either me or her father. It created a tense atmosphere. We agreed to a joint meeting of teams in Hong Kong within the month, to work out a test program. They sent me back to the hotel in one of the company cars. It was early in the morning in Hong Kong, but I happened to catch one of my partners in the office, to relay the good news by phone. That left an hour to spare for me to soak and reflect on the events of the day, and the probabilities of the evening.

12

THE COWBOY AND THE CHINESE LADY

⁕

The limousine picked me up according to schedule. It didn't have big steer horns on the hood which I half expected. Kenny Rogers' country-western played inside the car's lush interior; I became a movie star for the moment.

The chauffeur parked the limo in the garage underneath the building, personally escorted me to the private bank of elevators and accompanied me to the 47th floor. "I have orders not to let you out of my sight, ma'am," he said in explanation, pressing the doorbell outside the massive door carved with the 'A-G' brand. The door swung open, the chauffeur disappeared and a young, pretty Hispanic girl introduced herself.

"I'm Teracita, senorita, please come in. Mr. Gossett is waiting for you." She smiled as Tony came across the foyer to greet me.

"Welcome to the sky ranch, Kaytee. Ain't she a purty gal, Teracita, just like I told ya?"

Tony escorted me into the massive living room, and fixed our drinks. We stopped for a while at the windows, but eventually wound up on the couch, much cozier than I had intended. Soft strains of New York city flowed through the room. Neither of us said a word, caught in our own reverie. We hesitated to move or speak for fear of spoiling the special mood.

"Hungry? Let me show you what Teracita has arranged for our dinner. It should be a real surprise. Her brother Manuelo, from the restaurant downstairs, told her all about the 'Senorita especial' that was coming for dinner." He stood up, reached for my hand, unfolded me from the couch, and pulled me over to the dining area. The large formal dining room table stood unset, with a floral centerpiece and glass candle holders. A low table set for two was next to the window. Terracita arranged a complete steamboat dinner on nearby trays.

Pointing to the copper pot with the broth already steaming from the coals in the center flue, Teracita said, "Would you like me to prepare dinner, senorita?"

"It looks beautiful Teracita. You have already done all the work, I'll take over from here. Sit down, Tony, this is my favorite dining style. Just help me move the cooking pot to the center of the table." Putting an asbestos pad underneath, we put the copper pot into the center of the table. Teracita moved the trays of delicacies next to me. Fresh shrimp and thinly-sliced filets of fish, chicken, pork, and beef were ready for cooking. Another tray displayed fishballs, circles of squid, and the traditional quail eggs, along with vegetables, cabbage, lettuce, tiny ears of corn, and carrots, decorated around mounds of transparent rice noodles.

"No cowboy garb tonight." Tony said, handing his jacket to Teracita, loosening his tie and collar. He slipped off his loafers and easily folded his long legs to sit at the table.

"Not many Westerners can sit as you do, my compliments." I said, admiring the way he adapted to our way of life. For a moment I could visualize him on my own turf.

"Nothing like inviting a girl over to dinner and then making her cook for you," I said, with a wink. Shoes off, kneeling at the table, I began feeding the green vegetables into the boiling broth. I handed Tony a couple of chicken eggs. "Get to work hot shot, scramble these up in that bowl and dump them in, while I do the important work." With the larger pair of chopsticks, I took fresh shrimp, dropped them into the broth, and removed them a moment later, all pink and steaming; yes, the broth was ready.

Teracita watched approvingly, then disappeared, Tony added the scrambled eggs, and I made out like the contented Chinese wife. For an hour we gorged ourselves. I put the different delicacies in the broth, fished them out with the chopsticks or the small net, and dropped the tender morsels into our rice bowls. Teracita brought more coals and broth, appearing and disappearing without a sound. Finally, perspiration beading both of our faces and arms, I ladled out the remaining broth into fresh cups, adding only the rice noodles clear and invisible in the liquid.

"Lovely lady, that was elegant dining," Tony said, stretching out his long legs and leaning back against a stack of pillows. I did the same, unintentionally exposing one whole leg from the hip down in the open split skirt. When Tony reached over to slide a hand down one thigh, I reluctantly and slowly pulled back. We had talked little during dinner, now enjoying the languorous mood of soft music and full stomachs. I wasn't sure how I would deal with the tease of sensual reactions.

"Tell me more about yourself, Kaytee," Tony said, pulling back. He reached for a cigar, methodically removed the wrapper, slit the end, lighted it from a long match, and leaned back to exhale the first round circle of smoke. "Were your parents involved in the war during the bad times?"

"My father, because of his heritage, was a Confucian scholar, my mother a famous courtesan. They lived in Shanghai before the war, where I was born. From papa I learned the philosophy of life that says to enjoy happiness when you can. There may be times happiness may not be available. From mama I learned that food is more important to a man than sex, and that one should first please his stomach before his genital organs. Mama taught me to enjoy all pleasures by sharing the experiences.

"Now that I have your attention, may I tell you the story of the Confucius Jade?"

"Kaytee, with those beautiful legs, you have my undivided attention. I may have a problem concentrating on what you'll be saying." He wrenched himself up, giving me a hand, then led me back to the sofa. He went over the bar to get a brandy for each of us, and sat down in an armchair, half facing me. His craggy features broke out into a boyish smile, and said, "y'all got me roped and haltered, a'waitin to have the saddle throwed on my back. Time now to let me in on the secret."

"It's a strange story, Tony, one that I had trouble comprehending myself. On my way to New York for our scheduled meeting, My family asked me to stop in San Francisco. They knew I was meeting with you, and delegated me to carry a message. I have to believe in the fates decreed by the Immortals, more so than mere coincidence."

Tony interrupted in a disgusted tone. "Why me? I can understand our meeting for the business purposes; that's logical. This fate business is a little beyond me."

"Tony, hear me out. You are one of three men on this planet to hear about the rarest treasure in all the world. Few people know that you are a collector. I assume that your private museum is somewhere in this apartment. We also know that your treasures are purchased by a chain of agents. Only the most exquisite and rarest sculptures are in your collection. We also know that you are a student of karate, and run the Boston Marathon every year with a penchant for health and a wish for long life."

Smiling, I continued, "You drink mildly, smoke only an occasional cigar, trekked through the mountains of Nepal in your youth, climbed the five famous mountains of China, and have your body massaged by the best masseuses in the world. Yes, Mr. Anthony Gossett, we know a lot about you."

Tony was impassive, did not react to my smiles and looked irritated enough to send me home.

"You're angry at the invasion of your privacy. I would be too if I were you. I suspect you are thinking that I set you up, and you're ready to push the button to eject me. Please hear me out and then decide."

I didn't give him a chance to answer. "Our family has a rare treasure. You must listen quietly while I tell you the story of the jade, split by the Gods, that found their way into the family of Confucius..."

I spoke for an hour, relating the tale of the Jade of Shou Xing Laos. Tony sat transfixed, almost as though in a coma, as the words sunk in. For his own reasons, he never interrupted.

I sipped my brandy and watched Tony's face, the wheels turning in his mind, as I had seen him do with my advertising plan. Uncle Sam would be proud that I had carried off the initial presentation, in spite of the beginning. We made a mistake investigating his private life. Getting up, I walked around the room, giving him time to think. His furnishings were tastefully selected for comfort and use, not for show.

Teracita must have removed the remains of the steamboat without me noticing. I wondered how much the girl had heard.

Standing by the window, floating mentally out into the void beyond to see the city better, I didn't notice Tony coming up behind me, until I felt his arms around me, casually cupping my breasts as if we had been lovers for years. He turned me around, lifted my chin. I braced myself to refuse a kiss. I would love to be kissed and nuzzled by this wonderful man, but it was too soon, we both needed time. He didn't even try, and held me looser than I would have liked.

"Kai Tai Kong, you have complicated my life in a very short time. I believe the story you have told me, because I was once in the area you talk about. Burma, Yunnan, Kunming are all familiar places to me. I wonder at the coincidence of you standing here now. It's as you said. An unseen hand is directing us."

We began swaying to the music in the background, then dancing slowly to the soft rhythm. He pulled me tighter, or maybe I just moved in closer, my head on his chest, his chin nestled on top of it. Stopping for a moment, he reached down and pushed a control button. The lights went out, leaving just the candles, and the reflection from the windows, the outside looking in.

"Just close your eyes, honey, for a few moments, and then open them."

He was right, the night blindness disappeared and faint shapes began to appear, the view outside incredible. We barely moved to the music, letting the rhythm massage our bodies against each other. The alarm bells rang when I felt him arousing. He must have felt it also, as he pulled away slightly in embarrassment.

Switching to his cowboy humor, Tony cupped my chin so he could look right into my eyes, and said in a whisper, "Y'all best come over here little filly, afore the stud gets loose and starts chasing the mare around the corral. I see'd these broncos get riled up many a time, and they's hard to cool down. Let's mosey over and sorta talk over what kinda race we're gon'ta have."

Not bothering to correct him on the "little filly" talk, I mimicked him. "Wa'l padnah, what happens when the mares heatin' up and needs some coolin'. Seems like y'all need a cold water tank fer the whole dang herd."

That booming laugh came out again, echoing in the huge room, reverberating against the glass window. It was infectious. I began to laugh aloud with him. We both collapsed on the couch, tears streaming down our faces, unable to control ourselves.

Tony reached over, picked me up as easily as if I was a feather, and put me on his lap, my legs stretched out on the couch, my head and shoulders turned to him, noses an inch apart. My hands went around the back of his neck, and I could feel his hand on my ankle, sliding slowly up the calf, under the knee, moving over the thigh, and on up until one whole bare cheek was firmly in his grasp. We kissed softly, just lips meeting and working against each other, both of us hesitating to let go.

I pulled away, turned my head to rest on his shoulder, and said, "Time to take the filly back to her own stable, Tony, before we both get carried away and ruin a good business deal."

"You know, Kaytee, for a person that I didn't even know existed twenty-four hours ago, you sure have made some impressions on my life. A sensual, beautiful woman is in my arms that I don't know whether to attack or withdraw from. Every nerve end is telling me to be careful. The problem is, I don't know what to be careful of. For the first time in my life, a major business deal is insignificant.

"Visions of an Immortal God suddenly taking over my destiny, combined with a probable fight of my life to gain the immortality they represent. If I told anyone that knows me about all this, they would think I was either drunk or hallucinating. You asked to be home by midnight. Whether you like it or not, you are going back to the hotel right now. Then I'm going to wake up Teracita to give me a good massage, soak in the Jacuzzi and wait for the dawn to come up."

He bent down, kissed me again, lightly, squeezed my bottom, and abruptly stood up, picking me up with him, and setting me on my feet. "No, don't say a word. Kaytee, put your shoes on, and I'll ring for Johnny to come up and see that you get safely back to your hotel. Meet me at the office in the morning. We can work with Melinda on the program and save the next two evenings for my undivided attention. Call your family and tell them that I need some proof of the Jade. If as represented, forget about the other two buyers. Just name the price. I'll take it."

The phone ringing jarred me awake the next morning; it took three rings to bring me out of the dreamy fog. My partners were on the line from Hong Kong, wanting to know the scoop.

"We're on the speaker in the conference room, mousey." I recognized Rooster's voice and concentrated on tuning in with a normal answer. "Hi gang. We're in."

"Mousey, can you talk? Is someone in bed with you? What's the deal going to be?"

"No such luck. I'm alone, tired from a late night with the client. It looks like we are going ahead for the whole banana. Right now, I am supposed to be up and away for an early appointment. I promise to call as soon as I get time."

"Talk about Chinese torture. You really know how to keep us in misery."

"Relax guys, everything is all right. If I told you the whole story you wouldn't believe it anyway. Gotta go."

Room service sent up the whole works I ordered for breakfast, asking, sarcastically, I thought, how many people were joining me. Showered, robed, ravenously getting the first mouthfuls down, I tried to relax and recall everything that had happened the night before. The part that I remembered most was causing me to heat up again, and I could still feel the large firm hand holding half of my bottom. Giggling to myself, I tried to remember whether it was the right or the left one.

I lectured myself: Okay, K.T., enough of this nonsense. First, let's get through to Uncle Sam or Jie Lie, report in, and get an okay to show Tony the video. This secret agent stuff is exciting. Next get yourself dressed in something demure, and get over to Gossett's office. Linny is going to need some buttering up. Unless I miss my guess, you don't want to be on the wrong side of her. She could be trouble. Now what on earth are you going to do about Tony? The man's old enough to be your father, and is causing you to wet your pants like a teenage lover. You could really screw up the business deal if you allow this to become a love affair. The family is also depending on you, the only contact with a potential billion dollar sale. You are up to your tits in delicious dreams, K.T., my friend. You'd better start getting some answers going.

Critiquing myself was something I had learned years ago, often doing it while looking in a mirror. There was something in one of the Confucius sayings. I never could remember the exact quote, but the essence was:

Know oneself, for where is a better or truer friend?

My situation was like the candle burning at both ends. Here I am with three fires going on the same candle, one in the middle, and the others at each end. This is dangerous. I could get burned severely and the flames could engulf others.

Slow down K.T., let's use a little logic here.

13

MELINDA GOSSETT

—∞∞∞—

Extending the receptionist my card, I said "Kai Tai Kong to see Mr. Gossett or Melinda Gossett." A secretary showed me into the conference room and brought a proper pot of tea. I booted up the Little Tig Er, switched the file to NOTEBOOK.GOS from the menu, and worked on the outline. I'm a methodical lister, noting all the items I have to do, re-writing each morning, dropping completions and refreshing my mind on the uncompleted items. The notebook program was a good one, including calendars five years back and ten years forward, dates to remember that automatically popped as soon as you turned it on, and today's date and world time on order.

I called San Francisco that morning and related the strange reception of the information by Tony. "Uncle Sam, Tony expected the Shou Xing Lao to appear. He believed the entire story. The impression that I got was that he knew every place we were talking about and had been there. His message to you was straightforward: why bother with the other two potential buyers? All he wants is proof of their existence. How much do we want, and when can he see it."

"Kai Tai," the soft, knowing voice answered, "There is one problem I detect. You called him Tony, in a very endearing tone. Is there a relationship there you are concealing? If so, we'd better find another contact for him. It could be what my young lawyer grandson would call a conflict of interest."

"Absolutely not," I lied. "Gossett is a very earthy person and breeds familiarity. He pretends to be a simple cowboy one minute, and a tough businessman the next. Shall I show him the video?"

"By all means. You have fired the first barrel, now go with the follow-up. Please, Kaytee, try to remain with the script and don't get personally entangled. The family will have a meeting when you return to San Francisco this weekend. Ai Mei who is working with the Japanese contender will be here. Feng Wa will bring his report on the Sheikh. We want to pool our information and begin the second phase of our plan. Can you arrange to stay over the weekend?"

"The company is pushing me pretty hard, honored Uncle, but I will be there, as you wish. Please don't concern yourself about my personal relationship with Gossett. I am well aware of the responsibility you have entrusted me with."

"Thank you, Kai Tai. We trust you completely. Please be very careful, you could be hurt."

Thinking about that conversation, I remembered I hadn't changed my flight reservations back to San Francisco and then on to Hong Kong. There was a multi-use telephone instrument on the table. I punched what I thought was a button for the operator, intending to have her connect me with the airline. Instead the speaker came on. I heard Tony and Linny arguing. I should have turned it off, but as the not-so-secret agent of the Kongs, I justified listening.

"Well father," Linny was saying in her strident voice, "are you going to tell me about last night, or do I have to wheedle it out of you?" I visualized the six foot Melinda, with her father's shoulders and build, standing almost eye to eye with him.

"Damn it, Linny, you and that kid Teracita treat me like some dogie lost in the brush. Before she would give me my coffee this morning, I had to report on the strange mare in my corral last night. She's lucky I didn't wake her up to give me a rub down after the horse show. Both of you don't have to know everything I do, and keep score."

"Now, as to Kaytee, who irks you, she's as skittery as a new foal, and wants no part of an old stud like me. We had a pleasant dinner, watched the city lights until midnight, and then I sent her home. It was strictly a business dinner; the Phoenix Advertising Agency deal looks very good. I think we can make some money out of it. Get to know her and I think you'll like her. You may have to spend some time over on her turf, but do it, that is if you can tear yourself away from Edward for a few weeks."

Linny screamed back. "Leave Edward out of this! Just because you're anti-government doesn't mean you can put him down. I respect his job with the Justice Department. Are you telling me that an old warhorse like you didn't get into her pants, even with the soft lights and music, and the outfit she was wearing? According to Teracita, everything she had was peeking out from one opening or another every time she moved. By the way, what is this stuff about a jade figure? Is she trying to sell you something on the side? I don't trust orientals. You never know what's going on in their minds."

Tony's voice sounded irritated, but deliberately low key in contrast to Linny's loud shouting. "Melinda, that big mouth of yours is going to get you in trouble one day, and I don't like you pumping Teracita. She is too naive and thinks the two of you have to team up to take care of the old man. If you had half the finesse that Kai Tai has, it would improve your personality ten times. Now get your butt in the conference room with her and make friends. If I hear one word about your ethnic prejudices, I'll throw you out. You know I can't stomach any reference to the difference in people because of who they are or where they come from. I'll bet you are getting most of that crap from Edward. What you see in that horse's ass, I don't know."

Melinda's tone changed from screaming hellion to concerned daughter. "Easy now father, slow down or you'll need a couple of nitros. Remember what the doctor said about stress. All I want to do is protect you from designing females, which you have a penchant for. The way you're reacting, there is a lot of fire under that smoke signal comin' over the draw, as you would say."

I shut off the speaker. Enough snooping. Sweet-talking Melinda had a lot of hangups. It was interesting that she switched to the cowpoke talk when she wanted to calm him down. I gathered Tony had threatened to throw her out quite often. She ignored that warning completely.

My problem was, she knew about the Jade. Tony ignored her question, but I'm sure he hadn't missed it. We would have to find out a lot more about Miss Gossett. Obviously, she had a direct line into Tony's apartment with Teracita. There would be other company staff reporting in to her. Tony's mole was his own daughter.

Melinda found me quietly working on my notes a minute later. She must have been on her way in when the conversation with Tony occurred. "Sorry to keep you waiting, Ms. Kong. Father was on the phone with the Australian group and I had to backstop him with some information."

I responded sweetly, hoping the natural antagonism didn't show. "Aren't the new acquisitions over there going through? I like Queensland and the Great Barrier Reef area. Townsville, Cairns, and especially Port Douglas are bursting. That should be a lucrative market."

"You know more about it than I do." Drawing up a chair across from me, Linny sat down and tried to stare me down. "Where do you get all your information, especially some of the inside, really secret stuff?"

"You know, Miss Gossett," I dodged the question to cover up. "If you and I could get to know each other better, we might become friends. Why is it that I feel you resent me? The business relationship with your company and mine should be very good for both of us. Your father is a very interesting person. I assure you I have no female designs on him. I have my own love life in Hong Kong. Marriage is not in my immediate future." I finished with a brilliant smile and extended my hand.

Linny looked at me thoughtfully for a moment, then smiled and said, "Okay, truce, and I'll buy lunch." She did take my hand, but the feeling of resentment persisted.

Whatever her personal feelings, Linny proved to be very competent when it came to business. We roughed out most of the details of our prospective plan, each of us giving an inch but only when we had to on the fine points. It was past one o'clock when she flipped her notebook shut, and said, "enough for now, let's go to lunch."

It was after six. I saw Tony walking toward the white Mercedes convertible. I slunk down in the seat. He didn't see me until he opened the door and started to fold himself into the seat. "Wall look'it the stray that got caught up in the wire. Been askin' all over the place, where you got to. Best find out who left the gate open, no tellin' what will come in the corral."

"Jes lookin' fer a place to bed down and feed, pard, this here white lightin' with the forrin' name looked mighty temptin' to hitch a ride in, to the barn. Reckon you know the way, or do ya jes let this ani-mule have its head?"

Swinging those long legs into the improbable confines of the small car, Tony bent his head down to mine. I reached up to meet him. It was a light kiss, neither of us daring any intensity, but we held it for a long time. "Darlin', this here stallion can go either uptown to the ranch in the sky you were at last night, or head off into the hills whar thar's an ole stage stop inn that can get that bed and feed y'alls lookin fer. You've a mind either way?"

I would have loved to play the game. A night to remember in a mountain inn, separated from the world, a wonderful man to make love with and pretend to be a princess escaping her entourage for the night. "Tony, believe me when I tell I would love to run away with you for the night and forget the rules we both live by.

"If the offer is still open a few months from now I'll go any place with you for a night, a week, or more. Right now, the responsibility is too heavy on me. You know why. Phoenix is depending on me to be professional. The family's project is of worldwide importance." I reached over and put my hand on his, gripping the steering wheel. "I have a videotape to show you, proving the existence of the Confucius Jade. The Kong family is depending on me to get your opinion and decision."

We stopped for a light. Tony glanced over. "A guilt-filled night could ruin our relationship. Let's go to my place, rustle up some grub, and try to keep our passion on a low pilot light."

Without a grumble, Teracita had dinner on the table in a half hour. She arranged mixings to make our own tacos. Crisp tortilla shells, shredded beef, cheese, onions, shredded lettuce, and a salsa so hot, it brought tears to my eyes. Bowls of hot frijoles with cheese bubbling on the top. It was so tempting that I spooned it up like soup.

"Ready for the finale, Tony?"

Before he could answer me, the telephone rang. Tony answered and turned his back to me in embarrassment. "Yes, Linny, that's who I'm with and it is none of your damn business. Ms. Kong will be in the office tomorrow to work with you." He slammed the receiver down. "That girl is going to drive me nuts."

"She doesn't like me very much, does she?"

"Darlin', that female is jealous of everything and everyone that comes anywhere near me. When she finds out what you and I are talking about tonight, especially if it is going to cost me some money, look out."

"Tony, call her back. Invite her over to see the tape. If we're going to have a battle or objection, I want it right out front. There are too many problems in our relationship now."

"Maybe you're right, but let's do this. I'll have her come over, but in a couple of hours. I want you to run it through for me first, then let Linny see what we're talking about. All right with you?"

I nodded agreement.

Tony reached for the phone, turned on the speaker so I could listen, and punched an automatic dialing button.

An angry voice answered. "Yes, what is it?"

"Linny, don't take that tone with me. Please come over here in a couple of hours, I want you to see something."

"Dad, I'm not going to socialize with that yellow-skinned alley cat.

It's bad enough I have to do business with her, but there is no way I am going to sit and watch you play grab-ass while I pretend to ignore it."

"Linny, you got your tits in an uproar again. You're not too old for me to slap your face if you use that kind of language around someone I respect and admire. I'll expect you at ten." He pushed the disconnect without letting her answer.

"Whew, I'm sorry, Kaytee, there's no excuse for her temper and attitude. Please forgive me for making you two face each other."

"Never say you're sorry, Tony. I have met many hellcats in my lifetime. So far, none of them have eaten me, or taken a bite out of me. I can take care of myself. Go sit on the couch and I'll set up the video on your VCR. Yes, I know how to work it. We use them in the office extensively."

Setting it up, bringing the remote control with me, I snuggled up into what had become my favorite port, under Tony's big left shoulder. He reached over to dim the room lights. I flicked on the tape. An arm pulled me in closer, squeezed my shoulder and a hand dropped down to hold mine.

The screen lit up with the scene and background music of the Burmese mountains, rushing streams, torrential waterfalls. Tumbling through the rapids the camera work was so expert that I grabbed onto Tony's leg. I felt like I was in a rubber boat bouncing around in sheer terror of getting washed into the water. The scene finally reached the calm, silted waters of the Irrawaddy. The title CONFUCIUS JADE appeared, introduced by costumed young women sounding the temple drum. I relaxed, and felt Tony settling further into the soft couch.

When the figures emerged from the water and walked toward us, it was so real that I wanted to reach out and touch them. The only reaction I got from Tony was deep breathing. His hand, which had been caressing my thigh, suddenly stopped in place.

They faded from view in the finale. Tony reached over for the remote control unit, and started the tape over again.

'Confucius Jade' was on its third rerun. We heard the door chimes. "Tony, you forgot to open the door for Linny." He jumped up, and led her into the room. In the sweetest tone I had ever heard come out of her, she said, "Hi, Ms. Kong, haven't seen you since lunch-time. Please excuse me if I am interrupting your evening. Dad insisted I come over to see the ten o'clock rerun."

"Good evening, Miss Gossett. You're not interrupting. I agree that you should view this film. It's specially prepared for your father. My family, the Kongs of Yunnan Province, have a rare treasure that interests Tony. It's too valuable to bring around, so we made a visual presentation, to be seen by only three men in the world. One of those three is your father.

"Before you say anything about our business deal and me trying to pull something on the side, let me say this. The Phoenix Agency worked on our approach to Gossett for well over a year, and you know we made the appointment months ago. My family found out I was coming to see the Gossetts, and asked me to act as their messenger. That's all I am, a messenger."

Linny reverted, lovely face screwed up in anger, spitting out venom-laden words. "Whatever you call yourself, Ms. Kong, I know what you are. If you try to pull anything on my father that I think is wrong, you'll have me to contend with."

Tony started to say something, I could see his face bunching up in anger. "No, Tony, let me handle this. Linny, I have the greatest respect for your father. I'm proud that we are attracted to each other. I remind you, that we are both consenting, I repeat, consenting adults who like each other very much. If that doesn't please you, then you have a problem. I suggest you sit down, look at what we have to show you and listen carefully to what I'm going to say after it is over."

Without a word, she sat down in a chair facing the screen, while Tony punched up the program again. I smiled to myself.

The last scene faded from the screen to the beat of the temple drums. I flicked the rewind. Neither Tony nor I said a word, waiting for a reaction from Linny. We turned around to see her sitting straight in the chair, her face expressionless. Her bosom moved up and down in slow motion, as if she had reduced her breathing to a minimum. It was a waiting game. We just sat and held each other until Linny shook herself awake, stood up, and walked around the room, obviously collecting her thoughts. Finally, she walked up to the couch, faced us and said "How much?"

I pushed Tony's arm off my shoulder, unfolded my legs from under me, stood up to face her and said, "Linny Gossett, sit down next to your father and let me deliver the rest of the message from my family."

Both Linny and Tony started to say something. "Hold it. My turn. Now are you going to sit down, Linny, or do I have to give you an arm twist and a flip to put you in your place?"

Tony laughed that room-filling outburst of his, and grabbed Linny's arm to pull her down alongside him. "Go ahead, Kaytee, give it to us straight."

"The Kong's plan is to invite you and the other two interested parties to Fiji after the first of the year. On the night of the first full moon, in the Year of the Dragon, the Shou Xing Laos will appear. Our family expect a natural decision to emerge directed by fate, fortune, or the belief in the Jade of Confucius.

"We request you have one billion dollars, ready for transfer by electronic signal to our account. Exact instructions will follow. We assume you'll use your boat, The *Gossamer Gossett* sailing from the Gold Coast Marina in Australia. I'll meet you there and sail with you, bringing the rest of the details."

Linny exploded. "You people are nuts, out of your screwed-up oriental minds! If you think we're going to pay anything more than a fair market value for a trinket, you're mistaken. That is, assuming dad even wants the damned Jade. Frankly, I wouldn't give you two cents for it. For that kind of money, I prefer to buy a few more papers, or some real estate. Dad, you aren't considering this hokey proposal, are you?"

"Linny, there is a lot of wisdom in oriental philosophy. I enjoy collecting gemstone sculptures, and especially those of the Immortals. Shou Xing Lao has long been my favorite because of the longevity symbolism. I want to live a long time to enjoy what I've worked for. You should know that in the Chinese philosophy, longevity means the family line.

"This young woman who you have so crudely insulted is a descendant of a family more than seventy-five generations old. Now compare that with the Gossetts. My son isn't even married, and I suspect that he is more comfortable with men than with women. My daughter messed up her marriage, and is now glued to a man who hasn't the slightest interest in a family. That means I'm the last of the Gossetts. Our family line runs out when I die."

Tony stopped, got up off the sofa, walked around the room pulling at his right ear, letting the words sink in. He stopped where both Linny and I could see him. "I'm interested. The jade figures may be worth an incalculable sum. Kaytee told me of some of the happenings that followed their path. I believe them. If association will extend my life one day, one month, or many years, the Confucius Jade will be mine. Money is secondary. I suspect the other two rivals are as equally motivated.

"Linny, you're my daughter. You can help me to outsmart the others with that brilliant brain of yours, or you can fight, obstruct and confuse me. Think about it. Tomorrow morning I'll meet with finance and begin to accumulate the funds in an off-shore account. I hope you understand and will help me."

"You're a fool, father. They're ripping you off with sentimentality. It's your money, but remember, if senility creeps in, there are legal ways to stop even you from squandering it. As for your fortune-hunting little playmate, I'll take care of her in my own way."

Chin and mammaries jutting out, Linny stomped out of the apartment, leaving a verbal smoke trail in her wake.

"Wow, that woman has problems, Tony. Do you have any idea why her personality developed that way? You certainly have a compassionate nature. From what you have told me of Lauranne, Linny should have inherited calmer genes."

"It's my father's genes she inherited. He was a hard-nosed, bullheaded, country newspaper publisher. Pa stepped on anyone he could to get his way. Linny actually has a split personality. Half of her is intelligent, affable, and very generous. The black side is jealous, spiteful, narrow-minded stubbornness. She'll do what I want, because she intends to take over the business some day. Watch out for her."

I went over to Tony, took his big hand in mine, and led him over to the window, both of us looking out into the sky. "Tony, you were in a real dream state when we ran the Confucius Jade the last time. Would you tell me what you were thinking?"

Pulling me down on some floor cushions next to him, he put his arm around me, cupping me tight into his shoulder. "I can try, but it's hazy. The Shou Xing Laos are hypnotic, familiar, as if we have known each other before. With soundless words they talked to me, promising long life and happiness, and warning of possible unspecified danger. Is it possible I was just hallucinating?"

"Everything you say coincides with what my aunt Wan Yi, the family storyteller, experienced. Strange, phenomenal events have occurred in the aura of the Jade. I can tell you this, our family intends to use the funds to begin a University of Confucius. Open to everyone, we hope the world's present and future leaders will discover the power of the five virtues, and learn how to live with their own people and the rest of the world in peace. The evils of power and avarice are present in all societies."

Tony agreed. "The Anwar Sadats can use some help against the gurus, dictators, and militarists. The practical side of me would like to get the Jade. Part of me hopes for the return of my family nest. Tell me how your family intends to barter their soul for their university?"

"It's vague, Tony. It will be the first full moon of the Chinese New Year when you and the others meet. We believe the Shou Xing Laos will determine their own fate and yours when the three of you present yourselves."

The rest of that evening is a beautiful memory. Back in the real world, Tony kissed me goodbye at the airport. "Keep in touch, honey, I'll see you on board the *Gossamer Gossett* on New Year's Eve."

Book Three
THE IMMORTALS AND THE ELEMENTS

1

KUNMING, YUNNAN

—◦∞◦—

KONG WAN YI

The Master said, *It is these things that cause me concern: failure to cultivate virtue, failure to go more deeply into what I have learned, inability, when I am told what is right, to move to where it is, and inability to reform myself when I have defects.*

My second visit to San Francisco was for the fascinating meeting with our inner family group. Kai Tai, Feng Wa, and Ai Mei, our emissaries, reported their experiences with the three contenders for the Confucius Jade. I related the details to my adopted father and mother. Uncle Huo Huo was there. Mei Hua sat on a floor cushion, leaning against my knees. She was content to be close to me and amongst the family.

"There is much to tell, Father and Mother, about the meeting in Uncle Sham Choy's home in San Francisco. The plans are proceeding in an imaginative way that we never dreamed about. We are fortunate to have a family with such intelligence."

Deng joined us quietly, pulled up a chair, and lit his pipe, as usual not saying a word. He sat next to me, expressing, in his own way, his pleasure at having me home. "Now that you are here, dear husband, let me bring you all up to date. There is so much to tell about the events of the Kong Summit, as Uncle Sham calls it."

The three of them settled back in their chairs and I began.

"We gathered in the Choy apartment. Kai Tai, our cousin in the advertising business from Hong Kong, flew in from New York. Her mission was to meet with the media baron, Anthony Gossett. There is a slight problem there; we think she became enamored with the man. However, reception to the Jade was positive and she reported a strange reaction. When Kai Tai told him the story of the Jade, he became very remote as if remembering something connected.

Fan Shi grunted at this. I looked at him but he told me to go on. "Feng Wa, David Kong, a diplomat with the U.S. Department of State, managed to meet with the Arab Sheikh, Arum ibn Mohammed, through a son of the Sheikh. His story of the Palace of the Paradi in Eden titillated our younger generation. There were strange and beautiful women, palace intrigue and a luxurious living beyond our imagination. It was like the jade amulet and stories of intrigue in the books of Red Mansions.

Feng Wa reported the same mysterious reaction from the Sheikh Arum. He went off into a deep reverie while the account unfolded. It's as if both men were already familiar with the circumstances from another time and place." Fan Shi grunted again, and I made up my mind to question him later.

"The Sheikh is tantalized by the story of the Jade, only questioning why there were others competing."

Mother and Father were half asleep when I finished telling them about Ai Mei's experience in Kobe. Father just nodded his head when I came to the part about Ru Kokomoto manifesting a déjà vu attitude about the Jade.

I summarized quickly. "We hoped originally to intrigue at least one of the three men to own the Jade. Now all three seem to desire possession. Our video presentation convinced them of the reality. They dismiss the other rivals as unnecessary, and await a further move from our side. We worry. It's too easy; they are rich and powerful men, accustomed to getting what they want by any means available. Our plan is for a competitive bid arrangement in a remote area to ensure security. General Wei Tang is worried about foul play amongst them and possible theft of the Jade."

Mother and Father dozed during the rest of my report. Deng and Huo Huo didn't miss a word. Mei Hua was in her own world, oblivious of ours. "Dr. Jian Yi, you recall, is our Mencius connection. She reports a vital interest by the Mensa Society in creating an educational and physical structure around the teachings of Confucius. Their most important question is the possible location. Jian could not divulge that until after Father Fan visits with the Paramount Leader. Ren Quan, our financial advisor, is planning the technical and electronic equipment necessary.

The next day I discussed the trip to Lushan Mountain with Mother and Father, the momentous visit with Deng Xiaoping. Fan showed me the letter he had received from the great leader. It was so important, he had it framed in glass, fearing the paper would deteriorate from handling. The Great One brushed with an artist's expertise. I was sure it would hang in the family's archives one day.

"Old friend Kong Fan Shi, you warm the memories of our youth. It's well that you have returned from your self-imposed exile in Burma and are happy in your richer years in Yunnan. It would give me great pleasure to visit with you once more and relive the times when we were younger. You must tell me of the many years that have elapsed. In August, I retreat to the cool of Lushan Mountain to escape the heat of Beijing. Journey there, old friend, and we will meet. Enclosed is a note bearing my chop. It will facilitate any problems that may occur in arranging your trip."

Fan was very proud of the letter. His chess cronies looked in awe at the framed paper and accompanying travel pass, enclosed in a red plastic case. "Notice, Wan Yi," he said, "the pass says Kong Fan Shi and party. Chen and I would like you and Deng to come with us."

I laughed. "Deng would not take time out from his cooking, I know, but I wouldn't miss it for anything, Father dear."

"We're to leave the twenty-fifth of July and return the tenth of September, according to the schedule."

The day of departure approached, our excitement heightening until Mother Chen and I thought we would burst. "What clothes will we take for the interview with the Paramount Leader? What if he invites us to a meal with him?" I asked. "Do you suppose they wear the traditional Sun Yat-sen jackets and sloppy pants? We see mostly Western style clothing in Kunming, changed by the free-market place. We must be careful not to take too much. The cases will be too heavy to carry."

The night before we left, the family arranged a big party in the courtyard for the famous people that were going to visit Deng Xiaoping. Most of our local friends had never traveled any further than the Stone Forest. Uncle Huo Huo described our entire trip, proudly showing off the typewritten schedule.

Deng was as nervous as I that night; sleep was impossible. My mind kept going over all the details. I would be carrying the travel permits, a lot of renminbi, air tickets, and the very special pass Father had received from Deng Xiaoping.

Mother Chen rustled in the tiny kitchen, heating water for the tea. Deng was awake beside me, holding me close. We had been away from each other more than together since leaving Burma. Just before dawn, we coupled, not with the fervor and sweat of our youth, but with the slow merger of need for each other. After the wind and the rains, our bodies remained locked together, enjoying the warm comfort as much as the physical release.

"You are still a strong lover, my husband," I said, caressing his shoulder and back. "When I am far away, these moments recur and comfort me."

Deng's arms pulled me even tighter, murmuring "It's that way for me too, Wan Yi. You'll promise to care for yourself. My life would have no purpose without you."

It was an odd statement, somewhat fatalistic. I didn't tell Deng, but I had premonitions. Travel has its own dangers.

Mei Hua waited for us to say goodbye, no longer the tearful little girl worried about separation from her family. She was proud of her independence, caring for her Uncle Huo and working at the embroidery factory. "Mei Hua wish you safe journey. Here is gift to protect you." Her smile was like the Goddess we likened her to so often, Guan Yin. She handed each of us a small pouch, with the double happiness character embroidered on the outside. Inside we found a small smooth river rock, from her prized collection that had traveled so many miles. I shivered inwardly. Was this another sign of jeopardy ahead?

We busied ourselves with our cases, trying to cover up our tears, hugging her, touched by the personal and thoughtful gift. Finally we were in the taxi with Huo Huo on our way to the airport.

Airborne once more, the exhilaration of flight caught up with me again. Father was at the window. Mother sat between us, holding our hands tightly on take-off. She relaxed as the stewardess brought cups of orange juice, then the key-chain souvenirs of the trip. We talked little during the flight, still caught up in the emotion of the departure. My eyes closed, dreaming of the future.

Suddenly the Shou Xing Laos appeared, walking toward me. It had been many months since they had materialized in my thoughts. I concentrated, trying to read the lips. They were telling me something, waving their dragon-headed scepters to gain attention. I sensed they warned me of danger. My mind recalled Deng's words early that morning. Mei Hua's charm, in the embroidered pouch, was in my pocket. The dampness and sweat of fear came over me.

The plane vibrated; I awoke with a start. Mother shook me, mumbling incoherently, reaching across me for Father's hand. Unlike the international flights I had been on, the domestic pilots of CAAC do not make any announcements to the passengers. The stewardesses went up and down the aisle, calming the passengers, telling them the plane was safe. Father was calm, assuring Mother, holding her hand across my lap. I reached over and tightened her seat belt, telling Father to do the same.

The vibrating increased, and the plane shook so badly that all of the poorly stowed gear on the racks above us came tumbling down. Screams echoed through the plane from the bags, boxes, and cases hitting the passengers. Inexperienced passengers standing in the aisles tumbled over the sitting ones. I felt the pressure in my ears, as the plane descended violently. Oxygen masks suddenly dropped in front of us, few people remembering what to do with them. I strapped Mother's mask over her mouth and shouted to just breathe normally. Father watched and did the same, as I adjusted my own. Remembering the rest of the instructions from other flights, I showed my parents how to lean over with pillows in front of their heads. I thought of Deng's last words and the treasured good luck stones Mei Hua had given us.

The screams subdued into moans, as there was nothing anyone could do except cower in their seats. The stewardesses did their best to get masks on everyone and make sure their belts were tight. Father, looked out of the window, shouted over the din. "The engine fell off, like a giant hand ripping it away."

The plane suddenly righted from its dive, leveled off, and became so quiet we were afraid to speak. "It's all right now." The stewardesses quieted the passengers. "The plane can fly with the remaining engine, we're all right. We'll be landing in Shanghai in just a few minutes."

The injured aircraft pulled up to a gate as if nothing had happened. Inside was a mess with people fighting to get off, debris all around and the crew trying to attend to the injured. I cautioned Mother and Father to just stay seated. We let the anxious people crowd their way out of the plane, then reached down for our cases and proceeded out. Mother was calm; we were alive. Another link had been added to the chain of events. Our lives are controlled by our friends, the Immortals. No one would believe that the Shou Xing Laos had appeared just before the accident, but I knew they were there, and thanked them mentally.

"Kong family?" A pleasant-looking young lady bubbled happily. "I'm Wang Dai Jin, your national guide. Welcome to Shanghai."

She was young, in her twenties. I acknowledged who we were. She smiled. "I'm honored to meet the Kong family. Please let me help you with your case, Lao Kong," she said, taking it from Fan's hand. It was the old way, veneration deserved respect; I was impressed with our cheerful guide, Wang. "How was your flight from Kunming?"

Mother Chen just shook her head. I answered. "The plane lost an engine, scared us half to death. We were ready to greet our ancestors when the trouble cleared itself. Didn't the people on the ground know anything about it?"

"CAAC doesn't even tell itself when something happens. They never tell us anything, though Luxingshe is their biggest customer. That's awful, are you all right? You must have a powerful Immortal watching over you."

The car pulled up in front of the Park Hotel, a high-rise building of brownish brick on a corner right in the heart of the Nanjing Road shopping area. The lobby was unimpressive, with a gift shop and a coffee shop on the main floor. Wang had already checked us in, and we went right to our room, a pleasant suite with two bedrooms, clean and neat. The traditional porcelain tea pot and cups were on the table, along with a thermos of hot water. Our guide poured tea for us all, and then sat down with some brochures of Shanghai and environs.

"There is so much to see in Shanghai, and we don't want to tire you out." Wang produced a notebook and pen to write everything down. "First, you are scheduled to leave in four days for Lu Shan. Your ship departs at sunset on Thursday. That gives us Monday, Tuesday, Wednesday, and most of Thursday to program you. I suggest that we visit one major place each morning, leaving the afternoon for shopping or resting so that you don't get overtired. Please get some rest this afternoon, have dinner in the hotel dining room tonight, and we'll pick you up at nine tomorrow morning. I'll have a complete schedule ready for you by that time."

Mother and Father were excited by modern Shanghai. Visible construction changed its face daily. We visited the Yu Gardens and a jade carving factory outside of town the next morning. The three kilometers of shops on Nanjing road occupied our afternoons. Duo Yun Xian, the famous painting and calligraphy store, and Xinhua, the three-storey bookstore, intrigued Fan Shi so much that we had trouble getting him to leave. I bought bright posters and children's books in English and Chinese for Mei Hua.

Shanghai is crowded, hot, and uncomfortable in the summer, difficult to walk through or drive in with a car, but fascinating in its historic variety of life. The French used to call it the Paris of the East. A Paris that reflects the past tumultuous history, and the modern tourist assault, bringing more economic advantage than any of the prior invaders. There are massive modern hotels, reserved for foreign tourists. We, the masses, are physically separated from the tourists, lest we become tainted with western ways.

2

SHANGHAI TO LU SHAN TO QUFU

KONG WAN YI

The Master said, *To be fond of something is better than merely to know it, and to find joy in it is better than merely to be fond of it. The Master said, It is only the most intelligent and the most stupid who are not susceptible to change.*

Tsu-kung said, *The gentleman is judged wise by a single word he utters. That is why one really must be careful of what one says. The Master cannot be equaled just as the sky cannot be scaled. Were the Master to become the head of a state or a noble family, he would be like the man described in the saying: he only has to help them stand and they will stand, to guide them and they will walk, to bring peace to them and they will turn to him, to set them tasks and they will work in harmony. In life he is honored and in death he will be mourned. How can that be equaled?*

Ren – Human-heartedness; Yi – Righteousness; Li – Propriety; Zhi – Wisdom; Xin – Sincerity or Good Faith.

In politics, they stress the moral importance of human relationships, and in its last analysis, virtue alone constitutes the ultimate goal of man.

Three blasts on the ship's whistle tingled my back. We stood at the railing on the upper passenger deck near the bow of the coastal steamer. The Captain saluted us as he appeared on the bridge-wing to signal the lines cast off. There was a last flurry at the gangplank as two late passengers hurried aboard, swinging their carry poles with sacks that bowed their legs with the weight.

The gangplank rolled away. An officer fastened the deck-railing back in place. The deck-hands pulled the released midship lines on board. The aft-line loosened and hauled in, and the rumble of the winches helped to orchestrate the musical works of the ship's departure. We felt the engines rumbling below decks, and saw the wake of the propellers biting in, as the stern moved away from the pier pivoting on the bow lines. Hands on the pier released the bow lines on command. The ship backed into the middle of the Huangpo channel.

A tug took up position at the bow and helped to turn the vessel around in the narrow passageway. Five minutes later, all lines secured, the tug released its pressure on the bow. We headed downstream out to sea.

Eventually the Huangpo widened to the East China Sea. The anchorage was dotted with ships waiting their turn to enter the crowded waterway. Our ship, *Red Forty*, turned west through buoy-marked channels into the wide delta of the Chang Chiang, the mighty Yangtze River, water highway of China.

On the third morning, the *Red Forty* docked at Jiujang, and we became a part of the exodus. The ship's purser escorted his V.I.P. passengers through the pursers' office for the privilege of being first off the ship.

Excitable Wang, my name for our guide because she bubbled over with enthusiasm, settled us at a street cafe while she arranged for a van to take us up the mountain. The arrival port of JiuJiang has a constant flow of travelers visiting the mountain resort, Lu Shan. Further inland is the porcelain center of Jingdezhen, producing ceramic art for more than two thousand years.

The air cooled noticeably as the van climbed the narrow mountain road. It was a busy path, crowded with hikers, buses, cars and animal-drawn farm carts. At the top there was a central square, alongside a lake. Souvenir stores ringed the plaza, intermixed with food stalls. We drove up a side street to the office of the Luxingshe to find out where we would stay. Wang and I went in to get the hotel reservation. The Luxingshe clerk said "Sorry, hotels filled, no rooms."

Wang sputtered angrily, "But didn't you get our telex? My guests are very important people, here to visit with the Paramount Leader. We cannot tell them to sleep in the park. Show them your special pass, Wan Yi."

"Let me think," the young man said, flustered on seeing our document. "The hotels are filled because the Great Leader is here. The entourage with him is large. However, one of the homes originally owned by a Nationalist General is available. You must pay three hundred fifty yuan per night for it."

Wang negotiated, flashing the document in his eyes and eventually they agreed to give it to us for the three nights of our stay for the 350. There was room for our driver as well.

To Fan and Chen, we said, "we've found a mansion to stay in because of your importance."

The house, built of stone, was high on a hill overlooking the lake and valley. A wall of stone completely surrounded it. The caretakers unlocked the gate and led us up the steps to the house. Bedroom suites were upstairs, living and dining room areas downstairs, with servants' quarters in the rear. "Do you like your palace, Emperor Fan Shi?" I joked. "We should move here instead of the apartment we have in Kunming. The master bedroom alone is larger than our whole apartment back home."

Excitable Wang and the driver went off the next morning to see about our visit with Deng Xiaoping, returning smug and happy. "It's true, the Revered One will welcome you tomorrow morning at ten. He lives at the Mao Zedong summer home and museum."

The low rambling home nestled in the edge of a forest park was surrounded by an iron fence. A sign read 'SUMMER HOME OF MAO ZEDONG – OPEN DAILY 9:00 to 5:00.' Another sign next to it read 'CLOSED TEMPORARILY'. A pair of soldiers looked at our pass, checked their list, and opened the gate. Two more soldiers stopped us in the driveway of the house.

"Your pass please," he demanded, imperiously checking a note pad. "Kong Fan Shi, Chen Wu Xia, Kong Wan Yi may enter. Driver, move the car over to the visitors' parking lot over there. We will call you when it is time to pick up your guests."

Poor little Wang nearly burst into tears, wanting so much to be a part of our visit with the famous leader. She bit her lip and bravely said, "Don't worry, I will wait with the driver."

A guide ushered us down a long hallway, decorated with museum cases of memorabilia of China's leaders, Sun Yat-sen, Mao Zedong and Zhou Enlai. Other rooms we passed were rope-lined to control visitor traffic. Pictures adorned the walls, and showcase after showcase displayed hundreds of personal items of the leaders. Double doors opened into a large sitting room and bedroom. Jalousies led onto a porch beyond, and we could see soldiers patrolling the garden.

A small man stood at a desk in the center of the room, brushing characters furiously on a long sheet of rice paper. The round, unlined face looked up as we entered, mouth stretching into a broad smile. He put the brush into a porcelain holder and turned to greet us. Mother Chen and I held back as Father went forward with hand extended to greet the retired leader of the People's Republic of China. Kong Fan Shi, tall, slightly bent, bearded, large curved nose, greeted Deng Xiaoping, a small, stocky man with bright eyes piercing through skin-puffed eye pouches.

"Kong Fan Shi," he said, "it's been many years since we were in school in Chongqing. Was it 1920 when graduation threw us out into the world? You have time, I hope, to renew our discussions of Confucius and the socialist philosophy. Please, introduce me to the women and join me on the veranda. There are many arguments I must still present to you about the fallibility of your ancestor and his imperial ideas."

Taking the man's smaller hands in both of his large ones, Father clasped them tightly. "You were Kan Tse-kao then, old friend. My heart warms at the sight of you. Please tell me how to address the leader of China. May I introduce you to my wife Chen Wu Xia, and Wan Yi, our adopted daughter and daughter-in-law."

He bowed to the ladies and shook hands with them. "Xiaoping is fine, scholar Fan Shi. Friends and adversaries called me by many names while I was riding the waves of the political sea these past years. When I joined the party in 1925, I took the name of Deng Xiaoping to show my independence. May I inquire as to your health, Fan Shi?"

"I am well enough to climb Huangshan, the Yellow Mountain, but my jailers here insist it will be more than I can take. It would please me more to look as well and fit as you are. From what I read, however, life has not been that easy for you."

The two old ones talked as we walked outside and settled in rattan chairs on the porch. A woman brought tea and a tray of sweet cakes. Mother Chen and I proudly listened to the repartee between the old friends. It was like watching a chess game between scholars as they explored each other's technique. I imagined the two of them as students in their teens, debating and arguing. They had gone different ways in philosophy. History would record them kindly, if our plan materialized.

We expected to have only a short visit, and Father apologized for taking so much time. Talk is interesting, but our mission was important. I feared being dismissed within a short time. The opposite occurred, we were invited to have lunch on the porch with the Leader. He enjoyed the intellectual debate with his old friend.

"We eat sparsely, comrades," Deng said, pointing to the bowls of rice with cooked vegetables. "I've never enjoyed the large banquets that become so much of a show for foreigners and our own bureaucracy.

"It was thirty-five, the year that you went to Burma, when we suffered our long march to retrench and begin the fight all over. There were many times when we would have enjoyed this bowl of rice and greens as a feast. I can never forget the privation and the loss of life amongst our comrades. The Long March is etched into the soul."

Finally daring to speak, I said, "Honored Leader, we find ourselves in debt to the Immortals who generate our fate. It's a rare opportunity for people of our humble position to be in this house where Chairman Mao once worked and lived. Double happiness is hearing you and Father exchange thoughts."

"Wan Yi, you honor me with your presence. If you look back in the room, you will see a clothes rack with a robe of Mao's still hanging there, and his slippers are by the bed. On the desk where you saw me at work are Mao's brushes, ink slate, and chop." Winking, he continued. "The bathroom you used a few minutes ago is the same place he performed, many times. You sat on the same throne as he did."

Chen burst out laughing. "Wan Yi, this you must repeat as an anecdote for your children. They will realize how famous you are to have used the very facilities that the leaders of our country have honored their presence with."

Fan Shi and Xiaoping slapped each other in merriment, tears running from their eyes. The little man, shoulders shaking, recovered first. His face crinkled with smiles. "Thank you, good people. You bring light and laughter to my sober existence. Many matters that involve serious decisions affecting millions of people come to my attention. I treasure a gentle moment like this. I think that the Great Helmsman, if he is watching now, is amused also.

"Tell me, Fan Shi, you wrote of a special favor of weighty importance. In the days of the Emperor, I, as an administrator, would have appointed you Examiner of Yunnan. Today, I wield little power. There's a new leading Vice-Premier, and Secretary general of the Chinese Communist Party."

Fan pulled at his beard, thought for a moment, then answered. "I am happy that we have given you a few moments of humor. Schools have replaced the need for Imperial examinations by the official scholars.

"We have a mission of importance that will affect China and the entire world. We respectfully request your sage advice and need doors opened that only you can arrange. We know, by the changes you have brought about, that you are a modern person. We bring a chance for China to provide a method for the whole world to achieve world peace. Let Wan Yi outline our plans."

Everyone's eyes turned to me. I saw the tiredness coming to Father's eyes. I knew he couldn't trust himself to present the plan correctly. Each word would be important. We were asking a man who once criticized Confucianism publicly to accept the philosophy.

"Honored Leader, through a complicated chain of circumstances, our family has a rare treasure. Sculptures of jade in the form of the Immortal, Shou Xing Lao, and a mirror image. They are of a size and quality that have no recorded equal. My parents want for little, other than the chance to live the rest of their lives in the place of their ancestors. The Kong family debated on the future of the Immortals.

"We sought an answer that Confucius might conceive. The events that led to discovery of the Jade, and development after, prove a miraculous happening. Our ancestor fought against war and pursued education as the solution. The Confucius Jade is pre-destined.

"The Kong plan is to sell the Jade and create a university in the name of Confucius, to teach his ideals. We hope it will create a forum and spur world leaders to accomplish our ancestor's morals. Our family feels that the only place for such an institution is China. The particular place in China that would symbolize the Confucius doctrines should be the Master's birth-place of Qufu.

"We propose a neutral area, like the United Nations in the United States, or the Vatican in Rome. Such a territory requires complete independence. You can see why we are here talking to the one person in all of China who would have the vision and the ability to open the door."

Deng Xiaoping stared, immobile. His lack of expression frightened me. What response would we release in this person? He continued to lock my eyes without a word. Then he looked over to his old friend. "Help me, Kong Fan Shi. I can remember only part of a quotation that I believe Tsu-Kung said: *The gentleman is judged wise by a single word he utters.* What was the rest of the quotation?"

"I know it well, Xiaoping. It continues: *That is why one really must be careful of what one says. The Master cannot be equaled just as the sky cannot be scaled. Were the Master to become the head of a state or a noble family, he would be like the man described in the saying: he only has to help them stand and they will stand, to guide them and they will walk, to bring peace to them and they will turn to him, to set them tasks and they will work in harmony. In life he is honored and in death he will be mourned. How can that be equaled?*

"It's an apt and important thought," Deng said. "I realize how careful I must be in uttering even a single word. Your plan will cause havoc amongst the old men of the Politburo. There are powerful hard-liners in China that fear the doctrines of Confucianism. Such a task will bring the friendly dragons from the heavens to fight the devil dragons from the depths of the earth. You ask a momentous task from a mere mortal approaching the world of his ancestors.

"Tell me, friends, there are parts of the story you have painted over with a very wide brush. Is it your intention to keep from me the origin of the Jade?"

"Let me answer, Father," I said. "There's no way to hide from the all-seeing eyes of an eagle such as you, Honored Leader. Your adopted name means one who scales mountains and sees the world from the top, like the eagle.

"The origin of the Confucius Jade is Burma, never a part of any dynasty or tomb in China. My daughter Mei Hua discovered the rock of jade, guided by a being we believe to be one of the Immortals. The Shou Xing Laos were released from the rock by members of the Kong family. The entry of the Immortals into our lives infringed on no country's rights. We brought a videotape for you to see the reality of the treasure."

"Is there anything you wish to add, Chen or Fan?" Xiaoping said, turning to them.

"I have little to add, Honored Leader," Mother Chen replied. "All tales have divergent parts that could lead the listener astray. The Immortals have directed us, from the time the rock erupted itself from the Kachin Mountains of Burma. They engineered their release through the artistry of Kong jade carvers. The inventive minds of our family revealed the purpose of their existence. The Jade of Confucius bring us, K'ung Fu-Tze's messengers, to your doorstep. The Shou Xing Laos request your help to provide the land for the birth of a new era."

Deng directed an aide to set up the tape of the Confucius Jade in the living quarters. We watched the screen bring the Shou Xing Laos to life. At the end, Deng turned from us and left the house to walk alone through the forest garden. An interminable fifteen minutes elapsed before he returned.

We stood up when he entered the room and spoke. "I understand the immensity of your plans. The Immortals filled my mind, until I thought they were actually walking with me. You present me with the greatest task of my life, when I have few political tools to work with. I am constantly washed from one shore to the other by the hard-liners and the reformers. Let us retire for the afternoon. Your proposal wearies this ancient mind and tires the body. I need rest to consider your proposal thoroughly. Please return tomorrow and we shall discuss it further."

We arrived precisely at ten the next morning. This time the soldiers were more friendly, allowing Excitable Wang and the car driver to visit the museum part of the house. We joined the retired Vice-Premier. He sat in the same chair that we had left him in the afternoon before.

"Have you moved since yesterday, old friend?" Fan asked, as he got up to greet us.

The face, recognized around the world, wrinkled with a smile. "I spend my hours out here in the pure air. Beijing, and our meeting place the Zhongnanhai, have become so polluted that I savor every moment of this mountain freshness. Come comrades, sit with me, have some tea and tell me more of your plans."

It was late afternoon by the time we left Deng Xiaoping. His ideas expanded on our conception. "To complete China's part of the project, we will create a free area including Qufu and the nearby city of Jinan in Shandong Province. Taishan Mountain, with its seven thousand steps to the top, can provide a retreat for scholars. There will be no restrictions on arrival or departure of students or visitors within the enclave. We will declare it the autonomous territory of Confucius.

"The plan requires a considerable amount of political maneuvering within the National Committee. That will be my contribution." Deng's eyes webbed, the cherubic face smiled. "Please encourage your friends of the Jade to prolong my life long enough to see the completion. If America can fly to the moon, 'taking one step for mankind', surely China can create an international and free state to take a second step. When you're ready, I'll see that a working committee will open the doors you request. May the Immortals take care of you, Kong Fan Shi; you're a National Treasure."

The Great Leader remained on the veranda as we took our leave, his eyes closed in contemplation. I hoped that the Shou Xing Laos appeared and thanked him.

We took a train to Jinan, in Shandong Province, to visit Qufu, where members of the Kong family still live, cousins of the seventy-sixth and seventy-seventh generations. Fan Shi wandered through the thirty-eight buildings honoring Confucius as if it was his sole domain. He spent many hours in The Hall for Cherishing Ancestral Kindness. The Kong Mansion flows like the buildings of the Forbidden City, and is visited by thousands of our people each year. Government funds, they told us, are now allocated to renovate the buildings of Confucius and Mencius. Domestic and foreign tourists will pay many times the cost.

Kong Demao and her daughter Ke Lan, former residents and story-tellers of the mansion, told us of some of the sad events which occurred during the Cultural Revolution. Members of the Red Guard tried to destroy their own culture. The local people, distressed, saw the tomb and tablets smashed at the very grave of Confucius. The Mount Tai commemorative tablet, stone incense burners and steel inscribed by Huang Yangzheng were in pieces. During the night following the desecration, townspeople secretly came to collect and hide the fragments. When the era of the Red Guards passed into history, these people brought out the shards. The smashed relics were completely restored.

Our dreams became a reality in the aura of our ancestor. We envisioned students, leaders of the world, strolling through the Halls of the Confucius Mansion, worshiping the ideals of peace and education. They would take back to their part of the world knowledge that the divergent threads of mankind can be woven into a single blanket that would warm and nurture mankind everywhere. Confucianism and the five virtues would be repeated everywhere:

Ren - Human-heartedness; Yi - Righteousness; Li - Propriety; Zhi - Wisdom; Xin -Sincerity or Good Faith. In politics, they stress the moral importance of human relationships, and in its last analysis, virtue alone constitutes the ultimate goal of man.

We returned to Kunming, convinced that the Immortals had directed the decision of Deng Xiaoping.

3

VOYAGE OF THE SHALIMAR

KONG FENG WA

The Master said, *There are three things constantly on the lips of the gentleman: A man of benevolence never worries; a man of wisdom is never in two minds; a man of courage is never afraid.*

Today is the third of January. The *Shalimar* is to sail from her home port of Eden, through the straits of Hormuz and into the Arabian Sea. Our voyage will take us through the Indian Ocean and then to the South Pacific to the archipelago of Fiji.

Shalimar suggested I come aboard early with her to enjoy the boarding show. She brought three of her Filipino group, giggling and excited about the trip. The Greek coxswain on the launch took us out to the ship and tried to joke with the girls.

"There will be no fraternization, ladies. If I catch anyone of you cozying up to the crew, out you go, back to Manila. As for you, young man," addressing the sailor, "my troupe is strictly off-limits. You pay attention to your duties or the Captain will hear about it."

Shalimar led us below decks, getting her cluster settled. The three girls had one cabin to sleep in and another in which to store the mountain of costumes and paraphernalia they would need for the performances. Shalimar's cabin was next to the aft quarters of the Sheikh, and mine was directly across from hers.

"I arranged it this way, so you can slip over without the whole ship knowing about it. Now let's go topside and watch the rest of the entourage come aboard."

From the bridge, we watched the Captain greet the guests at the boarding ladder below us. Shalimar began a running commentary. "Captain Nicholas Palentafolous, a very capable sailor, you'll meet him officially later. Arriving is Abdullah, the Minister of Finance, and Assiz, the Minister of Security and State, you know them both. They bring two wives each. The women will share two cabins. The men have individual cabins."

The two ministers boarded first, ignoring their women and the pile of luggage. They barely acknowledged the Captain's salute and welcome, hurrying below. "Those two have plot-hatching time. They've been running around in circles ever since the Sheikh decided to bid for the Jade. I heard they're having trouble raising the cash Arum wanted."

Shalimar leaned over in a conspirator's pose. "If they could, they would steal the Jade and sell it back to the Emir themselves."

"Shalimar, do you ever get weary of the Palace intrigue?"

Laughing, she lifted the brim of the big sun hat she was wearing. Her green eyes, intensified by the bright sun, sparkled. "No, my young friend, the challenge, the game, being an insider, is my life's blood. One day I'll disappear, I hope of my own accord, but in the meantime, I love it."

A launch arrived with four more women dressed in their abaayas, eyes peeking through the shrouds. "They must be the harem contingent. Will they stay in seclusion during the trip?"

Shalimar answered. "They share two of the cabins and will team up with the other four wives of the ministers. They will stay in the inside lounge area, talking incessantly. I've listened to them for hours, and still don't know what they talk about. They try to outdo each other in claims about offspring and relationships with the Sheikh."

"Here comes Mustafi, with the working staff. They're Ceylonese and Filipinos, who will prepare the food, and clean up after the family."

The last group to arrive consisted of Arum, the Sheikh, and his sons Ahmed and Rashid. "Are Ahmed and Rashid the real favorites, Shalimar? Ahmed was a mess the last time I was here, and I really haven't gotten to know Rashid."

"They are the first and second born, thus favored. Ahmed continually worries about inheriting the throne, and someone getting in front of him. Frankly, I don't trust him at all. Rashid, on the other hand is an egg-head, very intelligent. He's an electronics wizard, educated by your finest schools. Rashid is okay, but Ahmed keeps him under his wing. They team up against the other brothers and sisters. How Arum puts up with them, I don't know. Just watch out for all of them. Selfishness, greed, and jealousy, combined with vicious personalities, are a bad mixture."

The Captain met the Sheikh at the landing, and they both came up to the bridge, acknowledging our presence with a nod. Within minutes, the anchor-winch started. The crew scrambled at the succession of orders coming over the intercoms. We could feel the engines rumbling below. The propellers bit the water; the ship gained headway slowly and headed out into the gulf. Shalimar disappeared after Arum and his sons came aboard. It was then that Ahmed came up to join me on the bridge.

"Prince Ahmed, thank you for meeting me at the airport last night. My previous visit ended with rancor on your part. I hope your anger has subsided, and that we can resume our friendship."

"I allowed the inner problems of the Palace to affect our relationship, David. It was unforgivable of me to remonstrate publicly about my father and Shalimar. You'll accept my apology, I hope?"

"For one of your position, Your Highness, an apology is unnecessary. Let's assume the happening was an insignificant aberration. Is your father in good health? I was unable to have an audience with him after my arrival."

Smiling, Ahmed replied, "Father is in excellent health, and regained a dozen years of age in anticipation of this voyage. It took a whole day to decide which four wives were to accompany him. The harem is still in an uproar over the selection."

"I guess that would be a problem. Was there the usual addition to the harem this year?"

"After you left, David, during the Islamic New Year on the 13th of August, Sheikh Arum ibn Muhammad al Parad took his sixty-fourth wife. According to Erik, the keeper of the records, I have three brothers and one hundred and two stepbrothers. There are also fifty-four nephews, and, with the latest birth yesterday, sixteen grand-nephews. Our family continues to grow."

"You don't count girls, do you Ahmed? I understand there are some pretty smart women amongst the female offspring. My wife has met a couple of them at school."

"Why should I keep track of them? They are of no importance, except for making alliances with other cousins and families. My foolish father has allowed a few of them to travel to the United States, unchaperoned. They discard their abaaya, uncover their faces, show their legs to infidels and dress in western clothes. It's against the instructions of the Quran, blasphemy, a sinful way to live."

"I disagree with you, Ahmed. Our belief is that women should have the same opportunities for quality of life as men. You shroud their bodies and pen them as animals to breed and service you."

Ahmed started to screw up his face in anger. I watched the effort he made to get himself back under control. "Enough of that, David. You will never understand. What of the rare treasure we are seeking? Can you tell me what it is, our exact destination, and who will be there?"

"Sorry, Ahmed. As before, my instructions are to talk only to the Emir. I can say, we expect to get the Sheikh to Fiji by the first of February. I'm hoping to enjoy this trip, visit a few places I haven't been before and relay any messages that come my way. The Ambassador has given me leave to sail with the Emir in the interest of good relations with the Emirate."

Ahmed bridled, and his face tightened with anger; he could no longer control himself. "You aren't going to confide in me, are you, David Kong? One day you'll regret this. When I'm Emir, I'll know who my friends are." Turning his back, he went down the ladder to the deck below. It was the second time he had used the phrase, 'when I'm Emir'.

I went over to pay my respects to the Sheikh. His regal profile fascinated me. A long nose, sensual lips and a strong chin outlined by the flowing gutra over the kefiya head covering were impressive. A gold agal, banding the head-covering, glistened in the sun, sparkling with tiny gemstones. His pure white dish dasha, blowing majestically in the breeze Lawrence of Arabia-style, completed my quixotic mood.

"Good afternoon, Your Highness. Technically, as a visiting diplomat, I should present my credentials and ask for an audience. Please excuse the informal approach. I'm enjoying your superb ship and looking forward to the excitement of the next few weeks."

"Consider the formalities attended to. May Allah bless this voyage, David Kong. Your message started this chain of events. I acknowledge your dual role. You have attracted much attention aboard this ship, my young friend. First Shalimar was at your side, then Ahmed. They are adversaries, yet both sought your company?"

"Like Allah, you are all-seeing, Your Highness. Remember, I'm a schooled diplomat, taught to hold my tongue and tune my ears."

"My son went to the same schools you did, but that basic fact escaped him. Would you care to tell me why?"

"Learning from our teachers is a habit of the Chinese, Sheikh Arum. We're imbued with it, a Confucian philosophy. The difference in our culture is a logical explanation."

"The desert is a hard place to exist in, my young friend, unless you know its secrets. Survival is an instinct we are born with. It's difficult for me to criticize those traits in my son. I have always loved to ride through the land, taking my direction from the sun, stars, and contours of the dunes. It's thrilling to come upon an oasis and bed down for the night by a campfire. I know I am in the middle of a sea of sand, quite like the oceans we are embarking on now.

"The desert is similar to the oceans, with the stars at night to guide and comfort. When the winds blow, the sea erupts and so does the desert. The sand is as blinding and dangerous as any hurricane on the waters. My son Ahmed has to survive in the sea of filial competitors I have sired. I watch to see if he has the ability to lead and command the lands of the Paradi one day.

"Ahmed is my first born, conceived in love in a tent in the desert. There is a special relationship of a first born son to man. There is a need to continue life, you call it longevity."

"I understand, Your Highness. What of our plans, have you given more thought to the Confucius Jade?"

"Your family's treasure has been on my mind constantly. The Shou Xing Laos have come into my dreams twice. We're getting to know each other, as if they guide my destiny. Somehow I feel myself following blindly the visions of the Jade, like the Holy Grail pursued by the knights of King Arthur's court. My courtiers question me about the quest. I answered that in only a few weeks from now, we will be in the South Pacific, competing with the others who have had the same vision.

"The Shou Xing Laos beckon, and so far Allah has not seen fit to interfere with the pilgrimage, as I choose to call it."

The call to prayer came over the ship's loudspeaker. "Please excuse me, I must go. We will meet for dinner on the after deck. Shalimar has promised entertainment for the evening."

4

VOYAGE OF THE GOSSAMER GOSSETT

KONG KAI TAI

The Master said, *Artful words will ruin one's virtue; the lack of self-restraint in small matters will bring ruin to great plans.*

My name is Kong Kai Tai. I am on my way to meet Anthony Gossett at the Gold Coast in Australia. We are to sail on board the *Gossamer Gossett* on its voyage to the Fiji Islands.

Two nights before I left Hong Kong to join the ship, I had a dream. I remembered every detail. Tony and I were on a white sandy beach, palm trees waving in the breeze. The surf rolled in and out over our legs. A green figure emerged from the sea at our feet. The Shou Xing Lao, shiny head gleaming in the sun, flowing robe and long beard dripping sea water. The dragon-head staff in his right hand waved in greeting. He offered a peach with his left. As the spray cleared around him, a slender crane walked delicately on its long stilt-like legs on one side of him. A small spotted deer leaped gracefully through the surf on the other. The light of the full moon passing through the figure, giving it an ethereal quality of liquid emerald. Shou Xing Lao grew until he was life-sized. The fine lines of the venerable face became crystal clear. Full, round cheeks supported eyes that crinkled in the corners and sparkled as he looked straight into my eyes. He raised the staff, and the dragon carved at the top breathed fire.

A gentle voice spoke. "We offer you and the generations to follow long life. May you have many sons and daughters. Guard your friend. Competitors are evil and jealous. One close to him has a lust for power. There are others with visions of greed. Eat our peaches for good health, commune with the other Immortals for wisdom and tranquility."

I tried to say something, ask a question, but the struggle for communication woke me up, wet with perspiration. White, gritty sand became a smooth white sheet beneath me. The strangest part was, I saw only one figure.

The helicopter circled the marina. Tony pointed out the sprawling Mirage Hotel, with its lagoons and the long, windswept, sandy shoreline. Inside the peninsula, pleasure boats lined the slots like toys. A four-masted schooner, larger than any of the others, berthed at the pier. From 1000 feet up, we could see a pile of supplies alongside, with tiny figures carrying them up the gangplank.

"The *Gossamer*," Tony said. "Largest sailing yacht in the marina. One hundred sixty-and-a-half feet long with a thirty-foot beam. Your home for the next six weeks, angel."

He hadn't let go of my arm or hand since meeting me in the Brisbane Airport. Without luggage and the helicopter waiting, we were aloft ten minutes after I landed. The welcoming hug and kiss left me a little disturbed. It was more perfunctory than warm. As soon as we were airborne, I looked up at the craggy face and said, "What's wrong, Tony?"

At first he tried to brush me off, saying nothing, holding my hand tight, turning it up and down nervously. "Nothing's wrong." He thought a minute, and then, resigned, shook his head. "Yes, something is wrong. I don't believe in dreams, never tried to remember them. Two nights ago, I had a dream, so vivid that even now, I can recall every moment."

"Tell me, Tony. Maybe getting it out will help."

He spilled out an emotional torrent that I couldn't stop. "You and I were on this long white sand beach, with a full moon shining. I saw palm trees, felt the warm breeze behind us. We were tickling each other, our feet at the edge of the water. Then a figure walked out of the surf, the Confucius Jade of course. It's been on my mind constantly since the video."

"Tony, hold it a minute. Can you remember which hand held the staff or on which side the crane was walking?"

"That's a strange question. Let me think for a minute. Sure. The figure was facing me, and you were on my left. As he walked toward me, the staff was on my right, as well as the crane."

"That's just it, Tony, the other one appeared in my dream or visitation, whatever it was. Did he talk to you?"

"That's what has me so worried. He said there's danger. Someone close to me is going to cause trouble. Others intended physical harm to me and a loved one. I'm worried."

We looked at each other, realizing what had happened. Tony brightened, apparently relieved. We would face the dangers together.

We landed within sight of the ship. Tony jumped out first. He gave me a hand down the steps, bending low to avoid the propeller blades. I could see a scramble of white uniforms and bare legs at the gangplank as we walked over.

I gasped, "You didn't tell me how big she is."

"You mean the boat, or the skipper?" he said, laughing.

"The boat, you goose, she's beautiful. I've never been aboard a sailing vessel this large. You may never get me off."

"No arguments about that, angel. You can stay as long as you want. The only problem you may have is sharing the tiny cabin with me. It does get cramped at times."

"I'll bet it's tiny. If I know your personality, it probably has a waterbed, steam room and dance floor."

"H'mm, never thought about a dance floor, but I guess we could clear a few square feet, if you like, for some good 'ole country-western foot stompin'. C'mon now darlin', let's meet the crew."

A bosun's pipe sounded its high pitched whistle as we boarded. Tony introduced the line up. "Captain Maurine Flauknet. Captain, this is my guest, Kaytee Kong."

"Welcome aboard, Ms. Kong, may I present my Executive Officer, Jenny Frobush, and the crew of the *Gossamer*."

I couldn't help staring at the woman. Captain Flauknet was almost as tall as Tony. A gold braid-encrusted officer's cap was cocked over one side of the long blond hair braided at the back of her head. As Tony had said, she was an incarnation of a Viking goddess, wearing brief white shorts, accenting long, tanned legs. A white shirt with gold epaulets tucked into the waistband of the shorts covered, but did nothing to hide, her feminine contours. Next to her stood Jenny, ranking second in gold braid, smaller, chunkier, a sharp contrast in size. The three 'decides', as Tony called them, wore sailor's middy blouses and denim mini-shorts.

We passed a group of Japanese tourists as Jenny 'piped' us aboard. I noticed their cameras clicking, recording the show. From the corner of my eye, I saw one with a video camera slowly sweep the ship from stem to stern. To my eye, he looked professional. I shrugged it off, more interested in greeting the crew.

"The decides are Josie, Annie, and Sakdi," Tony said. "We recruited Josie and Annie from the topsail schooner, Lindo, out of Saint Thomas. Sakdi is originally from Bangkok, our physical therapy and exercise leader."

We went toward the rear of the boat. Tony gave me a running commentary of the technical equipment, life boats, and Captain's gig. I was too tired to understand the explanations.

"I have errands to do ashore, angel. Why don't you take a bath and get some rest? Would you like Sakdi to give you a massage before you go to sleep? It will help you relax."

"Sounds terrific to me. I want to be fresh for the evening."

Tony went over to the wall speaker and flipped a switch. "Sakdi here, sir."

"Sakdi, I'm going ashore. Please come to the aft cabin and see that Ms. Kong gets bathed, massaged and put to sleep?"

"Aye, aye sir, leave it to me."

The rest of the afternoon was a dreamy blur, hard for me to separate reality from illusion. Tired from the long trip from Hong Kong, begun at least twenty-four hours before, I let myself go in the expert hands of the Thai woman. I remember Tony leaving and Sakdi coming in. Moments later, clothes stripped off, I was in a hot tub, sponged down and buried in soap suds.

"Just lie back and relax, Ms. Kong. Let me do the work." Her hands worked expertly from my toes to my head, cleansing every pore and crevice. Drowsily I felt her shampoo my hair.

Sakdi scrubbed off my make-up. "You won't need any of this goo, Ms. Kong. I have creams and lotions that will make you shine and look natural."

Finally she rinsed with the hand spray, emptying the tub. Then the warm feeling of water came seeping up again, until I was soaking in clear water. There was a low rumble, and the Jacuzzi jets in the tub began their soft massage. I gave myself up to the drowsiness, barely conscious of being helped out of the tub later, wrapped in warm towels and walked to the bed.

"We won't do much therapeutics, Ms Kong. That's it, just stretch out on your stomach, go to sleep if you like."

"Time to get up, honey, or you'll miss the sunset." Still deliciously sleepy, I murmured something and tried to snuggle back under the sheets. The rumble of the boat's motors and Tony's jostling forced me up very slowly.

"Don't look at me like that, Tony. I'm sure you've had naked women in your bed before. Go on out. Let me wake up, comb my hair and I'll meet you topside in a couple of minutes."

I found fresh undies in the drawer. Sakdi had laid out white cotton slacks which fit perfectly, and a colorful Ken Done sweat shirt. Tony had delegated the local shops of the Mirage Marina to supply a complete wardrobe for me. Even the canvas deck shoes fit my 4AAA perfectly.

Climbing to the bridge, I found Tony with the captain. We were motoring out of the narrow channel towards the bay. Maurine had the wheel and was talking to the speaker overhead. "Look alive now, Jenny, ready to hoist sail as soon as we clear the channel."

"Aye, aye, skipper, all ready on the foredeck." I saw her on the bow, standing by a stanchion talking into a head mike.

Tony explained. "We are a four-masted, square-sailed, schooner. This fellow Arthur Holgate, in Capetown, built a similar boat called the *Antares,* about two-thirds the size of the Gossamer. He uniquely conceived and designed it for a crew of three or even less if occasion demanded.

"Holgate sailed the *Antares*, single-handed, from the Cape of Good Hope to the Caribbean. When he arrived at Virgin Gorda, disbelieving immigration authorities accused Holgate of smuggling a crew ashore. Arthur took them out to sea, proving he could manage the steel schooner alone.

"I saw the *Antares* when sailing with the current owners, Cruises Antares, Ltd., and commissioned Holgate to build a larger one for me. The *Gossamer* carries nine thousand square feet of sail, auxiliary power by twin GMC three hundred sixty horsepower diesel engines."

"I don't know what a lot of that means, Tony, but I'm thrilled to be aboard."

"We can sail anywhere in the world. With the automatic windless equipment, we can be under full sail within ten minutes of the order. Watch as we stop the engines, and switch to wind power."

The Captain flicked toggles on the control board; the powered windlasses raised mammoth sails to catch the wind. The *Gossamer* slanted her deck and took off like a race horse, kicking up a foaming wake astern.

New Year's Eve was a whirlwind of local social activity, and then we headed out to sea. First port of call, Port Douglas on the Great Barrier Reef. We would be in Fijian waters in a month.

5

VOYAGE OF THE GOLDEN PEARL

⎯⎯∞∞∞⎯⎯

KONG AI MEI

The Master said, *To attack a task from the wrong end can do nothing but harm.*

I am Ai Mei Kong, representing the family of Confucius, on board the *Golden Pearl* sailing from Kobe, Japan to Fiji. As a gift for a very successful 'Year of the Pearl' promotion, Bloomingdales gave me six weeks paid vacation. The close quarters of a ship at sea made me an unwilling voyeur into the personal lives of the Kokomotos.

Nikko picked me up at Osaka airport. The drive to Kobe gave us a chance to gossip about the Kokomoto family. She made a statement that anchored itself in a back corner of my mind. I put it down to feminine wish talk at the time. "Riches and power in the hands of women could change the world."

This morning Nikko met me at the hotel for breakfast before proceeding to the pier. The *Golden Pearl* will sail at noon today, according to the schedule I received.

Before boarding, we walked slowly on the wharf, along the length of the ship. I had mixed feelings: the tingling fear of danger down my spine, repugnance at the war-like lines of the ship, and excitement at the thrill of adventure.

Nikko explained the craft's origin while we walked. "The *Golden Pearl* is one hundred and thirty-nine feet, designed by Andre Mauri, a Frenchman. The French firm of Chantiers Navals de l'Esterel, Cannes, built her. They are known for small, fast, naval craft equipped with the deadly Exocet Missiles."

A young man in a naval officer's uniform guarded the gangway. He checked our names off the passenger list and signaled a deck-hand to come down and take our luggage aboard. Another young ship's officer met us at the head of the boarding ladder. He saluted.

"Number six and number eight starboard side below, ladies. The sailor will escort you with your luggage. Miss Okusu, we have instructions that you are to have access to and command of the communications and security gear aboard. When you've settled, our comm-officer, Lt. Radin, will show you the equipment and how to use it."

"Thank you, Lieutenant. I'm familiar with every item in your installation."

I giggled at Nikko. "This is just like the navy. Are they always this formal?"

"You are in the navy, my friend. The Golden Pearl Navy, with Admiral Ru Kokomoto commanding. He will probably post a uniform-of-the-day for us during the voyage. Stow your gear, and get some warm clothes on quickly. We'll go topside to watch the noon parade."

My cabin, next to Nikko's, was larger than I expected, with twin bunks, a shower and toilet, desk and chairs. There were over and under storage drawers and bins for my clothes.

I grabbed a padded nylon windbreaker and joined Nikko in the gangway. "Nice. I'm surprised. It's so roomy."

We went up an interior spiral staircase, past the main deck, on by the second deck, and out onto the quarter-deck. "This is where all the action takes place, Ai Mei. Ahead is the Captain's quarters, the wheel house and communications center. We can watch for a while because all the officers are busy getting ready for the Admiral's arrival."

The ship's bell struck the noon hour. We saw three limousines drive up the wharf and stop at the ship's side. The loudspeaker sounded a shrill whistle. "All hands on deck, form up at the gangway ladder. Stand by to receive passengers."

There was a flurry of activity, feet pounded on ladders, sailors emerged from the hatches like ants from their ground hills. Two more officers joined the one at the head of the ladder. One had a lot of gold braid on his cap, epaulets and the sleeves of the great coat he wore.

"The older one is the captain. Next to him are the executive officer, second in command, and the three junior officers." Nikko explained as they took up position. Twenty seamen lined up in a double row opposite each other.

Ru Koko emerged from the first car, the door held open by the security guard jumping from the front seat. Stiff as a ramrod, the Admiral strode to the gangway, returned the salute from the deck officer there, and climbed the gangway.

At the Captain's command, "Pipe the Admiral aboard, bosun," he blew three short, three long, and three short blasts. Turning to his crew, the bosun barked out, "ten-shun."

"Hmm...they didn't check his name on the manifest." Nikko complained.

Following Ru Koko, like martinets, were Ichiban, Niban, and Sanban. A woman bundled up in a heavy trench coat, wearing a wide-brimmed hat, was the fourth person to emerge from the second car. The sons carried briefcases. The woman had a large carry-all purse over her shoulder. "That's our friend Yoko Kashimoto, under the big hat. She loves weird clothes."

The third limousine attracted the attention of the crews of the other ships, who were watching the scene. The first person to emerge I recognized as Nuki in ceremonial kimono and obi. Her hair, uncovered, was coiled high on her head with long ivory pins crossed inside the spiral. Her face, painted white, was exquisite, causing the audience to clap and cheer. The embroidered silk kimono moved forward, carrying the woman without a bob or ripple.

Pai Shan followed her, also traditionally dressed. Limousine attendants quickly emptied the cars of luggage onto the wharf. A brass-bound seaman's trunk and two white canvas sailor's seabags came from Ru Koko's vehicle. The second limousine disgorged a pile of nylon duffel bags of assorted colors. Nikko's luggage was obviously the battered leather one matching her shoulder case.

The Geisha's and her assistant's pile was the largest, with two chests, four full-sized suitcases, and two thick garment bags. All of the luggage was matched, and imprinted with entwined GY, the famed 'Gucci' pattern.

The entourage moved up the ladder, following their chief. "Permission to come aboard, Captain?" Ru Kokomoto said, as he set foot on deck. He saluted the flag of the Rising Sun and then saluted the captain. Returning the salute, the captain parroted, "Permission granted, sir, welcome aboard. The *Golden Pearl* is ready to sail on your orders, Admiral."

"I will join you on the bridge as soon as we get underway, Captain. Our first destination is Kagoshima. I'll require a continual weather report underway, and a seven-day forecast."

"Aye aye, sir." The captain saluted again, but Kokomoto had already turned, heading aft to the rear hatchway.

There was bedlam as the others came aboard. The bosun blew a short blast on his whistle. "Lively men, all hands to the cargo on the pier. Stack it in the saloon amidships. Passengers, please look to the executive officer for room assignments."

"Cabins five, six, and seven, sirs," he advised the three sons.

"If you are Miss Kashimoto, you are in number four."

The captain approached the two kimono-clad women standing away from the crowd waiting patiently for their turn. He bowed to the geisha, knowing their prestige and rank. "You honor us by your presence aboard. Please contact me personally if you need service. Your cabins are one and three. We have combined them to accommodate your luggage." He motioned to one of the sailors standing nearby, "Ahi is your steward. He'll show you to your cabin and explain the facilities at your disposal. Ahi is the only member of the crew allowed into Admiral Country, which includes your quarters. The steward station and small galley are the first deck above you."

Bowing slightly, Nuki answered, "Thank you for your courtesy, Captain. We are looking forward to a pleasant voyage."

"The loudspeaker blared, "All hands on deck, departure stations, on the double."

Admiral Kokomoto came up the ladder from below. Yoko and I both bowed, saying in unison, "Konichiwa."

"Welcome aboard, Ms. Kong. Please join me in my quarters, after we get underway."

The door chimed as I pushed the bell to the Admiral's cabin. A sign lit up. 'Enter.' A buzzer sounded, releasing the door catch. Kokomoto was engrossed in a naval chart laid out on the chart table. He looked up, pushed his chair back from the work area, and came over to greet me.

"Welcome to my modest quarters, Miss Kong. Hope you enjoy the facilities of the *Golden Pearl* and be comfortable during voyage. Are your quarters satisfactory?"

"Elegant, thank you, sir. It is my first sea voyage, and my good fortune to enjoy your hospitality. May I send a message to my family that we are at sea, proceeding on schedule?"

"Of course. Nikko will arrange any message you choose to send. Please avail yourself of any of our facilities.

"Come in, come in, let me show you around."

I slipped my shoes off in the carpeted entryway, the size of one tatami mat. It allowed for the swing of the doors and a place to remove footwear.

The chart table and desk area occupied the space of four mats to the right of the entrance. A bank of monitor screens was ranged above a panel of instruments.

"This is my work area. I can monitor the ship's most intimate corners, and Kobe headquarters. It duplicates the wheel-house equipment. Compass, depth finders, roll gauges, engine speed, fuel tank usage, and other performance recording equipment." On the desk alongside him were banks of switches and buttons controlling video screens, repeating from the bridge, saloon, engine room, forward of the ship's bow, aft from the fantail, and the passageways of the cabins. My mind lost the technical explanations as fast as he described them to me.

"Amazing to my non-technical eye, sir. I do hope there isn't a camera in my room that might inhibit me."

He laughed. I think it was the first time I saw him relax.

"Only at the telephone, Ms. Kong. You will find a disconnect switch if you don't choose to use the video system at the time the phone rings." I didn't believe a word of it, and vowed to check the room over for a hidden camera lens.

Kokomoto was in an ebullient mood, better than I had ever seen him before. He pranced and preened around, opening doors, showing the gadgets, proud as a peacock strutting around his peahens. A series of paneled screens separated the rear part of the cabin.

"The screens, inlaid with mother-of-pearl seascapes, were created especially for the *Golden Pearl,* by the artists in Yangzhou, China." A wall button started the panels sliding open, half to each side, shunting off on tracks, accordion stacking themselves.

The aft part of the cabin was another wonder. I gasped as my host stood back and let me take in the whole scene.

A ten-foot California redwood spa tub was in the center, with a raised deck around it to prevent the water from sloshing out. "It's moving," I said, as the ship rolled, almost tumbling me off the step I was standing on.

"No." Ru Koko explained. "The ship rolled, but the tub stayed level. It's mounted on gimbals, quite a sensation when you are in it during a heavy sea."

On one side was a washing area with a tile floor. It was equipped with small stools, wooden tubs, spigots, a hand-held showerhead, trays of soap, shaving gear, hair shampooing oils and colognes. A stack of the small towels used for semi-concealment of the private parts, and taking excess moisture off, were on a rack clip. Sluices drained off the water.

"A steam cabinet, massage mats, exercise equipment, complete health center. And that's not all." Ru Koko said, as he flipped yet another toggle switch. Two six-by-six-foot panels rolled back from the rear bulkhead, revealing, behind a glass bulkhead, the wake behind the ship churning the water in a deep V. It looked so close that I thought for a moment the sea could come in and drown us.

"My home at sea, Ms. Kong."

He broke the spell. "Have you heard anything additional from your family?"

I spoke in Japanese to make the association more intimate. "No, Mr. Kokomoto, I've received no messages. They expect me to contact them once a week at a certain time to advise them of the ship's progress. Can you tell me why you brought your sons aboard? They appear disenchanted and unhappy."

The boyish grin left his face to be replaced by a stern visage, implacable, Ru Kokomoto. His shoulders slumped and his stride slowed as he went over to the intercom. Flipping a toggle, he spoke softly into the speaker, "Pai Shan, tea please." A moment later the door opened without him releasing the lock. The women had open access to his quarters. The kimono-clad beauty bowed low, silently heated water, and prepared a tray.

Ru Kokomoto took up a lotus position on a mat in the middle of the cabin. I sat on bent knees facing him, not saying a word. Pai Shan set up a small folding table, served the tea, and quickly left us alone.

"My sons worry me, Miss Kong. They confront the evils of modernization that Japan has sought. Contrasting is tradition of our family, samurai, once trusted warriors of Emperor. I, Kokomoto, have wealth and power beyond my dreams.

"Every material object is mine, if I care to own it. Sensual pleasures are a part of my life. The Shinto Gods have seen fit to bless me with three sons, longevity of the Kokomoto lineage.

"You ask me why my sons are depressed. I am responsible. The blame rests on my shoulders, as well as the responsibility to rehabilitate them. I must try to save this generation for I may not live long enough to save the next. I will try to turn Ichiban from the drugs and crime involving him.

"Second son, Nu, must give up his infatuation with the woman Yoko. He will marry a samurai daughter and raise Kokomoto grandchildren. Sanban is weak, immersed in his electronic world. Maturity may take a few more years. I pray for him."

Ru Koko paused, sipped a cup of tea. I sensed that confession was difficult for this samurai warrior.

"I bring my sons with me. I hope that the Shou Xing Laos will help me, once they are in my hands.

"The Confucius Jade Immortals have visited me twice in strange places, at curious times. I recall their visits vividly. They warned me against evil within my own circle. Their admonitions do not leave me."

Ru Koko closed his eyes in meditation. I rose quietly and left the cabin.

6

THE SHALIMAR – BOMBAY, INDIA

——⊸❀⊷——

KONG FENG WA

"The Triumphal Arch, Gateway to India, on the Apollo Bundar," the Captain announced. Sheikh Arum, Shalimar, and I stood with Captain Palentofolus on the quarter deck, as the *Shalimar* entered the channels leading to the Indian port of Bombay.

The captain gave us some background. "Bombay has a fine harbor, used in trade for thousands of years. They built the arch seventy-eight years ago to commemorate the visit of George the Fifth, the British Monarch, Ruler of India at the time."

"Will we dock, Captain, or anchor and go in by launch?" Arum asked.

"Dock, Your Highness. We hoisted colors indicating your presence aboard, and also communicated that information to the Immigration and Customs ashore in Bombay. They'll send out a contingent to inspect us, and stamp our passports as the pilot takes us into the pier."

"Message from shore, Captain," the radioman said as he came up to the captain, saluted and returned to his post.

"It is for you, Your Highness." He handed the message over.

"Interesting. It looks like I won't be entertaining you at the Taj Mahal Hotel, like we planned. The prime minister happens to be in Bombay and has invited me to spend the day with him. A car will be at the pier when we dock.

"Send a reply, Captain. Express my thanks and say that I consider it an honor to join the prime minister.

"Shalimar, David, you'll have to do without my company today. Please enjoy yourselves. I'm sure the Taj Mahal Hotel desk will advise you of points of interest in the city. Years ago, before I assumed the throne, I enjoyed wandering the streets, visiting the bazaars, and bargaining for gems. Unfortunately, I won't have the same opportunity today. Protocol calls."

The Sheikh went below. The captain turned to the bridge. "All engines stopped. Lay to. Stand by the gangway to board the pilot and customs people." The staccato of orders sounded over the speaker.

We watched the Indian Navy patrol boat cut the water toward us. "We're getting royal treatment," the captain said. "The last time I anchored in this harbor, they sent a tug with a very disagreeable immigration officer." The captain then spoke into the intercom. "All passengers and crew intending to go ashore, please go aft to the saloon and bring your passports. The Immigration officials will board to grant you visas soon. The *Shalimar* sails at fourteen hundred hours tomorrow. It would be wise if everyone returned to the vessel tonight. We won't have time to search for you in the morning. The port watch has the duty."

I walked aft with Shalimar. "Shalimar, have you heard any more about the ministers and sons squabbling with the Sheikh?"

"David, what I've heard doesn't bode well. Arum is very introspective about it. He doesn't want to take any action himself, preferring to wait them out. The ministers are working on Ahmed to overthrow his father. The strangest part of the whole situation is what one of my girls overheard one night.

"She sneaked out to meet one of the sailors on the foredeck. They were going at it hot and heavy, concealed inside the launch, on the davits. She recognized the voices of Arum's two brothers.

"The Jade affair has Arum dazed and disoriented. There is something in its value worth far more than the billion dollars he has instructed me to accumulate. For the first time since he became Emir, his guard is down. Mustafi no longer sleeps at his doorway. The personal guard detail remained in Eden. It's the chance we've been waiting for.'

"Allah be praised, we can't murder him as he did our brothers. Times have changed. The people have grown to love him. Most of the Palace family are fiercely loyal. If anything happened to the Emir, they'd suspect us first.'

"We don't do it, penis of the camel. It has to look like an accident. Prince Ahmed must do it. That way we have a hold over him, and can control the country our way. Let me work on Ahmed. He's been trying to get one of those Filipino whores into his cabin. They've all sent him packing, and threatened to tell Shalimar if he tries again.

"I know Ahmed is plotting with Rashid also, and has lost millions of dollars, gambling at Monaco. He wouldn't like that information to get back to his father.

"He fears Shalimar as much as his father. The Red Witch is another date pit caught in my craw. Someday I'll get to her, off the ship or out of Parad, and give her what she deserves.'

"What may that be, my frustrated brother? Aren't your wives parting their legs enough for you these nights on board?'

"My wives are like yours. Their breasts hang like dung bags. They lie as stiff as dead fish, and smell about the same. Limiting us to two wives while Arum has sixty will be one of the first laws we'll change when we come into power. In the meantime, I'll find out how angry our young nephew really is. There is one other thought. The Jade may be worth more than the throne."

I broke in at that point. "Shalimar, how did you get the girl to tell you?"

"She is frightened of the ministers and Ahmed. They calling her a whore made her very angry. That's why she confessed her love affair to me.

"I gave her permission to meet with her lover, if she agreed to hide in the launch every night, and listen for me. The plotters think Mustafi bugged their cabins, therefore must meet outside.

"I suggested Mustafi do that when we sailed, but Arum nixed the idea."

"What happened at the next meeting?" I asked. "This is like reading a murder mystery by Agatha Christie. Which brother is the leader?"

"The girl couldn't identify which minister. She recognized Ahmed's voice though, because he keeps trying to get her in his cabin. One met the next night with Ahmed. The minister put a lot of heat on, first by persuading, then by threatening him. He tried to build up Ahmed's vision of being the Emir with all that power and money. At one time my girl thought Ahmed would agree. Finally, after an hour of prodding, Ahmed admitted, 'I fear revenge. Allah is in league with the Confucius Jade and the combination is too powerful to chance their fury. It's better to wait until a real accident happens.'

"David, you'll never guess what happened next. The sacrificial lamb attacked the lion. Ahmed is smarter than his uncle gave him credit for. He told uncle to leave the ship at Bombay or he would tell his father of the plot."

"So, which one are we losing, old money bags uncle, or the foreign intrigue one?"

"The Security Minister, Assiz, is leaving. I saw his bag packed, left outside his cabin door. He made some lame excuse to the Sheikh about being seasick."

Assiz waited imperiously by the gangway. He ordered a seaman to bring his bag and followed his brother Abdullah off the ship. They walked arm in arm up the pier to a waiting taxi, heads huddled in conversation.

It was a full day, and a full night, as much of it as I can remember. I recall the gangway ladder wobbling. A friendly seaman held either me or it still enough so I could get aboard. They taught diplomats to drink lightly. This time I was not working, and I lost control. My foggy brain recorded assistance from a red headed lady. She laughed at me, stumbling down the ladder to my cabin. I think she put me to bed.

The next morning, I, or the ship, was spinning around. I awoke naked amid the rumpled sheets. Somehow, I managed to get shorts and a tee-shirt on, find the saloon, and get some coffee with a dry croissant. Shalimar came in a few minutes later, fresh as a pink flower. With a wink of a very long, red eyelash, and a smile that showed every dimple, she said, "Hi."

"Not so loud, please. What's that supposed to mean? Did I do something awful last night? Whatever it was, I did wind up in my own bunk, though I don't remember taking my clothes off."

"You didn't. Chinese don't have much body hair, do they?"

"I'm sorry to have missed out on all the fun. I do hope you gave me a shower before you put me to bed, and took care of whatever else I needed."

"With all you had to drink, my young friend, I have to disillusion you. Your bamboo rod was as limp as a windsock on an airless day. It was interesting to get to know you, though, another entry for my diary. I will write your wife a note, advising her that you are excellent company and still monogamous."

Ahmed came in, looking no better than I. He nodded and went off into a corner to hold his head. Rashid followed him a few minutes later, cheerful and cordial, stopping at our table. "Wasn't the museum wonderful? I stayed until they closed. Did you hear all the noise coming from the captain's cabin last night, Shalimar? I wonder what was going on in there."

"Just keep wondering, Rashid. Everything was all right, just my night to take care of putting people to bed." She turned to me. "The three girls were in the captain's cabin, competing for prizes in belly dancing, or so they said. The prize was our Greek stud Palentofolus. I finally got them out after promising the skipper I would come back myself. I didn't keep my promise, so we may have lost one of our supporters."

"Oh well, shore leave, c'est l'guerre, Bombay. I hope the crew are all aboard. We are due to sail at fourteen hundred for Goa." I grinned at Shalimar, waved to Ahmed, and went back to my bunk to see if the ship would stop spinning and my stomach settle down.

Our next port of call: Goa, and the old Portuguese settlement at Fort Aguade. The Indians of this state are very proud of their heritage, and call themselves Goans, not Indians. There was no riotous shore leave at Fort Aguade. The weather was rainy and miserable. Arum ordered us on to the Maldives and Sri Lanka. From Colombo, we sailed through the Malaccan Straits and tied up in Singapore for a few days, our halfway mark.

Rashid and Ahmed constantly played chess on the afterdeck in a corner away from us. They were occasionally sociable, but often preferred to be alone. Abdullah, the Finance Minister, paced the deck above us. He disappeared into the communications shack several times a day. Arum spent most of his time on the quarterdeck and bridge, enjoying the mechanics of the ship, plotting position on the charts, studying weather reports. Each evening the men gathered around the oasis for dinner and the entertainment provided by Shalimar's sensual troupe.

Every Monday I made my transmission to the family in Hong Kong for relay to San Francisco. I heard nothing in reply, except an acknowledgement of my report.

The Sheikh had been strangely quiet since his brother jumped ship at Bombay. He was aware of the plot, even before Shalimar and I informed him of what we knew. Maybe it was intuition or another source of information. We noticed only the briefest contact between Arum and his family.

Shalimar and I were on the afterdeck, playing backgammon by the oasis. It was a perfect day at sea. There was enough breeze to keep the sails full and us cool at the same time. The quiet of sailing without engines creates a peace and contentment. I felt the call of the sailors' love of the oceans. The only sound disturbing the silence was the constant gossiping of the ship's harem in the saloon. Settling down to shipboard routines, the Filipino girls used the forward deck, rigged with a canvas awning. Mustafi and the Palace staff preferred the air-conditioned midships saloon. We rarely saw them except when it was time to dine.

Shalimar and I, absorbed in our game, didn't see or hear the Sheikh approach. The shadow across the board made us aware of another presence. He waved us back into our lounge chairs as we tried to get up to greet him properly. "Sit, sit, my friends. May I join you?"

"If you have any Singapore dollars, Your Highness, we will allow you to compete in our game. According to our navigator, the good captain, we'll be dropping anchor in Singapore harbor just after dawn tomorrow."

"Your financial requirements are too strict, and besides, I would not want to embarrass you with my prowess at this game. I'm the champion of my London club, rarely beaten by amateurs like yourselves."

Shalimar and I looked at each other, back at Arum's smiling face, and then to each other again. She said, "Your Highness, with a challenge like that, how could mere amateurs like ourselves resist? Please join us. How much would you risk on your reputation? Is the Royal Treasury solvent?"

I spoke up, "May this humble and poor Chinese boy suggest a mere pittance of one Singapore dollar per point. On a diplomat's modest salary, I could never risk the funds that you two wealthy personages could. Winner stays with the board, and a roll of the dice determines the first two players?"

"Agreed," Arum said. When the call to prayer comes, I'll pray for forgiveness for my sin of gambling."

We began playing, Shalimar and the Sheikh rolling high for the first contest. Shalimar played the game offensively, aggressively, knocking her opponent off the board at every possible opportunity, regardless of self-exposure. Arum was a skilful player, believing in position, counting the odds and doubling the bet only when he had an advantage. Shalimar simply doubled at whim, saying she had a hunch on the next roll.

"What have you heard, my friends?" Arum said quietly, as if talking about the game. Are there any new cabals forming around me?"

Shalimar answered for us. "It's strange, Your Highness, the tents are closed tight. There is little emanating from them. Abdullah communicates daily with garbled messages to Assiz.

"As for your sons, they talk for many hours each night on the foredeck. It's dreams they speak of, the changes they would make in the Emirate, uncles to dispose of, brothers and sisters used or rendered impotent. Rashid is weak and easily led. May I ask what sand Mustafi has stirred?"

"Not as much as you. Mustafi works well in the passageways of the Palace. Onboard ship it's more difficult for him, as the shadows do not hide his bulk. And you, David, is there any report from your family?"

"There has been a consistent badgering of Uncle Sam by a persistent journalist from one of the business magazines. He has heard rumors of the Kong family negotiating the sale of a rare treasure. A Wall Street Journal reporter wrote an article about certain Arab equity holdings being liquidated, forcing a sell-off last week. The market fell seventy-two points in one day, then recovered partially the next. I assume that plans are on schedule, and the Confucius Jade is en route to the same destination we are, or I would have been advised. May I be so bold as to ask if your brother, Abdullah, has provided you the funds you requested?"

"Oh, how providential of Allah to grant me this roll of double fours, even though He doesn't approve of gambling. Shalimar, you are now in a very difficult position, my corral points are covered, and you have two men dispossessed. It looks like I might gammon you, and with thirty-two already on the doubling dice, you stand to lose sixty-four Singapore dollars.

"Winning that bet should give me enough funds to cover all eventualities, David, to answer your question."

"I understand, Your Highness. It's comforting to know there are double wells under the oasis. Now Shalimar, hurry up and concede so that I may have my chance at the board."

"Well, just look at that, in bearing-off you've left a blot on your six point, Your Highness. My crystal ball reveals that I will return to the board with double sixes. Tell you what, I'm going to double to sixty-four and roll the boxcars, as the gamblers call them. If I succeed, you'll be on the bar, and I'll be the aggressor. As a matter of protocol, however, I wish you would refer to my markers as women, not men."

She rolled double sixes. Shalimar was out on the board with both of her 'women' and the Sheikh rolled nothing but ones and twos for the next six rolls. Unable to come onto the board, he barely escaped being gammoned himself.

The three of us were on the quarterdeck at dawn the next morning, as the towers of Singapore, the Lion City, came into view. A pilot tug came out to greet us, with customs officials aboard. It was a courtesy to the personal appearance of a foreign potentate. They cleared us en route, and the *Shalimar* went right into the wharf.

I stood with the captain on the bridge wing as we edged in for docking, enjoying the procedures. "Let go forward lead line," he ordered with the bull horn. A line with a leaded ball at the tip flew through the air to the dock, followed by the hawser pulled in and looped over the bollard. The bow officer signaled and a windlass began to tighten up on the hawser, bringing the bow close to the pier. "Let go aft lead line," the captain ordered. The aft hawser was soon pulling the rear of the ship in. "Double up the midships lines." Crisscrossing the ship's midsection, safety lines fore and aft secured the *Shalimar*.

A shore party moved a gangway over to our main deck level. The executive officer took up position.

The customs official that boarded us in the channel had stamped a visa entry in all of our passports, and everyone was ready to go the minute the ladder was down. Abdullah was the first one off. A taxi pulled up, opening a door for him. I could see another person inside through the rear window as the vehicle pulled away. The bulky figure looked to be a twin shape to Abdullah. Assiz was still in the game. Ahmed and Rashid walked down the wharf, arm in arm, their white robes looking incongruous in the Asian ambience.

"Goodbye, David, have a pleasant day," Shalimar waved as she went down with her three girls. "We are going to shop all day long. We'll be at the Shangri-La Hotel on Orange Grove Road about seven o'clock if you want to meet us. We're staying there while in port, and will be eating Chinese at the Shang Palace in the hotel. I'm giving the troupe a high-class fling."

A tour bus drove up next to the ship, and a pert young lady came aboard. "Lion tours to pick up a group of eight ladies from the *Shalimar*," I heard her say to the officer. The captain came up alongside me, and explained. "I have arranged a tour for the harem. Mr. Lee, the prime minister, sent his personal car for the Emir. They are conferring about a joint venture while he is here. That leaves you, Mr. Kong, what are your plans?"

"Captain, I'm very fortunate. A cousin of mine, who lives in New York, happens to be here on a work assignment. He promised to show me around. I'll be back aboard before we sail. Seventy-two hours, I understand, is that correct?"

"Yes sir, at fourteen hundred hours as usual, three days from now. There will be a skeleton crew aboard while we are here. Please leave a contact number, in case there is a change of plans."

The facsimile message from my cousin Scot was a little strange, in that I'd never told him where I was going. I didn't know his firm had clients in Singapore. There must be a simple answer for the coincidence of his job assignment and how he knew I would be here these three days. Uncle Wei Tang would have to be advised. He had warned us to report any unusual happening, no matter how trivial.

7

GOSSAMER GOSSET – LIZARD ISLAND

KONG KAI TAI

Dressed in full sail, the enormous nylon squares bellied to the wind. The *Gossamer Gossett* moved gracefully toward the cluster of islands visible in the distance. Tony stood next to me at the bow rail. He had one arm around my waist, the other pointing ahead.

"The world will hardly admit of an excuse for a man leaving a coast unexplored, once he has discovered it. If dangers are his excuse, he is then charged with timorousness and want of perseverance, and at once pronounced the unfittest man in the world to be employed as a discoverer. If, on the other hand, he boldly encounters all the dangers and obstacles he meets and is unfortunate enough not to succeed, he is then charged with temerity and want of conduct.'

"That's a direct quote from Captain Cook's log, Kaytee. Can you imagine him coming into this area two hundred years ago on the sailing vessel *Endeavor*? It was less than half the size of the *Gossamer*. A sailor, stationed on a platform at the bow, right about here, tossed a leaded line far ahead. The line straightened as the ship surged forward, and when it was exactly vertical, a yell would go to the bridge. 'Twenty fathoms! No bottom!'. Another sailor perched at the top of the mast, in a basket called the crow's nest. He watched for the telltale lightening of water color, indicating a submerged coral reef.

"These are still dangerous waters for any large vessel. It's to Cook that we owe the original charts of the area. Their depth sounding gear is slightly different than our electronic marvels. They depended on the lead line and lookout."

The voyages of Cook through the South Pacific enchanted Tony. Copies of the *Endeavor's* log were in the *Gossamer's* library. He quoted from them as we passed through the same waters.

Tony continued with the morning's lecture; I teased but listened. "As his log shows, Captain Cook, looking for a way through the reef, sailed right through here. Not knowing what reefs were close to the island, he went ashore in a long boat, and climbed that peak you see. From there he could see the break in the reef, 'two or three leagues away', as he said, actually about twenty miles from here. His log noted large lizards on the island. He named it Lizard Island."

"You would have made a good sea explorer, Tony." I looked up at his grayish red hair, tousled by the wind, his craggy face, now deeply tanned by the sun. His bronzed body was bare except for brief multi-color swimming shorts. Constantly oiling ourselves with sun-screen, I knew every inch of his body, intimately, as he knew mine.

The days at sea were sensual, and more exciting than I could ever have imagined. After the New Year's festivities, we set sail from the Gold Coast, letting the world and my inhibitions fade away. It was glamorous eating breakfast served on the fantail. Wearing little more than the briefest of jean shorts, or bikini bottoms, was erotic at first, then an exhilarating freedom took over. I understood the naturists.

Tony went over to the intercom, and flipped a switch. "Bridge? How long will it take us to get to Watson's Bay and anchor?"

"We'll take a sweep in front of the lodge to give the tourists a kick, chief, then heave-to in the bay. It'll take about an hour."

The drone of an airplane broke the silence as Tony and I climbed into the inflated Zodiac. Looking up, we saw the propellers of a Twin Otter circling the island.

"How long will we stay, Tony? Would you consider just scrapping the rest of our plans and getting off the world right here?"

"No schedule, Kaytee. I'll introduce you to some friends of mine who manage the lodge, maybe have dinner ashore with them one night, do a little fishing and diving. There are mesmerizing coral reefs to explore all around here."

The small rubber boat skimmed over the water. The reef gardens underneath looked like they were going to tear out the bottom, we were so close. I trailed my hand over the side. "Tony, the water is so warm, I can't wait to get in."

"Go ahead, jump in. I'll meet you on the beach."

He idled the outboard. I exchanged my thongs for swim-fins and put on a mask and snorkel, then rolled over the side. Watching for a few minutes to make sure I was underway, Tony waved and sped off ahead of me to the beach. The gardens teemed with tiers of coral, colorful fish, sea life, each conformation of coral more beautiful than the next.

For the last few feet I stood up to wade in, and saw Tony on the beach arguing with a woman. Before I could see who it was, she turned and headed into the main lodge building. Tony was fuming when he walked down to the edge of the water to greet me. "What's wrong, Tony, who was that?"

"You'll never guess who just happened to be here. My favorite daughter, Melinda, decided to join the cruise. And she brought that fop of a boyfriend she goes with."

"Linny's worried about your being out alone with the Chinese vampire that wants to sink her teeth into you and steal all your money. Well, so much for peace and quiet on the rest of the trip. How am I going to keep the two of you from each other's throats?"

"I'm sorry, Kaytee. Suppose I tell her to vamoose, blow off and leave us alone?"

"No, that's no way to handle it. If you and I are going to be friends, I'll just have to make peace somehow with your family."

It went better than I expected. Linny was cool but cordial. "I am sorry to bust in on you like this," she said. "There are some urgent business matters that need Dad's attention. The company simply can't do without him for weeks on end. It's urgent I join the ship; I'll try to stay out of your way."

"Linny, I have no desire to come between you and your father. My double life is that of a working girl and I happen to be a messenger connected with the Confucius Jade. Your father and I enjoy each other's company. Whether you come with us or not is up to you and your father. It's not my decision."

"Okay, truce, Ms. Kong. We'll stay at the lodge until Dad is ready to sail, and then come aboard. The ship is large enough for us to stay out of your way."

We sailed north from Lizard, stopping at Cooktown, where Captain Cook spent months repairing the *Endeavor*. Damaged severely on a reef, Cook careened the ship on the beach to do the work properly. We stayed ashore one night at the Wilderness Lodge at Cape York, the tip of Australia. I laughed at the 'BEWARE OF CROCODILES' sign on the beach, until I actually saw a pair of the monsters in a small tributary river we explored.

The tip of New Zealand, signaled by the Cape Reinga Lighthouse, was a memorable sight. "They call it 'Ninety-mile Beach'. The sand is hard enough to take tour buses up and down it, tides permitting." Captain Maurine gave me a ship's eye guided tour with the binoculars. We sailed further south, past scenic wonders like the 'hole in the rock', large enough to sail right through.

"Tonight we'll anchor off the village of Russell across from Paihia. You may remember an American author by the name of Zane Grey, who used to come here for fishing fifty years ago."

Tony and I spent the idyllic hours dreaming of a peaceful future. And present.

The hurricane-turned-typhoon hit us when we left New Zealand waters heading northeast to Fiji. Our delightful, peaceful odyssey suddenly turned into horror.

Tony rushed up to the bridge when Captain Flauknet called him. The barometer fell rapidly. I just followed along and listened. Captain Flauknet was engrossed in a heated discussion with Jenny, the navigator, huddled over the chart desk. We could return to New Zealand or try to out-run the storm.

"Chief, we're in trouble. Hurricane Elfreda is right in our path, heading southeast. Our northeasterly course puts us on a collision course with her. We're here now," pointing a finger to the junction of three lines on the chart, "thirty-one point five latitude and one-seven-six point three longitude. We're at least two-and-a-half days out of Fiji, and about the same distance from New Zealand.

"The storm pattern, according to weather reports from Vanuatu, is heading right over them now, toward New Caledonia. Port Vila in Vanuatu is recording winds in excess of one hundred miles per hour and accelerating. Elfreda is now rated a typhoon with those winds.

"My calculation is, the eye is going to collide with us in twelve hours, about twenty-three hundred tonight. We can expect to be blown east off our course. There is no way to predict the duration of the storm, wind velocity, or exact direction."

"Can the *Gossamer* weather the storm, Captain?" I blurted out.

Tony, Maurine, and Jenny turned around to see where the voice came from. They all laughed. Tony put his arm around me, and said, "Not to worry, angel. This ship could roll over twice and still right herself."

Maurine was more factual. "I've gone through worse storms in the North Sea and survived. The *Gossamer* is a well-built ship. We may suffer some deck damage, but don't let the Chief kid you. It won't roll over. You'd better plan on some heavy bouncing around though. The swells could hit fifty feet or more. That is going to put a lot of sea water on our decks.

"Chief, you better advise Melinda and her friend Edward to stay inside. If they need seasick pills, Josie has some in the sick bay.

"Jenny, round up Annie, Josie, and Sakdi. We need to tie down all the canvas except a small jib on the for'rd mast. Batten down the canvas with extra ties and set safety lines fore and aft on the main deck. If we have to get out on deck, we will need something more to hold onto than the rails. This is a serious storm. We don't want to lose anyone overboard. By the way, Sakdi is new to this. Keep an eye on her and make her stay below if you think she can't handle any deck duties.

"Set a watch on the bridge. You team with Annie, and I'll take Josie. Two hours on, two hours off, until the storm abates. Maintain enough speed to keep the bow into the wind. The jib should hold her head. Use my bridge cabin for relief. I don't want the crew running all over the ship. Let's get a move on."

"Aye, aye ma'am." Jenny saluted and was out of the wheel house, down the ladder, hollering for the decides.

"Waiting for orders, Captain." Tony grinned and saluted.

"Thanks, Chief, the deckies will handle the ship. You'd better see to your daughter. Get any loose gear in the aft deck and saloon, as well as your cabins, secured. You can expect a thirty degree roll or more. Ms. Kong, you might take over the galley duties. I noticed you have sea legs. Fill the thermoses with coffee and tea. Sandwiches are easier to eat during a storm like this. Make up some bags of dried fruit and nuts we can eat out of our pockets."

The wind was blustering as Tony and I went below. Linny paced back and forth in the saloon, the ship already rolling, rattling the galley gear. "Dad! How bad is it?"

"We're in for a typhoon, Linny. About as bad as they get. Where's Edward?"

"He wasn't feeling or looking too well, so I sent him down to the cabin with a handful of pills. Are our lives in danger? Maybe we can get a copter to pick us off?"

"Linny, anytime there's a storm at sea, there's danger. With luck, or if someone is watching over us, we may get out with a few nicks and bruises. I wondered why you brought the ninny along anyway. I thought he didn't like the sea."

Melinda answered as she did all criticism from her father. "You can never understand, can you? Someone actually likes and needs me. Edward said he just couldn't do without me for two weeks, and insisted on joining me."

"Okay, Linny, okay. Let's not fight. There is no way any aircraft can help us. We will have to trust in that big Dane up there to keep the ship headed into the storm. Get all this loose gear put away. Angel, check the galley to see if everything is tied down."

"Aye, aye, chief." Trying for a little levity, I said, "Tony, how about if I fix a lunch basket and we retire to that big water bed in our cabin for the duration? If we're going to tumble around, we might as well relax and enjoy it."

"Darlin', y'all do get a cowpoke all fired up. Ain't a half bad notion, 'cept we'd have to leave Linny alone."

That did it. Talk about firing up someone, the look on Melinda Gossett's face was sheer murder, with me as the intended victim. All the peace we had the past three weeks went by the boards.

With a venomous look at both of us, she exploded. "I don't give a damn what you two do. An old fart like you, playing around with a Chinese Lola is too much for me. I'm going out on deck to watch the storm come in. I need some fresh air." She slammed the door, going out, so hard that I jumped from the reverberation. Tony's warning to stay inside was cut off in mid-sentence.

"So much for a truce, Mr. Gossett. It looks like war from here on out."

"Don't worry, she'll come around some day. I apologize for the abuse. You don't deserve that kind of language. Go on below to our cabin. I have a few words to say to my daughter. I'll see you there."

"Tony, let it go. I can protect myself in my own way." I didn't like the look on his face, and if he lost his temper, I didn't know what could happen. "We have enough problems with the storm. We don't need a knock-down, drag-out fight with you and Linny."

For the next few hours we rolled in the big bed. The combination of the ship's tossing from side to side, and the waterbed itself, was a real turn-on. Tony's anger released in a frenzy of erotic sex that left us both gasping, wet with perspiration.

Suddenly there was a pounding at the door. Tony wrapped a towel around his waist and I pulled the rumpled sheets up around me. Padding over to the door, he pulled it open.

Edward fell into the room as the ship rolled. He looked awful, ashen-faced, disheveled, soaking wet in a tee-shirt and jeans. "Melinda's gone. I can't find her. I've looked everywhere. Mr. Gossett, we have to find her. Please help."

I rolled off the bed, grabbed a pair of shorts and a shirt, and threw some clothes at Tony.

"Calm down now, Eddie, we'll find her. This is a big ship and there are lots of places she could have gone. Now when and where did you see her last?"

"When the storm first started, I was seasick. Melinda got me some pills and I fell asleep in our cabin. About an hour ago I felt well enough to crawl out of the bunk, get a few raisins in my stomach, and went topside to look for her. The sea almost washed me overboard. I've never seen anything like this. The wind was fierce, the waves swept over everything. The only person in the saloon was Sakdi, curled up asleep on a lounge. No sign of Melinda. I managed to go up the inside ladder to the bridge. The Captain hasn't seen anything of her. She refused to let me go look for her on deck, and sent me for you. Please Mr. Gossett, we must find her."

"Kaytee, stay here with Edward. Bring me a pair of deck shoes."

"Oh no you don't, Tony. Where you go, I go."

"No time to argue. Edward, go back up to the bridge and tell the Captain that we're going out starboard side to look for her. Do not follow us. One lost soul is enough, do you understand?"

He nodded yes, and followed us up the ladder. Tony grabbed two red life jackets from a rack, strapped me into one and put the other on himself. He forced open the hatch to the main deck. The wind and sea spray were brutal, blowing my breath away; I grabbed on to the safety rope for dear life.

The deck lights gave us a vague glow to follow. Tony pushed me in front of him, tucked one arm around me, the other on the guide rope. He shouted in my ear. "Hold on to the rope with both hands, and bend into the wind."

The deck was chaotic, the masts creaking and groaning, leaning far over as the ship heeled. Massive waves broke over the whole deck in uniform intervals, appearing to get larger each time, viciously attacking us with tons of water. In between waves, we pulled ourselves forward on the guide rope. Tony's flashlight swept the deck ahead of us. We passed the superstructure, out on the open deck, inching forward, now subject to the full fury of the storm.

Across the deck, on the port side, we saw another light working its way forward. I could barely make out the form of Captain Flauknet as she got closer, parallel to us. The long blond hair streamed behind her. Her shorts and shirt were plastered to her skin under the red life jacket, as ours were. Pulling hard on Tony's arm, I pointed toward a huddled form ahead of us, wedged against the anchor windlass, immobile. Maurine must have seen it also. We worked our way over to the body. She got there first, crouching to her knees, lifting the head to see if there was any life. I saw a gash in Linny's forehead, as Tony played his light over the still form.

The sea hit us again, and I almost lost my grip. "She's alive!" Maurine screamed at us over the noise of the storm. Tony took off his belt, strapped it around Linny's chest under her arms, and looped his arm through it.

Hollering as loud as he could, Tony directed the return trip. "Kaytee! You lead off! Hold on to the safety rope with both hands! Wind your arms around it if you can! Maurine! follow us as tail-wagger in case we get into trouble! I'll drag Linny! Stop and hold tight when the waves hit!"

I started out on the port side, locking my arms around the rope, the rough surface and salt-water rubbing the skin raw.

We rounded the corner of the foredeck to go down the bulkhead of the saloon. I turned to see if Maurine and Tony were following. The captain had grabbed the belt around Linny with one arm, looped her other arm around the guard rope, releasing Tony to help me.

A scream formed in my throat. A tower of water as high as the main mast was headed right at us. I could see Tony out of the corner of my eye, crawling toward me, lightly holding on to the rope. He turned to check on Maurine in time to be caught in the wall of water about to engulf us. He grabbed for the rope again as the water hit, picking him right up off his feet. I felt his body crashing into mine, tearing my arms away from the rope. Together we washed down the deck head over heels. My back ached where he'd hit me, and knees and elbows scraped against every projection on the railing and bulkheads.

The torrent of water washed us aft the length of the ship, smashing us into the fantail windlass. Tony hit first. I heard the crack of bones over the storm as he took the brunt of the blow, stopping my body with his. I was dazed, Tony was limp under me. Minutes passed. I held on to him, wedging both of us in between the gear. Pain followed the numbness and shock. We were in the lee of the wind, but torrents of water continued to flog and tear at us.

I heard voices vaguely through the haze. Hands grabbed at me, intensifying the pain.

"Kaytee, speak to me. Can you hear me? Where does it hurt?" It was Jenny's voice.

Groaning, I mumbled, "Every inch hurts. Tony? Where's Tony?"

"So far everyone is alive. Both Linny and Tony are in comas. Tony's leg is broken in two places, his right shoulder dislocated and arm fractured above the wrist. Linny's head and scalp laid open. You're an absolute mess, scraped from head to toe.

"Josie and I have creamed you up with antiseptic salve. You don't appear to have any breakage. We managed to put temporary splints on Tony and tied down the shoulder. We've contacted a doctor in Suva and he is monitoring the three of you by radio. Melinda is worrisome. We sewed up the scalp injury but she is too quiet. The doctor advised we rig up an intravenous feeding until we anchor and he can get her to the hospital for x-rays. We've given you all some Demerol, so try to get back to sleep."

Waking up was slow and tortuous, and was made worse by my vaguely remembering a dream in which I was tumbling around the inside of a washing machine, trying desperately to get out. "You're awake, Ms. Kong? Welcome back to the calm South Pacific." Sakdi sat alongside me in the saloon, patching up my cuts and bruises. Something was missing.

"No wonder it feels so funny. The ship isn't rolling." I suddenly remembered. "Tony? Is Tony all right?" Struggling, she helped me sit up. Linny was on the lounge across from me, head bandaged, and sleeping.

"He is alive, out of the coma, and needs medical attention to set the bones properly. The way he's breathing we think he may have some ribs fractured. We've taped his chest just in case. The doctor warned us not to try and re-set the shoulder as the x-rays are necessary to make sure that there are no bone fragments in the way. Miss Melinda's still in a coma, pulse very weak. We've managed the intravenous with the doctor's help over the radio."

The ship was blown way off course, as it turned out, almost to the international date line. Four days later we sailed into Laucala Bay, Suva, Fiji.

Uncle Sam Choy had a medical team waiting in the harbor, boarding before we dropped anchor. The young Indian doctor and two nurses checked over Linny and Tony first, then me.

The doctor decided to take Tony ashore for x-rays and hospitalization. The temporary splints and cast had held him together, but resetting the broken bones might be necessary. Healing had already begun.

Dr. Hassan complimented Josie on the temporary cast on Tony and the stitches she had taken in Linny's forehead. My black and blues were already fading, the scrapes turned to scabs. The doctor prescribed a mild sedative for my back pain and suggested I didn't climb any mountains for a few days.

Melinda's problem was the most serious. Dr. Hassan warned us that head injuries such as she had apparently sustained could result in comas lasting months or years. He would give a better opinion after examining her in the hospital.

Moving Linny and Tony was arduous. They had to be strapped into metal stretcher baskets and lowered by boom to a waiting boat below. Tony grimaced trying to conceal the pain from me as they slid him off the lounge onto the stretcher. The doctor remonstrated with me to stay where I was until my head cleared. There was no way I would let Tony out of my sight. Hassan finally relinquished his order to a higher authority, a Chinese lady in love. Gingerly I climbed down the ladder, woozy from whatever sedative the doctor had given me. I vaguely remember being physically lifted by several arms into the boat.

8

THE GOLDEN PEARL – TYPHOON AT SEA

KONG AI ME

The morning after we arrived at Kagoshima was interesting. Yoko woke me with a knock on the wall between our cabins. We slipped into jeans and sweatshirts to see what was going on topside. "It looks like Number One is in trouble again," she whispered.

Two police officers shoved a hand-cuffed Ichiban up the gangway. We caught snatches of the conversation as the officers turned their prisoner over to the Captain. "Consorting with known criminals. House...drunk...tried to get away without paying...hurt three women... damages five hundred thousand yen..."

Two burly sailors took the prisoner down to his cabin on the captain's instructions to 'lock him in,' and invited the police to his cabin. They left a few minutes later, dismissed with, "Thank you for your courtesy, officers. The Admiral will be most appreciative. We apologize for any inconvenience."

There was a scene in the Admiral's quarters later that morning that we didn't see, but we could hear loud voices. A chastened Iu Kokomoto stayed in his cabin until long after we had left Kagoshima.

The weather warmed as the *Golden Pearl* crossed the Tropic of Cancer in a calmly rolling sea. A large electronic naval chart on the wall of the main saloon showed the ship's position, and the plotted voyage. The *Golden Pearl* was on the longest leg, a lot of blue water, with an occasional dot of island. Our first stop was Guam, bypassing Saipan. We topped off our fuel and fresh water tanks there. As a courtesy, we were given a tour of the U.S. Naval Air Station. The base commander kindly hosted a dinner for the distinguished guests. I, the unmarried American lady, was mobbed by a group of bachelor American naval officers and had a delightful evening.

The time sped by with quiet days at sea between island stops. I did participate in the ritual nightly family baths in the Master's cabin, but only when Nikko and Yoko were there and Ichiban was not. He continued to make passes at me, especially in the evening, after his father retired. One night, Nikko was up in the communications cabin, and Yoko retired early with a menstrual headache; the two younger sons played Nintendo in a corner. Iu drank straight shots of Suntory whisky, the steward refilling his glass continually.

I went out on the afterdeck to relax in the balmy night air. The wash behind the ship was electric with phosphorescence, and the sky alive with stars. The captain had warned us of an impending storm coming from the west. He expected it to engage us near the Solomons. For the moment, the night at sea was tranquil and magic to me.

The warmth of the tropical night made me drowsy. A hand on my shoulder startled me. "May I join you, Ms. Kong?" Iu's speech was slurred from the alcohol.

"As you wish," I said, wrenching my shoulder out of his grasp.

Iu flared. "You are untouchable, is that it, woman? I think you're afraid to have a man. Possibly you only like women, and that's why you spend so much time in the cabins of Nikko and Yoko. You only join the bath when you know I will not be there. Maybe the sight of a man's organ frightens you. Mine is twice the size of my father's. He has the penis of a ten-year old boy, and it takes two women to make it grow."

"That's enough, Mr. Kokomoto. The whisky makes your tongue strong. I have no desire to see your organ or listen to foulmouthing. Either you leave at once or I will..."

"I suppose, Queen Kong, you will go right to my father to embarrass me further. If you do, I will tell him that you spied on him at the Ryokan. You and the other two female dogs are plotting against him. I know more about you than you think. Drunk, am I? Listen to me, coolie woman, I can ruin your game any time I like."

"Your father would never believe anything you said. I have done nothing to endanger your father's plans." My mind raced, confused. How much did he know about my association with Yoko and Nikko? Maybe guesswork, but he could still stir up a lot of trouble.

"I...am...Ichiban. My father will believe whatever I say." With a derisive smile, he added. "What if I tell him that I caught you and the geisha having it on with each other in your cabin after he goes to sleep each night? What if he finds out that you have been joining Yoko and Nikko late at night after the baths?"

"But...but...," I sputtered. "None of that is true. You're just making it up. Why would you do that to me? What is it you want?" I became panicky. This monster could create enough false gossip to ruin the relationship I had with Kokomoto. It could even affect the Jade plans.

Sitting down on the lounge next to me, he grasped my inner thigh with enough force to make me wince with pain. I tried to kick myself free, and use the finger bending judo defense, but he anticipated and locked my hand.

"You... will come to my cabin, and do whatever I tell you to whenever I call. And you...will tell me everything that is going on with the Confucius Jade. I want to know where we are meeting, the others involved, and why it's so important to my father. The Jade should rightfully belong to me, as my father is spending my inheritance on it. Refuse me and I'll make so much trouble for you, your life will be unbearable."

"Okay, okay. You're hurting me. Let go and give me a chance to think for a minute." My mind raced for an answer. I must have time and get to the girls to figure out a counter-action.

He loosened his grip and then slid his hand up higher, trying to see how far he could go. He sensed my dilemma.

"Okay, let's talk about this. Maybe I can pleasure you in a unique way. My mother taught me many of the Chinese thousand delights." I let a half-smile escape, and managed to stand up, pushing his hand away.

"That's better. I knew you were the kind that needs male domination. Now let's go down to my cabin where you can show me some of those one thousand Chinese delights."

Relieved a little bit, I came back with, "Wait. You must be patient and let me prepare properly. I promise I'll come to your cabin freely tomorrow night. Yoko is expecting me now. We must keep our affair secret." I winked and gave him a pat on his crotch to seal the bargain.

He grabbed my hand, holding it against himself. "Now that's more like it. Tomorrow night then, right after dinner, and remember, if you disappoint me, I'll destroy you and your mission."

Giving it all the emotion I could generate, I freed my hand and edged away. "Promise me, Lord of Passion, avoid the whiskey tomorrow night. I want you strong and awake for me. There are tricks I want to show you. A strong bamboo rod is necessary. Promise?"

The scam worked. He let me go, and leered. "You worry needlessly, woman. I'm stronger than ten men. Many times I've had five women in one night."

Breathing a sigh of relief, I rushed below to cabin country. As quietly as I could, I knocked on Yoko's door. I slipped in with a finger on my lips at her surprised look.

"Trouble. The big bad wolf is at my door." We talked for an hour. I told her what had happened, and we caught Nikko before she went to sleep to bring her up to date.

"Let's throw the animal overboard," was Nikko's first comment. "There isn't a soul in the world who would even look for him, including his father. We'd be doing a favor for everyone."

"Murder occurred to me when he came up with that lesbian gossip, Nikko. I thank you for your support. It's my problem, and I have a lot more to lose than a toss in the hay with the monster. Let's sleep on it. By tomorrow we'll have an answer. I'll go back to my cabin tonight. The big bad wolf should be asleep by now."

"He was headed for his cabin with a full bottle of Suntory, the last I saw him," Nikko said. "Are you sure you'll be all right? You can sleep in my cabin if you like. Maybe we should make some noises for the devil; it might even be fun."

We all laughed at the half-suggestion. "Possibly. We could try it sometime," I said, "If I'm going to experiment with lesbianism sometime, you two bath partners would be a good start." They both stood in the passageway while I went to my cabin, looked around and waved, "All clear, goodnight, and thanks."

The ship was rolling heavily in the morning. Joining the girls for breakfast, weather was the main topic of conversation. The sea and the sky were grey, grim-looking. Ten-to-fifteen-foot waves lifted the bow up and slapped it down. The reeling deck made it difficult to navigate the passageways. The sky was ominous, completely overcast, dark clouds moving in a southeasterly direction.

Nikko brought us up to date. "The hurricane we expected is turning into a first class typhoon, named Elfreda by the weather stations. We were going to head into the Solomons to take refuge at Honiara. The winds would be dead on. According to the Captain, with our power we could make headway against them. If the storm held us back enough, there would be extreme danger close to the shoals. Typhoon-strength hurricanes can build seas fifty feet or more, and we'd be heading directly into the teeth of it. They decided instead to continue south and try to make Port Vila, Vanuatu. At least the storm will be pushing us in."

"What happens if we just stay out in the open sea? Surely this ship won't turn over."

"It's the force of this hurricane that apparently is worrying the captain. Elfreda has already ravaged Iria Jjaya and New Guinea. It devastated Port Moresby. All communications with the capital are out. This is one tough lady we are meeting. Listen! The Captain is giving instructions over the loudspeaker."

"Attention, all hands and passengers. Hurricane Elfrida is chasing us. We expect contact before or just at nightfall. Batten down all hatches, attach safety lines forward and aft on all decks. Passengers, secure all loose gear in your cabins. A flying ashtray or glass can cause a lot of damage. Wear life jackets on deck, beginning right now. Life-boat drill in one hour."

The drill was terrifying, the early force of the wind already creating havoc. The sailors made us climb into the launch, swaying on the davits, then lowered it halfway down. The swells heaved at the small boat, threatening to pull it down. Afterward, in the main saloon, we gathered, awaiting more information.

Nuki and Pai Shan were with Nikko and I. They looked strange dressed in borrowed jeans and shirts. Niban and Yoko were in a corner by themselves. Iu, feigning bravado, strode back and forth, flashing winks at me, whenever he thought no one was looking. Sanban busied himself with Nintendo.

The waiting was dreadful. Nikko finally said, "Ai Mei, Yoko, come on, let's go out on deck and watch the storm."

We put on life jackets and went out to the afterdeck to talk secretly. "Ai Mei, what are we going to do with old Itchy-pants tonight?" Yoko said.

I laughed. "That's funny, Yoko. Itchy-pants Ichiban. With this storm blowing around, maybe we shouldn't worry." We were standing at the rail on the lee-side of the superstructure. The crew stowed all the deck furniture below, the deck barren and slippery from the spray breaking over.

"Well if you don't like my idea of tossing him overboard, then maybe we should dope his sake," Nikko said, "How about I rig an electronic gadget that you can hook up to his clapper? We can then blast it off by remote control."

I laughed. "You gals are real friends. How do I get far enough away, when you set off the bomb? Ichiban looked pale in the saloon. We aren't even in the center of the storm yet. If he gets sick that will take care of his libido."

"Not permanently, Ai Mei," Yoko said. "We have to fight the dragon with fire, get some disinformation going about the monster that will nullify anything he can say. The finest defense is to attack. I'd like to know exactly who the gooks he met with in Kagoshima were. He is planning something." Nikko, usually well informed, had nothing to add. I thought nothing of it at the time.

Elfreda became stronger and stronger. Everyone was a little queasy, eating lightly, lazing around. We checked on Nuki and Pai Shan. Nuki held up well, but staying below in the cabin frightened poor Pai Shan. She also became very seasick. The medic gave her something to put her to sleep in the saloon.

In the meantime we took Nuki into our confidence, relating the problem with Itchy Ichiban. She had had her own problems with him over the years. "Don't worry what he might tell the Master. I have influence over Ru Koko. He would believe me before his son I'm sure."

The terrifying day went on. We tried to rest in our cabins. Nervous and physically uncomfortable, we went up to the saloon. We didn't dress for dinner, nor expected to dine formally. The Admiral showed up precisely on schedule, as if there was no storm. Iu started to drink, looked over at me, and put his glass down. Nu talked confidentially with his father about some business affair.

After dinner Kokomoto came by our table, as usual. "I'm sorry, we have emptied the tank and cannot have a communal bath tonight. You are welcome to come by for conversation, though, Ms. Kong. We do have matters to discuss."

"My pleasure, Mr. Kokomoto. I received a communication this afternoon from Hong Kong. They're aware of the storm and wish us well. They have arranged for our arrival in Fiji."

The table, bolted to the deck, rolled with the ship. Tableware and dishes became difficult to use. At least chopsticks made it easier to eat with one hand.

"The message is delivered," Nikko said. Our anti-Ichiban plot was started. "I sent it down to his cabin this afternoon. Are you still willing to go out on deck during the storm?"

Nikko answered, "If we wear the standard yellow rain slickers and hoods, we will look like the crew. Be sure to hang on to the safety lines. Yoko, are you sure your friend Nu is going along with us?"

"Yes, he worries about his older brother. The only one we have to keep out of the action is Ai Mei. Where are you going to be, Ai Mei, while the game is in play?"

"You just heard," I whispered. "The Admiral invited me to his quarters for a conference. I can drag out that out for at least an hour. Will that be enough?"

"More than enough," Yoko answered. "Our fake message advised Iu to meet his contact at precisely twenty-two hundred on the forward deck. So far Itchy Ichiban doesn't know Nikko broke his code. We think he is working on a plan to abort the Confucius Jade purchase. He's hoping to meet his contact tonight, someone on board this ship. That person is unknown, but if we make contact first, we'll find out.

"Ai Mei, you'll have control over Ichiban after tonight, we promise."

Nikko added. "Shore contacts relayed messages to Iu in the code I broke. He sends messages back to Japan that are relayed to someone in Vanuatu. They use the same route to answer. From what I can deduce, they are planning on either hijacking the *Golden Pearl* or stealing the Confucius Jade in Fiji."

The information shocked me. "You kept all this a secret? This is a nasty mess. Why don't you go direct to the Admiral?"

"He would never believe us. There is a reason to keep it secret. Your life and Ru Koko's will be in danger if you know too much. Right now, Iu Kokomoto represents the enemy."

I would have to get a message off to Fiji as soon as the storm was over. Uncle Wei Tang cautioned us to report all unusual rumors.

The Admiral was waiting. We talked of the Confucius Jade and what it would mean to the owner. The message, from Hong Kong, gave me permission to discuss the plans for the university. Uncle Sam wanted to assure him the funds served peace. There was to be a bidding sequence, a one-shot tender offer from each of the contenders. The immensity of the project and the gambling ploy impressed him. Ru Koko requested a visit with Wan Yi and the family when we arrived.

"There is something in my past I must confess to them."

I returned to my cabin, pretending to retire. Instead I kept my life jacket on, then put on the ship's uniform yellow rain slicker and tied down a matching hat.

The wind force sucked me out into the storm the minute I opened the door hatch. I made a grab for the safety line and locked an arm around it. Massive sprays hit me as the ship bit into the sea. I worked my way aft, hand over hand on the safety line. My arms looped around the safety line so tightly that they ached. At the end of the superstructure, I could make out two dim figures at the rail, huddled together.

Suddenly, hands grabbed my arms and waist, tearing me away from the safety line. They dragged me into a corner in the lee of a windlass housing.

"We told you to stay with the Admiral! Why are you here? Never mind. Just keep your head down, they can't see us."

Yoko and Nikko were my captors. We huddled close, talking in each other's ears over the wind. The ship dipped deep into the enormous waves, then shuddered as the screws came out of the water, spinning in the air. Time and again the swells swept over the entire vessel. We barely saw the two forms at the rail. Then one rose up and struck out at the other. They stood upright trying to keep a footing on the rolling deck and still punch at each other.

I screamed. "They haven't a chance. We have to help them. Both will go overboard at the next wave." We grabbed the safety lines and began working our way to the fantail. The next big breaker hit us without warning. The avalanche of water engulfed us and carried us toward the two combatants. They must have seen the wave, and, at the same moment, the three forms tumbling toward them. I vaguely saw arms outstretched to catch me before I crashed into a stanchion. Pain coursed through my shoulder. The last memory I had was of bodies tumbling against me and my head cracking into metal.

Lights exploding, my body was bouncing around, in what I perceived to be a giant pinball machine. The bumpers were actually people shoving me away as I crashed into them. Ichiban laughed as he kicked me toward Niban, who turned around and bumped me with his backside. Sanban, arms spread wide, tried to catch me as I spun by him, tearing my shirt off.

Tumbling down, Nuki, in her fancy kimono, waited for me. Pai Shan, across a narrow passageway, beckoned the safety of her arms. I rolled between them as they spun around, pushing me down a slide of colored lights. They blinked on and off as I hit sailor after sailor standing stiff as posts, each kicking me as I went by. Yoko stood square in front of me. She grabbed my pants at the waist as I tumbled past, succeeding only in tearing them off. Nikko was right behind her, feet spread firmly, arms extended to catch me, a smile on her face. Smashing into her, I could feel her hands grab the only clothes I still had on, bra and panties. They ripped off, as I bowled her completely over.

Nothing could stop the twisting and turning until I reached the bottom. Naked, arms akimbo, unable to control my fall, I saw a V-shaped barrier ahead, a row of bumpers tapering down to a black hole at the bottom. The bumpers were all clones of Iu Kokomoto, arms pushing me down from one to the other towards the abyss. They fondled, pinched, slapped, and poked at every part of my ravaged body, as they pushed me deeper and deeper. The hole swallowed me, relieving the terror of the fall.

The lights were softer now, a quiet glow. The cloud I fell onto rocked back and forth under me, gentle and soothing. In the distance I could see a pair of green figures, blurred, waving poles of some kind at me. They came closer and I kneeled in front of them, naked, shivering, shining with nervous perspiration. Lifting my head, my eyes focused on the jade Shou Xing Laos, my friends, simultaneously raising their dragon-headed staffs. They tapped my head, as if giving me a benediction. When I looked up again, they were gone, replaced by the smiling face of Nikko.

"You're awake, Ai Mei. Welcome back to the world of the living. We don't know where you've been, but with all the thrashing around, and the perspiration dripping from you, I would guess it was rough. Can you feel anything?"

"My head feels like a whole bunch of firecrackers going off inside." I tried to move a little. "Ouch, my shoulder. Your face is blurred. What's wrong with me?"

"Not much." Nikko smiled. "You broke your arm and dislocated your shoulder. Your head almost busted a stanchion on the fantail. Your body is a rainbow of blue bruises and red scrapes. The concussion is probably causing the blurred vision. Other than that, you are in great shape."

"What happened, Nikko? The last I remember, we tried to separate Iu and Nu."

She dropped her gaze into my eyes. "There's no easy way to tell you. The giant wave tumbled us in a mass, aft. Unfortunately you were in front of Yoko and I. The wave must have been 100 feet high, the captain said. When it passed, they found us. We had crushed you against the stanchion, badly hurt. I managed to lash a line around the three of us and waited for help.

"Both Ichiban and Niban are missing, washed overboard we assume. The Captain couldn't turn the ship around to search without danger of capsizing. Yoko is in the sick bay, badly bruised but otherwise all right. The medics pulled your shoulder back into line and put a cast on your arm, but we didn't want to move you any more."

"Oh no?... It's my fault... Kokomoto's sons dead?... If only I hadn't said anything about Iu."

"Ai Mei, we mourn the loss of lives, but their fate was taken out of our hands. How the three of us survived, we may never know. Nu was Yoko's lover, but destined for an unhappy future. Ichiban was a troubled son, his future also clouded. Sanban, the only surviving son will have to replace them both. In his father's eyes, it's a formidable task. Sleep now. When you feel up to it, we will talk some more."

The *Golden Pearl* arrived in Suva's Laucala Bay. Ru Kokomoto, in mourning, had not been out of his cabin since the fatal night. I sent a message to him, advising that the family extended their condolences and would see him at his convenience ashore.

9

SHALIMAR – SOUTH CHINA SEA

KONG FENG WA

"Storm warning, Your Highness. The Indonesian weather station at Ujung Pandang reports high winds and a possible typhoon heading south by west just below the equator."

"What is our position now, Captain?"

Pointing to the chart, "Here, sir, skirting the Indonesian archipelago. We have two choices. We can head south and make a run for Ambon in the Moluccas. I've estimated twenty-two hours at twenty-five knots, under maximum power. Or, if we let the typhoon chase us, the first safe place is Port Moresby, Papua New Guinea. The government there isn't too hospitable, but they can't refuse us refuge in a storm."

I was in the wheelhouse, trying with difficulty to see through the two men, both half again my size, crowding the chart table. "Does it look that serious, Captain?" I said.

"David, any time you have one hundred mile per hour winds in the South Pacific, it's dangerous. In any event we're in for a rough twenty-four hours."

"What's your decision, Captain?" Arum asked.

"Our best bet is to head south. If the storm turns easterly, we won't get the full brunt of it. If it bears down on us, we have a chance of out-running it."

"Our lives are in the hands of Allah and your good judgment, Captain. Is it all right if I alert the passengers? Few have been in a storm at sea before."

"Please do so, Your Highness. They're safer in their cabins or the saloons. Tell them to remain inside. The seas can easily mount a thirty to fifty foot crest sweeping over the ship. The *Shalimar* is a sturdy ship but a sea of typhoon strength will toss us around considerably. That's what scares most passengers."

"Come on, David, let's go below and warn everyone. I'll take the aft saloon and the port cabins. You take the midships saloon and the starboard cabins. Keep in mind exactly whom you have seen and warned. Meet me in the aft saloon when you are through and we'll check off the passenger list."

The Captain waved us off. "Thank you. I'll give you five minutes before I hit the loudspeaker for my crew. We have to batten down the hatches and secure the deck gear."

Mustafi and his palace attendants were in the mid-ship's saloon. The deaf-mute eunuch was stoic, as usual. His staff looked a little green. The ship was already heaving, the bow breaking the surface ahead, then slapping down with a jarring impact.

"Mustafi, listen carefully. If you don't understand what I am saying, pull my arm and I'll repeat it. How many of your staff are here now?"

He held up eight fingers, then reconsidered and held four in one hand and four in another. "Four men and four women?" He shook his head. "I can only see six here now. Where are the other two?"

He beckoned to me, and we went out the nearest door to find a man and woman, huddled next to each other, hanging onto the rail, afraid to move. We brought them inside, the wind and spray already fierce.

"Do all of you speak English?" I asked. Five raised their hands weakly. "Okay, let me finish what I have to tell you. Then repeat it to your neighbors that don't understand."

Speaking as slowly and in as short sentences as I could, I hoped they would feel better. Six of them left immediately, staggering and holding hands to their mouths. Mustafi, unaffected, rolled with the deck like a seasoned sailor. The other two women, both Filipinos, looked at me and smiled, holding their forefinger and a thumb in a circle.

"Don't worry, señor, we know about storms at sea. Our home is Mindanao, and the hurricanes come every year to our village. We fear and respect storms as the angry voice of the Gods."

"Bueno, señoritas, I am grateful for the help. Keep cold cloths on the sick ones. They'll have difficulty holding food down. They may sleep. Seasick pills make them drowsy. Please make sure no one goes out on deck. It's very dangerous. After you check on the people below, stow away all loose gear, dishes, glasses, anything that could fly around the room and hurt someone. Comprende, señoritas?"

"Si, señor, esta no problema. Will the passengers need anything?"

"We have snack food and drink available in the saloon. Hold off any further service until we reach our harbor."

"Mustafi, you all right?"

The big Arab nodded yes, smiling that crooked grin of his. He gave me a thumbs up and pushed me out of the saloon.

I found Arum, Shalimar and the three Filipino entertainers drinking cokes, sitting in the lounge chairs, and laughing about something.

"What's so funny?" I said, the ship's roll pitching me into the nearest empty chair.

"You should see the condition of Ahmed and minister Abdullah," Shalimar said. "I've never seen two sicker people. Their cabins stink with vomit. They fall out of their bunks to their knees every hour to pray to Allah for forgiveness and their lives. Rashid is enjoying their misery. For the first time in his life they need him to take care of them."

"And the harem, what condition are the ladies in?"

Arum answered, "We sent Assiz's two wives home from Singapore. My women, and my brother's, are holding their own. Two feel fine, apparently not affected by the storm, and are taking care of the others. Their biggest problem is fear of the unknown. I calmed them down. With good fortune and the assistance of your Immortal, David, we will arrive in Ambon safe. Have something to drink, and relax. Is everything okay with Mustafi and staff?"

"Yes, sir, I can't think of anyone unaccounted for amongst the palace entourage. Most of them are seasick. Two Filipino women and Mustafi are good sailors and will take care of them. I told the staff to forget us, as far as service needs, until we arrive."

"Very good, David. We'll be all right. I'm going up on the bridge to check with the Captain. Call me if there are any problems."

Shalimar and the girls relaxed, gossiping with each other. I rationalized to myself. Filipinos live near the sea, and are accustomed to storms. Shalimar is a survivor under any circumstances.

"How about a game of backgammon, David?" Shalimar challenged. "We can use the table board with the felt surface. The markers should hold okay."

"You're on," I answered.

Two and a half hours later we were still playing, the girls stretched out on the lounges sleeping. The inside passage door burst open. It was Rashid, frantic. "My uncle disappeared. Ahmed went to search for him. My father followed them, and hasn't returned. I'm afraid for them."

Shalimar leapt from her chair as if a rocket propelled her. Running to the door, she grabbed a rain slicker off a hook and was struggling into it when I caught her.

"No you don't. You stay right here," I said. "The situation is bad enough. Rashid, put on a slicker and life-jacket and come with me. Shalimar, get on the intercom and inform the bridge. Tell them we're going forward to look for them."

Rashid and I fastened the clumsy jackets on, and buttoned up the slickers. We had to push hard on the hatch to get it open against the wind. The light was fading from overhead clouds and twilight closed in.

Safety ropes crisscrossed the deck areas. Going forward, we headed right into the wind, the deck sloshing with seawater. Spray broke over us constantly. The ship crested, then dropped into a void. With the noise of the storm, there was no talk, just slow, agonizing motion. Hoping to find them on the foredeck, we inched our way forward. Massive waves stopped us, each time one of the monsters swept over the ship.

"Watch out!" I screamed at Rashid and tried to grab his arm. A surge that must have been fifty feet high was coming towards us. The bow clipped into it, burying the entire ship, up and over the bridge. I barely had time to twist my left arm around the rope, and grab it with my right. The bulk of water knocked my legs out from under me. My grip on the rope tightened with fear.

There was an empty deck behind me when I turned to see how Rashid had made out. The door to the aft saloon opened before I could turn back and look for him. A yellow slicker with a red head came out, heading aft. She returned a few minutes later, half-carrying, half-pulling a limp figure with one hand, gripping the safety rope with the other.

Shalimar looked up to see me heading toward them, and motioned me to go on. She pulled the door open. Hands reached out for the two yellow-clad forms.

I headed back into the spray, barely able to see. The water was constantly in my face, weak daylight fading. Hand over hand I pulled myself forward, passing the mid-ship's saloon, forward cabins, and finally moving out onto the foredeck. The stanchions, windlasses, and coils of hawser tied down littered the path, making it hard to get through. Suddenly a flood light hit the deck ahead of me. The Captain was out on a bridge wing above me, trying to help.

I muttered to myself, "Praise Allah, the Immortals, and the Captain."

The light played around to show me where to step as I carefully audited the surface ahead. Foot by foot it crept up to cover every part of the deck. Before it hit the men fighting in front of me, I saw the shadows ahead of it. The Captain must have seen them at the same instant. The floodlight illuminated the scene at the bow rail.

Wrapping both arms around lifelines, I stopped and stared at the stage-lit drama. Three figures struggled at the very tip of the bow. They all wore storm slickers and hats which covered their heads, making it impossible to tell who they were. One had a belaying pin in his hand. He held on to the safety rope with one hand, swinging the club with the other. The victim warded off the blows, struggling to hang on to the ropes.

Each wave bursting over the bow obliterated the scene temporarily. The third form slipped in a wave of water. He struggled to regain his footing. The bow heaved relentlessly up and down. The walls of water were an increasing danger. The bow rose, free of the surface for a moment. I could see again, powerless to help the combatants.

I uncoiled, one arm at a time, and reached forward as far as I could, twisting my arm around the rope. I grabbed tight and then released my other arm to repeat the sequence. The scene, in my mind, was in slow motion, struggling to fight the sea.

Approaching closer, I recognized Abdullah, wielding the club, Ahmed, sprawled nearby, and the Sheikh, blood running down one side of his face. Arum's right arm was locked around the safety rope, the left lifted to ward off his attacker. The ship settled in a trough. The attacker released his grip on the rope for just a moment. With two hands on the club he lifted it high overhead to make one last blow. The searchlight pinpointed a face twisted with rage, the anger ignoring the light exposing him.

Ahmed raised himself off the deck, grasping the situation. Letting go of the rope, he lunged at his uncle's legs, throwing him off balance. At that moment another monstrous wave crashed over the bow. The force of the water tore at my arms, lifting my whole body off the deck. I remembered a time once before when scuba-diving when a strong current suddenly took control at 60 feet down, along a cliff of coral. The elements had complete control over my body, frightening to the point of panic.

The ship shuddered. Its screws rose high out of the water and settled again. My feet found the deck again, and the floodlight re-focused on us. There was only the Sheikh to be seen, bleeding, legs buckled underneath, his body limp and slumped on the deck. His massive torso was held half-erect by an arm locked on the rope. I looked around for the other two, the Captain also searching with the light; there was no one else on the deck. I reached Arum and helped to pull him up. We both followed the path of the light searching amongst the bollards and deck gear. There was no one there.

Two deck hands reached us a moment later, to rescue the Sheikh. The sea swells became less onerous, tunnels of wind whipping around became flaccid. The sudden quiet, eerie, signaled the eye of the storm. We felt the *Shalimar* slowing, turning clumsily in the decreased turbulence. Searchlights on both wings plied the waters ahead. I walked upright, following the two crewmen supporting Arum between them. In the saloon, Shalimar and the Filipinos soon had the Sheikh, stripped of his wet gear and clothes, stretched out on a lounge. The women were toweling the shivering body and Shalimar cradled his head in her lap, exploring the damage.

Captain Palentofolus came down from the bridge. "We are circling to try to find the men overboard. There is little chance before we hit the outer perimeter of the typhoon. I ordered two life rafts deployed anyway."

The Captain sent one of the deck hands for the medical kit, and began working expertly on the wounded Emir. "A dozen stitches, Your Highness. A sailor learns how to tie knots. You will have a thin scar."

"Ahmed, my son, tried to save me. It's all so hazy. I remember Abdullah clubbing me. I remember Ahmed screaming at my brother to stop. Where are they now, Captain?"

My eyes met those of the Captain's as his head turned to me. He shrugged his shoulders and looked back at the Emir. "Your Highness, my sincere regrets. There is no trace of either your brother or your son onboard the *Shalimar*. You and Mr. Kong were the only survivors we found on the bow of the ship."

Arum looked up at Shalimar, then to me. I nodded my head. Tears streamed out of Shalimar's eyes. The Sheikh's eyelids squeezed closed in pain, and his head settled back limply, on Shalimar's lap. Demerol, administered by the Captain, slowly took effect. One of the Filipinos pulled a blanket up over Arum's shoulders.

"The ship is beginning to roll again, Captain. How much more do we have of this?"

"The typhoon is veering away from us to the east. We have to exit the eye and head for Moluccan waters, in the lee of Ambon. We should be in the harbor within twenty-four hours. Your presence will be necessary at an inquest when we reach port, Mr. Kong. What can you tell me of the accident?"

"Very little, actually. All I could see when I got up on the bow was the minister trying to club Arum to death. Ahmed tried to stop him. Both let go of their grip on the safety rope as that last wave hit."

"Can you tell me why they were there during the storm? We will have to have some answer for the authorities."

Turning away, I answered, "I have no idea, Captain."

We anchored in the harbor of Ambon. The edge of the storm swirled around us.

The next morning, the Captain went ashore and reported the deaths to Indonesian customs and immigration.

Mustafi came for me early in the morning; the Sheikh wanted to see me. Shalimar was in the cabin already when I got there. Arum sat up in bed, looking much better than when I had last seen him. Clear, piercing eyes shone through the bruised skin and bandaged head.

"Good morning, Your Highness. The Ambassador sends his condolences on the loss of your brother and son."

"Thank you, young Kong. The pain of losing my first born drives deep into my heart. It grieves me further that I am not there to console his mother. He was wild, but I know I could have taught him how to rule our people properly. Allah must have been very angry to toss him into the sea. I'm indebted to you for aiding me during the storm. What can you tell me of the events on the bow?"

"Very little, Your Highness. Your brother tried to club you to death. Ahmed attempted to stop him."

"Is it possible to cloud your mind? A death plot against me would shake the kingdom beyond reason. There must be no word of this leaked to the press, or back to Parad. Abdullah and Assiz plotted constantly against me. They turned my son against me. His memory must be honored. We can say the storm took their lives, and that my injuries were sustained trying to save Ahmed and Abdullah."

"I understand what you are asking, Your Highness. The Captain was on the searchlight from the bridge deck. He will have to report what he saw."

Arum answered, testily. "The Captain reported to me. He saw nothing clearly, except bodies hanging on to the safety lines. The wave that took them, he estimates, was more than fifty feet high, completely inundating the ship."

"What you ask is within the morals of diplomacy. Diplomacy, as they teach it to us, is to see only what is relevant. So be it."

Shalimar spoke up. "May I ask, Your Highness, what you three were doing there at the time!" How will you explain that to the authorities?"

Vexed, Arum replied, "It's my ship. I am the Emir. Stop questioning me. We are at sea, therefore sovereign territory."

Shalimar, in a soothing voice, pursued her point. "That's true, Your Highness. As I understand maritime law, any disaster such as this is to be reported to the authorities at the next port of call. The Captain of the ship is responsible for that. It may not be wise to put him in an untenable position."

I added my say. "Your Highness, if you ask such a favor of the Greek, he may at some time in the future demand an unsuitable return boon."

"The wisdom of youth, and common sense of a trusted friend. Allah is watching over me, and may indeed have saved my life. I will confide in you, but for no other ears. Rashid came to me. Ahmed and Abdullah were both missing. He feared for Ahmed's life. Ahmed was hurt and lying on the bow deck when I arrived there. A blow on the head waited for me. I admit, I should have been suspicious. Age affects my judgment."

The Captain returned from his official port call, accompanied by a civilian and two uniformed officials. In the Sheikh's cabin, the portly civilian in the multi-colored print shirt bowed slightly, in deference to the royalty present.

"I'm Boet Nanohey, Police Inspector of the Moluccas. Please accept my condolences for the tragic loss of your brother and son."

"Thank you, Inspector. Allah has summoned them for his own mysterious reasons. Captain Palentofolus requested permission for our ship to stay at anchorage in your territory until the storm abates?"

"You are most welcome, Your Highness. The Governor of the territory asked me to extend his welcome to Your Royal Highness, the Emir of Parad. When you recover sufficiently he will visit with you. Under the circumstances of your recent loss, the usual party formalities will be foregone. Officially there are some questions I must ask, Your

Highness. Would it be convenient now, or would you prefer me to return later?"

Arum assented and waved us out of the cabin.

"Thank you, Your Highness. If the rest of you," he said, turning to look at Shalimar and me, "would follow the constables to the saloon, they will get your statements individually."

An hour later the ship's launch took the official party ashore. Captain Palentofolus and I stood at the bridge rail, watching them go. "Are they satisfied, Captain?"

"Apparently. The inspector gave us permission to come ashore. He requested that I stop in later to sign the reports. The formal explanations are accepted. The Emir's and your story are not digestible to me, however. The ship is sovereign territory for His Highness, but I am Captain of the ship. There will be a reckoning one day. Tell me, Mr. Kong, just what is our mission in Fiji?"

10

SUVA, FIJI ISLANDS

―――⊶⊷――――

KONG WAN YI

Our ancestor, the Master, said, *If on examining himself a man finds nothing to reproach himself for, what worries and fear can he have?*

We waited anxiously on the porch of our hotel in Suva for the arrival of the *Gossamer Gossett*. "What are your thoughts, Wan Yi?" Uncle Sam asked. "You look far away from us."

"Those are precisely my thoughts, dear uncle. We are far away from China and Burma, where my life started. My thoughts are with Fan Shi and Chen Wu Xia. I feel their presence, giving me courage to go on. The Confucius Jade drew those fine ships and the people on them, to an unknown destiny.

"The quest for the Jade altered their lives, as ours were changed. Two of the ships' voyages have ended in tragedy, and the third endured serious injury. Responsibility weighs heavy on my shoulders. A feeling persists that there are still perils ahead, for us and the people we have affected.

"Gossett's ship is due within the hour and tomorrow, the *Shalimar* will arrive, according to Feng Wa's communication. The Emir lost a brother and a son. It will be difficult for me to face the Sheikh without guilt."

"Dear Wan Yi, you assume guilt that is not yours. The tempest caught the ships. The reports we received indicate culpability on the part of the people involved. You must believe in the inevitability of fate. Our ancestor, the Master said: *If, on examining himself, a man finds nothing to reproach himself for, what worries and fear can he have?*

"You reproach yourself unfairly, and thus you have needless worries and fears. Our fate leads us by the nose, as you well know, just as the oxen are. There is little we can do to control our destiny. Now my advice is to enjoy this tropical paradise called Fiji. Tomorrow, after Feng Wa arrives on the *Shalimar*, we will have a final meeting. Jie Lie is then going to take you to his favorite island of Qamea for a well deserved rest. Five evenings from now, the moon of the New Year will be full and the Shou Xing Laos will decide their fate and ours."

"You quote Confucius like Fan Shi, Uncle Sam. It's true, fate leads us by the nose, but doesn't lessen the pain caused by the ring through it. When is the rest of our family arriving?"

Uncle Sam consulted his ever present notebook. "Jian Yi, Ren Quan and Wei Tang have already arrived. They came into Nadi Airport late last night and are resting at the Regent Hotel. Jie Lie, Sha Li, and Rui Xia have been out to the resort at Qamea, organizing the assistance we will need. Ai Lin will take Kai Tai and Ai Mei to the hospital as soon as they arrive. David met cousin Xi Ku, the one he calls Scot, in Singapore, and invited him to join us on Qamea. Everything is ready."

Conversation lagged as we both lapsed into reveries of our own. The air was languid, the ship in the harbor drawing our attention. The *Golden Pearl* carrying an aura of grief, was about to weigh anchor and head out to Lacala Island near Taveuni. Malcolm Forbes had invited the three principals to use his resort as a headquarters during their stay.

Ru Kokomoto spent the morning with us, right on this porch. Ai Mei came ashore with the Pearl Emperor and his youngest son, San. My cousin Ai Mei, wrapped in bandages, fading bruises and scabs evidence of her horrible experience, introduced them, and immediately left with Ai Lin for the hospital. We insisted on a complete physical examination. Ru Kokomoto joined Uncle Sam and I on the porch. He sat straight as a ramrod, stoic in grief, his son silent at his side.

In stilted English, the Pearl Emperor spoke. "It is honor to meet daughter of old friend, venerable Kong Fan Shi. Ai Mei told me Immortals kind to him these many years."

Shocked for a moment at Ru Kokomoto's words, I remembered Father Fan's intuition before I left Kunming.

"The honor is ours. My father asked me to extend his wishes for your good health. It was his thought that you could be the same Japanese officer whom he counseled in Burma many years ago. He joins us in extending our deepest sympathy on your tragic loss."

"Yes, Wan Yi, I, that person, a half-century ago." A hint of a smile escaped from the corner of his eye. "Your family caused Japanese troops much trouble. Also your father talk me out of ritual hara-kiri.

Sons born because he stopped suicide. Shinto Gods bedevil samurai Kokomoto, saving the father, taking the sons."

A single tear showed the inner emotion on a tragic face. I instinctively reached over to touch his arm in condolence. The tear, ignored, ran down his cheek and splashed on my hand.

Searching for words, I hesitantly replied. "To lose one's family is to sever a part of oneself. It was my misfortune never to have known my father and mother, and I still mourn the loss. The years spent with your sons are a gift, their death a tragedy. It is good fortune that you have a son to comfort your retiring years."

The man's face softened ever so slightly. He stared at me, looked down at my hand still wet with his tear, and said, "You speak with wisdom of ancestor. My thought only to mourn lost sons." He turned to Sanban, acknowledging his presence. "We begin life together again, Sanban. Together we are Kokomoto samurai heritage."

San lifted his head, then turned to the smiling face of Uncle Sham. His eyes turned to penetrate mine with an unspoken question, and I nodded. "Father, you have allowed me to learn of the outer world and other philosophies. I will try to become a first son. We will learn to know each other."

The moment was tense with emotion; I gently changed the subject to the Confucius Jade.

Kokomoto said. "When Confucius Jade join Kokomoto, wisdom of Kong family also arrive. Tell me again origin of Jade? Miss Kong told part of story. She say Wan Yi carved Shou Xing Laos."

"My daughter, one gifted with the features of the Goddess Guan Yin, and whose mind remains forever in childhood, found the rock. Can you recall the mound at the bend of the river where the pavilion stood on our property?"

"Hai, hai, I remember. It was at point of land I knelt and prepared for honorable hara-kiri."

"The Jade waited there, buried in the silt of the riverbank. We know it directed our lives since it emerged. You were within its provenance. Therefore we must consider it more than coincidence that brings us together."

Uncle Sam had not spoken a word, awed by what he heard. "This is incredible. You were in Burma at the time our family lived there and met them?"

Ru Kokomoto actually smiled. "I was lieutenant in Imperial

Japanese Army, stationed Bhamo village. We believe Kong family hide American pilot and help escape. Serious military problem. If we prove American there, necessary to execute whole family. Now I know why spared. Shou Xing Laos, before born, protect them. Tell now, Wan Yi, where hide pilot?"

"There was a cave at the top of the hill overlooking the Irrawaddy, concealed behind the grove of trees. The American washed up on the shore, at the bend of the river. Deng and I, but children then, secretly hid him until our parents returned home that night. We nurtured him and then sent him on his way with our donkey, Hsu Hsu. He escaped over the Burma Road into China, we believe. We never heard of him again, because of the war. Hsu Hsu returned to us with a tiny American flag concealed under the saddle. The note attached said only, 'xie xie.'"

San Kokomoto spoke. "You never told us that story, Father. Would you have killed the Kong family and the American had you found them?"

"Yes, Sanban. True. Duty require execution of traitors and capture enemy pilots. Think, my son, strange happening save lives in presence of Jade. My life also spared. I must perform hara-kiri in tradition of samurai. Confucius descendant, scholar Fan Shi convince me, life more precious than tradition."

Ru Koko quieted. His eyes closed in meditation. Another tear made its way slowly from the corner of his eye, down the cheek. It fell this time on the hand of San Kokomoto, whose arm was around his father's shoulder.

The sea breeze blew gently across the porch. We waited patiently for the elder Japanese to return to us. As if a button had been pushed, his eyelids blinked. The pupils took seconds to re-orient themselves to the bright sun.

Ru Koko began again, moving from the past to the present. "Speak to us, Kong Sham Choy and Kong Wan Yi. What plans have Shou Xing Lao agents?"

Uncle Sham answered, briefing Ru Koko. "There are three interested parties, honored Ru Kokomoto. You will gather five nights hence, on the tiny island of Tui, twelve miles due east of Qamea. The first full moon of the Year of the Dragon is due to appear. The Confucius Jade has shown the propensity to give the illusion of life precisely at the peak.

"We believe the Shou Xing Laos will meet with you, appear to take on life, and help you decide. Each of you will tender an amount in excess of one billion dollars by electronic transfer to our accounts. Kong Renquan has arranged that only the highest offer will be accepted. Receipt of the transmittal will be relayed back to us on the beach, and delivery made there."

Ru Koko nodded, accepting the bidding process. "Ai Mei vague in details, but informed me funds will have special use."

I answered that question. "Our family will use the funds to begin a unique institution in the name of our ancestor. We have approval from the People's Republic of China to do so at the very birthplace of K'ung Fu-tze, Qufu, near Jinan, the capital of Shandong Province.

"The philosophical foundation of the University of Confucius is the five virtues of Confucius. According to our research, world scholars and teachers will attract leaders of nations. They will learn together how to live in peace with each other. Professor Kong Jian Yi will join you during your stay. She will explain the detailed plans, created by the disciples of Mencius. Cousin Kong Renquan will meet with you to explain the electronic means of the tender offers and prevailing bid."

Ru Koko looked at us with his slight, habitual, arrogant smile. "And what of the one named Kong Wei Tang, who arrived with the other two last night?"

It was our turn to be taken aback. Uncle Sham answered after a moment. "You are all-seeing, Ru Kokomoto. A wise man never underestimates a contender on the playing field. True, my cousin Wei Tang, the General, helps us with security measures. There have been rumors of possible danger, both from within and without."

"Please tell me what you mean by within, honored Kong Sham Choy."

"The answer to your question is unpleasant, under the circumstances, honored Kokomoto. Your number one son, Iu, had a plan to hijack the *Golden Pearl* and hold it for ransom or possibly steal the Jade. We believe there was an additional plot re-directing the money transfer to his own account in case the other plans failed. Fortunately we discovered the schemes and were prepared to defend the Jade. We were about to warn you of the possible hijacking, when we heard about his death."

Ru Kokomoto bowed his head, shaking it in disbelief. "You have proof? Yes, must have proof. Ichiban, terrible. Gods punish him. Gods punish father for evil. Sanban, you know of plot?"

"Only suspected, Father. I think Ichiban's friends in Vanuatu planned to capture the Jade. They gave up on the hijacking idea. Niban probably tried to talk Iu out of it. That led to the argument that caused both their deaths."

"And you knew, Sham Choy?"

"Yes, Ai Mei notified us when she found out, and General Wei Tang took the appropriate action to sanitize the Vanuatu connection.

Getting up, Ru Kokomoto beckoned to his son. He looked old and depressed; Sanban took his arm. "I will be at the place you say at the appointed time. For the second time in my life, I desire to commit ritual suicide from the shame and embarrassment."

I went to him, returning his bow. "It's a strange world we live in today, Ru Kokomoto. Grieve for your sons, but don't assume their guilt."

In contrast to his entry, his shoulders bowed as he left. His feet shuffled with age. Our hearts went out to him.

Aunt Ai Lin returned with a clean bill of health for Ai Mei. The medics on board the ship corrected the dislocated shoulder and set the broken arm skillfully. Her pain had dissipated, and the healing process was well along. They joyfully shopped in the local stores, returning with sulu skirts and wraparounds for all of us. We played around in the bedroom, trying the many different ways to wear the colorful garments.

"Now try this on, Sam." Ai Lin brought one over for her husband.

"You want me to wear a skirt? Now listen, Ai Lin, don't let this tropical heat melt your senses."

The gleaming white schooner, *Gossamer Gossett*, sailed into Lacala Bay thrilling everyone. The sight was wonderful. We watched the medical launch with the red cross approach and eventually take two stretchers off by boom. With the binoculars Uncle Sham identified Kai Tai climbing cautiously down the ship's ladder surrounded by helping hands.

The hospital room was crowded. Gossett was propped up in the bed, his leg in a cast supported by an overhead rig. Bandages were wrapped like a turban around his head and the shoulders, lightly bandaged, were held in place with an arm sling. The cowboy grin overrode the sight of damages, as he addressed me. "Madam Wan Yi." He took my hand and held it. "I'm very happy to see you again."

Everyone looked at the tall American stretching over the end of the hospital bed. Uncle Sham whistled. Ai Lin gasped at the words and looked at Kai Tai. She sat in a chair on Tony's unbandaged left side, massaging his hand. Kai Tai shrugged in a don't-look-at-me, I'm-as-surprised-as-you manner.

"You were the Kongs who rescued me in Burma in another lifetime, weren't you? Let me remember, the donkey's name was Hsu Hsu. I never knew if he found his way back after I left. A border friend offered to return him to your area, and then release him."

After the shocking experience of meeting the Japanese officer, Tony's words were half-expected. I squeezed his hand with both of mine in the sheer joy of the revelation.

"We found the flag and note under the saddle blanket, and knew you were safe. Was it a difficult journey?"

"I traveled only at night, and found many friends along the way. I decided that they would never take me alive. It would incriminate your family. I understand the old one and his wife yet live?"

"My Father Fan Shi and Mother Chen are well, now living in Kunming, their original home. Father cautioned me to expect some strange revelations when these meetings occurred."

Kai Tai, unfamiliar with Ru Kokomoto's meeting with us, looked at Tony quizzically

"Tony, why didn't you tell me before?"

Anthony Gossett raised his cast-covered broken wrist to interrupt. "Now simmer down, and let me tell you a story. It's hard to believe, but it's true. During the war, I was a U.S. Air Force pilot, flying the hump as we called it in those days. We flew from Kunming into India over the most dangerous flying route in the world.

"The ack-ack hit my plane over Burma, and my co-pilot was mortally wounded. I managed to lock the controls and jump from a thousand feet. I saw a Japanese patrol, chasing toward the place I would most likely land. Pulling on the shrouds with all the strength I had left, I managed to drop into the Irrawaddy River, a muddy, wide, fast flowing waterway.

"From there on I'm foggy, but I must have unhooked myself and floated down stream half-conscious. A young girl found me at a bend of the river washed up on the bank. If I am correct, it is to you I owe my life, Wan Yi. Her family hid and fed me. After a few days they gave me their favorite donkey to escape over the Burma road to China. I got out alive. Wan Yi, for the next ten years I tried to get a letter through to you, but Burma would allow no outside mail."

"I understand, Lieutenant Gossett. It was a difficult time for us too, as you can imagine. Another unusual coincidence: on the very bank, the curve of the river that you washed up on, was the original cache of the Confucius Jade boulder. My daughter found it there years later. The discovery started us back to China, eventually leading us to this meeting."

"Is it possible you're the American aviator the Japanese lieutenant hunted?" Uncle Sam interrupted, astonished at the repeat of this morning's surprise. He sat down heavily in a wicker chair, mopping the sweat off his forehead.

"That's more than a coincidence," Kai Tai sighed. "What is the story about the Japanese officer that Uncle Sam is asking about?"

I explained. "We had visitors this morning, one of the other contenders for the Confucius Jade, Ru Kokomoto, and his son. There was a terrible tragedy; both of his other two sons were lost overboard during the typhoon. There is a strange coincidence in the life of Lieutenant Ru Kokomoto that concerns you, Mr. Gossett. He was the Japanese officer in charge of the search for you, when you crashed in Burma. At the end of the war, he came again to our pavilion by the river, intending to commit ritual hara-kiri. Fan Shi convinced him that the loss of another life was a waste. That Japanese officer is Ru Kokomoto, the Pearl Emperor, a contender for possession of the Confucius Jade."

Gossett just shook his head and closed his eyes. Kai Tai, subdued and contemplative, folded herself on the bed next to him and leaned over to take his uninjured hand. Unconsciously, he put his arm around her shoulder and gently massaged her neck.

"Kaytee, please call the ship and see if you can find out what happened to Edward. It's strange he didn't come ashore with us to watch over Linny. The poor kid is still out. She should have someone with her when she wakes up."

"It is strange Tony, now that you mention it. I haven't seen Edward since I woke up. You know Dr. Hassan said Melinda may never recover. He wants to send her back as soon as transportation can be arranged. New York has better facilities to handle her case and keep her alive."

Gossett reacted violently, to our surprise. "Don't tell me about her not waking up. Charter a plane if you have to and find that nerd Edward. The least he can do is see to her comfort until I can get out of this contraption. That girl has worked her butt off to be a son and family for me until you came along, Kaytee. In spite of all our differences, I love her and will do everything I can to make her well."

Kai Tai was shocked into silence. Uncle Sham spoke up for all of us. "Don't worry Mr. Gossett. Kai Tai has already alerted us to the problem. We have a private medically equipped jet ready to leave for the States as soon as Dr. Hassan gives us the go-ahead."

He smiled. "According to what I've heard about your relationship with my niece, we consider you part of the Kong family. Your daughter is our daughter to be loved and cared for without reservation."

Gossett relaxed back against the pillows and pulled Kai Tai back to his shoulder. "Why I declare, you Confucians are a pretty good breed. Don't know as I want to change my name to Kong though."

"Not necessary," Uncle Sham replied with a grin. "Now as to our plans for the final bidding, we will have to modify it to allow you to make your bid from your hospital bed. Jie Lie will arrange a method to time all three bids."

Gossett had one comment. "Y'all are playin' this game like showdown poker with table stakes. Tell you what. I'll be right there on Tui, at the poker table, when that moon rings the bell for the game to start."

Uncle Sam smiled at the sudden turn of lightness to the air. He shook Tony's good hand and remarked. "Tell you what, after the third ship arrives I am going to go to Qamea, dope myself with kava, dance in the evening meke and see if I can wake up from this dream."

Tony put his good arm around Kai Tai, possessively. "Angel told me what she knows of the university plans. I hope you have a chance of putting it over. It's a magnificent dream, and I couldn't think of a better use for my money, *when* I acquire the Jade."

Sham and Ai Lin joined me for coffee on our porch the next morning as the sun came up. We watched the stately four-masted schooner *Gossamer Gossett* weigh anchor and move slowly out of the harbor as the *Shalimar* sailed into Lacala Bay. True to his determination, Gossett was back aboard. The two ships passed each other and exchanged courtesy flag signals. The *Gossamer* raised her impressive spread of canvas, billowing out with the morning breeze. It was a rare sight: two beautiful vessels passing peacefully by each other, the sun reflecting off the pure white hulls.

Uncle Sam chided me. "What surprises do you have in store for us when we meet the Sheikh? Surely, he will be the long-lost brother of Gossett or Ru Kokomoto."

"None that I can tell you, Uncle Sam. The revelations of the other two guests surprised me, in spite of Father Fan's intuition. He hinted to expect some strange disclosures. If we are to consider the overall developments, I would have to say there is probably a connection between the Sheikh and our family. Has Feng Wa contacted us yet?"

"Yes, he telephoned via the *Shalimar's* ship-to-shore communications. There is sadness at the loss of life during the storm. They will meet with us as soon as they finish customs and immigration formalities."

The tall handsome Arab chieftain in flowing robes entered our room without fanfare, accompanied by Kong Feng Wa and a beautiful red-headed western woman. His headdress was partially covered by a bandage taped to his forehead. Feng Wa made the introductions, and Ai Lin served coffee and tea; the royal presence created a formal atmosphere.

"It's an honor being in your company, Your Highness," I began, trying to ease the situation. "My family joins me in extending our heartfelt condolences for the loss of your brother and son."

"We bend with the winds of fate stirred by Allah," the Sheikh said. "I have many sons, but the loss of the first born is a deep wound, infected by the perfidy of my brother. I hope the Confucius Jade will bring me peace as well as longevity."

"You are aware, Your Highness," Sham said. "That there are two other persons as anxious to acquire it as you."

"Feng Wa has been most forthright in advising me of the others. There is an extra length of the straw in my favor, however. From the story of the Jade, I have learned it was born in Burma. I too, have been to Burma. This ruby ring I wear came from some interesting people I met there." He turned his hand into the sun. The blood red cabochon shot rays of fire in the reflection. "Many years ago, before my revered father died, I traveled with some Indian traders. We stopped in a small village, the name of which I cannot recall. I bought some rare gems from a Chinese family living there. The elder was a distinguished scholar and his wife a gem collector. They were gathering funds to travel back to China."

Uncle Sam dropped his head, and held it between his hands. Ai Lin said, "Oh no, it can't be!"

"Your Highness," I said. "Could the Indian traders be the family Karimganj by any chance, and the village Bhamo?"

"By the grace of Allah, that is the very name! Pray tell me how you knew."

"Our intrigue grows, Your Highness. The story I am about to tell you is more than a coincidence. The family you traded with is our own. Father, Kong Fan Shi, is the scholar you speak of, and Mother Chen Wu Xia, the keeper of the family treasures. If I remember correctly, you also purchased a magnificent golden pearl."

The red-headed woman they called Shalimar gasped and grabbed at her throat. She had listened carefully, without interrupting, after the greetings. Shalimar opened her palm to reveal a large golden pearl on a gold chain.

"Fate is stranger than fantasy. I recall a man dressed as you, talking for long hours with my father. I remember the two of you sitting by the shores of the Irrawaddy. The Confucius Jade, even then, lay at the edge of the river buried under the silt."

The Sheikh nodded his head in agreement at everything I said. I continued. "That's only part of the facts. We have also discovered that the other two contenders for the Jade have also at one time been in its presence in Burma. All of the strange visitations occurred long before my daughter discovered it.

"If I reach far into the realm of probabilities, the facts belie any attempt at fiction. It's impossible to dream a series of coincidences to equal this gathering.

"The aura of the Confucius Jade has been with us these many years. Now it brings the drawstring tighter around the lives of the Kongs, the Kokomotos, the Gossetts, and you, the Emir of Parad.

"The moon will reach its fullest four nights from now," I continued. "We will all meet on the island of Tui. Feng Wa will see that you have an electronic transmitter to make your bid, if the Jade seeks you."

That evening, we again sat on the porch facing the harbor. Each of us was in a private dream world, talking little. I felt the presence of the Shou Xing Laos. Their power, emanating from formation in the Kachin Mountains of Burma, began in another millennium. They would take us by the hand into the future.

11

QAMEA BEFORE THE FULL MOON

KONG WAN YI

Myself, the Choys, Jie Lie, Sha Li, Rui Xia, Ren Quan, Wei Tang and Jian Yi are at the resort on the island of Qamea. Kai Tai, Feng Wa and Ai Mei came over from their ships for a final meeting. Xi Ku, the young lawyer from New York that Feng Wa met in Singapore, also joined us.

The three vessels were all within a few miles of Qamea, anchored off the Forbes's island. Malcolm Forbes had flown in on learning about the coincidence of three such notable persons arriving in Fiji at the same time. The ships' crew were relaxing on the beaches, snorkeling and diving in the warm clear waters, resting after the harrowing battle with Typhoon Elfreda.

Uncle Sam was more of a clown than a serious leader of our expedition, attired in a loud Hawaiian shirt, a bright multicolored sulu skirt wrapped around his chunky body. His cherubic face and balding head were turning red in the sun.

"We are a long way from our living room in San Francisco," he started, after the chattering had died down and we settled in the sand. " In two days, we reach the culmination of our efforts. The beginning of a new era in the annals of the Confucius family will seep into history. General Wei Tang assumes leadership from here on, as the plan reaches finality.

"Our three emissaries have suffered much during the typhoon. They report their principals positive in their intentions to acquire the Jade. The tragic loss of life on two of the ships, and a near miss on the other, are events beyond our control. There may still be danger. Wei Tang will brief you. Please listen carefully. It's an old Chinese axiom that 'to enjoy life, one must be alive.'" We groaned at the silly humor of our uncle.

323

The General looked around. We were alone on the beach. The other guests at the resort had gone out for a dive. The Fijian work staff were busy at the other end of the beach bringing in supplies from the barge offshore.

"Kongs, you've each done a superb job. We're now approaching the final hour. Our beaches look peaceful and quiet. The Jade and I sleep together in the bure Sese, next to the main lodge. Be on your guard for any furtive movement, any incident at all that is out of the ordinary. Report to me quickly. From this moment on, Jian Yi and I will man the transreceiver twenty-four hours. Jie Lie has a new unit for each of you covering a radius of fifty miles. Plain language please. Don't bother to be subtle. If anyone is listening, let them. You all have your instructions. We'll meet on the island of Tui, tomorrow night. Please see that Ren Quan and Jie Lie are invited abroad your ship to verify the electronics for the financial transactions."

Chattering goodbyes, our group split up. Three small speedboats left to head back to their ships. The rest of us responded to the rhythm of a jungle drum summoning us for lunch.

The evening was intended to be celebratory. Qamea Resort arranged a special Fijian buffet and a meke. They explained that the meke is a drum-beat song and dance performance honoring the history and life of the Fijian people. After lunch, I sat on the beach with Wei Tang in the shade of the mangroves. We watched members of the family snorkeling and swimming on the nearby coral reef. The small boats anchored nearby. A breeze fanned us delightfully.

"It's a glorious day, Wei Tang. Why do I feel these trepidations?"

"Your mind clutters with the happenings of the past years, focused into the small lens of the moment. Why don't you try snorkeling like Jian Yi and Ren Quan? Look at them, floating along the reef. Underneath the water are coral gardens formed over thousands of years by millions of protoplasmic organisms. I counted dozens of varieties of fish breakfasting on the reef during my early morning snorkel. From the tiniest bright blue ones, looking like flowers in the coral branches, to some large enough to swim up to my nose and goggle at me. The profusion of brilliant colors, shapes, delicate fins, and their endless motion is hypnotizing. The current takes you down the reef without effort, and light tidal action waves you in and out as if in a rocking chair. Formations are a continuing array of cliffs, arches, caves, and fields, a kaleidoscope of scenes, another world."

"You'll have to teach me how to swim, Wei Tang, if I'm to enjoy your underwater world. Unfortunately, I fell into the Irrawaddy one day when I was very young. Deng saved me, but I almost pulled him under in my fright. I have never enjoyed the water since that time."

Jian Yi and Ren Quan swam up to the beach. Taking their swim fins and masks off, they dropped on the sand nearby. Jian Yi said, "I knew there was a life like this somewhere, I just couldn't find it. Do you suppose they would rent me a bure on an annual basis? My students could then come over for their study programs..."

"Careful Jian Yi, you might just find yourself waking up at home, and it was all a dream."

Ren Quan turned over on his back, folded his hands behind his head, and asked, "Are there any messages coming through this afternoon, Wei Tang? We asked our three to call in every three hours."

"We've given them a four hour window today, hoping they would all relax before the big night tomorrow. Kai Tai and Gossett took the *Gossamer* to some deserted beach away from everyone. He can enjoy watching all of his women diving and swimming off the ship. Kai Tai has whispered that the ambience is rather sybaritic on board ship. The Sheikh and Feng Wa have decided to spend the day trekking up to the waterfalls on Taveuni. Mr. Forbes provided a boat and crew for Kokomoto to go game fishing for marlin. Ai Mei wasn't too hot for that idea, but agreed to stay close to Ru Koko."

"I'm sorry for the worry I caused you, Wei Tang. I'm also uncomfortable about the night trip we must take to the island of Tui. What of the Jade and security if someone wants to make last minute trouble for us?"

Wei Tang carved a seat in the sand for himself, settled in it, leaned back, sighed, and finally answered me. "You are a bird with ruffling feathers, my dear Wan Yi. The weather prediction is fair and calm, with the tide coming in. We'll have two boats provided by Qamea. Koroi, the chief of the village, will take the fast boat with Jie Lie and Rui Xia ahead to prepare the site for the big show. We'll follow in the dive boat. Our three contenders are obligated to show by midnight, or are out of the running. With a full moon, it'll be like daylight, and the high tide will make the reefs less treacherous. Maybe you and Jian Yi would prefer to stay here?"

Jian Yi and I both looked up, startled at the suggestion. I answered for both of us. "No, we'll go. I'll control my fear of the water. Maybe

Koroi will bring me a few cups of that muddy water they call kava, to calm my nerves. They say if you drink enough of it, the reaction is narcotic. Please go on, Wei Tang."

"As for security, both Ren Quan and I believe the simplest methods are the safest. Our friends are back in their original wooden replicas; they look insignificant. There's a concealed beeper inside each case to alert us of any disturbance. We can follow them anywhere. Everything is in readiness, please relax and enjoy the day. Jie Lie and Rui Xia are monitoring the others and will let us know if anything awkward comes up."

"Thank you, cousin, I shall go back to reading the *Analects* to commune with my ancestor. His words of wisdom, like yours, are better than the kava."

Lassitude of the tropics took over all of us. No one predicted the typhoon of events that would precede the full moon on Tui.

The beat of the signal drums from the large main building called us to the meke and dinner. We sat on the steps while the villagers performed their delightful dance. Laughing children in their flowers and banana-leaf skirts completely captivated us. Make-believe warriors pounded their spears, to the beat of the drums, leaping around wildly. The women sat in a row, weaving their arms to the ancient stories they sang.

Cocktails, the magnificent buffet of local foods, and the constant music of the local guitarists singing their island songs, made a festive, raucous ambience under the fifty-foot high, log-fitted roof of the main lodge.

There was a lull in the music, and the conversation in the room had reached a cacophonous crescendo when Wei Tang's alarm beeper suddenly silenced the room with its high-pitched scream. Chairs fell over as Wei Tang and Jie Lie pounded out of the dining area, down the steps and over to the nearby bure. The bure Sese, Wei Tang's, was the first one next to the impressive central building. The dining area suddenly became a bedlam as the family rushed out after the two. The other guests, alarmed, milled around, and tried to find out what the commotion was about.

Wei Tang, from the porch of the bure, commanded the family crowded outside, "Everyone back to the main lodge. Please go back to your dinner. Sit at the exact tables you were at. Let me know who is missing. I'll be in soon and tell you what is happening. Please go back to your tables. Now."

Whispering amongst themselves, they returned as requested. I stayed with Wei Tang, Ren Quan and Jie Lie. He instructed the two men, "Activate Able at once. Communicate every five minutes. Be prepared to go to Baker."

Ren Quan and Jie Lie left at once. Koroi, the village chief, came up to the bure and waited quietly for instructions.

"The Jade is gone, Wei Tang?" He spoke tensely.

"Yes the disguised wooden figures are missing, Koroi, please have your people get to the fastest boat you have and scout the water nearby. There may be a boat waiting offshore to pick up whoever took them. If you can't intercept, follow."

Koroi barked an order to someone in the dark behind him. Two men rushed to the beach, and the sound of the engines taking off echoed moments later. I stood on the porch while Wei Tang and Koroi prowled the bure looking for clues.

"Nothing. They got away clean. It looks like a piece of the back wall had been previously cut out, then covered on the inside. That way they didn't trigger the alarm I set on the door. The signal you heard at dinner was a backup, activated when the figures were moved from the table. It could be someone here, at the resort, or an outside party. The thief had time to get to the beach, around the resort, through the jungle to the next beach, or over the hill in back of us. It's an island. They can't go far, unless they get to a boat."

Koroi spoke up. "My villagers are still here. There is almost a full moon. I can have them cover the whole end of the island."

"No, Koroi. There could be a great deal of physical danger. Wait until morning and then have your people fan out. Tell them not to look like they are searching, but to go about their normal life. Report back whatever they find."

Jian Yi came over. "Everybody is back at the tables, trying to eat dinner. The crowd was so boisterous before the alarm, no one noticed who was missing, if anyone. It was at least ten minutes from the time your alarm went off before we could take an accurate poll of everyone."

For the rest of that night, I kept getting up and going over to Wei Tang's to see if there was any news. Wei Tang remained calm, using his bure as a command post. The first plan petered out when they discovered that the trailing beepers had been immediately removed from the figures. They were the eyes, found on the ground in back of the building. Plan Baker was defeated when there was no movement on the beaches or boats. Plan Charlie, a poll of everyone supposed to be on the island, disclosed no one missing or unaccounted for.

Wei Tang admitted sadly, "It had to be someone in our family inner circle. No one else would have known about the basic precautions. The two possibilities are ransom or connivance with one of the bidders to suborn the sale. You will excuse me if I don't divulge any of the extended security plans."

MORNING BEFORE THE FULL MOON

Voices walking toward the beach awoke me early in the morning. I saw Jie Lie and the two girls, Sha Li and Rui Xia, heading toward the beach, carrying tanks and scuba gear. They took them out each morning before breakfast for a diving lesson off the beach. They stopped in front of my bure and talked with Xi Ku, who was just returning from an early morning snorkel.

Jie Lie said, "Scot. You're up early. It's not a good idea to go anywhere on the reef alone. You should have bugged me."

"I couldn't sleep anymore, and the water looked so inviting. The reef fifty feet offshore was incredible. Caves and wall formations had me snorkeling for hours. I can find my way without putting my head out of water. There were dozens of varieties of colorful reef fish this morning alone. Don't bother about me. Have a good dive."

I dozed, weary from the long night and worry. Screaming voices brought me up and to the door. The girls were running toward Wei Tang's bure, yelling hysterically for help.

Rui Xia, sobbing, blurted out fragments of the story. "Sha Li and I buddies.. Jie Lie ahead... around the corner of the rock point...current against us very strong...we stopped, watching a sand shark...pushed to the corner...Jie Lie gone...nowhere... thought he was playing joke on us."

Sha Li, calmer, picked up their story. "We looked in all the caves, sure he was playing games with us. Then we heard boat propellers whirling above us. When we got to the surface, hoping to get help, we saw a boat speeding away. We hollered at them but they didn't hear us. Jie Lie must have been aboard. He wouldn't leave us. Someone must have kidnapped him."

The girls couldn't give a description of the boat. Wei Tang admitted that Jie Lie had probably been kidnapped. He was an intimate member of the planning and hence, an excellent hostage.

Wei Tang gathered the immediate family around. "We must be calm. Whoever kidnapped Jie Lie and the Jade has a definite plan in mind. My counter-plans are working. We think we know who the perpetrators could be, but don't know where they are. My guess is they will contact us soon for whatever demands they have in mind. We can assume they know the urgency of the meeting on Tui tonight."

The demands arrived as Wei Tang expected. Qamea's facsimile machine whistled with urgent messages. Fiji's antiquated telephone system precluded any possible tracing.

KONG FAMILY - JIE LIE KONG MOMENTARILY SAFE. JADE SHOU XING LAOS TO BE LEFT ON NEXT BEACH AT HIGH TIDE IN DESERTED BURE. ANY BOATS OR PEOPLE ATTEMPTING TO FOLLOW WILL BE BLOWN UP. IF JADE IS NOT IN BURE BY THREE P.M. YOU WILL FIND DEAD BODY OF JIE LIE THERE.

Wei Tang checked with Koroi. High tide would be at 3:48 p.m. The second facsimile arrived ten minutes later.

FRIENDS OF SHOU XING LAO, CONFUCIUS JADE. WE ARE SAFE, HIDDEN FROM YOUR SIGHT. CAPTORS INSIST ON TITHING OF ONE HUNDRED MILLION DOLLARS ELECTRONIC TRANSFER TO FOLLOWING ACCOUNT: 602 ZIRA 455 5777 SON, BANK OF INTERNATIONAL COMMERCE, LUXEMBOURG BY SIX P.M. FAILURE TO COMPLY WILL RESULT IN OUR DISAPPEARANCE FOREVER. ACKNOWLEDGEMENT OF RECEIPT OF TRANSFER WILL DIVULGE OUR LOCATION IN TIME TO RECOVER FOR TONIGHT'S BIDDING.

We huddled, trying to ferret as much information as we could from the two messages. Wei Tang suggested, and we agreed, "We must advise our three agents at once, but keep the kidnapping secret from anyone else. They may be able to help. We must assume the possibility of it being one of the bidders or someone close to them. The influence of the Jade and the immense amount of money we are asking could make thieves out of anyone. Jian Yi, contact Ai Mei, Feng Wa and Kai Tai at once and fill them in. Now let's brainstorm what facts we have.

"Kidnapping, a hostage. We suspect someone in the Parad group, it is their style. Assiz is a possibility. The last we heard of him was when he left the ship in Bombay. Rashid is suspect. He could be conniving with Assiz. Giving up on killing the Emir, they would try to get the Jade and then ransom it off. Not a good plan, but then they didn't have a very good plan before.

"The Japanese son tried to use a Vanuatu gang to hijack his father's ship. Whoever he worked with could be continuing the plot. They might have hired a dive team to come over. By watching the island, Jie Lie's early morning diving practice was spotted. An unsuspecting Jie Lie would be an easy victim.

"Koroi, contact all of the nearby resorts to look for a strange dive boat. You must know all the local boats by sight. A strange craft would be hiding in some cove in order to save on fuel to wait for the rendezvous time. Look for a large antenna. They would have to have a facsimile machine on board to keep in contact with us.

"Ren Quan. Contact Sunflower Airlines as soon as Koroi gets off the phone. See if you can hire one of their planes to meet you at Matei Airport in Taveuni. Take Sha Li with you, and the binocs. We have five hours to find Jie Lie."

"What can we do to find the Jade?" Uncle Sam interrupted.

"That's your job, Sam. You, Ai Lin and Rui Xia get to work immediately to try and figure out who the Judas in our midst is. One of us, who knew all the plans, has decided to profit personally. Take another bure and work it out, member by member. When we find the person, I am going to take her or him apart, limb by limb. There has to be outside collaboration from the person who sent the fax.

"Scot, you're smart. Stick with me. Start working up a flow chart of all the facts we have on both kidnappings. Jian Yi, keep on the communications with each of our people after you notify them of the problems. Write everything down and shoot it over to Scot. Wan Yi, you and I are the command post. Please stay close and listen to everything that is happening. I may miss an obvious clue."

NOON

Wei Tang called a conference. Some facts were emerging. I listened. Ren Quan was aboard a Sunflower plane, and the pilot was flying a grid, with Qamea the center. He estimated they could cover twenty square miles before three o'clock.

Koroi had his two boats rigged with double forty Johnson motors. The two crews were armed with their coconut palm machetes and long, sharpened bamboo poles. He said quietly, "That is all the weapons we will need. My friends have checked out all of the strange boats so far. They are cruising around neighboring inlets with orders to observe and report only. We will find them." The gentle, graying-haired Fijian chief's nostrils flared as he spoke. His muscular body bulged in a singlet. I had visions of ancient Fijian cannibals raiding a hated enemy in another era.

Uncle Sam reported his team completely frustrated. "We have accounted for everyone in the family. During the meke, anyone could have disappeared for a few minutes to prepare for the theft. At the buffet, we were all milling around, deciding where to sit. Everyone was there at one time or another. The key period is when your alarm ticked off. Who wasn't at the table at that moment? No one can remember exactly.

"We reconstructed the scene. Sha Li would have been able to get up from the table, pretend to refill her plate at the buffet, jump off the back porch, get to Sese, enter, grab the Jade cases, and force out the eyes with the bug in them as she was leaving. She could have hid them anywhere, in or under a bure, or in a previously dug hole in the beach, and returned to dinner in a minute and twenty-two seconds.

"We did try to recall everyone gathering around the bure Sese, following you and Jie Lie. Scot is pretty sharp. By asking everyone, he was able to make a diagram of the scene, placing each one at the bure. He made another of the dining room, and exactly where everyone sat. After the moon went down last night, it would have been easy to remove the Jade and secure it in a permanent hiding place. Even a pit under the sand on the beach would be covered quickly, with the surf erasing all marks within minutes."

Jian Yi came in with a worried look on her face. She handed Wei Tang a facsimile message, apparently just received. "Another problem, General. Someone else is working on us." Wei Tang read it and then read it out loud to us.

"From The ROCK, San Francisco to R.Q. Kong Qamea, Fiji. Please verify new transfer codes and instructions received for your account, University of Confucius."

"What does that mean?" I asked.

Wei Tang looked at Jian Yi, and then back to me. "It means someone has broken our electronic codes and has devised a way to clear out our account after the transfer tonight. Now we have a third mystery to solve. It's already one o'clock. Jian Yi, get Ren Quan on the hookup. He will have to get to our modem right away to clear the lines, change the codes and work on tracing the break-in. We have a real smart cookie hacking our programs. It is fortunate that someone in Ren's office caught on."

Rui Xia was crying. "What about Jie Lie? His kidnappers aren't aware we haven't the Jade to trade."

"Easy, honey," Wei Tang said. "We will have something very soon. They have to move out to get to the rendezvous. Scot is taking a dummy package over there in a few minutes, in case they are watching from a land base. It will buy us time."

THREE O'CLOCK

The strain, coupled with lack of sleep the night before, took its toll on me. Aunt Ai Lin sent me off to my bure to rest. "I'll call you the minute anything turns up, Wan Yi. You look exhausted."

My body fought for sleep, but my mind countered it with the guilt I felt over the past tragic events and what was now happening. My eyes closed, and my mind wandered into one of those trances that seem to have a current awareness, yet transfixed in a coma.

The Jade Shou Xing Laos materialized. Unlike before, they were not moving, but seemed huddled in a cave, waving their rods, mouthing the word, help. The cranes and the spotted deer were clustered close by, as if all were in a cage or box. My mind strained to recognize the surroundings. It was not a cage, more like a cave fashioned by coral formations. Water surged in and out, sometimes obliterating them completely. I recognized odd-colored fish swimming in and out of the cave. One pair seemed more curious than the rest, continually swimming up to and then away from the Jade. Their black and yellow vertical-striped bodies were distinctive, impressed on my subconscious. The whole scene abruptly disappeared as Aunt Ai Lin shook me.

"I'm sorry to wake you, dear Wan Yi. You need the sleep so badly. They think they have located Jie Lie's kidnappers. Koroi has taken off with his attack team to check it out. Rui Xia went with them to keep the communications open. We should hear from them within the hour."

My mind was fuzzy. There was something I should remember. Did I dream? I took a quick shower to dispel the humidity and sweat from my short nap, still trying to recall something. Suddenly it came to me and I rushed over to the command post.

"Wei Tang, Wei Tang! Uncle Sam, Uncle Sam! I saw them! The Shou Xing Laos... came to me in my sleep, asking for help."

The family gathered around. Wei Tang, always unruffled, "Easy now, Wan Yi. This is important. Sit here and calm down. Tell us slowly exactly what you saw. Sha Li, write everything she says, word for word."

For the next half hour, I repeated the dream. Details of the scene became bolder as I added a rock, a fish and a wave.

Radio static interrupted the five-minute bulletins from Rui Xia as Koroi and his team closed in on the Vanuatu dive boat.

"...Ren Quan in the Sunflower airplane located them first, tucked into a cove on the back side of Taveuni. They passed over as if they were landing at Matei Airport...and then took another turn a few minutes later as if departing. Our two boats are approaching from either side... Koroi remembers the small inlet they are in, half covered with the surrounding jungle of mangrove trees.

"We are close to the... inlet now and can see the boat about fifty yards inside. A direct attack would be dangerous to Jie Lie. Our boat is going on past... the entrance. Koroi has signaled the other boat to do the same and take up positions, close to the banks on either side of the inlet...

"We'll wait until they exit. It's about time for them to go to the pick up point... Here they come, poling their boat out of the shallows. I can see one man at the helm, ready to start and gun the...engine. Koroi signaled his other boat. We're going to jam them from either side."

We heard the engines roar in the background, as Rui Xia left the line open. There were shouts, like battle cries, screams, and the sound of gunshots. That was worrisome; Koroi's men didn't have any guns. The tension for the next few minutes was unbearable. Finally Rui Xia came back on the line.

"...It's okay, we have Jie Lie. He isn't hurt. I couldn't talk during the battle. Koroi made me hide under the deck. Here's Jie Lie, maybe he can tell you what happened."

"I think we may call this the Battle of Taveuni...don't worry, Rui Xia and I are okay. I have a few bruises. Two of Koroi's men have some superficial bullet wounds. You don't want...to know about the gang of four and a leader that took me. When they wouldn't surrender, those sharpened bamboo poles flying through the air took down the...leader, an Arab in a white robe. Two others with guns were dropped when Koroi and his men boarded our boat. It's a bloody mess... two severed arms on the deck, still holding guns. The other two men have jumped in the water trying to escape. One of our boats is out circling them now. They haven't... a chance to escape. Koroi will return with me and leave his men to clean up the mess and notify the authorities."

"Jie Lie. Can you identify the white-robed man?" Jian Yi answered back.

"Yes...he taunted and beat me this morning. I wouldn't give him any information of our security plans. It's...Assiz. I recognize him from the photos David showed us. He is dead. One of Koroi's men chopped off the arm holding an Uzi submachine gun. It was never fired. Rui Xia became sick at the bloody mess. Koroi explained, 'no handguns allowed in Fiji.' We're on our way. Last transmission... Rui Xia and I have a little hugging and kissing to catch up with on the way back."

The bure Sese resounded with cheers. I didn't join them. The news about Jie Lie being safe was wonderful. But the toll of deaths as a result of the Confucius Jade was now seven. Would there be even more before the night was over?

The attention was back to me. We were sure the Jade was hidden on the reef. If we could identify the right place from my dream, there was a chance for rescue.

Scot returned from his errand of leaving a dummy package on the next beach. He was happy to hear the good news, and took over the job of recording my dreams from Rui Xia. They brought a book of photographs of reef fish and I quickly identified the two yellow and black ones - Emperor Angelfish.

Wei Tang was whistling with happiness. Jie Lie would soon be back, and we had a good lead on locating the Jade. If my dream was correct, they would be lying somewhere nearby on the reef, not more than fifty feet offshore.

FOUR O'CLOCK

"I have seen that pair of fish somewhere along the reef." Jie Lie said, as he was fitting on his mask and fins. "I don't think we'll need to dive very deep. Whoever did this didn't have time to suit up, get an air tank and go very far. Come on girls, get your masks on. The three of us are looking for the pair of fish first, then the small caves and recesses in the corals. The local fish have a tendency to stay in the same area, their home territory. When we find them, the Jade will be nearby."

We all sat on the beach watching the snorkels work back and forth down the reef, except for Ren Quan. He was in Nadi, working with his partners in San Francisco to straighten out the electronic problem. Uncle Sam had made a sand chair on the beach for Ai Lin and himself. Jian Yi and Wei Tang sat nearby in the shade of the mangroves. Scot had shied off from going out with the other cousins. He was walking by himself back and forth at the far end of the beach. Wei Tang watched him curiously and conferred with Jian Yi.

Aunt Ai Lin saw them first. She scattered sand all over a sputtering Uncle Sam in the excitement. The snorkels kept disappearing under water as they dived down on the reef. Then Sha Li surfaced, ripped off her mask and hollered. "We've got them! We've got them!"

FIVE O'CLOCK

The tired voice of Ren Quan reported in just after five o'clock. "We have it. The hacker was one of the smartest programmers I have ever seen. We hope there is a signature to the work that we can trace. There are not many people of this caliber in the business."

"How did he do it, Ren?" Jian Yi asked.

"Could be a she also, Jian, or more likely a team of people. They hacked our codes, inserted a virus to completely divert the funds after it hit Citibank. Citibank is working on the divergent addresses. Places like Luxembourg and the Bahamas are very uncooperative, even with thefts. They diverted to ten different accounts, which in relay diverted to ten accounts each. There were one hundred addressees that we know of that would receive ten million dollars each. It is possible there was further divergence.

"We were fortunate. One lone operator at the bank, working overtime, noticed the unusual flurry of activity. He contacted Rothschild at our office, and the bank's fraud team went to work.

"For safety, in case we didn't catch all the garbage, the whole program has been re-invented. We are now hooked up with Chase,

Bank of England, and Credit Suisse. We put our own virus in to cancel the whole program if any change occurs.

"Sunflower is sending me back in a charter. Have someone meet me at Matei airport in two hours. And Wei Tang. Save me a place on the launch to Tui."

"Ren Quan. Thanks." Jian Yi closed the circuit.

12

DESTINY AT TUI

———— ✸✸✸ ————

KONG WAN YI

Chief Koroi, Jie Lie, Rui Xia, Sha Li, and I were the first to arrive on Tui, in the fast boat. The diving launch with Wei Tang, Jian Yi, and Ren Quan arrived next with the team of Fijians from Qamea to act as guards.

"Spread your men out along the beach, Koroi," Wei Tang ordered. "Ren Quan and Jian Yi will stay with you to greet the other boats coming in. If there are any except the three we are expecting, use your walkie-talkie and warn us. Your men will have to carry Mr. Gossett up the hill."

We climbed a path through the palm trees to the top, where Rui Xia and Jie Lie were waiting. The entire perimeter of the small atoll was visible from there. A lagoon on the far side showed shallow water and a reef, leaving the beach where we came in as the only landing place. The crest where we stood was like the bald top of a mountain, with a single tree stump in the center. A circle of tall palm trees surrounded the crest, as if guarding the premises.

A remote-operated turntable was set on top of the stump, and I carefully unpacked my friends from their casing. The Jade was cool in my hands; I caressed the familiar shoulders and bald heads. We sat them on the velvet-covered revolving surface, a half-turn facing each other. I tried, unsuccessfully, to determine which was the Shou Xing Lao and which the reflection.

We stood back at the edge of the circle, completely entranced. There was not a sound as two burly Fijians carried Anthony Gossett up the hill, saddle-style. Kai Tai anxiously followed her injured dragon, constantly berating the carriers to be careful. She carried a legless chair back and pillows. The American, bare foot sticking out of the cast, relaxed himself on the soft sand of the ground and leaned against the chair back. He made them move him sideways to the Jade to get closer.

Kai Tai fussed over him, adjusting pillows and wiping a sweating face and shoulders.

"Okay Kaytee, enough. I'm here and as comfortable as I'm gonna get. Back off and leave me be."

Pretending a huff, Kai Tai answered saucily. "Talk about a mean Cayuse. You get a little banged up and start fidgeting like a bronco. If you need any help call someone else. I'll be busy for an hour or so."

She leaned over and kissed him, then walked back to our circle. I hugged her, knowing she was still nervous from the week's danger. "Mr. Gossett must be hurting a lot. It's some effort to come all the way over here in his condition."

"Wan Yi, Tony is one tough hombre, in his vernacular. That, combined with a stubborn streak and the arrogance of his money and power, makes me wonder if I should spend the rest of my life with him. He has asked me to marry him."

"You've put off your answer until the Confucius Jade is settled, I take it?"

She nodded in assent. "Here comes Ru Kokomoto."

Ai Mei followed Kokomoto into the circle, unrolled a tatami mat for him, then retreated to stand with the rest of us. We held hands with each other and stared at the Japanese mogul, dressed formally in naval whites. He bowed to Gossett, bowed to the Jade figures, kicked off his shoes, stepped onto the mat and kneeled down as if to pray, his eyes inches from the figures.

"What's his mood, Ai Mei?"

"Very good, considering the events of the past few days. He is absorbing the loss of his sons, and spending more time with Sanban. Yoko is a lost soul, retreating into her cabin, mourning Niban. Ru Koko has done nothing to assuage her grief. She refuses to tell him she is pregnant with Nu's child.

"Sssh. Here comes the Emir," I said.

Arum, the Emir of Parad, strode forcefully onto the hill top. Feng Wa followed behind with the entourage. Wei Tang pointed them to the still open space in the inner circle. Mustafi laid a woven prayer mat on the sand in the wedge of space. Arum swirled his robes about him, bowed to Gossett and Kokomoto, then settled himself down on the mat. His gem-set headband glittered in the moonlight, lighting the area. Fierce eyes narrowed and focused in their web of wrinkles on the slowly rotating Jade.

The moon rose tortuously. Ru Kokomoto sat as the Buddha Ho Ti, his hands, palm to palm, pointed upwards, eyes riveted to the rotating figures, hypnotized. He appeared to be transposed inside the liquid green, in total reverence.

The American, Gossett, twisted and shifted, trying to find a comfortable position yet stayed close to the Jade. Kai Tai helped to adjust the cushions. His upper body twisted to follow the figures as they slowly circled away from him, then came back into view on the turn.

Arum, the Arab ruler, remained stoic. His hand reached to follow the figures as if magnetized. His ruby ring caught fire in the moonlight, reflected into the green mirrors of the Jade.

Jie Lie rose silently and placed a small box with an antenna, prominent red and green buttons ready to send a signal, by the side of each of the bidders. The signals would go to their ships, and activate the relay authorizing or blocking the transfer of the funds. Their tender had been pre-set before leaving their ships. Our contacts reported that each of the moguls had spent hours in meditation. They could change the amount by punching a new set of figures into the lighted ten-digit keyboard below the red and green buttons.

Gossett, the gambler, twisted to his left to talk to the praying figure of the Japanese emperor. He spoke to him in a whispered tone. We strained uselessly to overhear. Ru Kokomoto shook his head negatively. Arum leaned over to Gossett, making it easier for the wounded American to repeat the message. The Emir nodded, acknowledging and agreeing. He pointed to Ru Koko and shrugged his shoulders.

The family of the seventy-fifth, seventy-sixth, and seventy-seventh generations of descendants of Confucius waited anxiously. We were dedicated to re-activating the five virtues of our ancestor. Within minutes, we would have the funds for the University of Confucius. Unless...

I looked at Wei Tang. Like Arum, he shrugged his shoulders. We had no way of knowing what the three were planning.

The moon rose higher, like a laser beam focusing down on the scene on Tui, the island of kings. Chief Koroi told us that the crown of this island inaugurated their leaders for centuries, also at the onset of a new moon.

The Jades became more molten in appearance as the light danced into their interiors. The flawless green Imperial Jade hypnotized all of us. From the expression of awe on the faces of the three rivals, I knew what they were seeing.

Shou Xing Lao striding toward them, growing larger and larger, until life-size. The dragon-head rod raised in greeting. A luscious peach proffered, the sweetness felt on their lips. Long slender legs of the crane lifting delicately as it moved alongside the Immortal. Dainty ears of the deer twitching and bending forward as it bounded ahead. Each move of the old one, every twinkle of the eye, was duplicated simultaneously by the other figure. They revolved around the tight inner circle, came within each man's ken, then receded, to re-appear as they came into focus again.

The moon rose to its zenith, and the focused beam widened into the light of reality. Audible gasps, sighs, and heavy breathing accompanied the phenomena. The Jade figures gleamed in their emerald beauty. They appeared to have life-like human form.

Vague shadows of other people gathered behind us but we were too intensely involved with the Jade to be concerned.

A figure separated from the shadows and approached Kokomoto. Wei Tang arrested it with a hand on its shoulder, then let it continue. The figure knelt silently by the side of the praying figure intent on the Jade. Ai Mei gasped. "Oh no, it can't be! Niban. He's alive."

Kokomoto became aware of the commotion and the person alongside him. He looked startled, disbelieving, reaching with a hand to tentatively touch the arm next to him. The father's hands went up to feel the cheek of his son. Nu's head bent down in respect for his father. Ru Kokomoto's arms went to his shoulders, pulling him close to reaffirm the phenomenon. He turned his attention back to the Jade figures, whose rotation stopped for the moment in front of them.

They spoke aloud in their native language. Ai Mei translated for us. "I feel reincarnated, cleansed, floating above, looking down on myself and my once-dead son." Pushing the shoulder of his son forward with him, Ru Kokomoto bent low to the Jade. "We owe you our lives, Immortal Ones, ask what you wish in return." The father and son remained bent over as the Shou Xing Laos rotated. Kokomoto sat back on the mat with his son, once again caressing his face. He punched new digits on the small transmitter and then pressed the green button openly for all of us to see.

Arum watched the scene across the circle from him, disbelief and astonishment on his face as a tall figure in a flowing white gown detached itself from the shadows and strode toward him. Feng Wa exclaimed. "It looks like Ahmed, but it can't be. I saw him wash overboard with his uncle the night of the typhoon. No one could survive in that sea."

The Sheikh stared in stunned silence. He made an effort to get up. Ahmed gently settled him back and on bended knee embraced his father, kissing him first on one cheek then the other. The whispered words carried to our ears. "May Allah forgive me for my sins, father. I am given a second chance by a power equal to Allah's."

The carousel stopped in front of the reunited father and son. Again Wei Tang held back his security men as Arum reached for a Jade figure. He held it up in the moonlight to commune closer with the Immortal. He kissed each of the full cheeks. Ahmed copied his father with the opposite figure, handling it fearfully as if it would break. They returned the figures to the carousel gently. Both men palmed their hands in prayer and bent their heads to the ground, sharing Allah's prayer rug.

Arum punched new digits into the transmitter but we could not determine whether he pushed the red or green button.

The Shou Xing Laos continued their journey around the inner circle and stopped in front of Gossett. We waited expectantly. Kai Tai had disappeared a few moments before with Wei Tang.

Two figures emerged from the trees behind us. The moonlight struck full on the exquisite tiny face and figure of Kai Tai. She was like a doll suddenly given life and motion. Her arm supported a larger person walking slowly into the inner circle. The pair moved toward the crippled figure on the cushion, then separated to kneel on either side.

Anthony Gossett was deep in the hypnotizing somnolence of the precious Jade, quite unaware of the pair's presence. Slowly, coming out of the trance, he turned to his right, recognized Kai Tai and inadvertently tried to put his injured arm around her. She pointed across to the figure on the other side. Melinda took his good arm and pulled it around her shoulders, snuggling under as she would a comfortable blanket. Gossett, suddenly realizing that it was his daughter, tightened the grip and pulled her tight to him.

I walked around the circle to see who it was and enjoyed a heart-warming intimate scene. No words were spoken. Tears flowed from the large, tough cowboy, hog-tied as he was with splints and bandages. Melinda and Kai Tai brushed happy tears from their own eyes and reached over to do the same for Gossett. They grasped each other's hands in front of him and he placed his own over theirs.

The moon, reaching its zenith, began a descent, fading the spotlight. Gossett, suddenly remembering where they were, turned to face the Shou Xing Laos. "Fellas, I don't know how you did it, but ah' sure am obliged. Whatever y'll need from me, you got." He reached down for the signal unit, pressed a new set of digits, looked at the two women on either side, as if to reassure himself, and pressed the green button.

A parent's loss of a child is an immeasurable tragedy. The hope that it isn't true is eternal.

Epilogue
REVELATIONS

KUNMING, YUNNAN

KONG WAN YI

If you believe, there is hope. Without hope there can be no belief.
There is no comparable saying of the Master in the Analects, but surely
he must have thought similarly.

Wei Tang confirmed the deposit of three billion and three dollars in the Confucius Jade accounts only minutes after the moon began to wane. Each of the three donors considered the Shou Xing Laos as theirs, but none required possession. The magnificent and symbolic Jade sculptures are permanently on display in Qufu at the University of Confucius. The impervious glass dome containing them rotates continually, exposed to the sun and the moon.

Etched jade plaques are at each of three delineated segments of the base, recording the donors' names for posterity. Each winter, to this writing, Anthony Gossett, Ru Kokomoto, and His Royal Highness, Arum of Parad, gather in the tower to commune with the Shou Xing Laos at the first full moon of the new Chinese year.

We had much to relate to Father Fan Shi and Mother Chen about the events which occurred in the ascending days and hours of the first full moon in the Year of the Dragon. They accepted the coincidence of the three men having been part of their lives in Burma without surprise. They believe that it is perfectly natural for a superior being to control phenomena and human lives.

Unknown to any of us except Uncle Wei Tang, Melinda had suddenly recovered in the late afternoon of the final day. Dr. Hassan, shocked by the seeming miraculous recovery, gave permission to have her flown over to the landing strip at the nearby Kaimbu Island resort, friends of the Qamea people. Their fast boat brought Melinda to Tui in time for Wei Tang to summon Kai Tai and bring them all together.

Melinda had been furious about Edward's disappearance and called friends in New York to investigate his apartment. They found a separation notice from his office on the desk along with a letter notifying Edward that he was liable on criminal charges for taking bribes. He was warned not to leave the country. His daily diary revealed he had been playing squash quite regularly with a Scot Kong.

General Wei Tang, already suspicious, forced a confession out of Xi Ku, Scot. Scot wanted to make big money quick and conquer the world while Edward needed funds to escape to Brazil where he couldn't be extradited. The conspirators concluded that if Scot could steal and hide the Jade, Edward would arrange the blackmail threats by fax from a small hotel on Taveuni. They almost succeeded except for the unique relationship of the Shou Xing Laos with me.

Melinda reported a strange dream. The Shou Xing Laos appeared in life-like form. As she remembers, they walked her out of the waters at the bend of a river in a far-off land. They sat by the shore in a beautiful red pavilion with turned up eaves and a green tiled roof. The Shou Xing Laos talked to her while two spotted deer and two red-headed cranes played nearby. Luscious peaches were offered to relieve her thirst.

The conversation was forgotten but by the time the dream faded, Melinda knew she had a friend in Kai Tai and a father who loved and respected her. Dr. Hassan was astounded and could give no clinical reason for the instant recovery, other that "it sometimes happens that way."

We believe the story David told us of Ahmed's miraculous return to life. The uncles approached Ahmed at the beginning of the voyage about eliminating his father, the Emir, and put himself on the throne. They would help cover the crime as an accident, install him as the new Emir and split the billion dollars.

Ahmed confided in Rashid and they agreed to refuse the uncles, one of whom left the ship at Bombay. The other uncle became more and more obstreperous during the voyage. He took it upon himself to summon Arum to the bow on a pretext. The storm was a perfect cover to kill the Sheikh and Ahmed and dispose of the bodies overboard. Rashid could be easily controlled. No one could prove anything.

The monstrous wave caught them both. Ahmed remembered the terror of tumbling around in the water, surely to drown. He was a diver, however, and reacted instinctively as he would have to losing his air on a dive. He had sixty seconds to get to the surface. "Don't panic," he told himself. A life preserver kept his head above the water. He held his breath every time a wave inundated him.

Somehow he survived the interminable night, daylight bringing the calm and the sight of an orange *Shalimar* life raft. Two days later, an Indonesian Naval craft searching for survivors of the storm found him.

Those two days gave him the time to reflect on his life, Ahmed told David. "We are given one life by a father and a mother, but a second life is bestowed by a higher being. I cleansed myself with prayers to Allah. The rescue craft came from the east. I pleaded with the rescuers not to notify the *Shalimar*. They sent a message to Wei Tang who provided the means for me to appear on Tui at the proper time."

The reincarnation of Nu Kokomoto was identically twisted, if one believes, as I do, that it could have happened the way he told the story. Ai Mei spent a day with him after his appearance.

He said that he had intercepted a message to Iu, who, in connivance with the drug barons of Kagoshima and the Vanuatu pirates, was going to hijack the *Golden Pearl* for the billion-dollar Jade fund. He could pay off all of his debts, and live the rest of his life in luxury. Niban tried to dissuade his brother and threatened to tell his father.

The resultant fight ended with both of them going overboard; Niban survived in the same manner as Ahmed. Ichiban never surfaced, he said. The second morning, Nu became panicky, he said. "I fought off non-existent sharks and in the haze saw an orange life raft with the name *Shalimar of Parad* on it." A passing vessel heading for Suva found him that day.

It was not difficult to trace the electronic theft problems to Nikko Okusu. Sanban had been taken in by her wizardry. She had convinced him that Ichiban and Niban were conniving to take over the company. In order for the empire of the Golden Pearl to survive, she said, they must divert an enormous amount of money. After they had conceived and implemented the plan, Nikko had added a further diversion, eliminating Sanban.

She refused to talk with Ai Mei. Yoko repeated what Nikko had once told her in confidence, before sailing for Fiji. "With that kind of money, I could live anywhere in the world. No man could ever dominate my life again."

Mother Chen accepted the survival tales, as did my astute Father, who commented: "Your epic covered the basic happenings, favorite daughter, but leaves more loose threads than an unfinished embroidery. The Japanese girl, Nikko, who conspired with the youngest son, how do they punish such crimes? What of our young relative Xi Ku, the traitor, and his friend Edward?"

Mother Chen and I both laughed. "We're delighted, dear father, that age has made no dilution of your deductive powers. You would have made a good operative for the Tewu, the spy apparatus of Mao's day. Drink your tea and be patient. It will take me many more days to recall all the incidents. Judicial apparatus must determine their crimes. Jurisdiction is a problem."

This is the life story of the Confucius Jade Shou Xing Laos, from their mountain fastness in Burma to the eternal dome at the University of Confucius in Qufu, China. What effects they may have on the future of the world and its inhabitants will be related by storytellers of the future.

Kong Wan Yi, Kunming, Yunnan, China

About the Author

A Certified Gemologist and Registered Jeweler with the American Gem Society for many years, Frederick Fisher and his late wife, Eileen, shared a passion for travel and "treasure-hunting" fine jewelry, oriental art and antiques. Until a few years ago, Fred and Eileen spent six months each year in Southeast Asia.

Fred first began wrting when he was an apprentice seaman in the U.S. Navy. He has written numerous articles for various magazines and newspapers and has published several books including *China Adventures, Love and Marriage,* and *Serendipity. Confucius Jade* was previously published in Singapore by Times International and is based on many years of extensive travel and encounters with the people in mainland China, east Asia and the Pacific Rim.

Fred lives in Sonoita, Arizona and still travels when he can.